MEET ME AT THE CROSSROADS

ALSO BY MEGAN GIDDINGS

Lakewood

The Women Could Fly

MEGAN GIDDINGS

MEET ME AT THE CROSSROADS

A NOVEL

AMISTAD
An Imprint of HarperCollinsPublishers

This is a work of fiction. Names, characters, places, and incidents are products of the author's imagination or are used fictitiously and are not to be construed as real. Any resemblance to actual events, locales, organizations, or persons, living or dead, is entirely coincidental.

MEET ME AT THE CROSSROADS. Copyright © 2025 by Megan Giddings. All rights reserved. Printed in the United States of America. No part of this book may be used or reproduced in any manner whatsoever without written permission except in the case of brief quotations embodied in critical articles and reviews. For information, address HarperCollins Publishers, 195 Broadway, New York, NY 10007.

HarperCollins books may be purchased for educational, business, or sales promotional use. For information, please email the Special Markets Department at SPsales@harpercollins.com.

FIRST EDITION

Designed by Yvonne Chan

Library of Congress Cataloging-in-Publication Data has been applied for.

ISBN 978-0-06-333797-8

25 26 27 28 29 LBC 5 4 3 2 1

PART ONE

No person saw the doors appear; that honor was reserved for a polar bear crunching a seal bloody, a murmuration making its clouds in the sky above the earth, a pair of black kites searching out grasshoppers in the soon-to-be kindling grass, a coati who had been asleep in the midday heat with its paws on its black snout, and a dog preoccupied with finding the rotting carcass it couldn't stop smelling. The animals, not understanding these things were doors, yet understanding they were not of this world, quickly left the area. Later, different people would go on television so intoxicated by the attention they were receiving that they were able to smile wide as they exaggerated and spewed out conflicting details. Some claimed to have heard a great voice coming from the air, encouraging them to announce the arrival. Others saw burning bushes singing loud the end of days. And one man, a farmer from mid-Michigan, was blunt and matter-of-fact in his perfidy. He was fertilizing soybeans, and then there was a door. It would not open. It would not burn. The door itself was a rich blue some days, one time silver, although no one else ever saw it that way, and sometimes, it wasn't even there at all.

In the days that followed the appearance, each country handled things differently. Four of the doors, because they were in not densely populated places, were unknown for years to people outside those countries. When they were found later, it was to some people's great annoyance. Because three had originally been sighted and collectively acknowledged—one in Michigan, one in Australia, one in Germany—they had given the sense that, finally, here it was, the end of days. Things in threes were always a warning. Despite arrests, despite violence, despite calls for common sense and patience, people surged around the doors. Ad hoc towns grew around them, sermons and prayers were held regularly, the surrounding grass and crops were destroyed by the pressure of thousands kneeling and waiting to see what all of this meant.

And for those who did not have faith, there was a swirling of opinions. Aliens! They were always pulling stunts on people, and here was another one, a step further from the flashing lights in the sky and sucking people up in tractor beams. Or maybe, finally, here was proof that we were all living in a vast, sick game of *The Sims*: See, the user had put the wrong thing in the wrong place, and here was proof that nothing mattered. Life did not make sense because we were pixels and blobs meant to be observed and tormented. Articles and theories and think pieces abounded. Maybe the doors were a trendy artist's conceptual piece. We would find out that each one of these stupid, overdiscussed portals was valued at a million dollars.

Then people learned they could not burn, that bullets bounced off them. They could never get soaked with kerosene or blasted with water, and when knocked on, they sounded like any other door. They did not open for any presidents or prime ministers or kings or queens. They did not open for scientists, not even the ones who spoke gently and dreamed about them. They did not open for the pope or the Dalai Lama or the popular televangelist from Southern California who wrote very dull books that could be summed up as, The only way not to be a sinner was to give him and his church a lot of cash.

One day, a man filled with grief and longing traveled to Australia.

His wife had died abruptly (many people were tubing, the inner tubes flipped, some people were lost, it was another horrifying thing buried in the news' miasma). Every day when he was in grief's clasped hands, she, the only she in the entire world for him, was always in the periphery. Church didn't matter any longer. Friends didn't know what to do with the intangibility of no funeral, only a potential memorial service. His father told him the only answer in times like those was to live. The man's wife had always wanted to see the Flinders Ranges (her laugh when she saw birds, her sigh when she saw beauty), so he flew to Australia. At the base of a mountain, he found a blue door and prayed. And after the fourth hour of prayers, the door swung open.

He walked and walked through an orange desert until he heard someone singing. He turned and there she was. The man walked her across the desert. Her hand was cold. I will stay with you forever, he said. This is the space where later, at their church, they invited people to testify. To listen to what God had given us: a chance to resurrect our dead. Yes, there were dangers to going through the doors, but this was all meant to be a test of his love.

And some people said his wife had never been truly missing. She had taken advantage of the chaos to run off with her lover but then things with the lover had been boring. The wife refused to talk about the other side. She would not answer questions about what it had been like to drown. She could not talk about what her body was. A blasphemy, some churches said. So, soon, most people ignored them. This is one of the things about living now, if a thing only stays mysterious, doesn't give a person money or acclaim, only seems to exist as a reminder of the universe's vast inscrutability, it is often deemed as being worthless or a grift. A minor tragedy of modern times might be how much comfort has become valued over knowledge or kindness or understanding.

But some families remained to worship. New people, who longed for their beloveds, trickled into these different churches. In Michigan, a new religion formed: the Church of Fortitude and Blessings was one of its many names. Ayanna's father was one of the first children raised in it. His parents, because they were more lenient than others and because theirs was a spirited kid who was good at math, still let him go to public school. He learned quickly not to tell other people about his faith. Services were on Tuesday nights and Sunday mornings. When he went and prayed before the door, he started wearing hats and hoods, hoping not to be easily recognized from a distance. Enough Black families had moved into the area that it was possible. And besides, Antony was pretty popular at school.

Don't worry, this is a story about Ayanna. Be patient. Soon, she'll be born.

Antony was popular at church too, because his mother was considered a seer. In those beginning days, it was more of a catchall term than just about prophecy. Think of it as akin to *nun*. She prayed, she kept everyone fed, and she knit sweaters and blankets while watching television and made them available to others in a small basket at every service. She encouraged a community to blossom. For a week before it actually happened, she had a recurring dream in which the door in Michigan finally swung open.

Each dream was the same: Walking in their old shopping market, picking up the Cheerios Antony loved, then heading to the milk aisle. There, next to a display for eggnog and eggnog-flavored nondairy creamer, was the blue door. A sound like a car crash from a distance where people ask what was that and then speculate about what it was. Peeking out behind floral curtains, they saw the people arguing in the street, the smashed glass, the red and blue lights approaching. The door swung open, and her own voice said, Don't let Antony come in here. Sometimes, it said, Don't let your kin walk these paths.

She didn't tell people that the door spoke to her in these dreams.

On the Saturday morning when it happened, she grabbed Antony by the hood of his sweatshirt and kept a firm grip on the black fabric. There was what looked like a path made of gold in the doorway, a boulder covered in rich green moss, in normal-looking grass. Another child, desperate to be the first person in the world to pass through the door, sprinted toward it and then was pushed out of the way by an adult man. A few people gasped. The child's mother yelled "asshole" at the man, and someone else turned and started scolding her for using that language in front of the children. A teenage boy chased the man—no one could tell if he was racing him to the entrance or teaching him a lesson for pushing a child. Antony longed to be a member of the scene, rather than an observer. He could sense all the gossip and bragging rights and attention to be harvested from doing something wild in this moment but would never squirm or push away from his mother. That was a story he did not want to have told about him.

The two squeezed through the door at the same time. One stopped immediately. The other went farther in, where he could not be seen.

"This is," he began, and then the only word that could be used to describe what happened is he popped. Turned into a splash of red and peach with fully intact pink fingernails. Outside, people sprinted away. Still, Antony and his mother did not move.

"You will never go through that door," she whispered.

He nodded. They were close enough that she understood he would never do that, but she was asking him, quietly, for reassurance and control. Telling him what to do gave his mother what she needed.

Then, the teenager walked out. A streak of red on his face, golden leaves stuck in the top of his thick, curly hair. In his hands, some golden rocks and three of the fingernails. Antony recognized him from school, not from church. He was older and ran track. Jumped hurdles in a way that made him look like a beautiful horse.

"Mateo," Antony called. "Mateo, you're fine."

It was the only thing he could think of saying. The boy was disoriented. He looked around and was weeping, not bothering to wipe at the flow of tears or the blood on his forehead.

"Mom."

Finally, she let Antony go. He ran to Mateo. The boy handed him the fingernails, the gold rocks. He was shaking and Antony kept patting him on the shoulders and saying "You're fine." It was a little awkward to comfort a boy older than him, but he knew it was the right thing to do in that moment. Antony's mother walked past him. She went all the way to the doorway and gazed in. A few people followed, and they stood in a concerned cluster. There was no sound coming from whatever world lay in front of them. A brief breeze that carried what smelled like a mix of lilac and rot and salt.

"Do you hear her?" a little white girl said. Antony couldn't remember if her name was Maddy or Addy.

No one knew what she was talking about.

The girl said she heard her mother's voice. "It's proof," she said, "that this is heaven. I thought I had forgotten her voice," the girl said multiple times, "but finally, I heard her again." She smiled. The girl said her mother was saying "Your hair is so long now." Her eyes were blue with flecks of brown, cheeks flushed as if she had braised herself in a too-warm bath. Antony's mother stooped down and asked, "How long has your mama been gone?"

"Three years."

Antony was listening to Mateo, who said he had seen pink figures walking the path. He was mad that none of the adults were taking care of him. Being kind and patient was hard. Some of the figures were people but very small, Mateo said. Some were stretched too tall, and a few were fluctuating between shapes. They were so pink they hurt his eyes. While Mateo kept talking and talking as if he had been there years rather than a few dramatic minutes, Antony slipped one of the stones into his pocket. He kept pretending the fingernails were also stones, because every time his brain remembered the pop, it took all his willpower not to succumb to nausea. There was hair stuck in the blood on Mateo's cheek. It felt disrespectful to drop the fingernails on the ground.

"I have to go to my mother," the girl said.

"Did you see what happened to that man?"

"But he was fine." She pointed to Mateo.

"We don't know why he's okay, baby."

Antony realized it was raining in little spits and mists. He turned, and almost everyone who had been at the service was in the barn that now functioned as the prayer center. They were smart enough to be afraid.

The girl squirmed, but everyone held on to her.

She lashed out and bit and scratched, but still everyone held. They let her hurt them. My mother, my mother, she sobbed. The girl bit Antony's mother's hand, and for the rest of her life, there was a scar on the soft part between thumb and pointer. Four teeth marks. The girl kicked everyone with her pink-and-white light-up tennis shoes. They flashed as she lashed out.

Mateo said he had heard his grandfather's laugh.

Antony took a step farther away from the door, pulled Mateo with him. He did not want to hear his grandfather or his father. Their soft, slow speech, the way they both coughed a little after eating in the exact same way, their cadence that he now carried in his voice. His mom winced sometimes when she heard him laugh now. There were already moments when late at night, awake at the time when all the world felt still, he felt sure he had heard someone saying his name. Antony would always tell himself it was a dream, but the way his body reacted made him feel certain that no, the voice had been real, had been his father's voice.

He would not tell Ayanna's mother any of this when they met at college. Not even one night when she would sit him down, tell him the worst thing that had ever happened to her because she loved him and wanted him to understand everything about her. He would not take her invitation to share. She had been raised normally. God did not lure people into traps in her religion. Her god was distant and judgmental, and all his sicko behavior was from thousands of years ago. Her god did miracles like putting a beautiful lady's face on a shirt, sending white ladies on daytime television angels, and promising eternity.

The door closed with a small thud.

The girl screamed at all the adults that had held her back, "I hate you. I hate you." Her voice shrill and young. It could've just been an I-want-that-toy meltdown at Target.

Later, when Ayanna's mother told Antony she was pregnant, he gave her the gold stone as a gift. He told her a friend had given it to him when he was a teenager and every time he kept it in his pocket, something wonderful happened. Meeting her at a party. Getting a full ride to the university. Good grades. This.

Opal took the stone gladly. It was not the response she had expected, but one of the reasons why she liked Antony was because she could never anticipate what he was going to say. She had seen it in his desk, in a small bag with what looked like, maybe, fingernails, dirt with flecks of gold, and another gold rock. What had she been looking for? An answer for why he seemed so much older than her or a reason for why he was so different from everyone else she had ever met, or to know him without all the effort.

"Where did he find it?"

Antony shrugged. "On vacation somewhere weird."

It was a tone he used only when he was lying, but Opal didn't know him well enough to know that yet. His eyes were soft, and she thought he might be thinking of their life together. They would be the ones filling drawers with rocks and knickknacks. A house filled with proof that they had traveled and loved. A year after Mateo had gone through the door, he had tried again. One of the fingernails in the sack was his.

2

When you meet at twenty in a crowded living room lit only with Christmas lights, twinkling purple-yellow-blue-white in a pulsating rhythm, when the music is so loud you have to lean in so that your lips are almost always brushing an ear to be heard, when you walk home together, and because you've had an unquantifiable amount of alcohol between the jungle juice and the shots and beers, and still you're talking and talking, and even though you haven't really, truly, purposefully touched yet, most of your brain power is spent on the heat of the other person walking home next to you on the sidewalk, how close your fingers are coming to brushing their hands or their thighs, and have you ever wanted anyone, truly, before in your entire life, and of course, when you kiss—finally—there is no room in either of your brains to think of consequences. And that's why, slightly before the time you're twenty-one, one of you is pregnant and both of you are casually saying things like maybe you were just not cut out for four-year college—you can make good money in HVAC—to prepare everyone for what's to come.

And when you get married at twenty-one and two weeks and at twenty-one and three-quarters, well, of course you haven't had the important conversations. You've been so busy listening to people talk at you about how long life is, how there are things you don't have to do right now, and what about adoption, what about you-know-the-medical-procedure-that-we-dare-not-speak-its-name because Opal is already the kind of nice lady who loses her mind every time the word is uttered, what about your degree, what about money, so the two of you make home a quiet place. The babies don't need stress.

By twenty-six, because you have not talked religion beyond basic platitudes about heaven and love, you have not talked rules and priorities for raising children, you have just been trying to keep your heads above water, and everything is trouble. It's the ordinary trouble that most people would say happens. And in fact, it isn't that unusual. For most people, faith is embarrassing to put into words. It's harder to explain exactly the way faith has added streetlamps and thruways into your life, your beliefs, especially if you're someone who doesn't regularly go to church or pray.

It's harder still if you're someone who grew up in a faith that was featured multiple times in *Dateline* episodes and later in annoying podcasts and who was regularly monitored by the US government to articulate why, suddenly, when you hear the flutter, your potential child's potential heartbeat, your brain leaps back to that red barn, to the blue door, to your grandmother leading a prayer among the surviving soybeans, and to when the smell of soil in early summer heat was its own promise from the god you knew. How could you have ever fought your girlfriend about what she wants to do, when your god didn't care about those things?

There's a place you hope your child is never called to, but every time you've glimpsed it, it has been more impossibly beautiful than the last time you saw it. Sometimes, the sky is cotton candy pink, sometimes pool-at-night blue. Where the paths are golden, where people bring back full silver and gold flowers and palms and pothos and quietly sell them to collectors for vast sums of money, even though the plants often die quickly when they're out in our sun, our cold. Where the voices of the dead can be heard, sometimes singing and calling everyone's names, where once, alone on a winter morning, you swore you heard the loudest voice of your life saying "Antony, Antony, it's okay to leave here," and you knew that was the voice of God, and your mouth crumpled into a gorgeous pink quiver, your eyes the warmest thing against all that January cold, and you were torn between wondering if you were delusional and narcissistic enough to have to tell yourself that God said it was okay for you to go away to college or if it was the truth, he loved you enough to tell you to go. That day, the air leaking from the open doorway smelled like bonfire and apple cider, and that, too, felt like a sign. The doctor said, Oh, it's twins, and Opal cried harder.

In your faith, heaven and hell are the same place, it depends on how your soul is judged. Your grandmother, one of the church's great elders, wrote out a theory that to walk through the door is to have your soul measured. Hell and devastation for a soul deemed unworthy, the ability to walk between here and heaven for those deemed righteous. There were arguments to be made that it wasn't so simple; the man who came and went the most was outwardly one of the biggest assholes in the community. He said that each time you came and went, it was a risk. You could bring things back. The one time you had tried to tell Opal a sanitized version of this while mildly stoned—that the universe's, the creator's, only desire was balance, so it seemed weird that heaven and hell were different places—you were awkwardly laughed off. It was strange to love someone who could believe the fundamentals of everything were so different from yours, but also exciting. Also frustrating. Also alienating.

And by twenty-nine, you are divorced. And despite being twins, the type of children that you have been taught famously always, *always*, want to be together, they are split on which parent they would prefer to live with. There is Ayanna, who wants to live with Antony, who loves her grandmother, who likes to go to the barn and pray for the good of the world, and who is considered a future seer in her church. She likes to hear the people say "and one day our love will walk back through the door." And there is Olivia, who wants to live with Opal and keep going to the Catholic school. She was recently voted the most like Jesus in their second-grade class, which is a high marker of popularity and actual kindness, especially for a little Black girl. Olivia—who can tell her mother is disgusted seeing the door—hates being in the dusty church, is always uncomfortable with Grandma Owens, and would like to make their life a little easier.

You, like most overworked adults, find it easier to think of the children more like illogical employees than family members who are reacting to your behavior. And even that is another discussion that should've happened: Do you want your kids to respond more to love or authority? Which specific ways do you want to avoid fucking them up? There are too many homework assignments and missing socks and there's not enough money to pay everything on time. You'll have the conversation next month, when you have time to go out to dinner.

So, to save money, you agree on a particular scheme: the girls will be together every weekend and every Friday night. They must do one sport together—easy, they love soccer. If they want to change the living arrangement and be together all the time, you must do what it takes to honor their bond as sisters.

Both of you will agree a year later that this is one of the big regrets of your together-life. You should have taught them to compromise, you should have encouraged them to do the harder thing rather than to make things easier for you, because, later, when the worst happens, you won't be crushed only by the loss, but by the weight of all the time they spent apart.

3

On the first day Ayanna saw the door open, she was seven and praying in front of it with her grandmother. At that time, she knew the following: like most things in this world, there were good and bad things about the door; it was where God lived; it might be where heaven was; if anyone wearing a uniform asked her if someone had gone inside it, she was supposed to say "never." The door had never called on her family. If she ever felt like it was, if she heard music, or if she smelled her favorite things, Ayanna was supposed to tell her father immediately.

When the door opened, Ayanna said, in unison with everyone else gathered, "Thank you, we are ready to listen." It had been three months since the last time it had let someone in. No one had died in eighteen months. Everyone was eager to gather new specimens, to draw maps, to further their theories, to see what had changed, to linger and hope to prove that their dead were not just voices and that the preacher in Australia was telling the truth. The people at that church wore blue shirts with the words DEATH CAN BE DEFEATED! printed on the front and back. For the first time, there was no golden path through the entryway. Instead, rich blue sky, navy grass, a silver mountain in the distance. Something glowing baby pink.

It was a little disappointing to Ayanna. A year ago, her father had told her that the golden path in his stories was real. It was where God lived. Once many years ago, God had spoken to him, and he felt sure now that it meant God had wanted her and Olivia to be born. That was how special they were.

Her grandmother was writing furiously in a notebook. Some people were sketching. Electronics didn't work within one hundred feet of the door. One of the scientists started to put on a special suit that was bright yellow and baggy. Ayanna felt sure she had seen this place before, drawn it too. She was in an art phase; both of her bedrooms were miniature art galleries. Walls were covered in her scribbles and landscapes and puppy approximations. All the blue crayons were worn to nubs. The silver markers that she used to draw what her parents called *v*'s were drying out and patchy.

Just like at the museum, Ayanna also made her own placards. This looked like God Teeth and Puppy Dog and maybe—she squinted as if it would somehow improve her vision—Cotton Candy in the Sky.

The pink thing blobbed closer to the door. Almost everyone around Ayanna moved or reacted in some way, but Ayanna took a small step forward. It was a little cloud, sometimes resembling a fuzzy dog, sometimes a face. *I love it, I love it,* she thought. It was talking in a high-pitched voice like a girl in an anime. "Can any of you understand me?"

"Yes," Ayanna said, "of course."

Her grandmother paused in her frantic writing to look at Ayanna.

"Who are you talking to?"

"Her."

Ayanna pointed to the cloud talking so quickly that she could barely understand it. It spoke of a daughter it wanted to apologize to, something about oranges, something about crossing over, silver, knocking on the wrong door.

Other people said they couldn't hear a voice, they heard what sounded like maybe a loud air purifier. *Whir, whir, whir.*

One teenage boy said he heard the words *paintbrush, melody, miss.*

"This is the first day of silver," Ayanna's grandmother said in her most officious voice. "Thank you, we are here to listen."

Most of the people gathered said it back to her like they did at regular services.

"Help me," the cloud said.

"How do I help it?" Ayanna asked everyone present.

"You don't have to worry about that," a woman said. "You're a baby. You don't have to worry about helping anyone but yourself."

Ayanna was offended by the idea that she was a baby, even when the word was said in a sweet, soft way like the woman said it.

The door closed with a slam.

THE WEEKS AFTER WERE filled with arguments and theorizing and extended services for the adults. For Ayanna, the weeks after were filled with blue dreams. Sometimes, mundane things like riding in the car or taking a spelling test or eating a popsicle, dreams in which everything but her was cerulean. Sometimes, she would sit up in bed and think of the fluctuating cloud and try to remember everything it had said to her. For the first time in her life, Ayanna felt true discontentment. It aged her in an abrupt way.

Ayanna never felt lonelier than on the days when she and Olivia were together. Olivia was talking about goals she had scored at school recess, about how she kept reading the same chapter of *Farmer Boy* over and over, about the boy eating all the delicious food, about how she had a First Communion dress, and it was the pretty one, not the one that Mom liked.

Her sister's voice sounded like her own, except slower, and she had a nasal Michigan *a* like their mom. Ayanna nodded along. Yes, the goals sounded great, yes, she would read the chapter too, and it was fine she wasn't doing a First Communion. She felt like she understood how her dad felt at breakfast sometimes. You just have to let the kid speak.

It made Ayanna feel so distant from her sister that Ayanna thought a lot about what she could do to bridge the gap between them. She liked Olivia and loved her. And they were twins. What was the point of being a twin if you felt that far away from your sibling?

She decided to go to church with her mom and Olivia for the first time in a long time. They woke up early on Sunday morning. Ayanna could tell her mom was pleased that she wanted to go to church with them. There would be doughnuts after Mass, and her mom kept talking about the ones with chocolate and pink sprinkles as if it were something Ayanna needed to hear about multiple times so that she wouldn't back out at the last moment.

"Wear my pink dress," Olivia said.

That was too far for Ayanna. She put on a pair of black cotton overalls and a frilly white shirt underneath it and white socks with ruffles around the ankles.

"You look very sophisticated," Opal said, and there wasn't a hint of patronization in her voice. Her mother's grip was softer than her father's when she was braiding. Her scalp had to work less because her mother knew what she was doing, loved the mix of textures on her twins' heads, the glissando between straight hairs all the way to the 4C hair they had inherited from both grandmothers. She liked to call their heads "the symphony" sometimes.

"Is there anything you want me to remind you about before Mass?"

"Can I sit between you so I remember what to do?" All the standing and kneeling and repeating! Usually her dad would be picking her up around this time. He would take her out to breakfast at the diner, where they always made her a smiling strawberry pancake and gave her milk in a coffee mug so she could match the adults.

Life would be so much easier if she lived here. There were no mysteries or fears in this house, in their church. Sometimes, Olivia cried when she did bad things and said things like now she wouldn't get to go to heaven. No one heard a mysterious voice. If they did, they would go and see a doctor. Ayanna didn't tell either of them about the door, even though sometimes her mother pressed her for more details. As far as her mother knew, the door had never opened and everything there was harmless and a little weird, but it was on her for falling in love with someone and having kids before getting real about things. Her mother tried to find ways to figure out what her daughter believed. Ayanna had been told several times by her father, her great-grandma who now lived back east, and her grandmother that telling her mom what was really going on might mean she could never see them again. Her mom regretted the custody agreement, was always looking, they said, for a reason to make things different. Grandma would sometimes sit next to Ayanna at the couch and say, "The courts hate Black men. They'll take you from him." There were so many things Ayanna knew and understood to keep inside herself.

Her mom's house, where almost every room was painted white or gray, where there were two portraits of Jesus, one original-flavored, a.k.a. white with sad big blue eyes, and another one where he was brown and laughing while wearing a red robe and handing a child a loaf of bread. The house always smelled like cinnamon-spice candles. The only room not gray or white was Ayanna's, painted a shade called "champion cobalt," and only because her grandmother had read an article that claimed children with blue rooms were more creative and calmer. In this house, they talked about spelling and watched PBS Kids shows and baked uneven cakes when good news happened. Mom oiled Olivia's hair and taught her things to worry about, like edges and ashy elbows and being good at math and laughing at boys' jokes to cover awkward moments. You lived and you died in this house, and that was how you wanted it to be because if you were very good, death meant a beautiful reward was waiting for you.

Because she spent most of her time with her father, it felt like her mom sometimes worried more about making sure Ayanna liked her and was close to her sister than actually telling her things about the world. It felt easier, but there were never times like when she was with her dad, where she could look at him and just feel her body relax.

At Mass, Ayanna sat between her mom and Olivia. She was more aware of them than the actual service. They sang the songs, did the hand motions, nodded along to the priest even though Ayanna could barely follow his sermon. He kept talking about wildernesses and deserts of the soul, and the sound of his voice was dry and reedy and made her feel tired. Olivia kept glancing at her, putting a hand on Ayanna's arm to make sure she stood or knelt with them. Both squeezed Ayanna's hands when the entire congregation held hands and recited a prayer.

The church itself was beautiful. It was like being inside an elaborate music box. Purples, gold crosses, dark brown wood, stained glass that seemed extra vivid because of how sunny the day outside was. The windows alternated between being representations of different saints and crosses and abstract patterns in white, green, and yellow. It was like a museum to their god. The music, too, made it feel like an event. An organ high above everyone that Ayanna was not allowed to turn around and look at. A man leading the song whose voice was so loud and rich.

The rules here seemed so simple. You believed in a family—the father, the son, the Holy Spirit—each of whom took turns being in charge. You listened to long speeches, and while there were parts that went completely over Ayanna's head, she felt like most of the time they were saying you have to treat others like you want to be treated. The part she liked best was when an older white woman read out things like "We wish for an end to the suffering of all people experiencing pain, anguish, and poverty," and everyone responded in one great thunderous voice, "We pray for them."

When there were speeches in Ayanna's church, they were about cultivating curiosity and the pleasures of the Unknown. The establishment had gone through so many names: the Church of Fortitude and Blessings (weirdly sounded kind of like a gym or cult!); the Church of the Blue Doors (too basic!); Curiosityism (too hard to say!); the Unknown Truths (felt too much like a band!); and the current one, Pathsong (already being argued against because it might sound too Christian!). She was learning about the need to be kind, to be curious and adventurous, to value knowledge and to accept that to be uncertain was to be in a necessary emotional space that could lead to true bliss and enlightenment. So many people came and went in her church that there were few generational families like hers. Ayanna's grandmother wrote in one of her texts, "This is a faith for those who are comfortable with wandering. To be lost is not to be in a negative state, but to embrace the fluidity of life. You come to Curiosityism to find a community that wants you to live, not to treat living like a frustrating waiting room, designed for you to make mistakes and repent ad infinitum."

Because of the way the church was set up, and because of Ayanna's height, she was not tall enough to be able to observe everyone around her. So she watched instead her mother and sister, as they knelt, as they stood, as they spoke their belief that the wafer in front of them had been transformed. Olivia smiled and it felt like a secret. Was she hearing God? The organ was playing an ocean of melodies and the stained-glass window nearest to them was a vibrant setting sun. You never have to be lonely if you believe, her mother had told her.

After, they went into the much more ordinary basement with its white tiles and fluorescent lights and waited in line for doughnuts. People kept coming up to and chatting with her mom and sister, telling Ayanna that they were so glad to see them all together at Mass as a family.

While her mom chatted with a group of people, Ayanna ate half her doughnut and turned to Olivia and asked, "Is it like this every week?"

"Sometimes it's different. Around Christmas or Easter or feast days. My favorite is May Crowning."

Olivia explained how the statue of Mary was front and center, how all the kids were encouraged to bring her flowers, and how they got to put them in vases that surrounded the statue. Once, Olivia felt sure that she had seen the statue gently smile at her after she offered it a bouquet of lilacs. It made Ayanna feel so much older than her twin to hear her say that. Why rely on imagination when you could actually see extraordinary things? She ate the rest of her doughnut and let her sister talk.

"Did Mary ever die?" Ayanna asked. "Did Jesus bring her back to life?"

"I don't think so. But he once brought back a friend."

Ayanna nodded. She went and got another doughnut, this time with sprinkles, and ignored the way her mom raised her eyebrows at a two-doughnut morning.

The adults around them were talking through complaints that ranged from work to neighbors to broken furnaces to whether there was a too-cool clique in a third-grade class that needed to be dealt with to aging parents who refused to stop driving. All the adults, even Ayanna's mom, were sallow in the fluorescents. A harmony of discontentment that felt hard to ignore, but somehow the adults could do it, maybe even embraced it. Some of the teenagers still seemed alive, laughing, and at one point pretended to crush milk pints on their foreheads. A lot of the moms were following their kids around and saying their names plus *no* over and over again, even to kids Ayanna was sure were older than her. It was too stimulating. For a while, she looked over the shoulder of a kid playing a video game, feeling calmer and more relaxed from watching him try to escape what looked like an especially dirty haunted house with three characters of indeterminate ages while a large man with a chainsaw chased them. So many khakis and polo shirts or blue slacks with brown shoes or beige sweaters with black pants that it felt like maybe there was a secret message or a pattern happening that she couldn't make sense of. Maybe it was because no one here had to ever worry about getting mud or blood or rain on them, because here everything was in order.

When she went home that afternoon, Ayanna asked her dad to drive her to the door. They sat together in the early summer heat, didn't mind their shorts were getting dirty, and watched it. Her dad was writing notes in his small, blobby script. Ayanna hoped to hear the voice again, to figure out what it needed. She wanted the door to open and wanted to hear a voice sing her name. For the first time in her life while looking at it, she didn't want to obey the rule about waiting until she was seventeen. Ayanna longed to walk through it, to feel the dark grass brushing against her legs, to see the mountains grow ever closer. She wanted to touch the golden rocks, push past the edge of knowledge and peer out unto the exquisite unknown.

4

At ten, Ayanna and Olivia had one of their biggest fights because Olivia said it wasn't fair that Ayanna got to celebrate Christmas. Ayanna didn't go to church, didn't believe in Jesus, and had barely even believed in Santa Claus. She had put in no effort, so why should she get presents and a long day in front of the TV alternating between naps and milky hot chocolates? Shouldn't she have to spend the day doing her religion?

It was one of the fallow times for the Church of the Blue Door. The door was in a stray-cat period—here one day, and open, then gone for three weeks, and when it returned, almost everyone in the congregation believed it looked different. The blue maybe less vibrant? The knob maybe smaller? Or maybe it was half an inch taller? There were enough arguments that instead of the planned church service of meditating in the barn, making a community service schedule, and praying for a kinder, smarter world, they spent a significant amount of time on an early December morning remeasuring everything, checking against the prior figures, and asking if the army would also be willing to compare against their measurements.

Early December, where the days are short and gray and to do anything beyond the bare minimum feels like an accomplishment. People needed holidays during this time as a thank-you note for continuing on to a new year.

Ayanna and Olivia weren't speaking, and Ayanna was refusing to go to her mom's house on their scheduled days. She told her dad that school was hard right now and she needed to focus. Antony didn't argue, he was too busy trying to figure out how to keep people in the faith. It felt like every year people were sliced off by their nostalgia for Christmas or Hanukkah, like they went home for the holidays, listened to their family talk about how weird their faith was over ham or latkes, got asked multiple times while trying on new sweaters and socks, "Are you sure that you're not in a cult?"

Antony felt the United States' biggest export was cults. Racism, capitalism at the expense of the planet's health, trucks that were so big you couldn't even see if a small child was crossing the street, not wanting to look at the truth of any situation unless the truth benefited you, the militias in the Upper Peninsula—those were cults. He was resentful, too, of all the cults in the news again. It seemed like thin white women with ghost-blue eyes were always writing their novels about them and then going on early-morning television to say things about death and dead actresses. There was the cult that a D-list celebrity had gotten into, filled with weird sex and what sounded like a lot of pressure to do Pilates.

When he walked in on Ayanna crying in her room, with math flash cards around her, for a moment, Antony considered quietly walking back out. He was tired both of trying to figure out insurmountable problems and of a quiet belief—that his ex-wife called "self-serving" and he called "healthy"—that his children should be allowed to have private emotions and feelings until they were ready to talk to him or they were clearly mentally unwell. He knew their mother was always seeking out their journals, asking their friends for info, taking them on car trips and asking them probing questions when they weren't able to go anywhere. Antony could see their teen years coming, and saw the tempest of slammed doors, sulky silences, and broken relationships those actions, if they continued, would bring.

Ayanna continued crying, didn't even notice him in the doorway. She buried her head into an oversized stuffed cat and yelled, "I hate you, Olivia."

"I'm sorry to walk in without knocking," he said. He tried to nod his head toward the overflowing laundry basket in his hands.

She kept her face in the belly of the cat.

"What are you and your sister fighting about?"

"It's dumb."

"Ay, tell me," he said.

Ayanna did not tell him then, or over dinner, or even after he had baked a yellow cake with chocolate frosting and presented her with a slice and a large glass of milk. It was only in the morning, after the first large snow of the season, when he called out to work and told Ayanna they were going to go sledding and watch a movie together today. Then, as their feet crunched on the snow toward the best hill in the neighborhood, Ayanna told Antony what Olivia had said, how kids at school were saying things like you had to be a good Christian to have Christmas, and she wanted to know why their church didn't have any holidays. Kids at school got Christmas and Easter, one of them had Ramadan—Antony guessed the breaking of the fast felt like a holiday to that kid—and Jewish people had all sorts of holidays throughout the year.

"I know you said almost everything on Earth is made up to help people do things or understand things," Ayanna said. He could not tell if her nose was red and her eyes were watery from the cold or from the emotions she was feeling. "But is it a real religion if it doesn't have holidays?"

"There are some faiths that won't even celebrate birthdays."

"I hate that."

Antony had not been sure he wanted to be a father when Opal had announced "We're pregnant," and the first year of twins, he was sure, had sliced at least twenty years off his life. But now that they were ten, their personalities were tangible, not in that liminal state where you had to wonder about how if the things you saw in them were just confirming your biases from when they were new. Ayanna, the wild one, their child who liked getting dirty, who wanted to run everywhere, and who had stopped nursing quickly as if even then she wanted to be independent. Olivia, easygoing—had slept through the night regularly as a baby—was obedient, but also had a dark side. The one who'd asked if it was true vampires did not believe in God, then was disappointed when the answer was, well, almost everything that has to do with God—crosses, holy water—hurts them.

But he loved hearing his daughters' opinions; the way Ayanna wasn't embarrassed to say exactly what she was thinking made him miss his sister. He liked direct women. Often, Antony felt guilty because he had a much harder time parenting Olivia, not only because of their schedule but because she was well trained in the obfuscation of her opinions and discomforts. Olivia was deeply invested in appearing nice. It was an uncomfortable relief to hear about her being mean.

"What would a holiday in our faith look like to you?"

She dropped the tow on her toboggan. Flopped into the snow and made a snow angel, fiddled with her mittens, and readjusted her hat. While she played and thought, Antony rolled a giant snowball, making the base for an inevitable snowman. Farther ahead at the hill, a kid was yelling at the top of her lungs, "Too fast."

"It should have really good food, we should have to do nice things for other people, and I think we should have to learn something."

He liked the idea of it.

What if, he considered while rolling the snowman's midsection, they had five days of holidays between the twenty-sixth and thirtieth.

It would overlap with Kwanzaa, but that was fine. Day one: Service. Day two: Knowledge. Day three: He couldn't think of day three. They went up and down and up and down the hill. Both yelling with delight at the final one where they wiped out and Ayanna lost one of her snow boots.

"We were going so fast, it felt like we would just fly into the moon," Ayanna said.

Antony laughed and helped her slide her wet-sock foot into the boot.

While walking home, Antony told Ayanna the rest of his idea. She suggested the last day be: Give Happiness. That wasn't snappy enough, but he liked the sentiment. By the time they had gotten home, the final two days had morphed into day three: Forgiveness; day four: Give Joy. Give Joy, there would be a party for all the members of the church, catered, and they would be encouraged to do a gift exchange, as well as adopt a family in the community to give them the things they needed for the next year all the way from food to small, nice things that would make their lives easier.

That night, while Ayanna and his grandmother slept soundly in the living room, even though they were claiming to watch a movie, he drove to the fields. Because of the cold and snow, the only people around were the military guys as usual. People already cared so little about the doors that only one of the military guys was carrying a machine gun in his arms. Everyone else was armed, but they no longer all had to patrol as if ready for violence. His grandmother had told him this would happen. The door had been met with so much violence and hostility when it first appeared. People tried to cut it, shoot it, smash it, set it on fire, legislate, and once they realized it was uncontrollable, unkillable, and unknowable, most called it a hoax or ignored it.

The solar lights formed a perimeter around the door, so the area was constantly lit up bright white. Antony hated it; he wanted to be able to pray and think without feeling he was on stage. Someone was in the barn, probably one of the teens having a hard time at home or one of the military guys making himself coffee for the cold night. He struggled to remember their names, all of them were Kyles or Mikes with short hair and square jaws. Antony did remember Malik, but that was easy, he always remembered the names of other Black guys.

In the white lights made even brighter by all the snow, Antony whispered to the door about his plans. It was still hard not to be self-conscious, even though all over the world there were people whispering to statues, to walls, to rosaries, and up to their ceilings, hoping for answers. It was one of the most interesting things about people, the way they often seemed more comfortable with objects or an unknowable God but, most of the time, could not ask for comfort from the people they knew best.

He wanted God to speak to him, to tell him this holiday, this religion, even the way his life was now, was going in the right direction. And what even was the right direction? He was thirty-one, and the contrast between feeling young enough to still be confused so often about life and feeling old enough that death—when he woke up in the morning and his back hurt or the idea of going to bed at ten was deeply appealing—was tangible in an unexpected way. I only have fifty more left, was a constant thought, and: I don't even know what "right" is.

The sound of a throat clearing. Antony leaned forward, until his forehead was almost touching the shut door. All these years with it, trying to understand and building other people's faith in the ways the door represented so many things—a path to God, a path to being comfortable with the universe's mysteries, an acceptance of death and change—and still, deep down, he was afraid of it. Antony never went through. He envied the people who could approach it and hear no voices. Every time Antony was near it, especially when no one else was around, he was sure he could occasionally hear his father from a distance. If not his voice, deep and slow, then the way his father whistled "Bring It On Home to Me."

"Are you okay? It's pretty late for you to be out here."

Antony turned; it was Malik.

"Thoughts," he said.

"Woman shit?" Malik asked.

"I wish. Would love all my problems to be she thinks I'm a scrub. Or does she like me?"

"Miss that time too. Wish I was fifteen again, looking in the mirror, hoping arm hair would appear. I used to lie awake at night willing my pits and chin to sprout hair, thinking that would make girls like me."

Antony could not relate to this. Girls had always liked him.

The snow was starting again. Antony watched some and wondered if that was a sign to go home. Despite himself, Antony opened his mouth and talked about how his daughters were fighting, how the church always felt (to him) like it could fall apart at any minute, and if he was even doing the right thing by raising his daughters around here. They only saw Black people they were related to. And, well, Malik. Antony and his ex-wife could agree on nothing. Dating prospects were all white women who seemed sweet, but he could see them earnestly saying things like "It doesn't matter whether you're black or white or green." He didn't want his kids around that. He wanted them to be happy with themselves, to love Black culture, and to find their places in it.

"There are white chicks and there are real ones," Malik agreed. "It's hard to find the real ones."

Malik proceeded to talk through some of his troubles, from how hard it was to make friends out here to how badly the Pistons were playing to wondering if his time in the service was done. At first it was annoying, but then, the longer Antony listened, the more he noticed how much it was relaxing him. Malik didn't want anything from him, really, other than to have someone who was willing, even for just twenty minutes, to care about him.

The door opened.

"Would you ever go through?" Antony asked Malik.

In there today, it was summer. The light bright, the trees green and gold. It was easy to see why his daughter loved it so much. His father was whistling again.

"Absolutely not," Malik said. Antony noticed how much the other man's posture had changed. "I hear the voices of every dead person I've ever known whenever that thing opens. In there is death."

"But you could bring them back."

"One weird white guy claims it happened." Malik had pulled out a cigarette. He rolled it between his fingers, tapped it against his lips. He was not supposed to smoke. Antony felt certain that if Malik ever smoked in front of him, it would mean they had worked their way into a friendship.

He could see Malik weighing two opposing thoughts: the pleasure of wanting to believe people were capable of miracles and the agony of knowing how often people lied to get what they wanted.

"Do you think all this"—Antony gestured toward the barn, the door, himself, as if that would be enough to communicate what he was asking about his faith, the way he had chosen to live his life—"is too weird?"

"I think everyone, whether they like it or not, is obsessed with death. If you have a religion, in some way, you're making a choice about what you think death is." Malik put the cigarette back and clapped his hands together. The snow came down harder. "Listen to me being wise and shit."

When Antony got home, Ayanna and his grandmother were awake again and splitting a slice of cake. The two of them were laughing together, and as he watched them in the moment before they noticed him, everything he was worried about felt smaller. They were on the right path, Antony promised himself.

5

Ayanna and Olivia prepared for Confirmation in their churches at the same time. Olivia, who was getting confirmed later than usual because her mother hadn't thought she was ready at fourteen, went to classes on Sunday afternoons in the church basement after Mass. There, she learned about the seven gifts of the Holy Spirit. She texted jokes to her friends under the table or read the one cool eighth grader's notes or continued her ironic doodle series of anthropomorphic household objects. There were kids in the class who cared a lot, but they were considered weird and kiss-asses.

Olivia spent a lot of time thinking about who was or wasn't popular or assessing where she was in the school social structure. She liked asking Ayanna about what made people popular at her high school, and even though the schools were twenty miles apart, it was clear that each one had its own culture and levels of attractiveness. Olivia wanted exactly what she had, an anodyne mid-tier popularity where there was very little to be lost and, as long as she kept things tight, where very little gossip could leak out about her. She was a defensive midfielder on her high school's varsity soccer team and was careful in her motions, more interested in containing other people than in making challenges. She straightened her hair and rarely went to parties where people drank and got into situations. Their mom was always telling her how to be the "right kind of Black woman": God-fearing, hair neat at all times (preferably straightened), no serious boyfriends until college, good grades, light-colored pedicures, deep clean your house every Sunday, no bra straps showing, a mixture of love and pity for Whitney and deep skepticism toward Mariah, ambitious but in a gentle way, and when the day came, be the kind of daughter who called every Saturday.

"That is nerd shit," Ayanna was prone to saying when Olivia talked out how often she worried about being in the "wrong" situation. "You can't control how other people see you."

Their mother had given up on telling Ayanna how to be years ago. Her feral daughter, Opal would sometimes sigh. It was foolish even to try to tell Ayanna anything—she was slippery and grumpy and confident enough even as a high schooler to correct people far older than her when they tried to tell her things about the world. Sometimes, this was fine. Ayanna's soul was old and *artistic*, Opal liked to say. Sometimes, it took all of Opal's willpower to stop herself from dialing up her ex-husband and destroying him on the phone for the ways he had clearly failed as a father.

Ayanna would rather talk about living on Mars than think about what her future wedding would be like. Ayanna was thinking about going to art school and was ignoring offers from Division III colleges to go play soccer on a full ride. Ayanna said that the only pro-life she believed in was a world without genocide. *You did this, Antony,* Opal thought whenever Ayanna was willing to share her thoughts, *and now I don't know how to make her right.*

Ayanna could not give her a sister a clear sense of how popular she was. She was in art classes and liked to paint her fingernails black, she was the striker of her high school's soccer team and had once gotten a red card for throwing a blue-flavored Gatorade after being subbed off after scoring two goals. Those things could be cool or dorky. Olivia wasn't sure. Ayanna still went to weird door church with their dad, even though more and more people were saying the doors were just a dumb hoax meant to be a distraction from what was actually happening out in the real world. Ayanna was in AP classes and wasn't embarrassed to say earnest things like "It's cool to learn new stuff." She talked about the racist things that happened at school, but when the twins went to the mall together, almost everyone who knew Ayanna stopped to say hi or at least waved. There were so many kids at Olivia's school who pretended she did not exist, whose parents had told them that she was not allowed to come to their birthday parties or sleepovers, and even the more "moderate" ones talked about how things were always harder when you didn't "grow up with your own kind." Ayanna did not diet before prom or homecoming, and Olivia had to take her dress shopping the night before the event. The only dresses Ayanna would ever agree to try on were either lustrous black or electric neons.

"I'm just not pastels," Ayanna always said, even when Olivia insisted that they could share the same baby blue silk dress because their homecomings were on different weekends. Their mom had convinced Olivia to go only with a group of girlfriends to "avoid temptation." Ayanna refused to share her plans.

"We're so different," they liked to say, Ayanna happily, Olivia contemplatively. They were rarely confused for one another, even though they were identical. Olivia, she thought maybe it was because of how they walked. Ayanna had good posture, didn't mind eye contact, and didn't feel obligated to smile. Olivia, when she was objective with herself, thought that she was always looking away from people, that maybe she smiled sometimes for the wrong reasons, and her mom said things sometimes like "You're so graceful, Olivia, you walk like you're dancing," even though that didn't make any sense to Olivia.

It was easier sometimes for Olivia to list what they agreed on. They liked harmonizing to "Tha Crossroads" by Bone Thugs-N-Harmony.

They liked Messi better than Ronaldo. They preferred spicy to sweet. They liked staying up late to read any book that had a love triangle and having big opinions about who the main heroine chose.

Olivia felt the distance between them acutely. When she asked Ayanna about her church classes, everything about them felt like half-truths. It was Ayanna and three other people, another teenager and two adults who had recently joined the farmlands. Their studies were spread across the seven tenets of their faith: service, curiosity, kindness, wonder, observation, listening, and courage. *How could someone learn "wonder"?* Olivia thought, but decided that to ask would make her sister feel judged. Sometimes the four of them would sit in silence for two hours, instructed to write down all the things they noticed, to be precise and vivid in the details. They were scolded for bathroom breaks or for taking more than an occasional sip of water. What was missed without that level of fortitude?

They were expected to volunteer their time not just at their church but also in their community. During the summer when Ayanna had begun her classes, she and Olivia worked at a food pantry, sorting cans, checking out the bread donated from different bakeries, making signs encouraging people to donate menstrual-health products and deodorant, and smiling at everyone who came in. It was one of the few places where people seemed too self-conscious to make small talk about the two of them being twins.

After one of these, they decided to throw a twins sleepover, elaborate and planned out, from the snacks to the movies to a promise from Ayanna that her sister could paint her toes something other than black. It was a rare night when their mom was out of the house, was away visiting her own mother for once.

They sprawled on the living room carpet, both facing the ceiling, and played their favorite game, Wild Thoughts. They told each other every thought they had stored up that felt too weird to tell other people.

There was an element of one-upmanship, but if they had been asked to directly explain how this was a game, what the rules were, who the winner was, maybe the only answer either girl would've been able to give was "Because we said it's a game."

"I have this idea," Olivia said, her tone light in the way that it seemed to be when she was about to say something devastating, "that you rarely tell me the truth. That everything you tell me about your entire life is made up just to be different than me. I don't know why I think you would do that, but sometimes when I think about how different we are, it feels like a prank you're pulling on me."

You were not allowed to disagree or comment, unless invited. A strict rule was to let the statement sit for at least twenty seconds. Ayanna's right hand twitched. She opened and shut her mouth. Her tongue felt large and dry, the way it did when she smoked weed at parties, but she was sober, and it was probably because her mom and Olivia liked the air-conditioning set to we-would-rather-freeze-to-death-than-see-a-drop-of-sweat. The twenty seconds went slow.

"Sometimes," Ayanna said, "I feel guilty that I went with Dad and that you should've went with him instead. I like that you and Mom are close, but you're both afraid of everything. I come here and sometimes I'm jealous of the way you can read each other's thoughts, know each other so well, and sometimes, I think, Wow, they're both so afraid of everything. I want to see everything, eat everything, I want to know everything, I want to sleep with different people and—" She paused at the thrill of saying something true and solid about herself and how she felt, then swallowed. "I want to have a big life. It makes me sad that it feels like maybe you could want those things too, but you care so much about what people think. Dad's not perfect, but he wants me to have a life."

"I don't care that much," Olivia said.

"You broke the rules."

Olivia sat up. She dramatically fell back to the ground in a way that had to hurt a little bit. Her hair was in a short braid with scraggly ends. She was wearing a matching pajama set with a cherry-and-lemon pattern. Ayanna had a matching set, but it stayed buried at the bottom of a dresser drawer. There was only one time when Ayanna had broken the rules. Last year, Olivia had said, "I believe that you do go to hell when you have an abortion."

Ayanna asked Olivia what her opinions were on Palestine, on Congo, on the pogroms that happened in India. Why was she so obsessed with something rooted in controlling women's medical decisions rather than caring about actual living people? Ayanna's father and grandmothers had worked hard in their church to set a precedent: they didn't think a medical decision had to become religious. She had talked at her sister about how the average abortion was for people miscarrying, how almost every single one was a medical decision, and Olivia had rolled away from Ayanna, curled into a ball with her forehead pressed against her knees. Ayanna still felt a sting of embarrassment about how she had reacted, kept thinking about the different ways that she could have said this that would have made her sister want to listen to her. But since that incident, Ayanna was precise and measured every time they played Wild Thoughts.

"I don't think you actually believe it's possible to bring people back to life," Olivia said.

Ayanna paused. It was complicated. She *wanted* to believe and knew that was the most important thing, at least to her. There was an embarrassing fantasy Ayanna liked to indulge in of going through the door, charting different paths, finding incredible plants, and stumbling upon a group of the dead and leading them back home.

"Go again," Olivia said. She said these words slowly, deliberately.

"I don't think Mom likes me as a person," Ayanna said. "Maybe it's because I picked Dad, but I think it was really fucked up they let us pick at all." Ayanna's heart was beating faster as she said it. She tried to sound mature as she continued. "Everything about me, she tries to change or diminish."

It wasn't that she said this aloud to have Olivia refute it, but in her sister's silence and the way she reached out and gently squeezed her arm, there was a confirmation. Ayanna felt that Olivia was intrinsically likable, both because Ayanna loved her sister too much to be objective and because Olivia was a person who liked to be kind. There was a part of her soul that enjoyed nourishing others. Olivia was the girl who didn't mind listening to other people's complaints, who people would sometimes chat with when she worked at her church's soup kitchen, and who seemed to already know what to do to make babies smile big and laugh when she was in their presence. But Ayanna also felt that their mom liked Olivia because she was comfortably obedient. There were no *why*s or *nope*s, no *doesn't sound right*s from Olivia. Even when their mom said wild things about other women or abortions or seemed to be leaning toward a kind of ashy-black moderateness— Why does everything have to be about race? was a recent go-to with her—Olivia would just let her go on. Ayanna couldn't handle the idea that half her genes were from someone who could be so ignorant, who seemed predisposed at times to never think about other people and their situations, but to comfortably judge.

But still, Ayanna could feel her eyes warming with tears, and was embarrassed that a small part of her wanted Olivia to interrupt. It would've been so reassuring to be told she wasn't seeing things right.

"I sometimes have this dream that I'm going through the door," Olivia said. "Yours, the one in the field. And each time, I have this big feeling like waking up in the middle of the night, and the next day is Christmas, and I'm overwhelmed thinking everything I wanted could be in the house right now. But what's there is nothing. A void.

I see nothing, not even space-dark, but my brain still tells me it could be something. After I have this dream, it feels like I'm being called to the door. And then I go online, and I read all these internet posts about them. How they're a hoax, and they feel bad for the people who still treat them as special. How they've been around through history, appearing and reappearing at will."

In a way, this wait was even more excruciating. There were so many things Ayanna wanted to say. She wanted to interrogate Olivia more about the dream. What did she mean by "called to the door"? Sometimes, these were signs of a vision to come. Or to be more aware of someone's behavior: people in the community who talked about these feelings were the ones most likely to enter and suffer grave consequences. The doors-throughout-history theory was one she believed. Ayanna wondered if she and her sister had actually been going back and forth with each other on Reddit about that idea without realizing they were talking to each other. Would she have named herself cornburger420? No, Ayanna knew her sister was not someone she was arguing with on Reddit, but she wondered what they would have made of each other in a digital space, no sense of their relationship, just words on a screen.

"Can I comment?"

"Permission denied."

"It's not fair that you get to break the rules and also police them."

"Is that your thought?"

"No, it's me giving you a yellow card." Ayanna lifted an imaginary card. She made her voice gruff and said, "Listen up, number five, we're here for a clean match, if I see you play like that anymore, I'll send you off."

"I think I'm scared because I like soccer better than school, but I don't think I'm good enough to keep going. And it's not like women can really make a living off it." Olivia laughed, and to Ayanna, the laugh sounded painfully adult. "Mom thinks I would be an excellent radiologist or lawyer."

"I can't imagine you doing either of those things."

The room was growing darker as they spoke. The only light was coming from the dimming sky. Soon, the streetlamps outside would turn on. A neighbor across the street might turn on her unusually bright string lights that looked like chili peppers. There was a comforting feeling of being bodiless in the growing dark, of only being two voices who loved the sound of each other's rhythms and cadences, that made Ayanna shake off any feelings she had about what her sister was saying.

"I think you could be great," Ayanna said, and she meant it. Tried to summon up all the conviction in the world, then reached out and felt around until she found her sister's hand. The exact same size, fingernails also short, a small patch of hair on the knuckle of her middle finger. She clasped her sister's hand, hoping the feeling would add to the reassurance of her words and give her the strength to not want to conform to their mother's idea of how her life should be.

They listened to each other's breaths and kept holding hands. A car drove by, music shouting out the window about every party being ready to drop. Someone walking down the street dribbling a basketball. A firecracker popping.

"I'm mad at Dad because he gave permission to a group of rich assholes to do an 'expedition of the door.' They're making a big donation to the church to keep us from protesting. It's one of the first times I've ever really judged Dad."

Five, ten, fifteen, twenty.

"You seem too smart to worship a door to nowhere."

"It's not nowhere." They didn't let go of each other's hand. Ayanna's voice was soft. "Sometimes, there's a place with golden paths and golden plants. There's music, laughter, and conversations in the air. You can smell your favorite things. There are large trees. Moss. Your beloved dead are there. Sometimes it's a meadow, always wrapped in the blue hour. It's always chilly. The grass is long, and there are pink things. Sometimes, they're in the shape of people or animals or clouds. I think they're souls. I want to cross through and explore either side. It doesn't matter, but I'm suspicious that there's proof, actual proof, because of the voices, the pink things, that everything is reincarnated. And I guess I'm mad at Dad because he won't let me go. The risks are too high."

"Why do you think that's proof? Maybe it's proof you've actually seen aliens? What if all of these are gateways to other worlds? All the stuff you like, it could be like, IDK, some alien technology to make you not be hostile to them."

Ayanna squeezed her sister's hand while she thought. Her immediate reaction was to feel incomparably stupid. How had she never considered that possibility? When her friends spoke about their religions, how they believed in heaven and hell, in the idea there were angels looking after them and their loved ones, she had a reaction that was sometimes a mix of be-nice-to-baby and of wonder at the ability of the human brain to believe. It wasn't that she wanted to take their faith from them, she wasn't like the boys at her school who liked to attempt to dress stylish and felt like the only way to exist in a truly moral way in this world was to be an atheist, but there was something about having tangible proof, about belonging to a religion, that encouraged and furthered a greater sense of knowledge that, she realized, could still make her smug and content not to question her ideas or the synthesizing she was doing of the research and ideas of the other people in her faith class.

"I guess," Ayanna said, "if that happens, I'll be a little disappointed. But it'll also be cool because I'll have discovered aliens. A Black woman making first contact will still put me in the history books."

"You'll probably get an awkward statue or plaque."

"Maybe it'll be a hot statue. Statues can be very attractive."

Olivia rolled onto her side and laughed. "Tell me, please, which statues do you find hot?"

"I think the ancient Greeks really appreciated a great ass."

Her sister laughed harder.

* * *

The expedition would have six people in total. Three billionaires who treated adventuring as a personality. They had climbed Everest. One had a ticket booked on a space flight that would shoot him up into Earth's atmosphere in a fairly rickety rocket. The richest of the group was obsessed with the idea Atlantis had been real, there was treasure, a whole culture to preserve, and when his fleet of Alpha-and-Omega Submersibles were ready, he would give humanity its greatest gift. End Child Hunger you silly twat, someone tweeted at him every single day, and his social media intern ignored it every time. The most annoying rich guy of the group was rumored to have once gotten very high at a party and said to multiple people, "If we had been born sixty years ago we could've gotten away with hunting people. Imagine how fun that could've been. Actually intelligent foes! Proof that you're truly an apex predator."

Even the champagne in their willowy flutes, the conceptual art of brightly colored balloon dogs, and the wood chairs custom-carved with lions' heads were embarrassed. Later, he would say it was a joke and he was so fucking tired of the way that everyone took everything seriously. Back in the day, we could be raconteurs and provocateurs— all well-functioning societies needed people who would push boundaries and force others to reconsider their positions in order to continue thriving. Everyone now was too anxious. There was proof of cultural stagnation all over the globe and it was because of fear. And for a little while, to prove a point, he funded some research studies to see if there was a correlation between hormones in milk and clinical anxieties.

The fourth member of the expedition was the most annoying one's sister. She was allowed to come as a nod to the woke values of today; she was practical and was also a decent amateur filmmaker. Her preparations for the journey were a mixture of intense personal training that involved running five miles a day wearing a backpack filled with rocks and digging and refilling a large hole on property her family owned, and using replica hand-crank film cameras to get around the fact that electronics did not work within a certain radius of the doors. The footage was important because there was no point of going elsewhere, of doing new things, if in the aftermath they had to spend all their time arguing with people about the experience's truth. We used to take a man at his word was one of the frequent conversational turns in the adventurers' group chat. We would look at the things he had accomplished, the way he spoke, where he was educated, and be able to feel the righteousness. Sometimes at night, she stared into her silk sleep mask and almost trembled with a mix of delight, excitement, and anxiety while considering what it would feel like to take historical footage that would be studied and discussed past her lifespan. No one watched her YouTube channel. Only her friends and her parents' friends had come to her most recent video installation.

The other two members of the expedition were men who had started a new company called DoorSherpas. This was their first journey as a team, but both claimed to have journeyed through different doors—Australia, Germany—and returned safely with rare plants to sell. Their promised services included protection from the unknown, setting up tents, carrying the biggest packs, first-aid and CPR certification, sabering off champagne corks, and discretion. Their original name had been Joe and Joe Explorers, but that was viewed as too down-market. Rebranding themselves as Sherpas, despite both men being originally from Ohio, added a layer of authority that lengthened their yearslong waiting list. One had gone through the door, not Australia but Michigan, when he was seventeen. He had been lonely and depressed and read speculation that going through the doors would change you if you survived. It felt like a low-key solution to all his issues. Either he would die in a way where he could not be saved, or he would be a different person.

On a bright Thursday, he drove the two hours and forty-five minutes to the door, stopping only to buy Takis in Detroit and wonder if he could convince any of the adults outside the gas station to buy him a forty for courage. When it was clear no one was interested in indulging a white kid's desire for an Olde English, including one man yelling at him, "Get your Ferris Bueller motherfucker ass out of here," he felt more than ready to see the door.

During the drive, Joe first tried to think of all the reasons he had to live. Listed off friends, family, but each name added to the list made him consider if those connections were even real. His parents were young and could have more kids if they wanted. His friends could be nice, but there was always a feeling that everything was superficial.

Did he truly know them? Did anyone even *want* to know him? All the girls he liked were out of his league, and at seventeen, that felt like one of reality's immutable laws. Joe's biggest crush, Lila (actually Lisa, but she had done a strategic rebranding in eighth grade), was currently getting made fun of because there was a rumor she had given one of the football guys head over spring break, just because she was bored. He listened to the same song he always liked to listen to, about being lost souls and maybe the only things in the universe that know anything are stars.

"I don't want to be anything," Joe said. It felt good and true in his mouth, so he said it again and again, until he wasn't even fully aware his mouth was still saying it. Everything in the world felt brighter. A bug smashed on the windshield, green and iridescent. Its leftover splat was art.

He parked his shitty car alongside the road; it was one his parents had given him because it still ran great except for the fact that anytime it hit seventy-five miles per hour it started rumbling and complaining as if it would explode. A perfect car for a moody teenage boy. Joe walked down the red dirt road underneath a canopy of trees. There were birds rustling the leaves, but they weren't saying anything.

"If one of you tells me not to do it"—Joe paused to speak up toward the foliage—"I'll stay."

They said nothing a person could understand.

There were three notes in the glove compartment of his car. One, kind, addressed to his mother. Another, true and rude and angry, addressed to his friend Dustin, who was the only person in the world that he truly liked. Any time Joe was his true self in front of Dustin, he felt better. The final, grumpy and terse, addressed to his father.

"I'm going to die with Taki breath."

If he had been able to laugh then, to hear how melodramatic his tone was, Joe would've gotten back in the car and driven home. Spent the drive sitting in the I-75 traffic backups around Flint, practicing telling his parents that he needed help.

The door was in the distance. There was no other blue like it in the world. It was saturated, deep, and maybe it was like a holographic X-Men trading card he'd had growing up. There were moments after he blinked when Joe felt sure he was seeing afterimages of the door. It was in front of itself, behind, sideways.

"I don't want to be anything," Joe whispered.

Each step was faster and faster. He heard his breath, kept resmelling the Takis, he was sweating, and there was dirt in the air. The door swung open.

There were people around it, an older Black woman who was writing in a journal, a guy wearing camo with a gun holstered to his side, and a middle-aged Black man who had taken his shoes off. He was leaning back, his head up to the sun, away from the door, and it was clear that the only thing he was aware of was the warmth.

Joe sprinted. He understood these people would want to talk to him, try to talk him out of things. No one wanted to see a teen die in front of them. And he felt a little guilty—as he ran the fastest he ever had in his life and blew past them into elsewhere—that they would see him pop out of existence.

The air was cooler. So many things were rich and golden, but somehow their shine didn't make his eyes ache. The air smelled like cotton candy perfume, gasoline, and the weird cherry cookies his mom and grandma made at Easter. Somehow the combination wasn't disgusting.

His heartbeat was loud, his hands wouldn't still, he was half crouched in a position that made him look as if he were preparing for a footrace. But despite it all, Joe was alive. When he calmed, there was so much to see. A path winding up toward a dense forest or down below to an area filled with golden ferns. Joe stooped and used his fingers to dig into the ground. The soil shimmered in his hands but was mostly black. Large bugs skittered from between his fingers. They were the first things that weren't flora, that seemed alive. On the ground were large seeds, akin to a pumpkin's, clinging to thready gold pulp. Another sign he was truly elsewhere. Last year, he had won a quiz bowl competition by correctly stating ferns used spores, not flowers or seeds, to reproduce. But here were golden seeds, here were bugs with a shine to them that maybe came from primarily eating these plants. A laugh in the distance, wheezy as if the joke heard was devastating and true. The seeds smelled like movie theater popcorn. Without thinking much of it, Joe ripped some off the roots, didn't care about the dirt because they smelled so good, and tossed them into his mouth. They still tasted like popcorn, but also of earth and a flavor he would later describe as aged cheddar cheese.

This was the part Joe kept to himself and never told his business partners: After chewing and swallowing the seeds, within five minutes, he had the feeling of his head getting lighter and lighter. His hands felt miles away from his torso. He wanted to clap or sing, maybe suddenly dance. There was a broad smile on his face, and Joe was aware enough to try considering the last time he had felt so good. Maybe seeing a Pistons game with his dad? The first time he had played "Come as You Are" on his acoustic guitar in front of other people? Then, a feeling of overwhelming lightness as he slowly sat down, thunk—*Maybe I am dying*, he thought—and lay prone.

For twenty glorious minutes, his body was a pond. Sometimes still and dead, but with ripple after ripple of that same smile, that urge to dance, that feeling that has no word in English, but the closest Joe could come to articulating it was: I-was-connected-to-everything-in-the-universe. Sometimes, he thought he could feel and hear gravity itself hugging him and telling him he had value. There was a resonance to everything. Even the bugs below had their songs.

When the high was gone, Joe gathered as many seeds as possible, being careful not to take any to delay his work. He ripped multiple ferns out of the ground, until he had give or take fifty seeds. He put them in his jeans pockets, not minding dirt or pulp or bugs. Life would be worth living if he could feel this way at least once a month.

Now, at thirty, during the few public events that Joe had done, he spoke slowly and confidently about things like man's need to conquer mystery. The reason humans existed was that the universe longed to be understood. People were naturally fact-gathering, pattern-understanding, relentless creatures. He liked to say things like "The most noble undertaking a person can take on is adding to the greater bubble of human knowledge." And that was why the doors should be explored and taken seriously. It was in the same lineage as why men went to the moon, why we scaled Everest. Eventually we'd be able to catalog every living thing in the oceans' depths. It was an approximation each time, but even the most incredulous person listening to him seemed to want to believe him. That was what people wanted to be sold in every venture, Joe would think while looking at the audience with their wide eyes and slightly opened mouths, a greater purpose.

The Joes called the seeds they sold "acre." Some people synthesized them into a drug that they called "CC," short for "cash crop." Other names were "cereal" and "slip." There was a popular rap song that called it "kino": Dropped some kino / saw time and space / and my baby mama's face. It was not a great song, but enough people liked it to constantly debate whether kino was CC or shrooms or MDMA. It was popular enough that the Joes could see their empire in the distance: a front organization of billionaire expeditions that went through official government channels, brief side trips to gather enough seeds to continue making acre, and incredible markups on both revenue streams.

Monetary donations to the churches associated with the doors would be handled by the rich people, and each church quietly had asked for a small percentage of acre. Most didn't take it recreationally, but as part of their church's most sacred rituals.

Ayanna's father had already received his cut. He was weighing the responsibilities he felt as one of the church elders to initiate his daughter firmly into the faith, and a parent's hesitation of wondering what would happen if his ex-wife found out that he had given this to one of their teenage daughters. They spoke regularly, they had to, but every conversation was seeped in the molasses of all the things they were keeping from each other. Even when they were together, though, being open and direct with each other had always been their biggest problem.

The expedition was in three days. Ayanna's ceremony was also in three. The twins slept in sleeping bags on their mother's living room floor. Both dreamed of a blue door opening. For Olivia, it was a mix of image and sound. Someone walking in high heels on a hardwood floor, a screech of water in an old pipe, and the sound of an ice cream truck playing a song about birds. There was an empty room.

Ayanna's: knee-length grass with a texture like velvet; four hands with yellow nails slapping and scratching their way across a golden path; a man she didn't recognize telling her once he had been the most famous cellist in the world and that had mattered more than being in love, but now he was dead and he understood maybe he had been wrong about sentimentality; her mother handing her a rosebush made of marble and telling her to please keep it alive; and an itchy feeling like she had forgotten something vastly important and would be scolded for her carelessness.

Ayanna woke up. Her sister's breathing was gentle, even. She listened carefully, let the rhythm of her sister's life as it moved in and out of her nose and mouth ease her back to rest.

6

"The first time the doors appeared was in dinosaur times, approximately eighty-seven million years ago, give or take ten mil. It was a great time to be a velociraptor, running among the tall grass and stones, chasing prey, speaking to one another through chirps and snarls and tail whips and wags. Dinosaur languages are almost impossible to translate into English because of their complications. Their bodies were certain, and they spoke in direct gestures but their conversations were nihilistic and circular. The first appearance of the door in their territory was treated as if it were just another part of the world, one without merit because it could not be eaten, it refused to be broken into parts, it could not be used as shelter, and its color was ominous. When it opened on occasion, only a few were willing to run inside. It smelled like freshly cracked eggs, raw meat, blood, feathers pecked clean and rolled lightly in desert dust, and glistening ponds on a too-hot day, but inside there were trees, bright soil, and stillness.

Remember, people have evolved to the point where we need brief, planned stagnancies. We call them 'vacations' and the average among us can barely afford them. A chance for a person to hear her own thoughts, for reverie, and a deep, dreamless nap in a very cool room on a hot day. For the velociraptors, and this should be obvious, stillness was death. Their religion was momentum and feasts."

Ayanna as an adult always paused here, certain that the previous paragraph had been written solely by her grandmother. The tell for her was the word *reverie*, her grandma's favorite. It was absurd to her that these were things she had grown up believing. It was a gift to her to see these things and see the hands of so many people she loved in the work of it.

Eventually, though, a door became another kind of measurement. Every time one appeared, species disappeared. They appeared again when the Neanderthals and *Homo sapiens* were in the midst of their great maelstrom of fucking and fighting. In some parts of the world, the appearance heralded in an age of prosperity. Hammers and shivs and slingshots were set down, the time instead spent exchanging information from the best animal blood and powders to use for healing and art to ideas of weather and migration. They showed their open palms to the doors, let their royalty and elders go through to either devastating or lovely effect, and for them, what were cities accumulated.

If Ayanna had lived a richer life with parents who didn't believe in traditional schooling, she could have gone to Spain and seen some of the art from this time. Where other people saw a series of ladders and dots, Ayanna would have seen doors. She would have seen trails that her peers in the church had sketched into their journals rendered as the complex dots. There wouldn't have been the queasy storytelling thrill of being "the first," but there would have been the very human comfort of legacy.

In contemporary times, the Michigan door was the easiest to get permission to traverse because the current administration felt they had bigger things to care about. Scientists and members of the armed forces went on a variety of expeditions and found the following:

1. There was never a guarantee that during the crossing you would be safe. For a while, they thought there was a pattern, six through, one no, then three through, two no, and it began again, but then

there was an expedition where everyone, one-two-three-four, popped quickly. After that, it was at random.

2. Everyone used the colloquial term *popping*, because *exploded* was too dramatic and *pop* felt matter-of-fact. They used it because even the *why* of it was still uncertain.

3. It was an easy way to make money and gain information by letting rich people pay for permits to go exploring and to promise that all things discovered on their expeditions were also property of the US government. It was also less of a burden on a military already struggling to recruit people to fight multiple wars. There were so many people needed elsewhere, why keep sending them to what felt like a beautiful, yet boring, national park?

4. The door would disappear again and might not return for hundreds or thousands of years. It was driven, like the most interesting things in the universe, by an unseen force. Even a scrap of information about where and how people were going elsewhere could help humanity leap a thousand years in development.

As an adult, Ayanna would read those rationales about the Michigan doors over and over in different declassified files about all the findings from artifacts gathered by and copied for her church, and theorizing typed up purposefully boring official reports given to Congress. There were three things she would consider the rest of her life. First, the idea these unseen forces were opening doors, giving people access to two static elsewheres, were part of the universe's weather patterns. That while we thought of weather as heat and liquid and air, forces such as this rippled across galaxies and the void. The second, which would have a profound impact on her life, was there were health impacts for people who had spent an extended amount of time traveling in these other spaces. Some people reported hearing voices, others reported seeing shadows and blobs, and some said that there were times when they fell into trances.

In those states, people sometimes spoke in a language that was still being studied, but every person, regardless of nationality, spoke it when in this state. Sometimes they wrote in a mixture of English letters, scribbles, and symbols that ranged from mathematical to cute little houses and cats. A sample sentence: A ~~~~~%γBD. To an older Ayanna, that sentence read "The silver mountains are where we go to be reborn." She did not tell people she could read or understand this language. It was too much trouble, and no one powerful seemed to consider the possibility that she truly knew things. They assumed she was too ordinary.

Finally, the third thing, what she had actually been trying to find clues of in her reading: there were four different accounts of people entering the door out into the blue meadows, as they were colloquially called. Most had to wander far and for long times before they saw her. But one account had her by the door. She was reading a book despite the dark, her bare feet pointed up in the air. The man who saw her said she had a lot of questions and that she insisted it was impossible for her to go back through the door and it was impossible to be lonely here even when you tried. Don't worry about me, she said to everyone who met her. Ayanna would read those lines over and over, wondering if, somehow, they were a message meant for her.

7

The morning after their sleepover, Ayanna realized she wanted Olivia to attend her ceremony despite all the obnoxious conversations she would have to have with her parents to make it happen. Olivia was in the kitchen making scrambled eggs and bacon. She was listening to gospel music and humming along in what could have been a kind imitation of their mother.

Ayanna strode into the room doing her best imitation of a hot TV lawyer, confident and deep-voiced, and said, "I'm going to call a family meeting."

Olivia ignored her and sang louder, trying to hit a note that you truly had to have a blessed throat to even attempt.

"I want you to come to my church's version of Confirmation."

Olivia stopped singing. She turned. The silk scarf she was wearing to protect her edges had come a little loose during the night and was looser still from her singing and dramatic gestures. It made her cute in a way that Ayanna felt sure she herself could never be.

"We can make it happen," Olivia said. She turned back and ground some coffee beans, despite not being allowed to drink coffee. This was for Ayanna. Mom said that coffee was for adults and it could stunt your growth. When she was eighteen, she could do what she liked with her body.

They sat at the table and ate breakfast, talking about the best ways to convince their parents. Ayanna felt nostalgia simmering inside her. As they ate and schemed, she could feel every breakfast they'd had like this together. The way their brains could sync up, how without saying it aloud, they could both communicate they loved each other not just as family, but as friends. Ayanna felt certain they would be doing this their entire lives, coming together for a meal one of them cooked and laughing their way through it. She was seventeen and felt certain in the way that only the very young or very rich can, that she could see the rest of her life spread out in front of her. All the times they would spend together until they were both ninety-four were there.

Olivia would sow the seeds by texting their mom and saying she wanted to talk about something important. Then, on the phone, she would tell their mom she was worried about college and how it would make it even harder to stay connected with Ayanna. Meanwhile, Ayanna would go home and talk to their dad face-to-face because he was hard as fuck over texts and baby soft face-to-face. She would say the truth.

Neither expected both parents would respond: "We should probably talk as a family about this."

That night they gathered for dinner at Ayanna's home. She knew there was a brief period of time when all four of them had lived here together, but could remember only the ways her parents spoke about that time rather than her own experiences of it.

"I still hate this rug," her mother said within two minutes of being there.

There was nothing noteworthy Ayanna could see about the rug. There was a small stain on it from when she had spilled some hot chocolate on it six years ago.

"Is this the same plant?" she asked while standing in the kitchen, rubbing her right fingers with her left hand. Ayanna's father nodded.

Her face was in flux between narrowed eyes and an occasional half smile. Nothing and everything seemed to please their mother as she continued looking around.

Ayanna and Olivia worked together on an elaborate salad to pretend they were not watching their parents. They peered at a cookbook and made a vinaigrette that turned out very poorly because neither was paying attention to the right amount of oil and lemon and seasoning to put in. It wasn't that they hadn't ever seen their parents together—they had been at soccer games and school plays and award ceremonies, often sitting together and chatting with a brusque intimacy that reminded their daughters they had known each other for more than half their lives at this point—but they hadn't been together in this house since the divorce.

It was, fittingly, a portal to imagining a different reality, one in which they had stayed together, in which they were all unremarkably happy and shared a rhythm and tempo. Ayanna could see afternoons where she and Olivia came home from soccer practice and each ate a bowl of cereal, then did their homework together in the living room. She would wake up at night and her mom would be in the dining room reading a book and slowly drinking a cup of nighttime tea. Their parents making a plan in the backyard for the yearly vegetable garden. All of them watching a movie together and splitting a large bowl of popcorn. There would be annoyances—someone always hopping into the shower when you were getting ready to take a bath; the loneliness of being around people whom you loved but could feel how emphatically different you were from them; bad meals; three out of four of them on their periods at the same time; parents arguing with each other about money; petty arguments with Olivia over who took the last Fruit Roll-Up—but there would be the intimacy between them that most of her friends took for granted.

"Be careful, Ay," Olivia said. "You almost got your finger."

Ayanna nodded and set the kitchen utility knife down.

She had done a terrible job of dicing the shallots.

The lettuce had been torn in a half-hearted way, demonstrating how little Olivia was also paying attention. Their parents turned toward them and gestured to the backyard. The girls went to them and together watched as a doe and two fawns sat in the grass.

"Dad," Ayanna said, "we should keep them. They would be great pets."

"We should probably get them to leave," her mom said. "They'll eat your whole garden."

WHEN THEIR DAD LOOKED at the salad, he shook his head at it. Everything was cut either too small or too big. The dressing somehow tasted sweet. Neither twin could agree on which one had accidentally added sugar instead of kosher salt. Ayanna couldn't stop watching her mother. She was completely unsure of what it was that was so annoying to her. It reminded her of when for a while her dad had been dating someone seriously, and during that time her mom had refused to meet her. She would not go to soccer games or pick up Ayanna if "Miss Ashley" was there. By this point, they had not been together for six years. Even middle school Ayanna could not fathom this. She'd had an idea of what it meant to be in love and saw no interest, no longing, not even friendship, coming from her mom's actions, even before Miss Ashley had started coming over for dinner. Her behavior during that time, and during this dinner years later, felt akin to acting out for attention. If that, too, was a part of being in love, then Ayanna figured, well, being in love was probably never going to be for her.

Olivia nudged Ayanna under the table.

Ayanna cleared her throat. She explained how much her upcoming church ceremony meant to her, tried to wax poetic about family, wove in some details about how these were precious times to have together, and in general managed to make both of her parents lift their eyebrows throughout. Her father's were raised because he couldn't help but find Ayanna inherently hilarious. The speech was terrible in its length and awkwardness, and she was being so weird, so unlike herself, that it felt like she was doing a bit. But he knew if he even neared a chuckle, she would be furious with him. Her mother's were raised because she had come in with the full intention of saying no, this would be impossible. She had not allowed Olivia to go to their weird but kind Wiccan neighbor's moonlight soul-binding ritual to her live-in partner. She had talked Olivia out of going to her friend Ruth's bat mitzvah. No temples, no mosques, no sweat lodges, just good old-fashioned pews. There was a precedent here to keep Olivia's path firmly set on being a good Christian. When she was an adult, she could make her own choices about faith experiences, but other faiths, well, those might be too confusing at this point in Olivia's life. But the speech, the earnestness, the way Ayanna's mouth had curled into a frown, how she kept saying Olivia was her best friend in the whole world, the stutter in the middle of the word *importance*, and the fact that for the first time in ages when she saw Ayanna, she didn't see someone who felt a little too cool for her own good.

It was childish, yes, to look at your child and feel this way. But you also, to be a good mother, had to see your child analytically and fully. You could parent someone well only if you saw them as they were.

And there was a relief, too, that her former mother-in-law, a woman who was not afraid to tell Opal her approaches to parenting and religion risked making her granddaughter simple and closed-minded, had not been invited over to dinner. It was a courtesy Antony had not done for her in the past.

Without her asking, he had pulled out the hot sauce and put it next to her glass of water. He had put extra salad on her plate and filled up her water when he had gotten more for himself. This, too, was simple but effective. There were so many complaints she still had about

Antony, and away from him it was easy to forget how courteous he could be. It was an indictment of the world, or at least the way that the average man Opal had met during her time in it behaved, that small things like remembering what she liked and making sure she felt taken care of during a meal still carried so much weight.

"What do you think?" Opal asked him.

He kept his face neutral. "I think." He paused and took a sip of water, then began again. "I think, despite everything, we're family. And our daughters want to be close and share experiences with one another. I see a lot of families now who don't bother being family. And here they are. Trying. So, it feels wrong to me to say no."

Antony took another long drink. "I want to be clear I don't think it would be wrong for you to say no. We've been talking about these things for seventeen years now. We are very different parents. This is just a for-me statement."

Beneath the table, Olivia took Ayanna's hand for a second and squeezed it to let off some nervous energy.

"Okay," Opal said.

"Okay?" Olivia said. "Okay!"

"Thanks, Mom," Ayanna said. She got up and hugged her mother around the shoulders with a quick burst and then went and sat back down.

"Can I go in the door?" Olivia asked.

"Absolutely not," her parents responded in unison.

Olivia apologized immediately, as she had her entire life. She swallowed what she wanted to say. The night before, she had dreamed she was at prom, walking through a crowd of women all in blue dresses while holding silver high heels high and dramatic in her left hand. It's here for you, it's here for you, people kept saying to her. An actor who played a melodramatic vampire boyfriend on her favorite TV show was there eating a baked potato with his bare hands. It was burning him, but he kept eating. Between steaming mouthfuls, he begged her to stay with him. But the door was open. She could hear violins and rhythmic handclaps and three voices harmonizing her name. Then, a woman she did not recognize, but whom her heart knew, came to her and said, "I need you to find Marlie Evans for me. I need you to tell her that I would never just leave her."

It was foolish, Olivia knew, to feel like a dream actually spoke directly to reality. You were supposed to chunk pieces off and think sideways. Losing teeth was a fear of change, not just am-I-afraid-of-getting-older? A snake was almost always sex. Et cetera, et cetera. But it was hard for these dreams not to feel like someone or something was talking to her.

Her dad was telling a story, something convoluted she couldn't follow because she hadn't been paying attention. Ayanna and her mom were listening, and Olivia noted how their facial expressions were exactly the same, head tilted in a way that showed off their half smiles, eyes a little squinted as if they could physically look for holes to poke in the story they were being told. *Was it the same in all families?* she wondered. Were there millions of people like her, watching two people united by blood who could barely agree on things like whether the sky was blue but who had the same exact eyes? She took a sip of water. Wiped her mouth with a paper napkin. Was love, at least familial love, allowing yourself to be tied to these people no matter how little you could understand them?

Then, the opportunity to tell them what she was thinking had passed because everyone else was talking about driving to the ice-cream stand they liked so much to get soft serve and maybe walk it off in the park. The fireflies were finally awake again. For so many years, Olivia had wanted this. The whole family laughing and talking and complaining about how quickly their ice cream was melting, and laughing harder at the mess. Someone walking past and thinking, Wow, the Owens-Morgan family likes one another so much. Let things be normal, she told herself, then shook the dream off and headed to the car.

8

The first ritual was Ayanna's least favorite. At 5:45 a.m., she put on her white linen flowy pants and matching tank top and walked to the soy field. She lay in the dirt at the base of the door and looked up into the sky and meditated on the church's doctrines. If Ayanna fell asleep, the ceremony would be over. She would have to wait another year. The idea here was for her to simultaneously root herself to this world while envisioning what she could do to make it a better place and to reflect on the sins and misdeeds and faults in her personality, which ones to accept as incontrovertible parts of herself and which to fix. Ayanna supposed she could daydream. No one would know what she really had thought. Everything was supposed to be written down after the hour's meditation, then burned in the barn. The soil was damp with dew, the sunrise fading to dad-jeans blue and soft wheat yellow. She wanted to paint it. Ayanna could tell her outfit was getting dirty. It was annoying, but the point of all the white was to carry the day's stains. They were another level of symbolism. White for all her higher aspirations and the colors of the day to symbolize that even when you agree to look outward, you should always stay rooted from where you came.

But she wanted this. So, Ayanna looked at the ways the blue became richer, how the clouds were hinting at a storm later that day, and told herself she would become a kinder person, someone willing to see other people's sides. For her entire life, she would find ways to make the lives of people around her better. Even if it was something small like buying a surprise dinner for a friend going through a hard time or recycling and continuing on at food banks and soup kitchens. She would walk farther than anyone else along the golden path, go to places where people feared to tread, and come back to add to a greater understanding of what it was. That was holy.

I will be kinder to people I disagree with, more willing to stand up for what's right, and I won't be afraid, Ayanna told herself over and over. She reached her hands into the dirt, felt how it was already warming.

The next step was to thank God, the creator of the doors, the creator of love throughout the world, and to feel the flow of it. When there was love, there was God. Where there was kindness, there was God. When there was natural beauty, there was proof of the being's great benevolent generosity. This was the part that always made Ayanna hesitate. To her, it felt ugly to think all these things were because of God. When she was in faith sessions, she had repeated these ideas back verbatim to please the church elders and her grandmother. But alone here, lying in the field, Ayanna thanked God not for being these things, but for having the generosity to give humans the capacity for these things. To be willing to love and to be loved in return, even when things between people could be so painful and confusing, felt to her like the purpose of existence. And to make yourself unavailable to these connections was a living death. They should be the most valuable things in a person's life, Ayanna felt. Already, there were people, especially boys at school, who said things like the measures of a person's life were the shoes they had, the house they kept, the car they drove. Maybe it was true their families had big houses, their lives were easier because they didn't have to worry whenever they bought things, but it still—although Ayanna knew she would never, ever want to say this to their faces—seemed a really empty way to look at life. Imagine having to think about the world in that way for ten years, let alone eighty or ninety. Would you even be recognizably a person after a life spent like that?

It was so embarrassing to think earnest thoughts like these. Ayanna covered her face with her dirty hands. Another unbearable thought surfaced: *Why can't I be cool?*

* * *

Most of the expedition was still sleeping. The only two awake were the DoorSherpas who were going through the expedition plans for the day. If the door opened to the meadow, they weren't going through because there would be none of the ferns they were planning on gathering. According to their contacts, there had been a National Guard member who had gone through the door three days ago and had popped, so the risk level of going through was very low. The pattern this summer seemed to still be seven safe, one death.

The Joe who had been through this door before was trying not to feel swept away by nostalgia. On the drive again, he had listened to the song on repeat, and while now it felt silly and theatrical, there had been a point when all the years had slipped away. He had raised his head up into a howl along with the singer, gestured along when the singer again sang about being so lost that only the stars could see him. Seeing the door again had been surprisingly like seeing an old friend. He hadn't felt the same way when he had gone through the other ones. But this one had given him a purpose. A dumb thought that embarrassed Joe: *Does the door remember me?*

The other Joe was far more focused. He was preparing the small breakfast bar in the Airbnb they were all staying at—none of the area's hotels had felt appropriate for how important the occasion was. Veuve, orange juice he'd paid some teens to squeeze, sparkling waters, and fruit that had originally been spread on a platter to look kaleidoscopic. The adventurers, as they liked to be called, had brought their own personal chef, a petite woman of Chinese descent with pink hair and tattoos of demons and forks on her forearms. They liked to brag that she had cooked for Oprah, but there was no proof of this on the internet. He was sure they would say it again while they ate their runny eggs with chili oil, their seed toast smeared in garlic, and their delicately cut avocados.

Still sleeping were three out of the other four members of the expedition. They had stayed up late drinking and already discussing their next adventure. Half wanted to take one of those quick trips up into the Earth's atmosphere, to feel the velocity and force of trying to escape and to see how truly beautiful it all looked from up there. A famous TV actor had cried and wasn't embarrassed about it, so it had to be pretty good. The other half had heard there was a jungle on an island off the coast of East Africa. Its inhabitants were famous, despite having no modern medicine and very little infrastructure, for living past one hundred. The nuts that grew there, buttery and delicious, were the secret to their longevity. The islanders looked good too. A sixty-year-old looked thirty.

"That's what you call an adventure? Gathering nuts so you don't have to do a skin-care routine?" one had laughed.

Another suggested he could bribe a senator he knew to let them stay in an area of the Utah desert that people were not allowed to camp in. It was a place where aliens kept crashing their ships. Several times nonhuman remains had been pulled out of the wreckage. They were divided between whether it was cool, gross, or boring.

"Get him on the phone and ask if they have any alive ones on a base."

One was quiet in the corner. He was going to find his son out there on the path. There would be no other adventures after this. *Tomorrow,* he thought, *I will hug him and apologize for everything I did wrong the first time.*

Nothing had been settled when they went to bed, but there was a glow all four shared from drinking too much liquor. They could feel all the books that would be written about them one day. Those texts would not include their conversation about whether they would have sex with aliens, if they would have to sign forms about whether or not they would if they visited Utah, and who the hottest alien to ever be featured on *Star Trek* was. Those conversations were not dignified.

Another member of the expedition who was awake was Margot. She was video journaling like she did every morning. The room she had was painted seafoam green, there were wooden children's toys stacked in a corner, and there was a shelf full of books that all had titles like *STEM for Babies*. Margot leaned against the wall, adjusted the angle of the camera until her jaw looked its sharpest and her nose looked its smallest, and then talked through her feelings. This, too, could be history. Margot talked through the weight-lifting routine of the past few months, the different films she had studied, from the *Roundhay Garden Scene* to *Battleship Potemkin*. She could hear the affectation in her voice, and kept willing herself to sound less self-conscious, less studied. It was why she had never really taken off as an influencer; someone had always written in the comments about how rehearsed she sounded, if they were being nice. More often she received the comment *this b is faaaaaaaaaaaaaaaaaake*.

"What do you say," Margot mused, "when you know your life is about to change?"

She had hoped making this video, because doing this was her

morning routine, would dampen the flames of anxiety licking at her stomach. And it wasn't like she hadn't asked herself this question before. If she went into her archive, she'd see she'd asked this the morning before she had headed to Oberlin, the morning before her first wedding, the morning before signing divorce papers, before joining the film conservatory, before what she had thought were monumental dates with so many people who only ended up disappearing in another month or so. If Margot had been a wiser person, she might have considered if making every life change a performance was actually harmful. If consistently trying to mold her life into something consumable was keeping her from being transformed. But instead, Margot watched the reversed screen as her face clenched with anxiety at not being able to answer the question. Lines around her eyes and mouth appeared deeper, a red zit was on her chin, her hair was too long, and was one of her ears drooping?

Margot took out her vitamin powders. One promised to give her the moon's wisdom, help with night vision, and soothe nerves. The other was for sunlight serenity and glossy hair. She chose moon's wisdom, poured it into her glass of tap water and swirled until the water turned light green. As she gulped down the bitter liquid, Margot read more of her novel. It was about a small-town couple; the husband kept engaging in affairs—with bank tellers, with the administrative assistant at his company, with the hairdresser—and the wife pretended to never know. None of the women were named, only given jobs. No one wanted to leave each other despite the affairs because they were always imagining "their sad brown apartments in poor school districts and they deserved better lives than that." On the plane, the novel had seemed hilarious and a little sexy. Now, Margot wondered if the book was saying something she couldn't understand, and if the writer should maybe be a little less smug about it.

And then, a knock at the door, breakfast was ready.

* * *

When Ayanna had reflected for a significant amount of time, five members of the church, including her father, appeared. They all carried shovels and dug around Ayanna. As they hollowed out a part of the field, they sang a song she didn't recognize about change and being alone and facing your life and maybe seeing the eyes of love. Ayanna had wanted a Frank Ocean song initially—which made her father groan—but hearing them sing this, she cried. Everything in the ceremony, she understood, was taking her to a point where she would feel moved, but that didn't mean it wasn't working. When they were done digging, they helped Ayanna up and over the holes. Her father handed her seeds. She held on to his hand and looked up into his dark eyes. She could not brush the dirt off her. It had to stay.

"I'm proud of you," he mouthed.

She planted the seeds, half plants from the other side, half a mix of bee's-friend pollinators she had chosen. In the distance, Ayanna could see Olivia was watching. She wondered what her sister made of all this, and was tempted toward embarrassment, until remembering that every week her sister agreed a thin wafer was genuinely Christ's flesh and ate it.

When Ayanna was done planting, dirt was thick beneath her fingernails. She was tired and hungry, but there were still hours to go. At the break between, Ayanna was allowed to eat. Olivia sat with her, kept refilling her glass with more and more water. She leaned her face forward, let Olivia use a makeup wipe on her cheeks and neck, even though it was against the rules. It was almost too much after all the thinking and emotions to have someone take care of her. Her sister's touch was soft, sweet.

"I cried a little," Olivia said. "I don't know what any of this means, but it still felt beautiful to me."

"I mean, it is a beautiful day," Ayanna said lightly. Her brain was everywhere.

"I think it's also because our family helped build these customs. I thought about Grandma. Remember how she says that every time you plant a seed, it's a prayer?"

Ayanna nodded. It was impossible for her to forget. Their grandmother said this every time she planted something, every time she saw the little sprouts of a new spring. There was something beautiful in it, yes, sure, but Ayanna thought it would take years before the saying would be meaningful again. She was supposed to have been here, but now that she was approaching eighty, the heat and length of the day would've been too much. Their grandmother would be the one at the end of the long day who would clean Ayanna. There were white washcloths and a steel basin filled with cold water, lavender, and ice waiting. She tried not to think about it. The longing to be clean and to cool off felt far more urgent than being hungry.

Her grandmother had told her there was nothing wrong with staying on this earth. If the door opened for her, it was just as fine to stay as it was to walk. Ayanna hadn't looked at her grandmother as she had said those things the night before. Her eyes had been on her grandmother's hands, her fingernails painted latte-color. She hadn't wanted to see her grandmother's eyes.

"I just thought it wouldn't feel sacred to me knowing that people had built these things," Olivia said.

"Didn't Jesus invent Mass?"

"What?"

"He was a real person, right?"

"I thought you were talking about the theory of mass for a minute, not like Mass Mass. I don't know. I'm tired." Olivia paused. "Do you think it makes me a bad person if I don't think so?" She drew a heart on the condensation on her glass. "Or, like, not a bad person, but a bad Christian."

"I don't know if I can judge," Ayanna said. It seemed like the only thing she had the emotional bandwidth to say at that moment.

"I just think it's better sometimes if Jesus is a story God told us. When I start thinking of him as a real person, someone who had a body. Ayanna, bodies are so gross."

"Body odor, farts, throwing up, backne, cankles, eye boogers."

"Exactly."

Olivia laughed. "Mom would ground me for this conversation. She can probably sense I'm having it right now."

Ayanna kept what she was thinking to herself.

* * *

The expedition members put on their hiking shoes, their expensive sunglasses, their vests, and tested the weight of their packs. Then, at the table, they signed another round of contracts ensuring that if anything went wrong, they could not sue anyone from the church or the Sherpa company or the US government. One of them wondered if he should have brought his lawyer to look over these final versions, but knew if his lawyer was involved, there would be no journey, only hopping on the phone and years of parsing sentences in size-ten font.

After the forms were done, they all took a formal portrait with the photographer they had flown in. Each was at an angle where they were looking into the distance, no smiles, and they were encouraged to "imagine oceans in the distance."

* * *

Sitting in the barn, Ayanna received a small backpack from her church sponsor. Inside were a water bottle, three small flashlights and backup batteries, a solar blanket, a small solar lantern, a waterproof notebook and three pens, a small first-aid kit, different dried foods, a mechanical watch that would still work over there, a golden pill, and a bracelet made of leather and black-gray beads. Ayanna put on the bracelet and examined the pill. In the dappled light coming from the barn windows, it was an optical illusion. It was simultaneously pill-shaped and looked like molten metal; it didn't seem possible.

"Ayanna, why do you walk this path?"

"I walk this path to see God's love." The words came out more passionately than she expected.

"Ayanna, why do you walk this path?"

"To learn about all the wonders of creation."

The church elder's eyes were kind. Ayanna could feel how proud she was.

"Ayanna, why do you walk this path?"

"To understand."

The only other acceptable answer would have been "to guide the dead back to life."

Then, Ayanna stood up, put on the backpack, and walked back out into the hot day. The blue door glistened in the humid air. Olivia, their father, and some others were spread into two rows, so Ayanna would walk through them. At each person, she paused and let them squeeze her hands or hug her. Ayanna was grateful no one said anything, only embraced her. To hear what they had to say would feel like she was walking toward death. For so long, all she had wanted was to go through, to see things for herself, but as she finally approached, Ayanna didn't feel any of the wonder and longing she'd had, only the fear she had long repressed.

When she approached her father and Olivia, Ayanna smushed them together with her arms, feeling both around her. If she said a goodbye, they wouldn't let her go through. The ceremony would be over. But she smelled them, both of their deodorants failing a little bit to combat the day's heat. Tried to hear the sound of their breaths and even each heartbeat. Olivia clung to her and whispered in her ear, "You'll be okay, you'll be okay."

It felt more like she was convincing herself than saying something she actually believed. But it was enough to make Ayanna press forward. Everything and everyone she touched, every sound heard, even the way her mouth tasted a little acidic from fear, was meaningful. If these were the last moments of her life, Ayanna was grateful to be feeling them so intensely. Then, the door followed its schedule, and opened. The mood shifted. It was not to the golden path, but to the meadow and its verge-of-evening skies.

She wanted to say "I love you" as she stepped into the new world, but that felt too much like goodbye.

9

Seeing Ayanna's shoulders, her bent head, feeling for the first time in their shared life like her sister was truly afraid, was too much for Olivia. Before anyone could react, she chased her sister through the door. She yelled something that some people said was, "If you die, I die," and other people said was just her sister's name or maybe even just a yell.

Then, the second unexpected thing happened, which was after Olivia chased her sister, the door shut quickly, reopened, and the meadows were gone. The path was there, but for the first time ever, it was snowing. Iridescent flakes large as moths gathered beneath a streetlamp. One person immediately began writing, but almost everyone else froze. A few heads swiveled toward the girls' father, but his eyes were darting from the door to the snow beyond already starting to accumulate on the golden branches to the military officers who were now running toward them to the expedition driving down the red dirt road in Hummers to a cloud that swirled up like a perfect soft-serve cone.

Out in the meadows, the twins looked at each other. Ayanna, a moonbeam in her still mostly white clothes. Olivia, in her sneakers and blue-and-white sundress, feeling the long navy grass tickling her calves and thighs. There was no door. In the distance, over her sister's shoulder, Ayanna could see light. She wanted to take a picture of

Olivia here, the light blue of her dress contrasting against the cerulean and indigo and navy of the landscape. Even in the whoosh of panic, she couldn't help but notice how beautiful all this was.

"We're alive," Ayanna said, then laughed because it was such an obvious thing to say.

"I'm sorry," Olivia said once, twice. "I panicked. I thought. I thought you—"

For so long in their lives, it had been a great disappointment that there was no special understanding between them. Everything had to be spoken aloud. They had not sensed each other when Olivia was in a car accident. They did not feel when something especially good had happened to the other. Sometimes, they lied to people who asked them about it, assured them that being a twin was special in a mystical way. You never feel alone, Ayanna had once said at a sleepover. This was one of the few times where they could look at each other and understand all the knotted-together emotions the other was experiencing.

"Well, we seem pretty fucked," Ayanna said, "but at least we're together."

Olivia sat down. She put her head to her knees, took a long, deep breath and released. Did it again. Another. "I feel like I'm on the urge of a panic attack."

"Verge," Ayanna said.

"I didn't believe you," Olivia said. "I mean, I did and I didn't. It seemed impossible, a door to elsewhere, so I feel like even when I agreed to do this, on some level I was doing you a favor because you had been tricked."

It didn't bother Ayanna. If this were dinner or if they'd been playing Wild Thoughts, maybe it would've bugged her. But there was no point now, and Olivia's actions showed Ayanna how little she understood the situation. What did the explorers she admired most do? They played unexpected circumstances cool in public and lost their shit in private. There was no privacy, so Ayanna resolved to be the captain for as long as she could. *It's beautiful here,* Ayanna thought. The sky was permanently in the twilight state where it was richly blue but never too dark to see. There were hills, and when she looked down, the grass shifted to lighter blues.

"What should we do?" Olivia asked.

Ayanna handed her a small slice of dried mango. "Eat this."

Olivia took it.

"What do you have in your purse?"

In the tote were four Band-Aids, four tampons, three different kinds of cinnamon gum, two granola bars, a Shakespeare reader with thin pages and small text, an extra pair of socks, a bunch of loose cough drops, thirty-eight cents, two hair ties, a cell phone charger, a small pouch with pink lipstick and two Advil in it, and sunglasses.

"This is helpful," Ayanna said. "We'll have fresh breath, and we can get fives on our AP literature exams because we have this to study."

Olivia didn't laugh.

"So, I think we have two options. We wait here and hope the door opens again. If we're lucky, it might open again in three hours if it's on the cycle I think it's on. And if I'm wrong, well, it might be two days. But we can be careful with the water. Oh, and I have food."

"What's the other option?" Olivia asked. She tilted her head up to the sky. No clouds, no stars, no moons.

"We walk north for an hour. Stop where we are, take notes and rest for thirty minutes, and then walk back here."

Olivia nodded. "That's the point of you doing this, right?"

"Yeah. Also, I think it will be worse for us if we just sit here. Like, emotionally. Just waiting, hoping that the easier option emerges, seems psychologically bad. For situations like this, I think it's always better to be doing something."

"How do you know?" Olivia asked. She stood up. Smoothed out

her dress and then pulled some of the grass out as hard as she could. The sisters peered down at the soil. It was unremarkable.

"I don't know," Ayanna finally answered, "but it feels right."

They started walking north.

"Oh, and one time I was home sick from school and watching the *Today* show, and they had these two college students on it who had been abducted from like a nightclub. And one of the girls admitted she froze in the van they were thrown in, like completely curled up like a pill bug. The other one went nuts. She didn't care they had guns. And was like punching and screaming and kicking and it saved their lives. The girl who did nothing is still in intensive therapy. The girl who went wild said she felt really good about herself. She had saved their lives."

"I've never seen anything like that on the *Today* show," Olivia said. "Every time I'm home sick, it's always a white family who adopted a chimp and then the chimp killed one of them."

Ayanna kept her hands in her pockets. She didn't want Olivia to notice they were shaking. She could keep her voice even as the adrenaline rushed through her, but it still felt like having drunk too many energy drinks. *It would pass,* Ayanna reminded herself. She fought the urge to hug her sister for so easily deciding to buy into the idea that this was normal. Took a deep breath and reminded herself to pay attention to everything here.

The sky never changed. Some of the grass went up past their knees, some was short as if it had recently been mowed. When she brushed it with her hands, it was softer than usual. Ripping grass didn't create a scent. Holding it up beneath her nose didn't either. Walking was slow progress because they were making sure to leave a trail, walking heavy, letting their feet stamp down what they could.

"How do the doors work?" Olivia asked.

"What do you mean, how?"

"Like is there something you can do to activate them? Are there things they like? Do you have to have A-negative blood type? Do they like singing?"

"They don't like anything. They are things."

"But this wasn't what you expected."

"Oh. Here is rare. It usually opens to a place we call the golden path because, well, a lot of it is gold. A trail, the trees, some boulders, a slope up to a mountain. In Australia, it opens to an orange desert." Ayanna's hands finally stopped shaking. She pulled them out of her pockets and stretched her fingers.

"Do you think that's heaven, and this is hell?"

Ayanna stopped walking. Olivia kept on for a few paces, then turned around.

"How could this be hell?" Ayanna said. "Do you hear screams in the distance? And also do you actually believe in hell? It seems like such a mean thing to believe."

"Why?"

"People getting tortured for all eternity, no redemption, fiery pits." Ayanna knew despite everything she said, the reaction she was having was that this could be true. She had never articulated it, but the idea of being in a place where nothing ever happens felt more in line with what she thought hell could be than any of the whole rivers-of-lava and demons-being-snippy-with-you-for-all-of-eternity did.

Before Olivia could answer, Ayanna saw in her peripheral vision a light pink light. She put her hand over her mouth. Olivia shook her head.

"Why are you being so weird?"

"Is there a light over there?"

* * *

Back in the field, everyone had decided the best thing to do was to be patient. No one had seen or heard a pop. The girls were fine. Their father had decided to treat this like a usual divorced-parenting problem, which is to say, he hoped it resolved and could be massaged before their mother had to be told or somehow found out on her own. He could not conceive of any possible way Olivia could tell her mother that she went through a door without it becoming a protracted fight. The only saving grace to this was they would be eighteen in six months. There was not enough time to have it become a legal fight as well.

It was still snowing in the golden path. Each pile on the branches and stones they could see looked in texture and coloring like jellyfish. It was beautiful and alien. But jellyfish were like that too, and their stings could be dangerous.

The expedition was there and all of them were delighted, although their crew was worried because they hadn't packed any cold-weather gear. They had paid one of the church members to go to the closest Walmart and buy windbreakers and sweatshirts and boot socks to wear as mittens. Antony kept thinking about his daughters, alternating between sending these people away and considering the amount of money they had given the church. Ayanna and Olivia, he tried to consider the least. Why had he let Ayanna do this at all? How could he not have reacted when Olivia ran after her? There had been a moment when she turned, where if he had reached and grabbed the back of her dress, or even said her name, it would have at least saved her. And what kind of parent was he to have let his seventeen-year-old daughter do something he would never do?

When Opal had been over for dinner, out in the garden, he had told her about a time when he had walked the golden path. He said he had heard the voice of God twice in his life. The lies came so easy. Once while walking alone in the snow and being afraid to go to college, and once while walking that path. He had told her the voice had spoken to him about bringing love into the world. He was still not sure what that meant, but it was what he wanted Ayanna to experience. Didn't she also think that God had a plan for their daughter?

Antony had purposefully echoed the words Opal's mother used to comfort her in bad times: "Remember, this is the Lord's plan. Even in the hard times, he's with you." He knew she had been told that when they were having marital troubles, had heard his former mother-in-law say it on a night when Ayanna had a 103 fever and wouldn't stop throwing up, when he was laid off from his job, during the storm that had knocked out all their power for an excruciating, humid week where they could not afford to stay in a hotel for more than one night and kept arguing which night it should be, which would make them more able to endure the rest of that unpleasant August. It had bugged him that there was none of this Lord's-plan talk during the good times, no "God has helped you find your way to one another, this marriage is blessed" talk. Nothing of that sort when he had graduated from college. None of God's will was apparently involved when they had found out they were pregnant with twins.

Opal had looked at his tomatoes, complimented how large the crop was as a response. If she had responded directly to what he had said, then there would have been trouble. But the redirection, Antony knew from their years together, gave her a chance to think. And if Opal was willing to not make a snap judgment, she could be persuaded. Was being able to know exactly how to get her to say yes proof he had truly loved her once? Was this way of going about it proof he had never loved her in the right way?

* * *

The Joes chopped some of the socks into makeshift gloves, passed out sweatshirts and parkas. They tried to make a joke about how this, too, was an adventure, but everyone ignored them. It was simultaneously too rehearsed and also not really a joke. No one was in the mood to do some community-building, half-hearted chuckles.

One of the women from the church was encouraging everyone to wait. She had a bad feeling about this from the unexpected snow to the switch from dark to light. There was adventure, and there was recklessness. You didn't go into the ocean in unsavory conditions unless you were trying to save a life. "We have to treat this like nature," she said.

"What do you know about the ocean?" Joe asked.

"I used to surf," she said.

"Oh, surfing," the other Joe said. "Hang ten, bro. Great." And that was somehow enough to make everyone ignore her advice.

It was so humid, everyone was uncomfortable. It was a day meant not for arguing outside in a field with little shade, but for lying underneath a powerful ceiling fan and slowly eating a bowl of ice cream. Everyone wanted to be in charge and didn't want to do any of the necessary thinking and compromising that came with being in charge.

"I think we should go for it," said one of the men. "Everything that gets written about in the history books is unexpected and difficult. Great men don't do easy things."

One of the other explorers couldn't help himself and whispered, "That's what she said."

A few people laughed in a half-hearted way. Only the explorers treated the joke as if it were funny.

"Look, we already signed off," Antony said. "I doubt we can say no now, but I do think you should be really careful. And it's fine to wait until things are more normal."

As he said it, Antony felt profoundly relieved to have an easy out. No matter what happened with these people, it was no longer his responsibility. It was ridiculous, he felt, to expect him to be in charge of anything right now. An oversized white truck was going far too fast down the dirt road in the distance. Whoever was in it was playing rap-metal, and as Antony watched, the dust kicked up by the truck's speed was moving to the song's rhythm. Everyone was watching him, but he kept his eyes on the truck, hoping they would let him be. For the first time since he was a child, he felt the urge to pray to Jesus. A God to make things right or at least to take on some of the responsibility of these moments.

"Let's fucking go," Margot said. It made her feel cool and tough to say. She had her film camera in her hands, cranking and saving these moments. Her brother's face framed with the open door in the background. He looked dignified, and like their father. It was one of the few things she liked about aging—seeing their parents' faces occasionally appear on her and her brother's faces, like headlights emerging from an early-morning fog. She felt the urge to say something to him, maybe thank him for this opportunity, maybe say, in some way, how important he was to her.

The plan was the expedition would be anchored on either side by a Joe. One through at the beginning, one at the end because the pattern when they had started planning this journey was thought to be five in, one at risk.

"We should go in together," Margot said to her brother. There was space if they linked arms. She expected him to say no, but he nodded yes. She realized he wasn't speaking much because he was scared. "Jason."

He nodded again and took her hand.

Margot wanted to say they didn't have to do this but understood this was what he was actually looking forward to. It wasn't finding new worlds or going on adventures her brother wanted, it was moments like this when he felt all of fear's monstrous pressure and then continued on. It was possible in these moments, when fingers stopped shaking, when the brain flooded with elation, to feel immortal. Only the dying and the wise can sit firm in their mortality.

Joe walked through, quiet and relaxed as if he were in his own home. He walked farther in and waved. "It's beautiful here."

"Let's go," she said again.

They linked arms and smiled at each other.

Through the doorway, it felt like being on an ascending plane. Margot could feel a shift in the air, her sinuses ached, her ears were clogged, and her whole body felt like it was being pinched by two large, calloused fingers.

* * *

In the beginning, Antony reminded himself, life was only chemicals.

In the beginning, there was only darkness and the patience of waiting for a voice to call forth the light.

In the middle, a man had to tell himself about faith to not panic over his daughters.

In the beginning, there was a fireball and now all life were children of the flames.

In the beginning, there was a hibiscus seed that needed love and a family of birds who could not bear to eat it. All the galaxies and planets and stars emerged when it bloomed.

In the beginning, there were all the worlds, then there was Truth, who searched the galaxy, trying to find where life should be.

In the beginning, there were two sisters who could never agree on anything, other than that they should never be apart. One became the heavens, and her hair became clouds and wind. The other became the soil, the roots, and the metals within. They held on to each other for all of eternity and that was how Earth came to be.

* * *

As the lights came closer, Ayanna and Olivia heard them speaking to one another.

"When you return, the first thing you should do is ride a Jet Ski."

"I will be a baby again."

"Tell me, what is a Jet Ski?"

"I miss water."

The lights were constantly changing shapes: tree and dog and human and elephant and cat and human and things Ayanna could only describe as alien. She saw they were surrounding an area of thick bushes with berries on them.

"We should pick some of those," Olivia said.

"We have no way of knowing they're safe. They look dangerous," Ayanna replied. The spirits continued to ignore them. Jet Skis were still a much more urgent topic of interest.

"So, you can go really fast on water?"

"And hold a beer at the same time."

"You can also do sharp turns."

"Once I was on vacation and fell off one when I was going really fast."

"Is that how you died?"

"No, I died from the flu."

"We have no idea how long we're going to be here," Olivia said. "This is the first sign of something livable. We'll forage it now, and if we get desperate, well, maybe we'll die quickly rather than starving to death."

"That was a really dark thing to say," Ayanna said. "I liked it."

Olivia fished the pouch out of her tote, took the Advil and lipstick out of it. Ayanna picked one of the berries; it was harder than expected. She raised it up to eye level, tried to see any true difference, besides texture, between this and a blueberry.

"It could be hallucinogenic or poisonous," Ayanna warned. Olivia had a very strict no drugs, no cigarettes, no vapes, no drinks life policy. Zero tolerance. She had spent enough time reading books about adventurers to know the first mistake many made was to eat something they knew nothing about.

"Do they smell like anything to you?"

"They have no smell," Ayanna confirmed.

The spirits crowded around them. It was mesmerizing to see them so close; their shifting was so fluid. Dog ears blooming on a young woman's face and then becoming leaves. Being around them felt like taking a large balloon and rubbing it all over your hair, then rubbing the balloon up and down your body. Every hair on Ayanna was at attention. Olivia's hair was also spread out and large, even the hairs in her eyebrows were wild.

"Weird, there's people here," one said.

"What are you talking about?"

"Two girls. I think they're twins."

The spirits were divided on whether Ayanna and Olivia were there. Ayanna continued filling the pouch. She guessed they had fifteen more minutes to go before needing to turn back around to where the door had appeared. The sensory back-and-forth between seeing the spirits around them and feeling nothing when they brushed against her was making Ayanna feel more anxious. Physically, her body was aware of Olivia's—her sister never triggered a feeling of needing personal space or alertness—and the long grass and the scratchy bush. Then, when she looked at the spirits, there was an immediate urge to run or back away, to find a way of giving herself some more room.

"Are you okay?" she asked Olivia.

"I'm fine. I think they're so cute," Olivia replied. "Especially the one that keeps going back and forth between cat and woman and blob. She keeps sniffing the air."

"I'm kind of freaking out."

Olivia took Ayanna's hand and walked her away from the bush. They sat down in the grass, and Ayanna took three deep breaths. Did it again, tried to visualize on a long inhale the breath going all the way into her lungs, into her stomach, down her legs, and into her toes.

What if we're stuck here forever? she thought. *What if I have to watch my sister die? I never should have asked her to come.*

"I think we should walk a little further," Olivia said. "I probably won't ever be here again. Don't you think it's impossibly beautiful? I know this is the wrong time for me to be filled with wonder and awe. But it's so beautiful, Ay."

Ayanna looked again at the grass, the pink spirits, the sky, the bush. Each one of them was teaching her a different understanding of the word *blue*. She let her heart thrill to it. Their father had once earnestly told them the secret to living well was that "you have to want to like things. Even enjoyment, enjoying things, whatever, is a skill you have to cultivate." "You're right."

They walked farther, saw a hill in the distance, ascended, and a sudden mountain range, silver and spindly, somehow lit from within. Above the mountains were clouds, as pink as the spirits, and Ayanna suspected that if she had binoculars, she would see they were not weather phenomena, but a murmuration of spirits shifting and talking with one another. Her soul swayed to the ecstasy as she surveyed the mountains and their shine, the distant vistas, the feeling of being the first. She longed for a canvas and paint, for months of time to capture it.

"Remember when we were eight," Olivia said, "and you told me one day you were going to find the Fountain of Youth?"

"We learned about it in school, our teacher kept saying everyone thought it was in Florida. It felt attainable."

That entire year she spent looking up facts about Florida, alligators, and the Everglades, and brainstorming what she would do if she found the Fountain of Youth. Sometimes, Ayanna thought it would be like a regular drinking fountain, dented and ugly like the ones at school, and waiting for her in a swamp. She would gather a bottle of it and save it to drink at the age she most wanted to stay. Olivia had told her maybe it didn't work like that, but instead worked to keep you young for longer, to live at your strongest for many, many years. Sometimes, Ayanna thought the fountain would be a creek or a stream, and they would have to test and taste many, and record how their bodies reacted. Maybe it would be a geyser pushing out of different parts of the earth. She had given up on it.

"Here's your first discovery," Olivia said.

"Ours," Ayanna said, and squeezed her sister's wrist.

They sat together in the tall grass, higher now than their waists, and worked together to draw a map. They tried to count their paces, give a sense of how long their strides were, and when they returned home would dry out some of the berries and grass to tape to the map. They decided that one day when they were credited for the discovery, they should be credited as the Owens Sisters. They could see the biography covers and test questions and Black History Month PBS program. They could hear themselves talking about the joy of being the first in a way that didn't point to oppression or being problematic, but to finding and doing something truly new. Here, finally, they felt like they understood what people thought being a twin was like, so in sync were their emotions and imaginings.

Ayanna noticed a flicker of green firefly light at what she estimated was about a half mile away. More and more of the fireflies appeared. They were forming a shape, low at first to the ground, that Ayanna thought was a bench, but it grew higher and higher, until the lights were clearly forming a door.

* * *

Margot's camera couldn't capture sound, but if it could have, each pop would have sounded like a firework arcing its way up toward roofs and stars. The footage through the door was hard to discern, what looked like light leaks in the camera taking up most of it, so a viewer saw only a back, a hood, and long white lines, but it was clear the siblings had to let go of one another to fully get through. Then, a tree branch jostled by the wind, Margot's brother looking up into the air, and then his head was gone and there was a soft zoom-in on what a viewer could easily mistake for a batch of red cirrus clouds that spread down and down until the entire body was gone, and all the bits of it were in the air for a gorgeous second, mixed with falling snow, each flake looking almost an inch in length. And the camera turned, and for anyone watching the footage, it felt like the camera was destroying every person it turned toward. Man after man after man popped like overfilled water balloons colliding with concrete.

There was something miraculous, some felt, in Margot's ability to keep filming. But, she would've said, the only thing in her entire life that had made her feel calm was video making. There was maybe a thought, too, if they were not going to be able to explore and voyage, at least they could achieve some form of glory by having a record. Few want to die, especially people like this, without leaving some kind of mark on the world.

The first Joe who went through the door ran away from it, his flight instinct strong, and Margot followed him farther down the path. Her footage stopped for a while, probably because it was too hard to run through slick snow and crank. Or maybe she was resting her hand. When the footage began again, Margot was in deep woods. Joe was ahead of her and there was a figure ahead of him, too tall, too thin, and Margot later would claim it, too, was made from gold like the trees and the path. That when it spoke, its voice was so loud she longed to cover her ears and she could not identify what it was saying but knew from its tone she should leave.

She fell multiple times, had to get seven stitches in her left forearm from the cuts, and the cuts themselves became infected and had to be studied. The wound kept reopening; the blood looked metallic to all the doctors she saw. They took samples and tried multiple ways of making sure the infection didn't spread. Margot small-talked through the blood draws, the poking and prodding, about the screenplay she was writing. It was called *The Expedition* or *The Golden Demon* or *I Plant My Flag*. It was feminist horror or maybe a faux documentary, or maybe it was both? Margot agreed to let her samples be studied, although she felt certain from the way the military doctors were acting that she didn't have a choice.

After the infections had healed, after the cuts became scars all her friends kept recommending really great plastic surgeons for, but for once, here were imperfections in her life she did not want to sculpt, aggressively crystal, green-drink-with-expensive-vitamins guzzle at, throw money at, or in any way pretend away. They were proof, for once, her life had been extraordinary. And sometimes, people DMed her after a live stream and said *your scars make you seem so real*, and sent a smiling emoji with large, teary eyes.

* * *

For the third time in his life, Antony heard what he felt sure was God's voice. As most of the expedition died, and his mind whirred toward an assumption that maybe the same thing had happened to both his daughters but he was lucky enough not to have seen it, he heard a voice telling him to atone. "Your greed caused this."

In his savings account was half of the million dollars the expedition had agreed to pay, the rest was in the church's accounts. He had done the negotiating, had agreed to make their time easier, had two daughters who would be going to college, and a shitty job. There was also the fact he needed his faith to give him something tangible. It had cost him a wife, and when people found out he belonged to this faith, they treated him like he was in a cult. So many dates and friendships had fizzled when they found out about his faith, as if believing in heaven or transubstantiation or different planets for the dead was any less strange. At least here was a door, here was elsewhere, and God had spoken to him.

"Your greed caused this."

Antony sunk to the ground and kneeled. His shirt clung to his back, the areas behind his kneecaps were sticky, and he could smell his armpits.

"God, please let my daughters be alive."

"You have proven yourself small and ugly."

"If my daughters return unharmed, I will—"

"You aren't in a place to bargain."

He gritted his teeth, folded his hands together, shut his eyes tight.

"God, I am not worthy of asking you for anything. I come to you." He could not think of a way to prove his fidelity to God. It didn't feel right to thank him, but also felt wrong not to express some form of gratitude. His knees were already wobbling, and he had never felt so old. One of the privates who was often assigned to patrol, the nice one who learned people's names, yanked Antony. He was saying, "You have to go, you have to go."

"I can't leave my daughters."

He looked up into the man's brown eyes.

"You can't hear it?" Antony asked him.

"All I can hear is you screaming," he replied.

They turned together toward the door. Things in the shape of people, but looked like black-and-white scribbles and static, were falling out. Each one took a few steps forward, then popped, leaving a black-and-white cloud behind.

* * *

The sisters were arguing about whether to go through the door below. Ayanna thought it best to turn around and go back—they were already behind the schedule she had set—and Olivia argued that if nothing made sense, if there were no guarantees, wasn't it better to try what was close and possible?

Ayanna was torn between wanting to say, "I love you, but your decisions have made everything harder today," and "I love you, and your logic does feel sound."

In the months leading up to this, Ayanna had read about the adventures of Sir Ernest Shackleton. A man who could not stop getting into the worst possible scrapes, who had cheated death so many times. He had survived ice floes, treks across the Atlantic in small vessels, madness, insubordination, the South Pole, multiple heart attacks. What had all that reading been about if not to take the lessons learned into this moment? You have to keep your crew loyal, Ayanna thought, and be willing to adapt to try to save your life. She could tell she was being too rigid about *how* things should be, rather than looking at the situation as it was. The minute you started making your decisions heavy, that was when you were truly lost.

"You're right," Ayanna finally said, "we should try."

They walked hand in hand, helping each other to keep balance as they descended down the slope. Close to the door, Ayanna thought it looked even more like lightning bugs had turned into a material that could be woven but was somehow shining. It was thin and only one person could go through it at a time.

"It doesn't even look like how we got here," Ayanna said.

"I'll go first," Olivia said.

Ayanna was so relieved, she felt ashamed. Caught in her feelings, she didn't say anything, not even thank you. Instead, she put her hand on the back of her sister's dress, squeezed the fabric between her hands as if she were a small, shy child clinging to her mother.

They stepped in unison, walking toward the door. Olivia opened it, paused, and Ayanna bumped into her.

"Sorry, it's warm."

Ayanna peered over her sister's shoulder. A normal neighborhood, ranch houses, trees, lamps. It wasn't where they had left, but it looked like a place where their cell phones would work again, where there would be people who would help them figure out how to get home. This was just one wild afternoon, Ayanna thought, we even have enough time to get pizza and rest.

"You know what, let's switch spots," Ayanna said. "I'll go first. You hold on to me."

Olivia didn't argue. She stepped away, then wrapped her arms around Ayanna's waist like they were hopping on a moped together. Olivia rested her head against Ayanna's back for a brief second, said something soft, but Ayanna couldn't hear the words, only the sound.

Here was where Ayanna went to her entire life, often at three in the morning. So many *should have*s: I should have said no, I should have said let's go back, I should have argued, I should have held on to her hands as they wrapped around my waist. I shouldn't have offered to go first when it looked safer. I should have let her go first. I should have been more serious.

Ayanna stepped through the door, and there was a moment when her heart felt so light, and she laughed with relief in the middle of a suburban street. Someone was grilling and blasting out soul music, and every smell felt so loud and overwhelming after elsewhere. Her phone was buzzing, text after text. And there was the twinkly sound of an ice-cream truck, calling everyone toward Bomb Pops and homemade vanillas. Ayanna turned, did a full circle, looked up into the air, looked toward the houses, and didn't notice the car coming toward her until the person started honking and rolled down their window and yelled, "Get out of the road, dumbass."

On the sidewalk were a long scrap of a light blue-and-white striped dress, a ragged cut from a skirt, and some long blue grass.

PART TWO

Once, the spirit sang that love was two intersecting paths. In a small ranch house, a mother converted her grief into red wine. She spoke to herself, to the wind, to God. Each utterance, a different attempt at penitence. If you apologize enough, if you make yourself small before glory, the universe will open its arms to you.

Sometimes, late at night, sometimes after enough prayer, the mother heard her lost daughter's voice, like music drifting in a window from very far away.

When you are lucky enough to have the dead speak to you, listen.

When you are lucky enough to be given a miracle, you must see it.

When you are lucky enough to be loved, you must treat it like a seed. You nourish it in yourself, yes, but you are meant to instill it back into the world. To not do this is a sin.

10

Ayanna felt like the first year of college was a complete blur. Most of it was because of grief—she had never felt so fucking alone in her entire life, and it was better, she knew, to let everyone think she was just a typical sad girl crying over some dumb boy than to try to talk about missing Olivia. In some ways it was better to be depressed because it helped her ignore the voices that tried to chat with her, the flickering shapes she could now see among people at the grocery store, or lingering in the city's complex alley system, and her longing to go back home, to wonder when the door would return to the soybean fields. Her parents did not visit her at college, but her grandmother came multiple times, despite the cost, to remind her she could not let sadness eat her whole.

Things snapped into place the second year, when she met Jane. They were in the same postmodernism seminar and sat near each other because they were the only Black girls in the room. Ayanna probably would have sat next to Jane anyway. During the first class meeting, Jane wore a white T-shirt, and written across it in all caps were the words *I EAT WHAT I FUCK*. The next class meeting, another white T-shirt, that time with the phrase *EAT PRAY BARF*. It was a level of affectation that, on a white girl or boy, would've made Ayanna feel exceptionally wary. The type of white kids who did this could be either the realest kids you knew or the type of white kids who thought the mixture of edginess and an enjoyment of Black culture made them special and who could send you things that used the N-word because "it reminded them of you." But here was Jane, a true Black weirdo of the highest order.

The third time she saw Jane that first week of classes, Ayanna was doing her usual walk around the city, trying to tire herself out. She listened to headphones and smoked one cigarette, long and pink with a gold tip. Ayanna needed both of these things to build a shield for herself alone in the world. The combination felt like it kept everyone but the truest nutjobs from trying to engage with her and gave her permission in this city just to wander. Here she was multitasking with her pretentious cigarette and listening to her private music—lately, mostly Alice Coltrane—and sometimes looking into different shop or restaurant windows to get a sense of what normal people were considering. They were having dinners where they looked a lot at their phones, they seemed interested in wearing tops that had keyhole sleeves and peplums, and it was rare to see someone whose smile completely reached their eyes. She refused to pay close attention to the spirits she saw. Ever present, wanting to speak, changing shape into swirls. Ayanna did not want to see a familiar face among them. *My sister is alive; I will find her*, Ayanna told herself on a regular basis.

"Ayanna?"

She turned and there was Jane wearing an eighties prom dress, turquoise with puffed sleeves and bows at the join between the sleeves and the bodice. Her hair, through an elaborate structure of gel and bobby pins and luck, was up in a mohawk. Her eyes were rimmed with black eyeliner to emphasize dark circles and lipstick had been applied to look like blood dribbling out of her mouth.

"I'm having a party; do you want to come?"

Ayanna surprised herself by saying, "Yes."

Later, she would describe this time as coming out of the first major depression of her adult life. The months before were still clinging to her, the crying, the anger, the stink of lying in bed and trying to force herself not to want death. It was a time when wanting anything positive felt like a surprise. There was a strange exultation when Ayanna could leave her room by herself or sleep through an entire night or look forward to eating the chicken broccoli bake in the cafeteria.

The party was in a public park. Everyone but Ayanna was wearing some form of partywear. Almost all the white people had gone ironic: thrifted prom dresses with maroon sequins, ruffled tuxedo shirts, or T-shirts screen-printed to look like a wedding dress or a tuxedo. Everyone else was dressed seriously and beautifully. A woman with skin so well moisturized that Ayanna made a point of pretending to accidentally brush her hand against her exposed arm to see how silky it was. So many golden jumpsuits and bright red heels. A light-skinned man with blue eyes like a nighttime soap opera star was fully dressed as a king. A crown tilted sideways, a red velvet cape he kept using for dramatic emphasis. Ayanna felt attracted to him but only because of the cape. Under the lights, there were shapes flickering between person, bear, stone, wave, zebra that Ayanna pointedly tried to ignore. No one could explain how Jane could get so many people to come to a party in a park.

No one could explain why Jane was also dressed as a zombie.

"Don't ask," a woman said. "The explanation will only make you hate her."

That was the first rule of knowing Jane. You had to accept she was whimsical, and the loveliness of the whimsy would persist only when it wasn't dissected. Ayanna felt the world needed more whimsical Black people, so she loved this rule.

No one mentioned Ayanna was the only one in jeans and a tank top. The king approached her and placed his crown gently on Ayanna's head. "Go forth and party, my good peasant," he said.

Some of the crowd was playing croquet. A few people were dancing even though there was no music, only the sound of many conversations and cars whizzing by on the slightly damp pavement. The crown was much lighter than it appeared. On the king's head it had truly looked real, but on her, it felt plastic and slippery.

"Do you have any nicknames?" A woman wearing feather wings was walking around asking people. Sunny, Baby, Pickle, and Chicken Sandwich emerged, connecting instantly over the fact that people refused to call them by their given names. Ayanna felt certain no one was nicknamed Chicken Sandwich and that this was a bid for attention, but walked on. Already Sunny and Pickle were holding hands and laughing. In the distance, Jane was having a tense conversation with two women in matching togas and with several cheap necklaces wrapped around their arms and foreheads.

"How do you know Jane?" Ayanna asked a woman wearing a domino mask and a Burger King crown by the coolers.

"I don't know her. I know Stephen." The woman pointed to a crowd of men who were all laughing over something on one of their cell phones. "He deals corn."

"Corn?" Ayanna made a show of looking through the cooler, trying not to acknowledge how uncool she was being. I'm twenty years old, she thought, and I don't even know what the good drugs are.

"Acre." She laughed and took a sip of a very uncool wine cooler. "If you're a cop, you have to tell me."

"I'm a cop."

The woman laughed harder, but Ayanna knew she was overdoing it to be kind. She took a canned cocktail and walked toward the group. Seeing a bunch of guys together looking at a cell phone always made Ayanna cautious. There was a good chance they were all laughing at a dumb *Naruto* meme, but there was just as good a chance they were looking at some exploitative porn thing or something that might make it clear that oh, these are hateful people.

Ayanna didn't have to ask or do anything. The one wearing a velvet suit jacket and no shirt handed her two small packets and asked for seventy-five. A first-timers discount.

"I only have fifty on me."

"Take me to coffee and I'll agree to that."

"Whoa," one of the guys in the group said, "someone is smooth."

"It was fine," Ayanna said, "not that smooth."

Despite what he was wearing, Stephen didn't look stupid. A beautiful jacket with a nice pair of black jeans, black Sambas, short black socks. Annoyingly, his chest looked like it was worth showing off, but Ayanna was trying not to give him the attention he so clearly wanted. He smelled good. If he were rich like some of the kids in her classes—heirs to different food- and Earth-killing businesses, and some celebrity's kids—he would have smelled far worse. Every kid someone whispered to her about always smelled like they had taken a solemn vow to work out every morning for three hours, eat an everything bagel, then rub themselves with cumin and lemon. There was a hint of what perfumers called "musk," maybe pepper? Pepper in a good way. Although, Ayanna realized, all those kids she knew were white. Black rich people might actually enjoy having money instead of pretending they didn't.

She shrugged and handed Stephen her phone and fifty dollars.

"Okay, let me try again." He kept his hand on the one he'd placed the pills into. "You have beautiful eyes."

"A little generic, but still nice to hear." Ayanna watched as he put his number into her phone, called his own. "I mean, I'm sure you could pull a lot of interest just by going around this party, leaning in and saying a little softly, 'Your eyes are incredible.'"

"Is it really that easy?" a different man asked. His fingernails were painted a matte navy. He was wearing a T-shirt like the ones Jane usually wore, except it read: *EVEN PROM KINGS ARE TYRANTS.*

"I like your shirt," Ayanna said. She assumed he was Jane's boyfriend. The idea made her feel more comfortable chatting with him. There were so many people she knew who overlooked bad behavior in their romantic partners. Felt like it wasn't their job to take up all the places where their parents had failed and educate them: "He wasn't homophobic, he just didn't know better"; "He called women 'bitches' because a girl had been mean to him in high school"; and "He was just kind of uncomfortable around Black people because his grandparents lived through the riots." The excuses were baffling but seemed to be socially acceptable. Ayanna felt like she was often treated as if she were being childish and unreasonable when she scoffed at the excuses. He can drive, he can vote, but how dare he have to consider other people's feelings? But Jane was somebody who had little patience for people's thoughtlessness. On their first day of the postmodernism seminar, while looking over the syllabus, she had raised her hand and asked the professor, "Why is everyone on this syllabus white? Are there truly no postmodernists of color?"

When the professor had talked around the question, Jane had let her finish, then in an uncomfortably kind voice said, "It's fine. We all mess up sometimes."

One of their classmates had laughed a little, and Ayanna assumed Jane would never return to the small seminar room with its brown carpet and dust smell. But she continued attending. It was clear the professor did not like her very much, but Jane persisted in raising her hand, engaging with the texts, and sometimes referencing writers and artists who were not on the syllabus but had contributed to a multicultural understanding of the topics at hand. While Ayanna was slowly reading *S/Z* and trying to understand some grand unified theory of what postmodernism could be, she could at least say that she was getting an education in how to respectfully stunt on your professor.

This is all to say if Jane was principled enough to clearly engage with a racially myopic authority figure, to continue doing her own research and reading on top of her course load, it would be deeply disappointing if her boyfriend was trash.

The presumed boyfriend said, "Are you Ayanna?"

It was a delight that Jane thought about her enough to tell other people about her. "I am."

"Felix." He held out his hand. They shook, and the rest of the group started talking about where to go and drink next. In the crowd, there was a flicker of pink. Ayanna tried to ignore it.

"Have you ever taken these before?"

He smiled. "That's a story for another time."

Felix was making long eye contact. His eyes were soft and dark. There was a look in them that reminded her of the way her eyes looked now, always a little too shiny, always a little too tired, always looking for something to make living feel worth it. She slipped the pills into her front jeans pocket to give herself something to do. When he continued watching, Ayanna took a long drink from her previously ignored canned cocktail. Plastic and strawberry taste.

"What do you think happens next?" she asked.

"I think all souls are reincarnated. I was once a bird, I think."

She made a show of looking him up and down, didn't mind that he had taken her vague question as an existential one. "A puffin."

"You flatter me." He rubbed a hand on the top of his locs. Felix made a show of observing her, made a frame with his hands. "I can see all your past lives. You were once a snapping turtle. You were once a photographer. You were once an incredible cook. You were a dinosaur."

"I am an incredible chef. I make the rat from *Ratatouille* look like he's working a McDonald's drive-thru." Even Ayanna laughed at herself. She took a breath and looked away from Felix.

"Once I thought I was going to be an explorer. I would see something new every day. I wanted to go to the bottom of the ocean, I wanted to go to Mars, I wanted to go places people had never even conceived were places to go, I wanted . . ." She trailed off. There was something about him that made her keep talking when normally her guard would be up.

He gave her a look she couldn't read. Felix gestured toward her. "Let me show you something."

They walked deeper into the park, past a couple leaning against a large oak tree and kissing. *Imagine being so into someone else*, Ayanna thought. Their kissing was a duet in two-four time. A small part of the park was fenced off. An unruly patch of woods. Felix helped her hop it, then pulled himself over it. It was darker and quieter.

"Do you remember the doors?" Felix said. "You know the ones."

She froze, but he wasn't watching her. His eyes were on the fallen branches and the roots he was navigating over.

"Well, they were real. They let people go to other places. Woods. Meadows. Mountains. All kind of like here but wrong. Beautiful, but wrong. Not a hoax, though. There was even a church upstate."

Ayanna couldn't speak. Her mouth was dry. She rubbed the top of her right hand. Was it possible he was leading her toward a door? The desperate rush of wanting to run ahead and see if really, truly, there was another. The nauseated feeling of wanting to stay absolutely put until her heart calmed.

"Anyway, one of the professors here is studying the doors. I mean it's harder for her to do it than it was a few years ago. If you like adventure, let me show you something cool."

Felix walked and walked, keeping his hands on the tree trunks to stay balanced. Branches reached for him and still he persisted. Ayanna followed, trying to keep her eyes on his back. The white T-shirt was a little tight and she could see how sharp his shoulder blades were.

In a hollow, there was a little drop of the golden path. Short and twisty, about eight feet long and three feet wide. There was the moss. Some ferns grew next to it. Bright somehow still, despite it being the gloaming time. And on the other side, the high navy grass of the plains. Felix was explaining something, but even though he was close, she couldn't hear him. Her eyes were on the blue, the gold, the ferns.

"How did this happen?" she finally asked, her voice small and squeaky with confusion.

He didn't answer. She walked and stood on the path. For a moment, her brain told her she could smell Olivia's apple shampoo, feel her short fingers against her arm. Ayanna was crying. A voice she didn't recognize said, "I knew you would come."

"You've walked the path, haven't you?"

Ayanna let herself feel for five, ten, fifteen, twenty. Took in a deep breath, released it slow. Again.

"I don't know what you're talking about," she said, and walked away.

11

For six weeks, Ayanna had gone to the door every day. She'd taken off her shoes, let her toes push into the warm dirt and sharp pebbles, and asked it to give Olivia back. She'd begged and pleaded with it. Sometimes knocked and slammed herself against it when no one was around to stop her. The knob changed sometimes: once a mouth with long, straight teeth, sometimes patterns with spirals and flowers and dots, and a swirl of clouds around the knob's full moon.

Where were her parents? Drinking, fighting, talking in her father's garden. Drinking, fighting, talking on her mother's front porch. Drinking, fighting, talking at night in the road, on the phone in their separate houses, walking together in the park. Only the grandmothers rolled their eyes at this behavior. Other adults spoke to Ayanna about grief; it was normal for them to behave this way. They had lost a child. Bourbon, beers, red wine, bottom-shelf gin, top-shelf tequila. Tears, arguments, walking into a room and feeling like she had almost caught them embracing. Sometimes her dad said today would be the last one like this and then Ayanna would come home crusty and tired from sun and pleading, and he would be asleep in the backyard next to the packed tomato plants.

"I'm still here," Ayanna said to her mom, to her dad, to the adults at church who tried to get her to understand her parents' perspective, to the door, but was met with silence.

Her mom did not respond to texts from her. When Ayanna brought her food and water, she ignored it. Only when she was drunk was she willing to look at Ayanna. Once, she spoke to her like she was Olivia.

"I love you," her mother had said. She'd hugged Ayanna close, let her smell sweat and alcohol and lavender soap. Ayanna had accepted it. She was too tired to be angry.

The next morning, her mother was gone.

Ayanna's grandmother sitting at the table, opening the bills and taking Antony's debit card from his leather wallet, her grandmother talking to the police officers in the station, on the phone, her grandmother telling her she needed to get ready to go back to school, her grandmother telling her that she could talk to her, her grandmother saying the words *mental health advocate* like it was a new technology she had never heard of before, her grandmother suggesting she call some friends and go out, her grandmother trying to pass a soccer ball to Ayanna and the ball instead hitting the shed with a loud, satisfying thunk, her grandmother doing dishes and crying and then saying she always cried while doing dishes, that's how much she hated doing 'em, why haven't you noticed before, her grandmother telling Ayanna they should go get her hair braided for the school year.

Grief time was different. Dinner was sometimes at four in the afternoon, at midnight, never. Mundane things—scrubbing the shower, weeding the garden, making toast—were hills to trudge up. Time never made sense. Ayanna would sit in her room and think she had been crying for hours to find out it had only been three minutes. Conversations would take hours but when Ayanna reflected on it later, only five minutes' worth of information had been said. How could it take her hours to say, "It hurts"? Ayanna's brain was sinkholing with it; even thinking Olivia's name plunged her elsewhere sometimes.

Every night, Ayanna told herself in her too-cold bedroom the door would open again to the blue grass and blue sky, Olivia would be there at the entrance. Everything would be fixed. She would no longer be alone. Ayanna had written out a long apology to Olivia. She would take her to dinner, would buy her ice cream, rub her sister's feet. She would do what Olivia wanted and go to the same college as her and they would be roommates. They would eat breakfast together almost every morning and study at night in the same bed.

On a Sunday night, the door opened to somewhere new for the first time since that day. A swamp with squat pink trees and long trailing branches, orange water, and what looked like lily pads made of bronze, each the same as the other. *A month ago*, Ayanna thought, *what a thrill it would have been to see this.* She lifted her head, stopped slumping. This one, it had a smell too. Like rotting pumpkins mixed with fresh-cut grass. The sky, a true black. It seemed as if all the light Ayanna could see was coming instead from the water. One of the trees closest to the entrance was covered in fuzzy green fruits.

I should walk through, Ayanna thought, *and disappear too*. But it would be her luck that the very next day Olivia would return, looking for her. When someone was lost, it was better to stay put.

The lake rippled. There was a mist too, she realized, lighter orange but it did nothing to make the sky feel lighter. She watched it for what felt like hours but was probably, Ayanna figured, maybe fifteen minutes. The mist swirled and shone, the water, Ayanna felt more and more certain, was warm, a few times it fizzed up as if it were carbonated and then stilled again. When the door shut, Ayanna was relieved. But was it a brighter blue now? The knob was no longer ornate; it had turned into a plain silver. Then it became brighter and brighter, until

Ayanna had to shut her eyes. Even closed, she could see the intensity through her lids. Ayanna covered her eyes with her hands, drew her head to her knees, and still, pain. A creak, a pop, and the air was sauna-hot and dry, Ayanna raised her eyes, blinked at painful red-and-white spots in the corners of her vision, and the door was gone.

It will come back, Ayanna thought, and wished she could ask it why this time had been so dramatic. She walked back to her dad's car by straying into the woods, not caring they belonged to a neighbor who hated the church. Wending their way between the broken branches on the ground and roots was a flock of wild turkeys, a mix of the dead and the spirits of their kin. Small heads and waddles. The spirits shifting between cloud and outstretched wings, all of them making strange hisses and garbled complaints until she backed away slowly. One of them had what looked like a bag of Chips Ahoy! in its mouth.

She took a picture but the dead did not appear in it. The living turkey with the cookies looked smug. He had found something delicious. Ayanna wanted to show Olivia. Later, in the middle of the night, she woke up and researched whether turkeys can eat chocolate. The answer was not really, and she lay awake wondering if the flock would die from eating the cookies, and feeling certain it would be her fault.

That night, Ayanna and her grandmother ate a pizza together in the backyard. It was chilly for the first time that summer, a wind pushing both of their hair away and then slapping it against cheeks and foreheads. Ayanna's grandmother was asking her again what had happened when they had gone through the door.

"I saw spirits," Ayanna said. "Some spoke English, some spoke maybe Korean, and some spoke a language I had never heard but I felt like I had once known or understood it."

"Once, we all spoke the same language," her grandmother said. "Not just people but everything living. We were able to understand the exact meaning of the wind rushing through trees. Dog barks. Other people too. There's a song of the universe that we all felt."

Ayanna chewed on an especially large mushroom she had picked out of the congealed cheese on the pizza box's bottom. Her heart thrilled for the first time since she saw the silver mountains. She could barely make out the garden. The idea of being able to hear the secrets of plants pushing out from the dirt, to hear what algae had to gossip about, and to walk out into a world filled with more and more things to know.

"Maybe, if you have to see them for the rest of your life," Ayanna's grandmother said, "you'll at least get a chance to learn that language."

Ayanna nodded. She didn't care if her grandmother could see it or not.

"Maybe," her grandmother said. She stopped and shook her head. "I don't know why I'm saying that word so much. But maybe when we die, that's the payment. Your soul returns to that language. If it's willing. And now you have your whole life to learn that language again."

Ayanna was too angry at herself for becoming a person who cried when she heard the word *death* to hear what her grandmother was saying. She stood up and went back inside. She scrubbed the kitchen clean. Her father was out again. The countertops and knives gleamed.

Then, in the morning, it was reported for the first time since they had all appeared, all the doors were gone. *It will be fine,* Ayanna told herself. She picked all the ripe tomatoes—the heirlooms, the Romas, because her dad had called San Marzanos pretentious, the big yellow boys, the little cherries she still liked to squish between her fingers to feel like a giant—and put them on the table. Ayanna made sauces, she had learned how to can, it would all be fine, the doors would come back, Olivia would return, she sliced tomatoes and covered them in basil, olive oil, pepper, and salt. She did not go to the field and watch the scientists gather soil samples. She did not go to school the next week when it started up again. She did not ask her father what had happened to make her mother stop coming over.

"I THINK YOU NEED to go live with your grandmother," her dad said on a Tuesday morning while Ayanna watched *The Price Is Right* and made a salsa. A college bro was shaming himself at Punch-a-Bunch. Every punch, an epic fail for both prize money and his own dignity. He was punching in a way to clearly make himself feel tough while doing it. A *kee-yah* there, a grunt over there. He didn't even look blazed. Ayanna shook her head.

"I'm sorry," he said while Ayanna diced poblanos.

"Do you think I should cook these first?"

"Ayanna."

"Why not Mom?"

"You know Opal doesn't want to see you."

Ayanna watched her hands chopping. Encouraged herself to say everything she had been thinking these weeks while he drank and cried and ignored her. She was going to yell at him, to demand that he be there for her, to ask him what they could do for Olivia. If anyone knew anything about the doors, about what to do, it would be him. It would feel good to finally say everything brewing inside.

Ayanna's father was crying. His eyes were red and the way his lips were crumpled, she felt like he was far younger than she would ever be again. She wanted to cut off her own pinkie. She had read people did that in some countries as a path to a sincere apology. She wanted to walk around her life, offering her right pinkie to everyone who loved Olivia. If she said that to Olivia, Ayanna knew her sister's face would scrunch up with concern and glee and maybe she would say something like "You can't culturally appropriate an apology, Ayanna." Her father was saying things like I can't do this, I'm sorry, I don't know how to be a good parent, I don't even know how to be a person, and she could not bear to fully listen to what sounded like her father breaking up with all the responsibilities that came with raising her. Ayanna put the knife down and went to her bedroom. There, she pulled all the clothes out of her closet, looked at her books, and wished she had gone out into the orange swamp. Her pinkie was so small. What was the point? She knew it would have been better to have walked through the door when it had opened, slipped her shoes off and waded into the orange water, leaned back into its carbonated orange warmth, looked up into the black night, and let herself slip down below the surface.

12

In her dorm—after showering and changing into Olivia's cherry-and-lemon pajama set—Ayanna took one of the golden pills. She drank a glass of water in a quick gulp and then flopped back onto the bed. The ceiling light looked kind of like a boob. White walls, white sheets, everything she had brought to live in this single stowed in the blocked-off closet. Only the desk looked vaguely lived-in, with her laptop, some pens, and the off-kilter stack of books. "How can I do this for another sixty or seventy years?" she asked herself. There were no answers available, and she promised herself she would ask herself again tomorrow. It was easier some mornings to want to live when the sky was bright blue and the trees were crisping from green to brown.

Ayanna's brain stewed in anxieties. The doors had disappeared two years ago, so there was no point in speculating. Accept the things you cannot change and gather the wisdom to see the world in all its possibilities. She could stop trying to look through and ignore the dead and try to find Olivia among them. It had been two years, could Olivia still be alive? Ayanna pressed her right hand over her heart, hoped it would calm her down. The hardest thing was to decide which world she wanted to accept: a world where her sister was alive but struggling without help or a world where her sister had died two years ago.

For a little while, Ayanna scrolled through the strange-sightings forum, hoping again for a sign. A door discovered in an idyllic grove, a ring of mushrooms, a dank basement. Instead, it was a long discussion about the number of people who claimed to have seen lights in the distance drawing them in and sometimes becoming a man's shadow. Mostly, the man stared. But some said he came closer and spoke their names like an evocation. He stayed in your dreams after if you didn't give him money or a secret. The man stood in the corners, laughing, while you dreamed about your days. Everyone wanted to be interesting enough to be cursed. Everyone wanted to believe that even the unreal could be controlled. But whenever the extraordinary came into their lives with all its unruliness and depth, they always tried to look away because it couldn't be bought.

Ayanna sighed. She wanted the pill to immediately kick in, to give her the promised feeling of intense obliteration she longed for. Ayanna deleted her rant that the supernatural did not operate under the logic of capitalism. "Don't post while getting high," she muttered.

You were supposed to take this pill intentionally, not while scrolling on Reddit, Ayanna reminded herself. When the elders in her church had taken it, it was part of a sacred ritual. First you prayed for everyone you loved and could ever love. Name them: *Olivia, Dad, Grandma*. Tell yourself what the therapist encouraged: I love myself. I love being alive. I can build a life. I am not alone, there are people who care for me. Ayanna. Ayanna. Ayanna. I want to love myself. She wanted to be enough of a cheeseball that she could name every person she had met at the party. *Will my heart be open to them and maybe their future friendships?* Was the only way forward to be as earnest and open as you could stomach? Ayanna stretched out on the floor, tightened all her muscles for fifteen seconds, then relaxed them. Did it again while naming herself as one of her loved ones. She didn't believe herself but she tried.

Then, you were supposed to envision a better world, Ayanna reminded herself. No poverty, no homelessness, a place where everyone was treated with exquisite value, that was what her church had taught. War would be considered the deepest shame. We did things to mitigate climate change. We accepted hope over cynicism. We understood that compromise could be painful, but it was always better than violence. Life was sacred and to walk through a door and bring back life was honoring that. Her brain started to float. Maybe, she considered, the world would be a better place if all mayors and presidents were golden retrievers. A dog society. "I love myself," Ayanna said, finally aware the drug was starting to work, but it still sounded like a lie. She tried to tense her legs again, but they ignored her.

Next, challenge yourself to make the world a better place. Even when it feels hopeless. To continue living, and Ayanna could almost hear her father's voice at its warmest and most earnest, to continue living you have to want things to be better. Think of the small, kind things you can do when big changes are out of reach. Nothing will change if you don't ever try. Figure out ways to advocate. There was heat on her scalp, it felt like her hair might fall out. Ayanna's brain looped between a scheme to become a billionaire's altruistic ex-wife, wandering the earth ending childhood poverty and starting arts scholarships, and the loopiness of sending postcards to different people urging them to reelect President Rover, a good and just boy who believed all humans should get universal walks and health care. Nothing will change if you don't ever try.

Ayanna added another step to the ritual. "Olivia, Olivia, Olivia," she said aloud. You had to say things in threes, she knew, to really mean them. *I am so tired of being alone, Olivia*, she thought. It was too honest to say aloud. She wanted her sister's spirit to come to her and promise to never leave. She wanted her sister's spirit to come to her and say: I am still alive behind the doors, and this is when they will return. And if her sister would not come to her. She said the name again, the name sounding more like O-lif-euh by the fifth and sixth attempts.

In high school, a girl had told Ayanna that some doctors speculated that when you died, there were ten minutes or so where you knew you were dead because your neurons were still firing, where you could hear the world around you but could also know this was the end. There was no life flashing before your eyes. There was only the anxious rush of your brain attempting to reassure itself and cling to life when facing the eternity of nonexistence you were rushing toward. When her brain moved into the void, her hands uncurled until fingers rested flat on the rough sheets, shoulders moved away from ears, even toes and arches let go of their rigidity. The release of being nothing that came from the pill.

After five minutes or so of this, Ayanna felt aware of a presence on her bed. It was talking to her for a long time, something that was a mix of saying things about a daughter, a digression about what was the most romantic song in the world, and Ayanna knew she was high because the voice kept insisting it was "I Know What You Want" (featuring Mariah Carey), and she thought maybe it was her mother, finally ready to forgive her. Was her mother dead? Did her mother like Mariah? No, it was always Whitney for her. But the woman was saying, "You have to find Marlie Evans, you have to tell her where my body is, you have to tell her I love her, I love her, I wouldn't ever leave her."

She slept a little, then felt a hand on her face. Lips on hers. Ayanna opened her eyes and a man was there that she didn't know. He was saying, It's you, Liana. A layer of pink light was around him, and as he touched her face, the man sometimes shifted from what looked like a donkey to another man's face to an apple tree.

"I'm not Liana," Ayanna said.

"You were her. I can hear her voice beneath yours, I can see her life pulsing in your heart."

"No."

"We're meant to be together."

He told her about a time when they were walking together on a rainy night in May. Every light they saw felt like a chance for him to say how he felt. But the conversation kept wandering to a book Liana had read about a bunch of rich English and American people who were vacationing in Italy and treating limoncello like a potential wellness cure. And as she spoke about this, her thoughts were wending toward how throughout history liquor had probably always been treated that way, and he was thinking about her hands, how sometimes the first thought when he woke up was, *What is she thinking?* Ayanna couldn't help but be moved a little. She could not tell if this feeling was simply because of how passionately this man was speaking or because maybe he was right. No one had kissed her in years. She had told Olivia that in her first year of college, she was going to get a 4.0 and get railed in the arboretum. Instead, Ayanna had struggled to get a 2.7 and only got asked out by the weird, mean kid in her freshman comp class whose idea of feedback was to tell everyone to write better.

Once, she'd been a woman named Liana who talked about novels while walking home with men in the rain rather than whisper words of deep and vast erotic anticipation. Outside Liana's apartment, this man had said, "Do you think you could ever be in love with me?" And she had shaken his hand and went inside.

"Do you remember now?" he asked.

"I'm sorry, but I don't think so," Ayanna said.

He slapped the pen-and-pencil cup off her desk, then left, walking right through the heavy wooden door.

The rest of the night was spent spinning between what felt like only half-heard requests from different spirits (a goodbye, a bank account number, something to do with stolen slingbacks), a long dream—Ayanna hoped—that involved being in a Wendy's and trying to stack twenty chicken nuggets on top of one another in a great leaning tower before being allowed to eat them, and then a phone call with Jane where Ayanna agreed to play on her soccer team. "Why are we having this conversation at four in the morning?" Ayanna said twice, and Jane replied each time, "Hey, asshole, you called me." Sometimes for brief moments, Ayanna was on the path again, walking toward a pair of silver mountains in the distance. They alternated between the light blue every distant thing on Earth seems to have and a liquid silver. One of the few things Ayanna remembered reading and enjoying from her first year of college was an essay most of her classmates hated about longing, loneliness, the color blue, and how, maybe, at least in her interpretation of it, life might be a series of figuring out what amount of distance you needed from ideas, from people, from yourself.

When Ayanna woke up in the morning, she planned on having a big breakfast, writing a reading response, then spending the afternoon stoned again. In the cafeteria, Jane was waiting for her. She was wearing neon-green soccer shorts, a T-shirt with the phrase *Goal x Hunting x Association* on it and on the back, just her first name, *JANE*, with the number sixty-nine. She was wearing cat ears and carrying two pairs of keeper's gloves.

"You're still wearing your pajamas. We have to be there in twenty minutes."

Ayanna grabbed a banana and a cup of to-go coffee and changed. She put on a tank top, her old black soccer shorts, the long socks, and threw her shin pads and cleats into a bag. As she was tying her hair back, Ayanna realized that despite feeling a little off from the night before, this was the most she had felt like herself in years. She stepped over the pens and pencils on the floor and tried to remember when she'd bumped into them.

"I have a shirt for you," Jane said. Ayanna opened the door and took it. Number ninety-nine.

On the walk over, Jane explained the team's current drama. Their usual striker had broken up with their sweeper, and the team was taking sides. Multiple times she informed Ayanna about the necessity of scoring goals in this game, that a win would really bring the team back together. So far, they were top of the league despite being all women and artsy enbies. She did not explain why the team had to be brought back together. Injuries were alluded to as "complex interpersonal relationships." They had beaten the bro team, Hat Trick Titans, 1–0 on a muddy Tuesday night. Several members of the team were still talking about getting a commemorative tattoo for that victory, but Jane thought it was cheesy to do things like that for an intermural soccer team, especially in year one.

"Why did they break up?" Ayanna asked. "What did the striker do to have to quit the team?"

Jane continued talking. The team they were going to play wasn't very good, so it would be a bad omen if they lost. People were already out drinking, preparing for the football game that was hours and hours away. Two frat dudes were screaming at each other about who had cheated in a game of cornhole. They were so loud that Ayanna's head ached. She longed for the big breakfast she had promised herself, but instead drank for a long time from Jane's water bottle.

"Acre can really dehydrate you," Jane said. "Next time, make sure to have two Gatorades. One for when you take it, and one to drink immediately the next morning."

"Thanks, Mom."

Jane rolled her eyes.

"Do you know someone named Marlie Evans?" Ayanna asked.

"Are people actually named Marley?" Ayanna could tell by the way Jane said the name that she envisioned it spelled with an *-ey*. The name was, somehow, even weirder than weird Jane could imagine.

At the field, it became apparent the reason for the team break was Jane. The aforementioned sweeper greeted Jane with an enthusiastic kiss, and they walked together arm in arm to the center of the pitch. While the two led team stretches, there was a mix of conversations that ranged from "They're cute together" to "These shitheads couldn't wait even a few weeks to flaunt their relationship." It became clear Jane had slept with at least two other women on the team.

It didn't matter. Ayanna stretched her hips and her legs, her eyes automatically looking at how poorly the pitch was maintained. She liked using the proper English terminology; running on the pitch felt like poetry, running on the field felt like being a startled cow. Dips on the sides, areas where the grass was patchy. Together, the team jogged a lap around. The other team mostly appeared to be doing yoga together. All in child's pose, except for one guy who was juggling, knee, head, foot, knee. Ayanna felt certain he was the only one who cared about winning. Sensing that desire made her want to score six goals. She warmed up, doing trick shots hitting the crossbar and goalposts. It felt good to refuse to let herself put the ball in the net. There were people watching her follow this pattern, but for the first time in a long time, the only things her brain cared about were the ball, the angle at which she hit it with her foot, and the pinging sound whenever she connected.

When Ayanna's anxiety was truly bad, she walked around listening to guided meditations. One of her favorites was a woman with an indescribable accent saying to imagine your soul was "a tender, little soap bubble floating in the empty majesty of your lungs. Picture the iridescence, purple, green, blue, pink against all the clear. Add layers for the complexity of your life experiences and emotions." Each person had this tenderness inside them. Listening helped sometimes, sure, although other times even the thought of visualizing her soul felt painful and cruel, but this, Ayanna thought, was what she should have been doing. Here in the repetitive motions was the nothingness she had longed for.

"Take a minute and eat a little more." Jane tapped Ayanna on the shoulder. There were a bowl of orange slices and water bottles next to a rickety bench. Ayanna ran to them and drank for a long time, squirting water into her open mouth. Even the dribble of it down the front of her shirt was nostalgic. The orange slices tasted extra good. Jane told her they were going to play a 4–5–1.

"I haven't played in two years." Ayanna held a strip of orange peel in her hands. "Feels like a lot of pressure."

"The other team calls itself the Fighting Grandmas. I don't know how many more ways I can tell you they're terrible."

"I don't know if this is right for me."

Olivia would've laughed at her for saying that. She would've said, You are one of the most competitive people alive. You don't like yoga because there's nothing to win.

"Their defenders have scored more goals than their striker."

Ayanna shut her eyes. She tried to lose herself in the warm sun and gorging herself on orange slices.

"If we lose, we lose," Jane said.

But they didn't. By the end of the first half, Goal x Hunting x Association was up by two. A brace scored by Ayanna. The thrill of trapping the ball on her chest, the pain of it, but still the control of moving her body through the air and risking falling or slipping or miscalculating where the ball would hit. It was still hard; the way Ayanna approached the ball was as if she had spent the last few years of her life crying and occasionally smoking, and not lifting weights. Yet she knew that night she would lie awake thinking about the goal she'd scored on a breakaway where she breezed past the guy who cared too much and slammed the ball into the top corner. The way it felt to trust herself took Ayanna's breath away.

"You are our Messi," one of Ayanna's new teammates said.

"He's a winger," Ayanna replied, but was sure no one heard her, as most of them were hugging and yelling like she had just won them the World Cup.

"Offsides, offsides," the boy who cared too much yelled, but everyone ignored him. He was clearly wrong and furious.

At different points during the match, he'd kept yelling "offsides" at Ayanna. He received a yellow card from the referee for pretending to give out his own yellow. The boy who cared too much was furious that Jane was wearing cat ears still while keeping goal. He felt it was disrespectful and dangerous. She should get a yellow too.

In the past it would have been annoying to Ayanna, but she was too much in the zone to care. Running, shooting, yelling, "I'm open," pretending to shoot an arrow into the air after finally getting her hat trick. In a way, she was feeding off his dreadful intensity. Each outburst made her more focused, every time he tried to rattle her made her want to thank him. The game's ninety minutes—even though she knew her whole body would be sore for a part of the next week—were the best she had felt in years. Positioning her body with the farthest-back defender, storing up the energy to break into a sprint whenever a midfielder set up a run for her, feeling the lengthening of her stride. When she used to run like this, Ayanna had imagined herself as a horse on a beach. But there was no need for whimsy here, there was more than enough pleasure in focusing on controlling her speed, controlling the ball, positioning her body to take accurate chances. This was an intelligence and understanding she had missed.

After, they went to the bar that only carded people at night and ordered pitchers of the cheapest beer. People's friends started rolling in, and even though Jane was busy flirting with both her sweeper love interest and the bartender with two lip piercings and an impeccable cat eye wearing a they/them pin, Felix and Stephen showed up fairly quickly.

Ayanna attempted to avoid Felix, who was clearly trying to figure out what to say or do to make them comfortable with each other. *I just want,* she thought while doing a shot with all the offensive line, *one day like this. No path, no sister, no death, no big conversations.* She got into a spirited debate about Megan Rapinoe, into one about Liverpool versus United, into one about Coors versus Miller, into Austen versus Brontë, first as literature then as cage fight. Austen was voted as the winner even though Ayanna could not follow the logic. Brontë, moody with a pack of sisters and a love of drama, felt much scrappier to her.

A girl was telling Ayanna a long, dumb revenge plot. She was going to sleep with her ex-boyfriend's father or older brother to teach him a lesson. Ayanna kept asking her, "What lesson are you teaching?" And the girl kept saying back, "If you don't get it, you don't get it." Ayanna shrugged. Her left foot ached, right shoulder too. She paused to talk to Stephen, who handed her a shot.

"Should we cheers?" Ayanna asked.

"Let's do something else," Stephen said. He had a new haircut, she realized, hair long on top, short on the sides. "Let's say something at the same time."

"What do you mean, the word *something*?"

"Just any random thought, no questions."

It felt dangerous to Ayanna, but she shrugged. This was college.

"I ate turtle soup this summer. But now when I'm awake at night, I feel guilty about it," Stephen said while Ayanna said, "Sometimes on days like this, I wonder if I died and I just don't know it."

"What?" they both said and then slammed their shots. Ayanna was surprised to get the appeal of it, the sweet of bourbon, hot in the mouth and throat.

More than a little drunk, she encountered Jane, who was fussing over the jukebox.

"'River Deep Mountain High' or 'I Would Die 4 U?'"

"'I Would Die 4 U.'" Ayanna let her hair out of her ponytail. "You know how there's all that gossip about how at the Olympics everyone is fucking each other because of sports energy and like competitive energy?"

"I've never heard about this in my entire life."

"You should read about it," Ayanna said. "You're living it."

Jane laughed. "Maybe my next shirt should be *SPORTS ENERGY IS FUCK ENERGY*."

"If you do it, please make me one."

Jane was delighted. "I knew it. Just like sensed that underneath all that big sad-girl energy there was someone interesting in there."

Felix came over to them while Ayanna chugged some of her beer to avoid having to react to the words *big sad-girl energy*.

"I heard you destroyed the other team."

"Hat Trick over here did. I mostly got to daydream and look at butts for ninety minutes."

When Jane had walked away, Felix cleared his throat.

"Look."

"You don't have to."

"Please."

Ayanna took a deep breath and looked beyond him. On the bar walls was a series of drawings of famous celebrities merged with dogs. Michael Beagle Jones. Marilyn Poodle Monroe. The bar had to not care about IDs because of how uncool it was. Ethan Husky Hawke.

"I just want to say sorry. I clearly made you uncomfortable and put you in a situation that you didn't want to be in. And I know even now you probably don't want to deal with me. It's just important to me that I at least apologize." Felix's voice was low and friendly. She could tell he didn't expect her to say, "I accept your apology," or explain.

"How did you know about it?"

"Oh, I'm a research assistant for the professor. If you ever want to know more or meet her, let me know. But truly, we don't have to talk about this ever again."

He paused and turned toward the jukebox. "It sounds like Jane is in a mood."

Ayanna nodded. If she hadn't been drunk, she would've walked away by now. Instead, she turned toward him. He seemed sober. "Why do you study it? The path?"

"Because." He cleared his throat.

"Do you want to go get something to eat?" Ayanna asked. She wanted to make a good choice, not just keep wandering around on a belly full of fruit and beer and too much water.

Over baskets of chicken strips and french fries, Felix said the professor was building the Institute of True Reality. A rich donor had given her a bunch of money to do it. The ideas would include a variety of different disciplines over time. For example, there was a scientist theorizing that aliens were potentially already among us, but because our eyes haven't evolved enough, we can't see them. There are many different forms of matter and there are so many things in the universe that are limited by our potential for understanding. It wasn't publishable yet, this was all speculation, but it was one of the things. There was also some virtual reality stuff too, but Felix found it embarrassing.

"There are also cultural ideas." Felix paused and considered a waffle fry. "Am I talking too much?"

Ayanna shook her head no, mouth too full of chicken strips to want to say anything. This, too, was exciting. She thought maybe her ideas about education and learning had been deeply childish because she had never considered it was possible to discover or theorize new things just by sitting in a quiet room and having an imagination. She thought he was still avoiding her question, there seemed to be something personal involved here, but Ayanna didn't want to push. Felix told her one idea of an invisible reality made evident was through art. What some religions might call a soul might actually be the human brain's ability to develop different ways of seeing. Different realities might have tangles that could be seen or understood by sensitive brains.

"Isn't that offensive to artists? Doesn't it discredit their imaginations?" Ayanna asked. She didn't like that her brain was immediately thinking of an opposing example that there was a possibility people were so powerful—and they weren't aware of it—they could conjure things that could change reality.

Felix paused. He was smiling a little bit. One of his front teeth was crooked and bent in toward the other. There was a birthmark, darker brown, beneath his left eye. A pack of cigarettes was peeking out of the pocket of the light blue button-down shirt he was wearing. Ayanna couldn't tell if she was noticing these things about him because maybe he would become someone important to her or if the intensity of a conversation about ideas, of how seriously he was speaking, how his dark brown eyes were kind, made it feel like having a crush. He was a man who actually allowed himself to find women funny. He had apologized to her for making her feel uncomfortable. It was annoying how just these moments of respect did so much. There was still so much to learn about living at twenty, but Ayanna had a strict rule about men: don't date anyone who won't laugh at a woman's jokes. No smiles, no kind gazes, no "Oh, that's funny," only genuine laughs. Felix's laugh was a little deep, sometimes close to a snort when something really got him.

"I think it would depend on the artist, right? Toni Morrison talked about feeling voices move through her when she was working on her novels. Several writers and artists have embarked on different forms of mediumship, like Lucille Clifton. So, I think some people would find it very offensive, yeah. But others might think it's an even greater testament to their art, they can look and commune with invisible realities and sources and still make something understandable and beautiful for those who can't."

A theory, long denied, was moving from seed to bloom in Ayanna's brain.

"Can I visit the institute sometime?"

"I can talk to Professor Collins, but I'm sure she'll say yes."

One of the few childhood memories Ayanna had from when her parents were still together was of her mom telling them very earnestly about how the world was made. There was nothing, and then there was light, and then there were birds. She had not realized her mother was remembering and reciting from the Bible. The story had never done what it was supposed to do, which was make her feel sleepy and relaxed. The idea of the darkness and the void and that someone—although even then she knew it was not a good idea to refer to God as just some boring old someone—had woken up one day and seen they could make a void into something beautiful.

She had a similar feeing in this moment listening to Felix speak, here was someone who was talking and giving her the tools to build a life. She wanted to be that to someone else. It was the most she had wanted something in two years. Ayanna looked away so Felix couldn't see how wet her eyes were.

Once, the spirit sang of a wedding between worlds. There are fields that burn, there are cities swallowed whole, and in each of these seasons, new questions arise. The purpose of the audience—of each great congregation—is to watch and try to understand. There are seasons of birds and of seeds spread by the winds, and these are meant to let the souls speak the necessary truths.

After a season of flame, the doors were born to usher in the next bloom.

When the winter sleeted in, the doors were meant to hibernate.

In death, there is life.

In life, there is all.

Everything has a season.

13

Professor Collins was a Black woman who challenged Ayanna's understanding of age. Her face looked young and smooth, she laughed often and, for an academic, seemed unusually focused on having fun. Her hair was a mix of grays and whites and piled on top of her head into a braid crown. When Ayanna entered her office with Felix, Professor Collins hugged Felix and acted like an aunt. He should eat more, how were his grades, should he be here right now or should he be studying for midterms? Ayanna had never seen an older person who looked so cool in her black jeans, black T-shirt, black boots, and bright waxed cotton-print blazer thrown over her shoulders. Most of her professors wore plain blue sweaters and overpriced brown dress sneakers with big white soles.

After a few more questions like that, she sent Felix to the marked-off woods to take photos, record observations, and meditate within its bounds and write down any "unusual phenomena" he might experience. Then, her red glasses sliding down her nose, Professor Collins turned back to Ayanna.

"How much do you know about the work we do here?"

"I don't, really," Ayanna said. "Felix has told me things."

Professor Collins laughed, though Ayanna didn't think what she had said was funny.

The office was painted a rich blue; with the blinds closed and the room illuminated by a paper table lamp of deep orange and a bamboo floor lamp, it seemed to have the texture of velvet. There was a large painting in her office, black background, shapes of many different blues—aqua, cerulean, navy, cornflower—and light yellow. A Post-it note next to it had the words *The courage to venture to the edge of reason* on it. Ayanna's postmodernism professor had a cross-stitch on the wall that read *The most important arguments you can have are with yourself.*

"LET ME TELL YOU how I came to this," Professor Collins said. Her voice had a little rasp to it. Ayanna assumed Professor Collins must have seen the meadows or even walked through the door. The room was clearly speaking to that space. Ayanna was torn between admiring the place and wanting to immediately walk out.

"For a long time, I studied different Black spiritual practices around the world. Many of us are Christians now, but a lot of us believe the world of the dead is side by side with the world of the living. And I'm sure you heard the story, right? About the preacher who brought his wife back?"

Ayanna nodded. She tried not to think of the story any longer. Last year, at the height of her depression, she had watched over and over clips of the wife being interviewed on *At Home with Simone*. The wife wore a frilly white dress and a vacant look. If you wanted to believe her, the look seemed to speak to her always seeing elsewhere now. If you didn't want to believe her, the look seemed to be on the face of a liar trying to avoid eye contact. The wife spoke about dying, about being alone and elsewhere, and the joy she felt when suddenly her husband was there. It was interspersed with what felt like clear fundraising for their church.

"I grew up believing that might be possible," Ayanna said. She reminded herself to be brave. If anyone was going to take it seriously, it would hopefully be this woman. "I might still believe it's possible. Or at least I want to."

"I take it you've had an experience with a ghost." Professor Collins pulled out a notebook. "Can I take notes?" Then she laughed. "I love having a job where I can say 'You've had an experience with a ghost.'"

"Sure." Ayanna ignored the ghost question and barged on to what she wanted to speak about. "I was raised in, our faith had a bunch of different names, but in the Church of the Blue Doors. You might also know it as Pathsong." Ayanna realized the professor didn't mind her interjections about herself and, in fact, seemed to be relieved not to have to keep talking.

She did not tell Professor Collins about the Olivia of it all, but she described again walking not out onto the golden path but instead into the vast wilderness with its long, blue grass, its perpetual blue sky. There were lights among the grass, and they spoke to one another. Some knew who they once were, some knew all the things they had been, and a few refused to acknowledge their new realities, speaking about going to the office or about stocks as if they could not see anything around them. Ayanna described seeing what seemed now in retrospect like a vast parade of them moving toward the silver mountains. Some of them were shapes and spoke in languages unintelligible to her. I know this sounds crazy, she said more than once, until Professor Collins told her to stop saying that. I see them still, sometimes, all the time if I'm being honest, I just work really hard to ignore them, Ayanna admitted. She told the professor about the ways the meadows made her understand the color blue, how there were berries growing there, how a door had formed from what looked like bugs. She paused, thinking about her sister's arms around her stomach, her head against her back, her dress, the strip of it that she couldn't throw away, the weight of Olivia as they stepped in unison through the new door. *I keep looking for Olivia in the dead;*

I keep trying to ignore the dead because I don't want to see her, Ayanna thought, but did not say.

The professor's eyes were soft. Ayanna realized she was still standing and talking. And had she been talking too quickly? She had the feeling of having finally said something important, but still saying it sideways, so the boulder remained, but she could feel the beginning of an important erosion. Ayanna felt the urge to leave and do her after-therapy routine, writing down everything clarifying in her palm-sized journal, then eating a bunch of popcorn in an attempt to feel only salt and butter rather than emotions.

"Let's take a minute and have some tea." Professor Collins turned on a kettle. She produced two mugs, a box full of teas that looked expensive compared to Ayanna's usual two-dollar box of night-night tea.

"Do you think there's something special in tea, something we don't know about"—Ayanna tried to get comfortable in the chair, but it was impossible—"that actually makes us feel psychologically more in place? Like a chemical that interacts with our brains like Zoloft or Lexapro?"

"Don't overthink things." Professor Collins was going through her bookshelves while the kettle burbled to itself. "Sometimes, people just need to feel good and reassured. It's a lesson I wish I had known at your age. Find ways to have small pleasures that don't directly hurt other people. Don't teach yourself to tear apart everything you like."

She said it like it was just an ordinary thing people said to one another within knowing each other for thirty minutes. There were people, adults, out in the world who could treat the world with intense attention and wanted to enjoy themselves. And then didn't feel shame at all for encouraging other people to feel the same.

Once the tea was settled and steaming in their mugs, Professor Collins turned back to Ayanna. "What do you think this other place was? Don't tell me based on your faith, don't be afraid of being embarrassed. I'm not here to judge." She pushed the glasses back up, they teetered and slid again.

"I think there's a reality where all souls go while they're waiting to be reborn. And we act like Earth is the only place with life, but there's as good a chance you'll be born on Earth as you will be reborn on any planet sustaining life. The, I don't know what word to use, people, I guess. But there were people there who felt so profoundly other, yet we all go to the same place." Ayanna hadn't expected to say it so calmly.

What she did not say aloud was, "And maybe the ghost state is just spirits waiting for the people they want to be with to also die. Which means, maybe, Olivia, even if she died, isn't avoiding me or furious with me but she's being kind and waiting for me." And then she thought, *No, she's still alive*. But even that thought felt like a lie.

The professor was silent for a long time. Ayanna couldn't read her expression, but thought her hands were shaking. On the desk was a plant with pink-and-green leaves in a planter designed to look like a greyhound. A stack of books in different languages and different subjects ranging from cave art to mediumship to a history of the Terra Nova expedition. Outside, it was gray and threatening to drizzle. The leaves on the trees around this building were still green and refusing to admit October was fast approaching.

"One of the hard things about running something like this," Professor Collins finally said, "is people don't want speculation, but hard data. I'm the type of annoying person who feels most alive when she's speculating."

"I'm sorry," Ayanna said, but felt immediately certain it was the wrong thing to say.

Professor Collins waved it away. "I'm not saying I don't believe you, or what you're saying hasn't given me a lot to think about, but now you've given me a new problem. How do we even prove this?"

Ayanna tried not to think at all, only wait. Her left shoelaces were far dirtier than the right. She wanted to stand up and look closely at the painting on the wall because the other woman's brain was somewhere else and for her to interrupt or try to speculate would be unhelpful. And besides, Ayanna could tell all her ideas were bad. There seemed to be nothing they could do beyond waiting for a door to appear.

The last time she had spoken to her father, he had claimed all the church's texts had been seized. They would probably sit the rest of their lives in government storage. If they filed claims to get them, there would be endless runarounds. He had said it was better to move on in a situation like this rather than to let all the red tape, all their denials, chew at him. If she told him about this place, about her interest in getting involved, he would say, "Haven't you been hurt enough? Don't you want to live a life?"

"My church had paperwork," Ayanna finally said when the silence became unbearable. "Part of our faith was to acquire knowledge about what was truly out there."

"I'm sure it's gone." Professor Collins gestured to herself a little, in a way that made Ayanna certain she was having a profound back-and-forth with herself. "You know, nothing like this has to be solved immediately."

"Should I go?"

"No. Let's go out to the woods for a minute. Felix's out there."

They left in silence and walked to the park. It started to drizzle, but Ayanna thought to remark on it would be annoying. There wasn't any need to hop the fence with Professor Collins. Before, Ayanna had missed the card reader attached to it. With a quick scan of the professor's university ID, the fence clanked open. In the woods, the drizzle was reduced mostly to a soft patter on leaves. She peeked at her cell phone: an invitation from Jane—with a crystal ball, a strawberry, and a glass of champagne next to it—to hang out. She assumed the crystal ball meant getting stoned but wasn't sure. Ayanna considered telling the professor her other secret, since her time in the meadows, the spirits asked her for things.

There was still a tightening in Ayanna's chest and throat as they approached the path, but she knew it was coming. Felix was talking to some people; she had thought he would be alone out here. Ayanna told herself she could not meet any more people while being a complete emotional mess. If one more person kept giving her soft eyes, making references in some way to being gentle to herself, she would scream. On all levels, she knew it was better than the year before when it seemed like no one could see or cared to see that she was having a complete mental health crisis. But Ayanna longed for the impossible: to be neutrally seen.

Felix was there with two people who were clearly professors. One was sitting on the ground and drinking from a water bottle. The other was complaining about how their laptop didn't work here. Felix was lying on the golden path, clearly trying to meditate, but couldn't focus because of all the chatter.

"Hi, everyone, I want to introduce you to our new work-study student, Ayanna," Professor Collins said.

"Ahnna?" the under-the-tree professor said.

"A, as in the letter, yah-nuh," Felix said.

Ayanna hadn't realized this whole thing had been a job interview. It was too lucky to pass up, though.

"She was a member of Pathsong growing up," Professor Collins said.

"I have so many questions for you."

The professor under the tree turned out to be a creative writing professor. It was hard not to wonder if she was the one Jane had last year. Jane had told Ayanna not to bother taking an intro to creative writing class. It was either people writing vague poems about being sad or referring to their genitals as peach pits. The professor had assigned an anthology where every story seemed to be either about a white guy who was a bad husband and/or father or about someone who had been molested and somehow thought they were too good for therapy. And then the professor had the audacity to get bored when everyone kept writing semioffensive stories about sexual violence despite her choices in course texts. They read a few stories by Black people but they either talked with what Jane called "massa accents" or every part of their life was fucked and despairing. Jane was still an English major because all her comms classes were too stupid, but she had no idea if she could finish the degree.

What became increasingly clear from talking with both professors was that neither was sure how much they could publicly accomplish as part of this institute. The other professor, who was an astronomer, seemed happy to take the money from the donors, because it was fun to consider how these doors broke so many understandings of the universe, but also said they would be surprised if the money didn't dry up within the next three years. Good for the CV, though, they kept saying. Their nail polish was golden and peeling. There was one other professor who had an affiliation with them, a religious studies and gender studies professor who was away researching in some archives in Indiana. Felix was enthused and dubious. The donors, as he put it, were rich people who wanted to find a way to become even richer by charging people to bring their dead loved ones back to life. They wanted proof the doors worked, *consistently*, then wanted to find a way to seize the means of production.

"Capitalism has people even wanting to get rich off grief," he said while shaking his head.

"We are here to see and document the best way to engage with 'spirits,' with the doors gone," Professor Collins said. "And whatever the donors do with that information, we have to learn to be okay with that."

After another twenty minutes of chatting, Ayanna promising to let the religious studies and creative writing professor do a joint interview of her, Professor Collins said it seemed like the work studies were free to go for the day. They could put down five hours of work on their time sheets.

As Felix and Ayanna walked through the woods, Ayanna asked if he was going to hang out with her and Jane on Saturday. Felix offered Ayanna his arm as they negotiated some high roots and the slippery ground.

"Be careful with Jane," Felix said. "As long as you're friends, she's the best."

She wondered why he was saying this.

"She's my friend. Maybe my best friend in the world," Felix said. "But in a romantic relationship. Yikes if you want more than fun."

He let go of her arm and looked ahead.

"Sorry. You just seem like you're coming out of a really bad time. And people can change. But I've never met anyone like Jane who so absolutely does not want to be in love and knows it."

"Do you think she really feels that way?" Ayanna asked. "Or is it an affectation? It feels like almost everyone on the soccer team thinks they can change her, and that's part of the appeal. I kind of assumed she was leaning into the appeal of I-can-fix-her. 'I can be the one who makes her fall in love.'"

Felix shrugged. "I don't think she's that cynical. But I'm sure it's one of those reinforcing cycles. People find you attractive because they can tell you're emotionally unavailable, you feel good because people find you attractive, and then, well." He used one of his fingers and made a motion of creating a perpetual circle. Today, his fingernails were a shiny black. She could tell by what he was saying, how he was saying it, that he had also been going to therapy for a while. He was also older, having taken a few years off because of family issues, he had said—although he'd said it in a way where Ayanna could feel the distance—but it was still wild to Ayanna to hear anyone around her age articulating something like that so thoughtfully. "Anyway, I doubt I'll be hanging out on Saturday. I have an exam on Monday."

She nodded despite the fact he couldn't see her.

"If you want to come here on Sunday and try Professor Collins's meditation plan with me, we can both get paid, and I can talk you through part of the ideas and theories here."

She said that would be great, still a little amused by the idea of how easily she had been given the job. Finally, growing up in a weird religion had done something positive for her. Ayanna watched him walk ahead of her, looked at his locs from behind, how beautiful they were. With the rain beading on top of his hair, Felix was a freshly watered plant. She liked the way he tried to move through the world, wanting to be precise with and kind to people even when he was saying borderline judgmental things.

There was something, too, that made Ayanna sure he had lost someone important to him. She took a deep breath, focused, willed herself to look, but there was no spirit hovering around him. Yet there was another sense Ayanna felt she'd gained from traveling through the door: the ability to see whose personality had been formed around mourning and those who had lived only in the lands of minor inconveniences and forgettable heartaches.

"I'm a twin," Ayanna said, because for the first time in years the urge was there to say it. "Well, was. I don't know how to put it yet."

She would never have said it if she'd had to look at his face. Ayanna noted the way he stopped walking for a half second, how he stopped himself from looking back at her.

"I guess I'm telling you because I don't think I can imagine Jane being my girlfriend. She reminds me of how I felt around Olivia. My sister. I mean they're nothing alike. Probably would've hated each other. But she gives me that feeling of having someone who always wants to see me." Ayanna left out, thinking it was too weird to say aloud, some of Jane's appeal was she seemed so completely disinterested in being in love with anyone but herself. Her guiding focus seemed to be a deep cultivation of herself and her ideals. Almost every woman Ayanna had ever met seemed to have internalized the idea that being a woman was to always seek some external approval like from God, from daddies of all genders who encouraged please-like-me-at-all-costs mentalities. It wasn't that people who weren't women didn't want approval, but Ayanna felt regularly to be seen by other people as a woman meant you were expected to build your life around wanting approval. Hanging out with Jane was a reminder not everyone felt that way. The closest thing Ayanna had to having future plans was a desire to care about other people but to never let their opinions about her be the North Star of her life.

Ayanna realized some of the ease she felt with him came from not having to find a way to ever tell him, "The world is full with spirits and I can see them." He already knew this information, accepted it, and wanted to know, to see more. It was hard not to be jealous of how comfortable he was with all this.

A tree branch almost hit her in the face. Ayanna ducked and nearly tripped into Felix's back. She caught herself on a tree trunk and scraped her hand a little bit. It had only ached to refer to Olivia in the past tense. Ayanna watched blood bloom out, how it became thinner in the rain hitting her raised palm. Felix was still walking ahead of her, unaware of their near collision.

14

Jane hadn't mentioned Stephen was coming over with her, and it hurt Ayanna's feelings a little. It made what Felix had said to her about Jane feel less like a kindness he was trying to do for her, and maybe more like the result of the three of them gossiping about her. Did they all think she was another one of Jane's intermural soccer WAGs, eager for two weeks of good sex and six weeks of hurt feelings? There was the possibility, Ayanna thought while pulling out art supplies and putting her nice, expensive pens into neat rows, that what she'd thought were new friendships were nothing. She was an anecdote to those people. Someone whom they would call Anna or Anya Who Played Soccer with Jane for a Fall Semester. Stephen was telling a story about going to the Alpha Phi Alpha step show the night before and watching them dance against some Korean B-boys.

"Why didn't you text me?" Jane kept saying.

He showed them a video of two guys doing what he called "an airflare."

"The human body is incredible," Ayanna said. As always, seeing someone accomplish something physical and beautiful relaxed her. Sometimes, when she couldn't sleep, she watched footage on YouTube of synchronized swimmers or elaborate gymnastics routines.

Ayanna waited for one of them to pull out the edibles or the acre, but instead Stephen pulled out a Ziploc bag filled with what was clearly tea. She waited for him to explain that it was drugs of some kind but instead he busied himself exactly measuring out three cups and going down the hall for water to put in Ayanna's kettle.

"There was this artist, Lucille Hayden, who said this was part of her process of speaking to the divine," Jane said. She winced when saying the words *the divine*. It was another thing Ayanna liked about her, the way Jane's facial expressions couldn't help but betray how she really felt. She'd been reading on the internet that if you drank this tea, meditated, then approached a canvas or a piece of a paper, it would help you channel spirits or God or the universe's knowledge—whatever your flavor—while creating. Automatic writing or drawing, feelings of transcendence or of being a part of something bigger, it could all happen. It wouldn't be a fake glow like MDMA or shrooms.

"What is God?" Jane asked them when Stephen had returned.

"I'm an atheist," Stephen said.

All this drama over tea, Ayanna thought.

"Black people aren't atheists," Jane said. "Even when we say we are, we're still spiritual."

"No." Stephen shook his head. "I don't fuck with that. No angel bullshit. No deep force that Black people connect to. None of that."

Jane shrugged. "You should have to go through time and tell your ancestors this. I bet they would beat your ass."

Stephen rolled his eyes. "I bet my great-great-great-grandfather was an atheist too. I bet he was working the fields, worrying about massa, and thinking there was no way there's a God because he let this happen."

"Everything and nothing." Ayanna finally answered the question.

Neither of the two of them seemed to know how to respond to that. Ayanna felt like her dorm room was exceptionally small. The love seat she had wedged in could barely hold both Jane and Stephen. The minifridge was stuffed now with iced tea and Gatorade. She could feel the box of Olivia's things under the bed: her shin guards, her Bible, the pajamas, her stuffed bunny with the weird red eyes, nail polish, journals, a bonnet, and all the photos of them from over the years in a Ziploc baggie. Outside, it was one of those fall days when it looked as if at any moment the gray clouds would burst into a cold, loud rush. The wind was loud and filled with leaf fragments and plastic bags.

"Okay, let me try this again." Jane clasped her hands together. "I think we should take a minute and meditate on what it means to ascend to a higher plane. Even if you don't have a faith, there has to be a state of bliss or ease you would like to be in."

"You would be great at selling people tummy teas and crystals," Ayanna said. "Just use that tone and blink less."

"I think that's only a business for blond white ladies who think you can season things by throwing some figs in," Stephen said.

"Come on," Jane said.

"She's got cult-leader charisma," Stephen said. "We're lucky she's not evil."

They both laughed while Jane waited for them to finish.

"Why do you want to do this?" Ayanna asked. She sat on her rug, wrapped her arms around her knees.

"This is what college is about."

To Ayanna and Stephen, this seemed like an obvious and dumb lie, so they laughed harder. If they wanted to do college, they would go smoke a joint and watch a movie, they would go to the curated dance party across town and find someone to dance with and hopefully hook up with, they would watch couples fight at a frat party while bros yelled too loud about flip cup.

Jane told them when she was in second grade in her private Catholic elementary school, she had been voted the person in her grade that was most like Jesus. She had received an illustrated children's Bible for this accomplishment and a little certificate her parents had kept. She had decided after that to be a nun and devote her life to Jesus. Jane ignored their questions about how she was like Jesus. In a lot of ways, Jane continued talking, this was one of the happiest years of her life because she had dedicated herself to being good. Making sure everyone got invited to birthday parties, giving people gifts, being kind to other kids when they were being annoying, doing her homework on time, rarely yelling at her brothers, writing her grandmothers letters—all these things kept her busy and focused on making other people feel loved. But then, it got exhausting to be good all the time. Whenever she acted out, her teacher or her parents would somehow bring up something like "Well, this isn't very much like Jesus, is it?"

"I didn't need one of those dumb bracelets," Jane said, "because it was always on my mind."

"What bracelet?" Stephen asked.

"How do you not know what a What Would Jesus Do bracelet is?" Ayanna asked.

"He has fancy parents that moved him all over the world. A year in Berlin, a year on some island, California."

"California is not fancy," Stephen said. "California is mostly highways and dust."

Ayanna had imagined every child in the world, at some point, had been given some sort of similar gift. If not WWJD, she had assumed it was WWM(uhammad)D, WWB(uddha)D, WWA(braham)D, WWD(alai)L(ama)D. All of these kids wearing brightly colored bracelets, encouraged to collect them and to think deeply about how often they were failing. It felt right. Ayanna had worn hers for a while because every kid at school who was cool was wearing them, because Olivia liked to wear a rainbow of them on her left wrist, which seemed elegant, and because it had pleased her mother. Her father had asked her why she wore it when she didn't believe in Jesus, and she had shrugged and said, "It's pretty." It was clear to Ayanna in retrospect that he was trying to figure out if her mother had forced her to wear it.

"Let me tell my story." Jane dramatically threw her head back, as if it would fall off if she had to keep listening to their digressions.

She continued detailing the ways that being told she was like Jesus was a curse instead of a blessing. There was a day when, finally, they read the scripture about Jesus just fucking losing it in the temple. He's angry about the people turning God's home into like a mall, was how Jane summarized it. And he knocks over everything, orders people out, he causes a real scene. And it was such a relief to Jane because now there was proof he wasn't unattainable, that he was a person just like everyone else, someone who could do miracles, and be lovely and warm, but was also capable of upsetting everyone around him and being embarrassing in public.

Ayanna was engrossed in what Jane was saying and in trying to avoid catching Stephen's gaze. Their friend was feeling bad. There was something a little hilarious to Ayanna, and she suspected to Stephen too, that Jane's way of wanting to address this problem was drinking a spiritual tea and doing some guided meditations and art instead of talking to them directly or seeing a therapist.

"But our teacher said this is one of the few times where Jesus probably should have used his words or maybe prayed on it for a while." Jane crossed her arms. "And that was kind of the end of faith for me. But there were months where I was floating away, only thinking about kindness and goodness. I want to be in that state again for even just five minutes."

Ayanna thought that was impossible now that Jane was an adult but didn't see the point of saying the thought aloud.

"Have you considered MDMA?" Stephen asked. "Jacob would give you a reasonable price."

"Also," Jane continued, "I got thrown out of school in seventh grade for kissing Ivy Simmons after a basketball game, and it made my parents send me to live with my aunt. I want to feel like I did before the moments I got caught with Ivy. Big and, like, beloved and blessed."

Stephen squeezed Jane's shoulder. "Okay. Let's try." He looked around the room. "Is this spiritual enough, though?"

Later, whenever people were surprised Ayanna was friends with Stephen, she always thought about this moment. The way his eyes were so tender to Jane, how it was clear to Ayanna that deep down he thought this was so, so stupid but he was willing to let his friend do something stupid and safe to make herself feel better. Ayanna had forgotten the grace that comes with deep relationships. The way things no longer were a waste of time when done in the service of making a beloved one feel a little more at home in the world.

They turned off the overhead light, turned on the desk lamp. Overhead lighting was not spiritual. Stephen and Jane argued briefly about what was spiritual, he thought they should put on Coltrane; *A Love Supreme* is the sound of the universe. What about *Eternity*? Ayanna was about to suggest, but Jane spoke first to say she felt he was just trying to be interesting with that suggestion, and they settled on a three-hour YouTube mix that was a compilation of nature sounds like whale song and birds in the rain, and Enya with no lyrics tracks. There was some mumbling about conflating spa capitalism with true spirits, but everyone was tired of arguing. They would all drink the tea slowly, eyes shut, taking deep breaths and thinking a word over and over.

It felt, Ayanna also kept this to herself, like a lot of effort. She longed to tell them spirits were everywhere. There was one downstairs in the laundry room, always wisping around the lost and found, searching for a misplaced T-shirt. Another was always in her academic adviser's office, consistently moving between bookshelves, window, and drawers, replicating the patterns of its probably mortal workdays. This didn't mean there was a higher power. As far as Ayanna could tell, all it meant after these years of seeing them was that existence was impossible to quantify. People had no idea all the depths and complications of what living could be.

Though she could see the similarities to her former church's rituals, Ayanna refused to think of this as a spiritual experience for herself. All she wanted was to chill and have fun. She could already have smoked a joint and spent a nice afternoon walking around town, sketching things or listening to Earl Sweatshirt and people watching. She could have taken another pill on her own the night before. The tea tasted terrible, like the Throat Coat her grandma liked to take instead of NyQuil.

Meditating was fine; Ayanna refused to use a word actually important to her or consider anything about her life, so she settled on *Panenka*. It was a favorite word, something she had always wanted to accomplish, and just beautiful in sound and rhythm to Ayanna's ears. It was nice in an unexpected way to lie on the thin rug in her dorm room and think, *Panenka, Panenka, Panenka*.

She admitted to herself after two rounds of thinking Panenka that she was also scared. It would be embarrassing to talk to spirits in front of Jane and Stephen. It still felt—despite Professor Collins, despite her grandmother, despite Felix—like it could be a symptom of mental illness.

Panenka, Panenka, Panenka. Relax. It was only tea. *Panenka, Panenka, Panenka*. She was only syllables and breaths.

A woman was speaking to her. She was saying, My name is Valerie. We've met before, but you keep forgetting. I forgive you for that. I need you to find Marlie Evans. M-A-R-L-I-E. She's wasted so much of her life trying to find me. I was the love of her life. We fell in love when she was twenty-one and I was twenty-one. You need to tell her I didn't leave her. There was an accident. Her voice was a whisper, close to Ayanna's ear. The room, Ayanna opened her eyes, was filled with a pale pink light.

15

"There is a space between the worlds," she heard herself saying. "A crack where some souls go, so they stay half here, half there."

"Stop playing," Stephen said. "You're doing real Ouija board behavior."

The room was there, but for a moment all Ayanna could see was a woman's face, eyes dark and wide-set, thin eyebrows, and a mouth small and full, a little rosebud. Then, it was gone, pink static instead.

A voice was saying, "The place where every world needs to bleed together, so life's tides can continue. Each life like a mushroom, connected across different forests, times, journeys," and Ayanna could hear herself repeating it back to the voice.

Nothing was below Ayanna. She could feel only air beneath her back. A soft hand she didn't recognize, too soft, was touching her cheek.

There was no formal name for the place where Ayanna and Olivia had gone. Some called it the meadows, others the blue lands, a few people called it Indigo, as if it were another country. But there was a feeling to being there, among all the stillness that was impossible to recreate on Earth. Ayanna felt it in these moments, she could hear voices, was aware of her own breath, but there was a stagnancy in the room that she heavily associated with that place.

"Her name is Marlie. M-A-R-L-I-E."

Ayanna was aware of the small room around her, of Stephen sitting cross-legged and shaking her foot, trying to wake her, of Jane sleeping curled back into embryo position, and of the feeling like her own body was walking up a rocky slope. Ascending and almost slipping. The hairs on her arms were standing at attention. Valerie was saying Marlie's name again. Someone was knocking on a door in the distance. An urgent rhythm. *There is nothing fun about this,* Ayanna thought, and the coherent thought echoed in her mind. She thought she could see the word *fun* in huge font on the back of her eyes.

"Liana," another voice said. "You've returned."

"Go away," Valerie yelled.

Stephen was wiping chip crumbs on the rug next to her arm and muttering about needing a vacuum. He put his hand in the one-inch space between where Ayanna's body should have been and the rug. His face was expressionless.

She was at a party and wearing a blue dress with gold buttons down the bodice, a thick white-lace collar, and small white gloves. There were people dancing close, the lights were low and meant to mimic candlelight, everyone was sweating. The sweat was thick on the nape of her neck, tangling up the kitchen of her vast mane of hair. She turned and there was a man watching her, mouth a little open.

There was a feeling as if someone were sitting on Ayanna's stomach, holding her supine. Dry mouth, locked in place above the rug, the top of her head too hot. She did not want to have a vision, to be swept away into someone else's life. Ayanna tried to say, "Stephen, shake me, wake me up, help," but nothing that could be understood came out.

A couple behind her was kissing deeply, each trying to take all the breath from the other's lungs. People were dancing. Everyone smelled like beer and sweat. Any person who somehow still smelled of shampoo or nice perfume became the most attractive person in the room.

He said, "Why did you shake my hand last time? I've spent a week trying to figure out what that meant."

Her brain was fuzzy, but she could recall the rain, the lights, telling him about a book she only half remembered. It was about a couple who drank too much limoncello and argued in the Colosseum. She remembered, too, that she was also lying in a dorm room wearing a big sweatshirt and was too stoned to get up and get a glass of water.

He said, "Just let me kiss you once."

She realized she was married, and that was why they were so miserable.

"Do you remember now, Liana?" he asked.

"My name is Ayanna," she said. "I am a twenty-year-old college student in Michigan. I am looking for my sister. I don't think I ever want to get married."

"I'm waiting for you still," he said. "If we're reborn together, we have a better chance of finally being together."

At the party, he put his hands on her face. They were somehow cold despite the heat of the room.

In her dorm room, she gasped loud, as if stepping into a pool, having been assured it was heated but finding it was as cold as the night air around it. Ayanna fell to the floor.

"Are you okay?" Stephen asked. "Jane? Can you hear me? Ayanna's really scaring me."

"What was my name?"

"Your name is Liana Nelson." The mouth saying it was soaked in gin. She could not imagine, despite all this, ever wanting to be in love with this person.

In the real world, someone had slapped her face. Not hard, but enough to startle. Both spirits were gone.

Stephen was saying something, the lights were flickering. Highlighters had lifted off Ayanna's desk into the air. Stephen made her drink some Gatorade. He kept a hand on her wrist. It was gentle, like he was trying to feel her pulse. She tried to focus on what she was drinking but had never thought blue Gatorade had a taste beyond soft salt and soft sugar. The way he was holding her wrist made Ayanna feel like he loved her. It wasn't extraordinary, though. Every time someone gently touched her, to let her know her bag was unzipped or to steer her away from some obstacle, it elicited that same whoa-are-they-in-love-with-me feeling. *I must be lonelier than I could ever understand*, Ayanna thought. Stephen was talking to her in a low, soft voice, asking her if they needed to go to the ER. She wanted to call Felix on the phone and tell him everything she had just experienced. Stephen promised he would never tell anyone about this. It was too weird.

"Did I say anything?" Ayanna asked.

"You said a lot." His eyes were wide. Stephen looked like the kids in afterschool specials who had just seen their friends take too much LSD and jump off a bridge.

"Did I say any names?"

"You said Marlie Nelson and Liana Evans."

She tried to stand up. Felt as if her legs were across the room and kept sitting. She asked him to write the names down for her, then eased herself down to the rug again. Jane seemed asleep, a small smile on her face, even breaths, arms and legs relaxed. For a moment, it looked like her desk lamp was floating in the air. Ayanna shook her head and shut her eyes. The room spun, she walked again elsewhere in her memories, calling her sister's name.

When Ayanna woke, the sun was setting, and the little lamp was fighting against the growing dark, making a puddle of golden light around them. Stephen was ordering a pizza. Jane was crying and typing something on her phone. In Ayanna's hand was a pen. Next to her was a notebook. Over and over, she had written the name Marlie. Ayanna turned the page. In a mix of her print and old-fashioned cursive, loopy and lovely, were pages of text.

"Did I write this?" She knew the answer but hoped to be wrong.

"Yes, and it scared the shit out of me," Stephen said. "You were writing but your eyes were closed. Sometimes, you spoke but the words were mushed together. It was the longest hour of my life."

"An hour," Ayanna muttered. She remembered at most ten minutes.

There were drawings on some of the pages. Mostly small and intricate: a necklace, a lake, figures dancing at a party. A face on one page, a woman with a Cupid's bow and an open mouth with slightly crooked teeth. Her hand had paid special attention to the eyes. The irises resembled television static and there were dark abysses of pupils where the page was thin from the force of her hand. No hair, no eyebrows, and a scribble of a left ear.

One of the hardest parts of being very depressed for Ayanna was feeling afraid of her brain. There was an ease and confidence she'd had with herself before losing her sister, that had been easy to take for granted. Ayanna understood she was annoying sometimes, focused too much on her own feelings than on those of other people around her, but it was fine. It was like her inability to understand geometry—frustrating, but also able to be accepted. To be a person was to have faults. But when depression had curled itself through every fold and crease in her brain, there were days when the only positive at the end was Ayanna had not listened to its quiet appeals to end her life. Sometimes her brain made what felt like very reasonable and measured arguments that if she believed the golden path, the meadows, the mountains were all some form of a vast afterlife, well, what was the point of feeling this bad? She could try again in a new life. Someone could always bring her back. This world was ugly and cruel and filled with unkindness, and it was probably dying anyway. Every day, another public shooting, another record catastrophe, and people saying, Look, these things are fake, so we don't have to try to make things better. And if not that, people seemed to go out of their way to reaffirm their commitment to wanting other people to suffer. They thought it was interesting to say people were getting worse and to be self-pitying about their time on Earth.

Why be alive? Ayanna would think while lying awake at night, feeling wired and listening to the snores of her freshman-year roommate. And then, she would take a beat, feel ashamed for the previous thought, and try to list off all the people who would feel something if they heard she was gone. She knew this too was an issue: you couldn't only live for other people, but it was the easiest thing Ayanna could think of in these moments.

Looking at these pages, Ayanna felt the familiar twinge of distrust. Here could be proof she was not feeling better like she thought she was. The medication she took every morning, the biweekly conversations with the therapist, the journaling where she tried to sit and kindly speak to herself weren't working. Here was her brain gnawing and scratching itself again.

"I bet this tea was laced with something," Stephen said, but they could both hear the lie.

She waited for him to talk about the levitating or the way the objects had moved. Ayanna knew she had not imagined it. They looked at each other. His eyes were very shiny.

"This is going to sound like a joke, but have you considered having an exorcism done?" Stephen was not smiling. "That was one of the most fucked-up things I've ever seen."

He told Ayanna once when he was a child, he had gone with his dad to tour a cabin. Stephen had been only seven at the time. It was fun to go somewhere alone, just him and his dad. But everything about the cabin had felt wrong. While his dad had followed the realtor, Stephen had walked into the study. It was a beautiful room, still filled with old books, a beautiful rug, and this glistening desk with roses carved on the legs. It felt like being in an illustration, he said. But every time he pulled a book from the shelf, Stephen saw a man's face with large pink eyes. His teeth were long. Nothing the man said made sense. His face was in the desk. His face was reflected in the window. He kept saying nonsense words and making noises. "I was sweating so hard, my shirt clung to me," Stephen said. "I ran out into the living room and barfed on the floor."

"Did your dad buy the cabin?"

"No. He was so busy making sure I was okay, someone put in an offer within hours, and things just felt right."

"Please don't tell anyone about this." Ayanna wasn't sweating. Everything felt mostly normal except that she was so thirsty. The first Gatorade had already been slammed. She was halfway through the second.

"You should talk to Felix," Stephen said. "I think you were doing automatic writing. He's obsessed with it lately."

Ayanna ran her fingers over the drawings in her notebook. Felt again the force she had used to make the eyes and lips. She turned to Stephen. He smiled at her, relaxed as always.

"Oh. And who's Olivia?" he asked. "You talked to her for about ten minutes."

Ayanna refused to look up and meet his gaze until she was sure her face would be still and relaxed. When she spoke, Ayanna was relieved her voice was only slightly higher than usual. "Did she say anything back?"

Stephen raised his eyebrows; he was more uncomfortable than she had yet seen him. "Ayanna?"

She tried to say it was a joke but knew by the way Stephen and Jane were looking at each other that they did not believe her. The room still had a pink cast to Ayanna. She took a breath, let out another, the easiest way to ignore the spirits was to focus on the living.

"Are you okay?" Jane asked.

Ayanna put her hands over her eyes. Another breath, another. When she looked up, Jane and Stephen were clearly so uncomfortable that Ayanna longed to run from the room, never go to classes again, and start over somewhere else. There was a spirit she refused to look directly at behind Stephen's head. She focused on his face. He was mouthing something, but Ayanna could not tell whether he was trying to comfort her or express fear.

16

Ayanna's mother had not invited her to the memorial service she'd had for Olivia. Ayanna had found out from the texts and messages from old friends in common, and from family members, that her mother had told everyone she was "unfortunately too sick to attend." Some people took Opal's words at face value, and some people sent Ayanna well-meaning messages about taking care of herself and said things like just because funerals helped some people, didn't mean they were always the right thing for grief. It was irrational, but she was furious that no one seemed to see the truth, her mother just didn't want her there. It had happened a year after Olivia's "accident."

She typed out so many texts in responses that ranged from I wasn't even invited to it to she blames me to I don't think I have a family anymore, then deleted each message before sending. Ayanna was used to asking Olivia what to do about their mother. If Olivia said the sky was artichoke green, her mother would be willing to say, "Okay, baby, tell me how you see it." If Ayanna said, No, Ma, the sky is blue, her mother would most likely say, "Well, how do *you* know."

Oh, the way Ayanna's mother could say "you" with so much incredulousness. Sometimes, Ayanna wished she had recorded the way her mother said it so she could play it for her therapist or for the few friends who knew what was going on and sometimes said, "Don't worry, the two of you will be family again."

It's not unnatural to be selfish. There have been times throughout history when for humanity to survive, let alone thrive, selfishness was necessary. People had to eat as well as they could, they had to not see other people as people, had to view the world with a hardened heart and not risk their own health just to keep the species going. That type of animal fear, it was probably evolving inside humans alongside genes developing immunities and other environmental adaptations. But Ayanna felt at heart, most adults she met had never truly reckoned with this part of human nature, and how much it developed a comorbidity of self-absorption. So many people who just because they felt an intense feeling—good or bad—who weren't able to hold both the weight of that emotion and to consider how their actions as a result of that emotion impacted other people.

Ayanna's father had said nothing. He had gone, sat in the back, accepted a few condolences, and called Ayanna that night to tell her to give her mother some more patience. They were hurting, but she was *hurting*. Ayanna didn't have the energy to keep fighting. "Sure, Dad," she said. In the following silence, his breaths were even. In the next room, her grandma was playing some violent multiplayer game. She had read video games helped the brain rewire itself after trauma. Ayanna's father breathed and her grandmother shot and shot and shot.

Sometimes, she was able to even feel a little sorry for her mom. Ayanna knew Opal's faith was real; her mother truly believed in God and heaven and angels. There was a story she often told of hearing a voice on the way to work saying "Opal, Opal, go this way." So she didn't follow her usual route to work for once and avoided a ten-car pileup. That was enough for her to have firm proof angels were real and they were looking out for her. She always told Ayanna and Olivia to listen for the small voice of God because he was always watching and looking out for them. It had taken all Ayanna's willpower not to mention the roadwork and slowdowns also happening on the usual route, the first time she'd heard that story. Her mother wanted to be special in God's eyes, and who was Ayanna to try to take that from her? But the thought was also annoying because it felt indicative of their relationship, Ayanna doing and thinking about ways to make her mother not just love her but *like* her, and her mother too self-absorbed to think about her as a person worth seeing. In these moments, when she was optimistic, Ayanna wondered if she had ruined everything by picking her father and considered apologizing. When she was feeling realistic, she knew apologizing might embarrass her mother and make the situation between them worse.

Oftentimes, though, Ayanna thought about how her mother had lied about what happened to Olivia. She claimed the girls had gone to a state park together to swim and hike. Ayanna had napped by the lake, and when she woke up Olivia was gone. Even worse to Ayanna, there had been a police search. No one could find Olivia—of course—but they did find the remains of another girl no one had reported missing.

She did not understand why her mother had concocted such an elaborate lie. She didn't want to consider why her father had agreed this was the right idea. She did not understand how her mother had gotten away with it. She didn't understand how everyone who had questioned Ayanna had believed her.

Maybe because it shared a glancing resemblance to the truth. Maybe it was because at the heart of it, no one really cared that much. And Ayanna had been able to tell the truth through all the questions: One minute she was there, the next gone. Yes, she had run to a neighborhood nearby, panicking. There was no one who her sister was afraid of or talked about. She hadn't seemed distressed. Yes, there were things that worried her, things she was sometimes upset about, but that was normal. Ayanna could tell that the more times she answered those questions, the more people believed her and thought her sister had died by suicide. Here was another typical Midwestern family refusing to see how depressed one of them was. Here was another Black family who believed in prayer and sweating it out instead of pharmaceuticals. The state park had different areas that historically had seen deaths. Especially because no one could find Olivia's cell phone. And a kid Olivia had known from school talked about how Olivia sometimes wrote sad poetry and then ripped it up when a draft was done. Another boy had said he and Olivia had been sort of talking but then he had gotten back with his ex-girlfriend and she had refused to talk to him because she was so upset.

If it were possible to talk to her mother in a way that wasn't painful, Ayanna would ask her, Why did we have to lie?

If it were possible to talk to her father in a way that wasn't painful, Ayanna would ask him, Why did you leave me alone with all this?

And the truth, as she understood it now, when they all were in the old living room together, and her mom was finally quiet after hours of alternating between crying and saying a range of things—should never have trusted you, why did this happen to her, you fucked up, I hate you, she was my child, how could I have ever let you into my life—was embossed forever on Ayanna's brain. But she kept coming back to looking at her mother's crumpled face, her father's face, blank and eyes flat and bloodshot, and thinking, *I have to remember this. It's the last time we'll be a family.* The only times she felt like crying were when her mother said something cruel and Ayanna noticed her own head was automatically swiveling toward where Olivia liked to sit on the couch. The blanket there still smelled like Olivia and spilled coffee, but it could do nothing to make them all treat one another better.

Stephen had told her that what she said to Olivia was I'm sorry, I miss you, please come home, I'm sorry.

AS AYANNA WAS GETTING ready to go have brunch with Stephen, Jane, and Felix, she looked at her phone. There was a message from her mother: Hello. I have been trying to contact your father, but he has not responded to any of my messages. Tell him to call me.

Ayanna put her phone down. She rubbed her eyes, making circles with her palms, feeling her soft eyelids and long eyelashes, and taking one, two, three deep breaths. There was the impulse to immediately text back you didn't invite me to my sister's memorial service. Another to pick up the phone and force her to speak to her. Yet another to remind her mother they hadn't spoken in years. The phone buzzed and buzzed. Her dad was in Europe. He had not returned to the US since deciding to go and walk the Camino de Santiago. They had not spoken on the phone since the start of school. He wrote her emails, long and ponderous, about the nature of life, of faith, about once being able to walk between worlds and now trying to stay fixed on the beauty of this one. You never walked between worlds, Ayanna thought, when she read these. I did, and now I'm alone and like this.

Sometimes he complained about the diet he had put himself on, mostly vegetables and fruit, porridges, and whatever he was served when visiting a monastery because he would not be rude. A few descriptions of landscapes or people or children playing sports with one another. She did not respond often to these or find them charming. His desire to find peace by walking a path dedicated to a god he did not believe in felt disturbing and out of character. It was also easy to consider that he had crossed an ocean to avoid her.

Ayanna picked the phone back up. Another series of texts from her mother: ??

Last night, your sister visited me. She told me where I put the necklace I've been looking for and asked for grandma's cookie recipe.

Bullshit, Ayanna thought. She could call her therapist's office and ask for an emergency session. Or could spend some time in bed journaling. The room felt too bright, her eyes were itchy, and Ayanna picked up the phone, put it gently in her trash can, fished it out, put it back in with more force and threw some note cards from her desk on top of it for good measure, heard it buzz against the metal, reached in again, then shoved it into her bag. What was the point of dealing with an unsolvable problem immediately? Her walls felt very white, as if someone had come in during the night and painted them a starker shade.

It was impossible to believe her mother, a woman who believed angels spoke to her, who had refused to let her attend Olivia's memorial service, who had spent years now reaching out only to be cruel.

Yet Ayanna's hand reached for the phone. She wanted to ask for the details, had there been pink light, what had "Olivia" looked like, what had her mother been doing before this visitation. Ayanna scrolled back up, reminded herself that this was all couched in an effort to get Ayanna to make her father talk to Opal. It was probably a lie. She had promised herself to stop trying to have any kind of relationship with this person.

Another buzz from her phone. It was Jane telling her they were downstairs and waiting for her. Ayanna slipped on a coat, looked another time at hair, and fought to put on her knee-high boots. Her face in the mirror had a slight yellow cast to it, as if she were recovering from a long illness. Eyes, bloodshot. Lips, chapped. There was homework and reading she could be doing.

DOWNSTAIRS, IT WAS A petty relief for Ayanna to see Jane looking just as bad. Her edges were dry, she was wearing big dramatic sunglasses that kept slipping down her nose to reveal puffy, red eyes. She was not wearing one of her white T-shirts, but a large black sweater with pilling beneath the armpits and on the wrists. Stephen greeted Ayanna with a hug and a soft "Are you doing better?" And Ayanna tried to ignore Felix as this happened because she knew that to hear him talk in his slow, kind voice or to see him look at her with eyes brimming with empathy and interest would result in her crying and sobbing in front of them. *Jesus, if you're willing to help a nonbeliever,* she thought, *please let me be cool.* She imagined religious teens all over the world kneeling in front of crosses and thinking the same thing and felt almost like herself when her mouth twitched up into a smile.

Jane and Ayanna were silent on their walk, while Felix and Stephen argued over some book they were reading for class. Felix felt certain the way the last section was written was proof the main character had died because it switched over to letters rather than narration. Stephen was telling him he was overthinking it, the author was probably just bored writing everything the same way and wanted the freedom to be poetic and make the readers feel, you know, closer to the story. Both agreed, though, that Stephen's argument would probably get him a B- on the upcoming paper, even if it felt intuitively right to him.

Ayanna turned to Jane to say something banal like, "I could really use a cup of coffee," but saw a tear streaking down her cheek. She felt the urge like she did with Olivia to wipe it away, but instead gently looped an arm through her friend's. They walked down the street with linked arms. Jane cried a little more quietly, and Ayanna resolved to keep all her crying to the shower she would take when she got home tonight.

When Jane was done crying after two blocks, she turned to Ayanna and said, "Thank you."

She wanted to respond with something nice or funny, but all her tired brain could think to say was, "Feel it, girl." Luckily, Ayanna didn't say that aloud or she would have run home in complete disgrace. Instead, she settled on squeezing Jane's arm, trying to get the pressure she used on her own arms and shoulders when she felt deeply anxious.

It felt like luck that there was no line to the trendy breakfast. It was a blessing when the waitress immediately, without asking, plunked down four coffees, strong and with so much caffeine that Ayanna immediately sat up straight.

"You all look like you need something special. Not being rude here, just being direct," the waitress said. She was an older woman who had dyed her hair crimson. When she spoke, all her *a*'s were short, nasal Michigan *a*'s, the kind where you could hear how Michigan's ancestors had turned Grand Blanc from something regal, spoken with a kind of dignity, into something that sounded like Grand Blank, a name for a city, sure, but also ugly and hilarious.

"We need something profound," Felix said. And that was another thing she liked about him. He was someone who didn't mind playing around with people he didn't know. Felix's phone was put away. Everything he was doing and saying showed how he wanted to be there.

The waitress looked like she was genuinely thinking this through. "You have two options, then. Our homemade corned beef hash on top of smashed potatoes with a chili egg or our Dutch baby pancakes with maple-cider syrup and bacon. Everything else is delicious, but probably not right for your situation."

"We'll have two of each," Felix said, and no one argued with him or asked to see the menu.

The restaurant was decorated to look like it was truly someone's eccentric home. In the room behind them, people were sitting on love seats or in custom chairs meant to look like ugly recliners. The mugs they drank from were all vintage. Ayanna's mind had a picture of Garfield saying "I hate decaf." There were family photos on the yellow walls. She could see Felix's face only if she turned completely. She was aware of his arms, the one inch of space between their knees, how he was also turning to take in the room. Ayanna wondered if he was doing the calculations she always did in a new space, the quiet checking to see if she was the only nonwhite person. He kept scanning, paying attention every time someone came through the door. There was a long table, though, of Korean kids, dressed nicely like they might have come from church. A spirit was wisping around, following a waitress, but Ayanna felt only positivity coming from it. She wondered if last night had changed something somehow. Before, it had been easy to resist the urge to see—it had taken effort to hear and understand what the dead were saying, meditation, work she had resisted doing, and now, the spirit was just there. Ayanna realized one of the conversations she was overhearing was it trying to get the waitress's attention for more coffee.

She shook her head. *I don't want to think about the dead. I want to be here.* It didn't make the ghosts go away, but it helped her refocus on the living.

"Is this place too cool for its own good?" Stephen asked.

It was a ridiculous statement, Ayanna felt, coming from someone who was wearing a beautiful floral jacket over black jeans, an oversized white T-shirt that she had heard him tell Felix was from Japan, and fresh-out-of-the-box Jordans. Everything about him spoke of his willingness to put in effort.

Jane, clearly feeling better, argued it was impossible for something to be too cool for its own good, unless they were talking about someone doing too much K. The world needed pretentiousness to make life worth living. If everything was always trying to be ordinary or ignored, people would never have capital-*E* Experiences.

"I don't feel cool enough to be here," Ayanna said, "but I also feel like shit."

"Do you want me to go get you a Gatorade and some aspirin?" Stephen asked.

Jane smiled and looked away.

"No, but thanks for the offer."

Ayanna's phone was buzzing in her pocket. She pulled it out automatically, and found several texts from her mom. She willed herself not to read, but saw the words typical, why are you like this, and don't respond. Before, her mother had never been this aggressive over text. Sometimes in person if Ayanna "wasn't behaving right," there were outbursts, but here were blocks of text on her home screen that were both anxiety-making and proof she could show people the next time they earnestly said things like "Your family is all you got" when they heard she was estranged from her mother.

"Who's blowing up your phone?" Felix asked, then moved away from her. He smelled good, like fresh toothpaste and cedar. "Sorry, I shouldn't have looked."

"My mom," Ayanna said. She tried to find an urbane and relaxed way to put it and tried out, "We aren't close."

There was a moment when Ayanna was tempted to tell them the whole thing, from walking through the door with Olivia, to it letting only one of them through, to her mom's lie. She didn't know what she would do or say, though, if someone asked why she kept repeating it. And it would be worse, too, if they judged her. It was a relief when Jane spoke up.

"I don't speak to my parents because they're homophobes," Jane said. "Being gay is a white-people thing, I guess."

"My dad has never told me he loves me," Stephen said. "I can't even remember the last time he hugged me. Also, once I heard him refer to me in a meeting as his 'African American son.' And it made me exactly sure why he and my mom hate each other now."

"I have a beautiful and respectful relationship with my parents.

We're best friends. I'm always looking forward to spending time with Timothy and Suzanne," Felix said. He laughed. It was a pleasure to hear him laugh because it was raucous and so out of sync with the measured way he always spoke. "Nah, they're always on me to cut my hair, to wear nice clothes, to become a lawyer, to pledge Alpha Phi Alpha, to be safe. I have parents that met at a frat party. They're both copyright lawyers. They would sue my ass if they heard me refer to them by their first names."

"Well, cheers," Jane said, and they clinked their coffee cups together.

AFTER BREAKFAST, JANE ASKED Ayanna if she would do a favor for her. Ayanna agreed, and they walked together to the Catholic church. Mass had just finished and there were still people outside talking to one another. They walked in and Jane sat in a pew, pulled out the kneeler, then crossed herself.

Ayanna, unsure of what to do, treated the area in back with candles and statues like it was a small museum gallery. She stuck her fingers into the holy water, remembered to make a cross, and for a moment, it felt like her mother and sister were in the vestibule talking to other congregants while she was left to explore. All the lit candles were in long blue containers, and Ayanna wondered what that was about. An organist was practicing for the next Mass, a song Ayanna remembered from going to services on and off over the years with her mom and Olivia. It was a song about eagles, maybe? It seemed impossible for anyone who was not truly talented at singing to hit all the notes, but the melody made Ayanna's eyes feel a little fuller.

One of the things she liked least about churches was that they tended to be places where spirits liked to congregate. Before, it had been one of the few places where there was no effort. There were so many dead that the rooms in a church were always glowing and pink to Ayanna. The dead seemed to like to follow their routines: grocery stores, liquor stores, churches, gas stations, hospitals, bingo halls, and fast-food restaurants, most often Wendy's. In this church, they were interspersed throughout the rows, present enough that to Ayanna the air felt a little thicker. A spirit was sitting directly in front of Jane, but neither noticed the other.

A statue of Jesus presided over the lit candles, his carved hair lush and voluminous, his eyes blank in the white marble, his nose perfectly unremarkable. He had cheekbones and a chin that would make him always get noticed in a crowd. Ayanna thought, as she continued looking at the statue, that everyone rendered Jesus conventionally attractive, not just because he was in charge and everyone wanted to listen more to handsome people, not just because it would maybe feel a little blasphemous to render God's son as a real uggo, but because maybe it felt like a bigger deal if Jesus was hot and he decided to never have sex. They wanted to give people no room to say "Well, look at him, of course he was celibate."

"Do you want to light a candle?"

"I shouldn't," Ayanna immediately said. "I don't go here."

She turned, realized what she'd said was weird, put her hand over her mouth. A priest was standing next to her. He was the youngest priest she had ever seen. Black with skin so moisturized and perfect, it felt like she was in a Catholic-church-themed photoshoot. Sell perfume with your holiest face. He was smiling and his teeth were a brighter white than his robe. He fished around for something in his pockets and pulled out a lighter. It was cheap and decorated with a polar bear wearing sunglasses. Jane used a matching one to light joints.

"We have these here to give our parishioners another way to pray. Especially in fall and winter, fire feels hopeful." He had a Nigerian accent that made the words feel like a melody.

The priest pointed to a painting hanging up on the other side of the vestibule. It was clearly an amateur's work. In it, a woman in a light blue robe, a halo around her, was skating alone on a pond. The landscape was firs and angels and crosses. The priest explained it was a parishioner's rendition of Saint Lidwina, the patron saint of ice skaters. She was a woman who'd had a tragic ice-skating incident, became briefly paralyzed, then because she embraced God, never had to eat or sleep again. Her body parts could help others. A flake of skin or a lock of hair given to another could destroy a lingering ailment. Ayanna could not figure out where he was going with this. The priest kept smiling. "Even in the depths of great suffering, you can give of yourself."

He handed her the lighter. If he had not been a priest, if she had not been in his church, Ayanna felt certain she would have been more annoyed; a woman can't even be paralyzed from a tragic ice-skating accident without having to figure out how to be responsible for other people. But she had come here freely. Ayanna turned the lighter over in her hands. She was tempted to treat it like a birthday candle, make a wish for herself, but instead thought, Olivia, Olivia. She lit one of the candles in the red holders. Olivia preferred red to blue. The night before, Ayanna had dreamed they were together again in the meadows. Olivia was showing her a bush, the leaves aqua, and the fruit growing off it were clearly strawberries, but Olivia kept calling them a word that sounded like *zeezle*. Every time Ayanna tried to ask questions, all either sister heard was a sound like gargling. It used to feel profound when she dreamed of Olivia, but lately, it had only seemed like proof of how guilty Ayanna still felt. *Olivia, Olivia, Olivia,* Ayanna thought again.

"What's your name?" he asked.

"Ayanna."

The priest leaned over and lit another candle. "This is for you. I will keep you in my prayers."

Ayanna smiled. "Thank you."

OUTSIDE, JANE SAID HE was the most conventionally attractive priest she had ever seen.

"My sister would have been so uncomfortable if he had been her priest," Ayanna said. "She would have had to find a new church."

Jane paused. Her eyes were wide and Ayanna could see what looked like a mix of curiosity and, maybe, pity. "You never told me you had a sister."

"We're not close," Ayanna said. "Olivia's been away for a long time."

Jane did not seem to notice the strange phrasing or the way Ayanna looked away. It had taken all of Ayanna's willpower not to cross her arms or move her lips into what Olivia called the "clear lies" position.

It was a beautiful fall day—blue skies enhancing the hearth-fire beauty of all the trees. Ayanna felt like it was the first autumn she had ever seen and enjoyed. Her phone was buzzing again in her pocket, but she refused to look. Jane kept glancing at her as they walked back to the dorms but seemed mostly immersed in her thoughts. They were talking about soccer in a half-hearted way, about whether Ayanna should invest in new cleats, she had always wanted Predators, and if the team should practice on Tuesday night, but each could tell the other's mind was elsewhere. Ayanna was considering going back to get her headphones and take a long walk. Maybe buy a cup of apple cider. It was suddenly beautiful enough that maybe walking out in all these reds and yellows would give her the clarity to figure out what to say or not say to her mom, how to write the paper she had due, how to tell people about Olivia, how to be kinder to herself, how to figure out who she even was to herself, how to get to a place where every time she thought about Olivia, the thoughts weren't new bruises, but proof of how much she loved her sister. Ayanna felt a sharp mix of hopefulness and pain when she thought, *I want to like myself again.*

THEY SPLIT WAYS AROUND the dorm, and Ayanna checked her mailbox. In among the mailings for student tickets to art events and political postcards urging her to vote was an index card. Written on it was *Liana, I can't stop thinking about you.*

She read it again. Decided it must be a dumb prank from Stephen and Jane or maybe from her freshman-year roommate or even something someone had found a way to stick in the wrong mailbox, and she chose to ignore it. Stephen and Jane made sense to her; people were always trying to turn the inexplicable into something they could control. Make it a joke, ignore it, try to develop it into a hoax or something only you could understand. She shrugged. Whatever they needed. Ayanna walked upstairs, pretending to be very interested in the rest of her mail. She half convinced herself to go see *Carmen* the night before Halloween. The person who had been texting her was Felix, reminding her to meet him in a few hours at the woods. She felt a little burst of excitement and told herself it was nothing.

In her dorm room, there were several note cards on the ground matching the one in the mailbox. A few with the name Liana written on it, filling up the space. Some with messages like *I lie awake at night thinking about your eyes, every time I see something beautiful I want you to see it with me, every morning I long to hold your face in my hands, please be with me, we are soulmates, Liana, the rarest thing in the entire universe.* The handwriting was curled and condensed, looking at the shapes, but not the words, each line looked like it was composed out of hairs from her head.

Written on her desk in lipstick: *Liana.*

There was a smell in the air, like rotting meat forgotten in the back of a refrigerator. She opened a window, but still it persisted. She lit candles, scrubbed her desk clean with paper towels and the lavender-scented spray she liked. The smell was maybe stronger, as if it were trying to fight back. She looked under her bed, in her dresser and desk drawers, in the closet, but couldn't find anything that could be the source.

Something zipped from beneath the door, another note card. It read, *leave him, please, I can't take this.*

Ayanna opened the door, but no one was in the hallway. There was no sound of doors being shut or footsteps. The only noise was her neighbor on the right, singing gospel with too many notes for her mouth to handle and cleaning again. Even the harsh chemicals, the bleach, the lemon, couldn't fight the rot.

* * *

The tree near the fence was covered in crows. They were silent, and as Ayanna tried to count them, she realized she had never seen so many in the same place without being filled with their caws and discontented cries. Her grandmother had told her that contrary to popular belief, you should never see crows as bad omens, but after her dorm room and the night before, it still felt like a bad omen. From her bag, she fished out a blueberry scone left over from breakfast and crumpled it in her hands, tossed it in their direction. Ayanna's approach to all superstitious thoughts was to face the thing distressing her head on. She told the crows to enjoy the snack, and watched as a few, then many, leaped up and started eating.

Felix walked up wearing headphones. He swiped his card on the gate and waved Ayanna in. He was carrying a duffle bag that wasn't fully zipped. A large book was poking out of it.

"What are you listening to?" she asked.

He took his headphones off and offered them to her. Tina Turner's voice was sweeping through them, and Ayanna half shut her eyes as she walked behind him, even though she should have been paying attention. The ferocity and freedom of Tina hitting the loud notes made her feel settled. She had planned to show Felix the note cards, to confirm this wasn't something Jane or Stephen would do. It was the type of paranoid, insecure thought she hated, that these people she was starting to really like were befriending her only because she was lonely and easy to tease. But would he be friends with people who did that? Although, to be fair, there was something about him, maybe it was the fact he was so earnest, or maybe it was because he was a man who cared about making sure other people felt comfortable, that made people behave a little softer around him. There was a bubble Felix created where people gave one another attention, were willing to be a little more vulnerable, and felt comfortable laughing.

Oh, Ayanna thought, *this is getting into crush territory.*

Almost everyone she had liked in high school was on the mean side of personalities. Sarcastic boys, boys whose only personality after she got to know them was being good at school, boys who read political blogs with the express purpose of wanting to argue with their conservative teachers, boys who said barely anything 90 percent of the time and then, when alone in their car, instead of intensely making out, all they wanted to do was talk about how alone they felt, boys who played their guitar for her and thought playing some dumb, easy song from 1972 was enough to say something meaningful. These things felt like a direct contradiction to why he was so appealing to her—Felix was someone who seemed like he would tell you he loved you easily. Worse to Ayanna, he seemed like the kind of emotionally mature person who would tell you he loved you and be fine with the fact that you might not immediately say it back.

When the song was done, Felix told her about his love for Miss Tina. How in love he was with her voice. How she could even turn "What's Love Got to Do With It," a song Miss Tina famously hated, into something so fucking profound. His voice was soft in a way that made when he did swear feel funny and charming. "The power in her," he said, shaking his head with admiration.

Ayanna almost walked into a low branch, ducked and avoided it, but still got some of it tangled in her ponytail. Felix turned and helped her untangle her hair, picked leaves out from the ends, and her heart felt so big and warm in her chest with his nearness and the tenderness of his fingers. He is the kind of person, Ayanna thought, that people probably regularly get crushes on; this is nothing. She touched his headphones that were now slung around her neck.

"Are you okay?" he asked. "It seems like you're having a rough day."

Ayanna told him maybe she was feeling hungover, then the rest of her thoughts kept coming out, from hearing from her mother for the first time in years, to the note cards under her door and in her mailbox, to being told twice about a woman named Marlie. How more and more she wondered if once she had been this woman named Liana. Felix nodded as she spoke. Put his hand out to touch her arm, then pulled back. She was surprised Stephen and Jane hadn't told him what had happened yesterday. While they were quiet for a moment, Ayanna realized she had said, "The world is full of spirits, I see them everywhere, they speak to me," and he had treated that as perfectly normal.

"Well, what do you need right now? Do you want me to listen, do you want advice, or I don't know, something else?"

"I don't know yet," Ayanna said. "Oh, and my room smells like ass, and I can't figure out where it's coming from."

"Do you still want to do this work today?"

"I would like to have money."

She continued: "What do you think this is all about? Work." Ayanna could tell how awkward she was being but could not crawl out of the deep crevice of discomfort she had built.

"Oh, that Earth is purgatory." Felix shrugged. "Or maybe it's a beautiful vestibule for the rest of the universe. Or for other dimensions. Or maybe it's a vast experiment in loneliness. Sometimes, it feels like we learn about a new world or a new galaxy every other day and yet, still, we're alone."

She shrugged. All options felt possible and deeply depressing. Once, when she was a child, her mother had told her the story of Genesis, of God creating the sea, the skies, the animals, and man. But Ayanna had felt it wasn't beautiful or miraculous; even young, she had thought, Oh, he was sad. That's why Earth is here. Ayanna had told her mom, "God was lonely and he made some toys," but her mother had hated that. Opal had told her, "Life is a beautiful gift. God was being generous. God is never lonely."

At the golden path in miniature, Felix pulled out what looked like a custom Ouija board. All the letters of the alphabet and the *yes* and *no* were present, but on the sides were: *please find, please tell, I'm sorry, I need*. Ayanna picked it up and felt it. Smooth. Close up, there were gold lines in it. The wood was lighter than it looked. She was disappointed that it felt so ordinary in her hands. No electric shock, no frisson of recognition, or even a hint of the thrill she used to feel seeing the path.

"This is made from one of the trees over there, isn't it?" Ayanna felt a little sick imagining someone bringing an axe through, destroying some of the natural beauty. Then, she considered whether that was hypocritical. Ayanna had seen adults return with bags of ferns, roots dangling with golden seeds and metallic bugs.

"There's a big trade in wood, seeds, ferns from the path. Rich people collect, and I mean, you've taken acre. The high-end versions of it can only be produced by using the seeds in the base of the ferns there. Although most is synthetic now. But I feel you, it still feels off." Felix was putting down what could only be described as offerings. A wooden bowl filled with pristine fruit, incense that loudly smelled of tea, a bottle of wine, and a bouquet of irises.

"They like presents," Felix said. "You get much higher rates of responses, though, if you have a sense of what the person you're trying to contact likes. Gin, cigarettes, luxury perfume of a certain scent, their favorite clothes if you have them. It helps. Most of the time they'll eat and leave and ask for a small favor, but the right gift can make them tell you secrets."

As Ayanna watched, she wondered if there was anyone who Felix was missing and hoping would move the board's planchette. Ayanna wanted to hear him talk about all the people he had ever loved, all the pets, the places he'd been to that had changed him or given him a sense of who he was. What if he was doing all this just to talk to the soul of a beloved dog? Would that be alienating or endearing? Was it possible to have a real relationship—platonic or romantic—filled with mutual understanding and trust if the other person hadn't suffered as much as you? Ayanna took a breath. The way her thoughts were starting to feel fixative gave her a feeling she had described to her therapist once as "thoughts over easy." He hadn't really gotten what she meant, but it was the only language that felt right to her.

Felix took the board and planchette and sat cross-legged in front of it. A spirit muttered, "I asked for a well done steak, not this." Shut his eyes, took a deep breath, and made a whispery sound between his teeth that made Ayanna feel like he was attempting to shush someone politely. She watched Felix for a little while, but then felt too self-conscious staring at him. A cloud like a three-fingered hand hovered up above him but near his shoulder, a spirit she knew he couldn't see.

Ayanna wanted to try, despite knowing well it was a bad idea.

"They're being weird today." Felix studied the untouched bowls. "I'm not trying to be rude here, but I feel like it's you."

"Maybe no one wants to talk to you." She said it with a smile.

"I misspoke. I'm trying to say, but I can't think of how to say this in a not weird way: there are things around you that are maybe crowding everyone out."

"What are you talking about?"

Felix asked to see the note cards from her room and mailbox, and the notebook she had mentioned from the day before.

"Look at these," he said. "There was one who kept saying, 'Liana, Liana, Liana.'" She scratched her arms. The spirit was here. Felix was right. But she did what felt like the safest thing to do when a man was constantly trying to get her attention: ignore him.

Felix had her walk away until she was at the edge of the copse. From there, Ayanna watched as Felix shut his eyes. It still took a while, but soon the spirits were gathering around him, until the area was filled with a pink fog. She could see the twist of shapes in it—a horse, a bat, a teenage boy with bad posture, a woman in a ball gown, a bear, a river, mushrooms, a child. The fog was thickest over the offering. After a few minutes, they started to disperse. Felix waved Ayanna back over.

The fruit was down to seeds, shreds, and a few small bits of flesh. One iris stem remained, the incense was in bits, and the wine was tipped over, a cork and a small glug giving itself to the ground.

"They usually only interact with things they loved. You should see what happens if I put out a full nice sheet cake or french fries. But they rarely touch people on purpose."

Ayanna wasn't really paying attention to what Felix was saying. She was wondering if she sat here, with this board, with Olivia's pajamas, if she could talk to her sister again. It was an accidental cut to think like this, to know the thought meant at least a part of her had accepted that Olivia was dead.

Maybe, if she had the right tools, Olivia would come and speak to her. Ayanna wondered if apologizing would make her feel better.

As Felix packed things up, Ayanna formed a plan in her head. She would steal the board, put out all of Olivia's things, and wait as long as possible.

Then, she paused. As long as Olivia never came to her, there was the possibility that, somehow, she was still alive. Ayanna let out a breath. When had she decided her sister was dead? When had she stopped believing that if the doors came back, so, too, would Olivia? Ayanna stood up and walked out into the woods before Felix could notice.

Her body pulsed with the desire to punch one of the thick tree trunks until the bark made her knuckles bloody. Hit herself in the head with the sharpest, biggest rock she could find. She had given up. She might spend the next few days eating as little as possible as a form of penance. Ayanna had a piece of paper in her wallet on which she had written down what to do when she felt so angry that she wanted to harm herself. She didn't look at it.

17

Jane was planning an elaborate Halloween party at a friend's off-campus house, the Goal x Hunting x Association had won another two games, and Ayanna, despite everything, felt like to the rest of the world it seemed like she was thriving. Four goals, two perfect midterms, a hair day where two other Black women called out compliments to her on the street, and an interesting assignment from Professor Collins to meet with a faith healer who claimed to have received his powers from walking through the door. She wasn't sleeping well at night. Sometimes in class, a small, clear voice would cut through her note-taking or her arguments with other students to ask, "Why are you still here?"

When she talked to her grandma on the phone about soccer, about going to movie nights at Stephen's apartment, about eating vegan red-bean-and-corn-bread bakes with Jane every Wednesday night, about the work she and Felix were doing together, her grandmother said, "Hearing you sound like this, it makes me feel so good. I was worried about you for so long."

It was impossible to tell her grandma how complicated it all was. To sit on a couch next to Felix and want to reach for his hand one moment and then on the walk home think, *It would be so easy to disappear tonight.* To laugh so hard she cried when Jane told her about a night out at a drag king show. Then to decide in a quiet moment that she didn't deserve to eat for the rest of the day. To stand in line with Stephen to buy limited-edition shoes that looked like beige sleeping bags and to listen to him talk about how your drip should be constantly evolving, and somehow, this, too, was so much fun but her own brain was whispering below it all, "You aren't the one who should be here." Her grandmother promised to bake cookies for all her friends. She was coming to a parents' weekend in early January and expected all of them to take her out for lunch.

The only way for Ayanna to keep her brain quiet was to constantly be doing. So she threw herself into work. Extra credit, morning runs, and additional research for the faith-healer interview. Ayanna watched clips from a broadcast of *At Home with Simone*. The show was kitschy with all of Simone's obsessions with diets, cashmere throws, and authors who were always lying to Simone even if it was just the simple repeated phrase *I'm so happy to be here*, and the way that Simone couldn't stop bringing on dubious square-jawed medical professionals to cart around wheelbarrows of fat or tell people the secret to keeping away Alzheimer's was to drink a smoothie made from celery, apple cider vinegar, and ground pink Szechuan peppercorns. But still, she couldn't help but smile watching the opening credits, and how her parents had encouraged her to call the host "Aunt Simone."

Ayanna remembered quickly why she had found Simone so interesting. Some of it was the musicality of her voice, the high and low notes that made even a cursory "Folks, it is a Tuesday afternoon" beautiful. But in her long opening discussion, during which Simone looked at the camera, it still felt radical to see someone be so Black on TV. From talking about a news article that suggested baby powder and hair straightening might be contributing to higher than average cancer rates in Black women to the ways that winter Tuesdays always felt like a new *innovation* in misery—and you could hear the relish she took in making the *o* in *innovation* long and theatrical—and then to a long story about taking her mom to the church, and her mom was so old now, she was clapping on the ones and threes.

"Let me tell you," Simone said, "about a young man who is working his way toward sorting out all kinds of people miseries. His name is Matthias, formally known as Matthias of the Lord's Path, and he's here today to tell us about his journey."

Matthias of the Lord's Path could easily have been Matt of Varsity Tennis. He was probably nineteen at most, but tall with the broad shoulders of a man who went to the gym and lived on a diet of unseasoned grilled chicken breasts. He was white with very blue eyes and wavy brown hair in a trendy cut. There was something about his face that kept Ayanna from thinking he was "too handsome." Everything symmetrical, unremarkable ears, but maybe it was the way he jutted out his chin—he always looked like he was on the verge of saying something harsh.

"When I was five," Matthias said, "I was at a festival with my parents and a woman collapsed in front of me. While everyone tried to figure out what to do, I heard a voice telling me to kiss her left hand three times. I was always hearing voices then. My parents had raised me in one of those blue-door churches. I had run through our door when I was even younger and played out among the golden paths, not a care in the world, while my parents were too scared to follow me in. They had to coax me out with a candy bar, but by that point, I had eaten some dirt and some leaves."

"What is it about kids, they always be dirty," a woman yelled from the crowd, then was shushed immediately. There was no room for attention seekers in Simone's audience.

Ayanna's heart was too loud. She paused the video, took a long drink of water, and paced her dorm room. It could be a lie. Everything he was saying so far was pretty generic.

She unpaused the video, leaned closer.

"It was strange, the leaves tasted like popcorn. I don't like popcorn anymore because of it." This was the only thing he said that felt true to Ayanna.

"The woman," Simone said gently. She smiled, her teeth so white against her signature Simone's Red Passion brand lipstick.

"The voice insisted to me, kiss her hand. The woman had gotten back up, she was slurring, and people were arguing whether this was diabetes, a seizure, or a stroke, when she fell again. I rushed forward and kissed it." Matthias then described the hand, how it smelled like roses, how her fingernails were painted eraser pink.

"Then, she woke up," Matthias said. He made a face, like a fish gasping out its life on a boat's floor.

Ayanna sniffed. The room still smelled a little, like a refrigerator filled with meat and produce abandoned for a sudden long trip. She paused again, stood up, and cracked the window. Outside, it was pouring, the wind ripping off any tentative leaves and slapping them into gutters and swirling them along the sidewalks.

Later, the woman had tracked down Matthias's family and told him his mouth had felt like a burn each time on her skin. The woman had been living with brain cancer, but when she went to the doctors after that, all her scans were clean.

"She told me I saved her life." For the first time, Matthias smiled. "I've been chasing that feeling ever since."

The Simone studio audience broke into rapturous applause. What Matthias was saying was very nice, Ayanna conceded, but infuriating because no one was asking for proof. She felt certain, looking at the freeze-framed image of him smiling and all the women in the studio audience behind him applauding, that if he were a woman, or not white, or even less attractive, there would be at least one person who couldn't handle what he was saying. It was too simple for someone not to doubt. We live in a world, Ayanna thought, with doors that people ignore or still call hoaxes, a world people call flat, filled with disease disbelievers and people who refuse to believe humans have ever even been to the moon, a world where when you read about history and see all the cruelties, all the wars and violence people have inflicted on one another and did not question, it often seems impossible that people are still alive at all. But this dude can claim to heal people with his hands? Sure. This is the thing everyone seems willing to believe.

Maybe the Simone studio audience, though, was the wrong place to look for dissenters. Famously, they all received gifts from Simone—bags filled with retinol, cashmere shawls, candles promising to smell like a romantic night by the shore, granola bars promising to make your face less red and your eyes clearer, and assorted other objects that spoke to aspirations of having a life only involved in the mathematics of maximizing comfort. There were many popular videos on social media of people going through their Simone gift bags and ranking the gifts, estimating the costs, and talking about how wonderful the experience was.

Then, Simone reminded everyone that Matthias was a child of miracles. His mother was "the famous pastor's wife." The camera moved in closer and closer to Simone as she told the story Ayanna had heard so many times now: a grieving man, a blue door near a mountain range, a long walk home. And now the new addition: a child.

The first round of questions Ayanna composed for him all had the same how-dare-you vibe. The second felt better, a mix of genial questions, then potential follow-ups that would make him have to be explicit about what he was saying. What she wanted him to directly say was this: No, going on the path does not give you healing superpowers. No, I don't want to encourage people to risk their lives going through the doors in the hopes that they, too, will be able to cure cancer. Yes, I am ashamed that I exploit people's fears and grief to encourage them to give me an "offering" in exchange for a "healing session." Yes, I am a grifter. I am the son of grifters. She wavered here. Ayanna was deeply annoyed with herself that this was the myth she did not want popped. *Even if she's dead, I want to save her*, Ayanna thought.

On the Matthias of the Lord's Path website, there were vague descriptions of healing sessions and prayers from him, and you could buy candles consecrated by his hands or oils he had blessed. The cheapest item on the website was seventy-five dollars. Matthias also did corporate events.

She looked at the Post-it next to her laptop: *MARLIE NELSON* written in Stephen's all-caps-only handwriting. Ayanna was tired of procrastinating, and finally searched. All that came up were the exploits of a high school volleyball career and some wedding registries that were filled with baskets and cocktail shakers and gray cashmere throws. None of these Marlie Nelsons seemed like they were the kind of people a ghost would desperately be looking for. They all seemed like wholesome people who liked volleyball and never would have someone from the other side desperate for them.

Felix texted her to tell her the writing professor was losing it in Professor Collins's office again. She was telling Professor Collins about a dinner she had gone to with a very famous author and it felt like being back in high school. They could not figure out why the creative writing professor was working with them other than because Professor Collins seemed to like her a lot and said things like "Ernestine is the best reader I've ever met." They—Ayanna and Felix—felt they worried far more about credibility and standards than Professor Collins did. It wasn't that she didn't take the work seriously, but they felt like her concerns were nebulous and maybe even too playful. The creative writing professor was complaining all writers wanted to know was who had money, who was fucking whom or fucking someone over, and things about the capital-*I* Industry.

I am also deeply invested in that gossip, Ayanna texted him back. I would rather lie awake at night considering all the possibilities of who is secretly fucking and thinking no one knows than whatever she thinks is more interesting than that.

Then, she was embarrassed by the text and added a hahahaha to hopefully make it less awkward that she was texting him, in a way, about sex.

Are you nervous about the interview today? Felix texted. I can come if it'll make you feel more comfortable. But you'll crush it either way.

Ayanna weighed the offer for a few minutes. Thanks, but I got this.

Before he responded, she typed: Why doesn't anyone ever talk about how haunted dorms are? Why is it only houses or graveyards?

Fr, Felix responded, the most psychologically dark place I've ever been is Bursley. Filled with anguish, anxiety, and rage. Swear to god, saw a ghost there my freshman year, peeing out a third floor window. Everyone used to also say sixth floor was cursed floor.

Cursed floor? Ayanna immediately texted back. She wanted to go, see how many spirits lingered.

A shooting happened there a million years ago. People used to make dumb dark jokes like B6: Where Roommates Go to Kill. It's fucked because people really did get murdered there.

Do you think just because someone died somewhere, it's haunted?

Three dots coming and going. Ayanna looked at her hair, considered putting on some more makeup, examined what she was wearing, a black dress she had worn for school award ceremonies in high school. It had made her feel grown-up, but now seemed, maybe because it was baggy in a way it wasn't then, a little childish.

He didn't respond before Ayanna had to leave. She walked to the nice coffee shop with her headphones on, ordered them both cappuccinos. It was her first one, and Ayanna was surprised at how little she liked it. Bitter, tasteless foam. The coffee shop with all its smells and people picking at muffins and scones made it impossible to ignore how hungry she was. Ayanna took another sip while scanning the shop. Sitting at a table in the back was Matthias, dressed all in navy blue. He was closer to thirty now. His skin had a shine she associated with seeing people in movies and knowing their faces were coated in makeup, the world and all its light in service of underlining their beauty and health. He was holding a cake pop in his hands and inspecting it as if he had never seen anything so strange and potentially delicious.

When Matthias noticed Ayanna approaching the table, he set the cake pop down and smiled. She expected bright veneers, but his teeth were the most normal thing about him. A normal person's idea of nice teeth. They shook hands, and Ayanna introduced herself, recorded herself asking if it was fine if she recorded him and promised that this interview wasn't going to be published, but would be used only for research. He was also more than welcome to request that his responses be anonymized. She set the extra cappuccino in front of him, but Matthias ignored it.

Up close, his eyes were very blue. One of Ayanna's least popular bits was that blue eyes were overrated. It had gotten her booed on and off for two hours on a long bus ride home from a high school soccer match. Blue eyes were for zombies, wolves, and weird fish that looked like they had men's souls stuck inside them. Blue eyes were invented by the sunglasses industry to keep people squinting; no one throughout time had them naturally, a time-traveling executive for Oakley Incorporated had genetically modified ancient people to have light-colored eyes to sell more sunglasses, then destroyed his time machine and all time machines when he returned to the future. Blue-eye propaganda had worked so well that you could stick a pair in the eyes of someone who had a terrible personality and looked like they were actively dying from a medieval plague, and still 50 percent of people would ask, "Is he seeing anyone?" Ayanna smiled at him as she sat, while wondering how much people bought into his "healing" because his eyes were blue.

"You've been through the door," he said.

Ayanna nodded, a little annoyed.

"My dad was an Air Force officer, and my mom is German," Matthias said. "We grew up in the Church of ParadiesTur. You're Pathsong, right? No Jesus, just doors."

"That's not quite right. We didn't worship the doors or treat them like God. We believed God made the universe and thus the doors, but we were concerned more about believing in a creator who wanted his people to be curious and brave."

"Are you implying that most Christian faiths aren't that way?"

Ayanna surprised herself by laughing. "Why are you grilling me?"

"I could tell by the look on your face walking up—you don't believe me at all. You're not here for a nice conversation."

She sipped again. It took all her willpower not to wince. The baristas were listening to a country song, clearly ironically because of the multiple yeehaws they kept doing while heating up different sandwiches.

"What kind of face would have made you trust me?"

Finally, he relaxed. Matthias put his hands up in the air, waved them around like he was clearing smoke. "Okay, maybe I've just come in defensive."

"Sometimes in the US we call how you're acting 'coming in hot,'" Ayanna said.

"I like that." Matthias took the offered drink from her. "Whenever I come to universities, all people want to do is fight. They think a sign of immense stupidity is to believe anything at all. Universities want people to spend so much time thinking about thinking, the only thing they end up believing in is thinking. They shouldn't exist. They're making people worse."

Everything he said sounded rehearsed to Ayanna. Even the way he smiled self-consciously while finishing that last sentence felt calculated.

"I don't want to fight with you." She had shown up ready to, but listening to him spout off, Ayanna was already bored. It was ridiculous to her to fight about universities, about learning. It was weird to her to see someone so young doing oldhead talking points. Conservative kids she knew weren't arguing against universities, they were arguing against affirmative action, saying things about the quality of education and how it should be governed by a free marketplace, or talking about how they often felt prosecuted or punished for their beliefs by their power-tripping graduate-student instructors. Ayanna wasn't interested in those fights either, because they never felt like building understandings, they just felt like a game of Liberty Chicken—each complaint escalating toward the ugly math of trying to figure out whose freedoms were truly being curtailed. She could not understand how someone who believed he was blessed by God, was making money going around touching people, wanted to play those games too.

Ayanna made eye contact with him and asked a question she hadn't planned on asking. "What do you think the doors are?"

"No one's ever asked me that directly." He tapped the table, gazed into the distance. "I think they weigh your soul. In ancient Egypt, they believed your heart's weight was impacted by all your actions during your life. And the Egyptians were on the right track. Our souls change shape, color, and texture based on the things we do in this world. The doors know, and they give out gifts and punishments in return."

On the café table, someone had written in Sharpie *Stephen King is a CIA plant*. The baristas were still acting like they were main characters in an indie movie, no one had ever had so much fun pouring low-fat lattes. Ayanna's hands were shaking, and she put them on her lap under the table. Behind her, it sounded like someone was trying to lay down an ultimatum. "I told you I loved you six months ago," the girl kept saying, "and you said 'thanks.'"

"I can't tell what you're thinking," Matthias said.

She knew her great-grandmother had posited the same thing. Ayanna's father had said it was just a theory and there was nothing wrong with theorizing. But Ayanna felt like it was a sin in its own way to use something inexplicable as a way to judge others. It was a family shame.

"My sister is the best person I have ever known." Tears—angry, small, seeking to further infuriate her—were dripping down her cheeks. "The universe did not punish her. She was good and kind and—" Ayanna cut herself off for a moment because what her mouth wanted to say was, "a universe where someone like you can even remotely think he is better than her is disgusting and cruel and I don't want to be in it. You are a grifter. I don't want to live in a universe that would ever think *I* am better than her." And she cried harder, because speaking had made Ayanna acknowledge it again: Olivia is dead. She is not coming back.

"I didn't mean to offend you. It's just what I think." Finally, he seemed like a person. "I didn't know about your sister."

"How many people have you cured? How do you keep track? Why are you the only person to have gone through and come back that can suddenly heal people? Why is your mom the only person to ever be found in the doors and brought back?"

"I'm sure," he said, "if you're here, there's something different about you now."

"All experiences change people." Ayanna took her napkin, dabbed at her eyes. She remembered the mascara, gingerly brushed on in a moment of self-doubt, and now there were thin teary lines of it streaked on her cheeks and nose.

"Tell me about the time you went through," Matthias said.

"We're here to talk about you."

"When I look at you," he said, "I can see how much it hurt you."

"Okay," Ayanna said.

"In my church, we knew God had sent the doors to find those who most belonged in heaven or who could bring people closer to it. If you died in the journey, that was also his kindness. He didn't want you to suffer and be tormented in hell. It was a blessing. We're already living in the end of the world. We actually had an afterlife. My mother returned to this world because she is good and kind and how a woman should be."

One of the great faults of Pathsong was how often it flip-flopped on the idea of an afterlife. One church elder's writings was about her hypothesis that the doors themselves were made of souls. Finally, enough intelligent people had died and had sort of Voltroned their remaining spirit energy into making these gateways. Another had said, pragmatically, "If we want the church to survive, we have to believe in paradise." He had proposed that heaven was a great golden castle, large and immense for everyone, filled with beautiful art, and finally a chance to rest and think. The golden path if followed for days would take you there. You had to pray and reflect and acknowledge the complications of your inner self to have the castle's gates open for you. "We want people to have something to yearn for," he had said.

"We should get back on topic." Ayanna went to one of the questions she thought would calm him down. "What does it feel like to help people?"

"It's the greatest gift of my life. And a responsibility. I heal."

Matthias uncrossed his arms. He rumpled his hair with his hand.

"What do you think the golden path is?"

"Sometimes, heaven. Sometimes, hell. Sometimes..." He scratched at his hairline. "What's the word for the place between them? All my brain keeps coming up with is 'pavement.'"

"Purgatory?"

"Yes."

"Are you saying you think it's all of these places at once? Or are you saying you're not sure?"

Her voice was steady again. Ayanna was still holding herself very tight, shoulders toward ears, but couldn't help it. She wanted to snatch the cake pop he'd discarded and eat it in one big, ugly bite.

"I am unsure. Sometimes, I think it could be whatever you deserve. Sometimes, I think we'll never know."

He continued: "I have a question for you."

"Okay."

"May I touch your hand?"

"Why?"

"I think it could help you understand."

"I'm healthy. I don't need anything. Thanks." She had never said the word *thanks* so tersely.

"No, you're not."

Ayanna crossed her arms.

"Please don't touch me."

"I know who needs me because I have two ways of looking." Matthias smiled.

He was looking into the distance as if behind Ayanna was an audience who loved and admired him, not a couple arguing about "what it means to be in love."

"I can see the person in front of me and if I focus, I can see their aura. The average person's aura is beige, neutral. There are people with different colors all the time—you are not beige. All auras become a deeper and brighter pink the closer a person is to death. The other commonality is sickness, it's gray spots. I look at that woman over there"—he pointed—"and see her seasonal allergies. Ragweed. There's a small area over her sinuses. If I went into a hospital, I could tell you where someone's cancer is, whether someone was truly physically ill or if their symptoms were mental."

"I'm fine."

"You're anxious and depressed. There's also something around your eyes I've never seen before. Blue and death-pink."

Eyes back on the table, down to her brown loafers, on her feet crossing and uncrossing below the table. She had completely forgotten what Professor Collins wanted her to get from this. Ayanna decided that if the professor didn't like the interview, she would just quit. It was fine. Everything felt wrong.

"Where do you think the doors went?" she asked. "Why have they been gone for so long?"

Matthias reached for her, quick. Ayanna backed away, almost tipping her seat into the woman behind her.

"I asked you not to touch me."

"It will give you peace."

Ayanna picked up her bag, didn't risk reaching for her napkin or cup.

"For special cases,"—Matthias stood up and wiped some crumbs off his pants—"I do this for free."

She walked away, could feel him behind her, close at her heels. Ayanna assumed he wouldn't reach for her in front of all these people. She was torn between making a scene and feeling the mix of uncertainty and fear thumping in her chest. Matthias was well-dressed, he clearly had money, and she might only be seen as a Black body having a mental health crisis in a cute coffee shop that people loved to take pictures of maple lattes in. The pleasure of going to aesthetic places and being briefly ensconced in a world of good lighting, beautiful wood, and food better looking than most of the faces around you. The danger of being out in the world and seeing the faces swivel toward you over and over and trying to determine why you would even think you belong in a place as lovely as this. So, instead, she walked a little faster, dodged all the people waiting for their eight-step drinks, did not notice when one of the baristas waved at her—a girl from the soccer team—and did not pay attention when opening the doors.

If Ayanna had been paying attention, she would have looked before rushing out of the coffee shop. This block was notorious for people breaking the law and riding their bikes on the sidewalk. Worse, many of them rode their bikes really quickly on the sidewalk because they were the kind of people who were very scared of riding in traffic, but who didn't want to extend any courtesy to pedestrians. Enough people had gotten hit in the neighborhood that the city was threatening to send out additional police officers to ticket bicyclists who were disobeying the law. Even Ayanna's most abolitionist-leaning friends were torn on this one: they were definitely unhappy with the idea of more police officers on the streets, but they were also tired of living in fear of some frat dude who insisted his name was Nico, not Nick, running them down on his rich-kid bike.

So Ayanna rushed out, she did not see the bike coming at her quickly, or somehow even hear the girl yelling at the bicyclist already. She was saved only by Matthias pulling her back quickly, and his hands were so hot, like they had been baking for thirty minutes on 425, and she yelped an unseemly and embarrassing little noise, and the too-fast bike rider turned with a surprised face filled with freckles, then ran into another person and fell off his bike. Everyone was yelling at one another, the bicyclist was trying to blame Ayanna for distracting him, Ayanna was talking to the poor guy on the ground who seemed dazed and was saying he was going to be late for class, and Matthias was trying to talk to Ayanna, and a white girl with her hair dyed half white, half black was saying, I am an EMT, but not doing anything other than announcing her status as a trained medical professional, and a random guy from the coffee shop was yelling at the bicyclist, saying that he better not run off, I'm watching you, bro, and so many people were stopping to gawk at the situation. A few people with phones out, but some stunned enough to just watch.

The guy who'd been hit was bleeding a little bit on his arm. He stood up, as Ayanna offered him some Band-Aids from her bag. A girl with maybe too much hair waved at him, but he did not notice, and she kept walking to class with her headphones on. There was a cigarette on the ground, still smoking, and Ayanna realized it had been knocked out of his mouth by the collision. He seemed like the type of white guy Ayanna liked best, quiet and polite, alternative enough that you could look at him and think the odds were higher that he was not racist, and who probably, when he was drunk, would be able to tell you an actually funny story. It was a lot to pin on someone based merely on looks, but Ayanna was trying to make sure she saw at least one person in this situation as a person. She wanted to help him, felt it a relief to think briefly about someone or something that was not her or the situation she was in.

"Do you think you need to go to the hospital?" Ayanna asked him. His eyes were bright, and he was clearly listening to her.

"I can't believe I got hit by a bike."

"People are assholes," Ayanna said.

She was trying hard to focus on him and not herself.

Matthias did the sign of the cross and came over to the man hit by the bike. "You are bleeding internally."

"What?"

He quickly put his hands on the man's face. "God is with you."

"I feel asleep," the man said. "That's the only thing that can explain this." He winced and put up one hand, trying to get Matthias to stop touching him.

"You're going to live now, my brother," Matthias said, and let go.

"If I don't"—he turned to Ayanna—"I need you to tell my friend Kiki that I was in love with her. Her boyfriend sucks."

He made Ayanna text Kiki's name to herself, as well as her phone number from his phone. She saved the number as "Actual Person Named Kiki." Then, someone came from the coffee shop and asked if they needed to call the cops or the hospital, and everyone started taking off, except the bicyclist, who was saying performatively, "But my bike got wrecked."

"I saved his life," Matthias said. "And maybe yours too."

Ayanna waited to feel different. She had felt the burn of his hands through the back of her coat and on her right hand and wrist. The urge to tell herself it was anxiety or panic was there, but she knew it wasn't true. In some ways, it was what she had longed for, some magic way that wasn't pills and talking and processing to return herself back to who she'd been before. Felix had texted back: We want to think that haunting is about the living, but all the explanations are with the dead who owe us nothing.

"Which way is my hotel?" Matthias asked.

"You're staying downtown?"

Her phone buzzed in her pocket. Ayanna didn't care that she was being rude. It was Jane: Are you OK? Heard you got pancaked by a bike.

"Your hotel is north," Ayanna said. She shook her head. Apparently, nothing interesting in this city could happen without someone texting Jane about it.

They walked in the same direction a little more. Matthias's entire affect seemed different. He was giddy: his walk almost a dance, and a grin that Ayanna would describe as unhinged because it did not waver.

"Have you ever saved a life?" Matthias asked. "It's the most exhilarating feeling in the world. I feel so alive. I live in miracles. I was born of them. I give them. Praise him!"

Ayanna knew it would be better if she walked straight to the bar that never carded her and bought a shot. But there was a question boiling in her with each step she took away from the coffee shop. *I used to be someone who wasn't afraid of saying what was on her mind,* Ayanna thought. It was another thing she mourned. When death steals someone precious, it's hard not to miss all the other, smaller things it stuffed into its pockets alongside the beloved.

"Can I ask you one more question?" Ayanna asked. Her voice was high and shaky. She realized she had no idea where her feet were taking her.

"Sure," Matthias said. He seemed completely transformed to her out in the yellow fall light. His face and eyes bright with ecstasy, the wind blowing his longish hair, and a dimple had appeared in his cheek.

"Do you ever see the dead?"

"No," Matthias said, "that's impossible. The dead are dead."

"Then what about your mom?"

"My mother drowned. God brought her back. My dad had to do a pilgrimage of true faith." She could hear how he was parroting someone else. "And God rewarded him."

"But do you really believe this?"

On the street around them, there were mostly students trudging to class or in and out of the coffee shops and corner stores. The tree closest to Matthias was dotted with little pink spots. She guessed maybe it was a whole flock of sparrows who had suddenly died and did not want to be apart. Two blocks over was a street she always avoided because one of the most tangible spirits Ayanna had ever seen lay in the alley between the road and the parking structure. They had jumped and remained in front of the graffiti that read *Krave* and was embellished with three messy hearts. All it ever said was "I did this," and Ayanna could not tell if the spirit was referring to the graffiti or death.

That was the world she lived in. No one full and intact returned and lived again.

When she was thirteen, Ayanna had read about how different cultures designated some places as sacred because they were so beautiful that spirits—the kind people said were impossible, like dryads and naiads and demons—revered them. A waterfall in Europe, woods in Japan, a swamp in South America. Misty blue grottoes scattered across the Mediterranean that grandmothers worried about not just because of the tides but because of the somethings that loved it. It made her want to go to all these places; now, everywhere was potentially those places.

"You don't have to be alone," he said. "Let's spend the day together. If you just listen, I'm sure God will give you peace."

Matthias had the look on his face of someone who was used to getting let off the hook for his bad behavior. One smile and one moderately nice thing probably did feel like an apology to most people. Here he was putting in an effort. Ayanna turned. She jogged and crossed the street before he could react.

18

After typing up the interview notes and sending them to Professor Collins, after spraying and wiping her room again because when she returned, the rotting-meat smell was so bad as to feel almost viscous and capable of attaching to her for forever, after going to her mailbox and finding another batch of note cards that had only the sentence PLEASE KILL YOURSELF SO WE CAN BE TOGETHER written on them in all caps, after ignoring texts from everyone because she could not handle interacting with anyone, after eating a cup of chicken tortilla soup, because it was the most appealing option on the dorm menu, and staring into the void, after reading some of another book that seemed only to be saying in different ways, Wow, books are made of words and every reality created by books is false because man is fallible and anything can be misconstrued, Ayanna longed for sleep. She turned over the day in her head, and looked again at Stephen's notes. Instead of Marlie Nelson, she decided to search the name "Marlie Evans."

Ayanna scratched her nose and eyebrow, didn't let her eyes focus on the screen. Every day for two years, she pingponged between anger and denial and depression and bargaining. Everyone kept acting like one day she would wake up having ascended to acceptance, a beautiful new life, where yes, her sister had died, but it was only trivia rather than a wound. There was no point any longer in pretending she wasn't interested in what the spirits were saying. None of these things would undo everything that had happened. For two years, her grandma and therapist kept saying "You have to move forward." They said variations on "Healing only comes through living." She read the results. There were six Marlie Evans that immediately came up on the search. The one who seemed the most likely to have a ghost looking for her was an eighty-two-year-old who lived in the same city as Ayanna. The first hit for her was about her long-running book club. Over the summer, she had celebrated forty years of bringing Black women together to read. Ayanna laughed when she realized the author at the featured event was the creative writing professor. They were celebrating the release of her third novel, which was about a Black woman who was an assistant professor and a writer trying to date in a college town while dealing with racial trauma and not getting paid enough for her previous books.

"Big imagination," Ayanna muttered, then felt a little guilty reading how kindly Marlie Evans had welcomed the writer, how earnestly she believed that all Black books mattered because Black Americans were developing a cultural heritage in a nation still hostile to the idea that there were many different ways of being American, and how reading was one of the most remarkable things of being human. She had been a schoolteacher.

Tired and knowing she would overthink it in the morning, Ayanna wrote two emails. One, first, to the professor, asking if she would be willing to introduce her to Marlie Evans. And the second to the book club's email address where she first wrote a long, rambling message about Valerie, the visitations, the way that Valerie was still obsessed with Marlie and wanted her to know she had never meant to leave her, then realized if Marlie was anything like either of her grandmas, she would think Ayanna was an insane person and never respond to that message. So, she backtracked, deleted the email, and wrote an email about her interest in the book club, which was true, and asked if they were taking on new members.

Then, Ayanna reread her dad's latest email. He had been at a beautiful monastery where no one spoke regularly, let alone spoke English, but they'd fed, clothed, and kept him safe for five days. Each day, three times a day, he did the stations of the cross and focused on the idea that suffering was inevitable, that without suffering, it would be impossible for people to understand how wonderful grace was. The only thing that kept her from writing a scathing email back was for the first time he had written I miss you. She responded back I miss you too.

People kept texting her, asking if she had been the one hit by the bike. Ayanna inspected her wrist where Matthias had touched her; it felt wrong that there was no mark. Felix texted with an offer to bring her dinner.

She put on a sweatshirt and jeans, took a bag and tucked a joint and some acre into it, and left her dorm. Without much contemplation, Ayanna walked to the gate surrounding the woods. There were no spirits and it made the world flatter. She looked around, then hopped over. There wasn't a headstone or marker for Olivia. She thought if ever there was a time in her life where she had money, one of the first priorities would be to do something good in her sister's name. Olivia who worked with her at the soup kitchen and pantry, Olivia who had once written an essay that true patriotism was striving for an America that lived up to its best ideals and that meant getting rid of childhood poverty, Olivia who could be such a brat and a snitch but who was also, at the heart of it all, good.

Her father had written in his most recent email: A part of the path is marked with silver seashells, others yellow, some with a sword driven through. Silver Spanish Saint Seashells for the Suffering, a tongue twister prayer. I like them though because they are simple. All shells have mysteries. Your mother and I used to want to go to Prague and walk the Charles

Bridge. It's supposed to be lined with a century's worth of saints. It protects the city. Now, I think it would be too much to bear.

I don't understand life at all, Ayanna. I walk around and even on the path, I meet miserable people. I meet people who think their divorces are the equivalent of true suffering. I look at all these people and think why are you here instead of Olivia. The shells make me think of going to the beach with the two of you when you were kids. Every shell you found, each of you tried to blow and make music. I know I haven't learned enough that I think the shells on this path have anything to say to me. I am fasting and not sleeping much. I like myself this way. It makes me too tired to lie.

That was his response to her message: Will you be around at Christmas?

From the park in the distance, she could hear what sounded like a contentious basketball game. A man yelled, "That was a technical foul." It felt late to be playing basketball, and to be keyed up enough to yell about it. Any basketball after ten thirty should be melancholic practice meant to hit the perfect three-point shot or a sensual game of H-O-R-S-E between two combative lovers. Ayanna didn't feel anxious being alone in the dark or in the woods. It felt, alone like this, like she was going home.

At the path, Ayanna sat cross-legged. She thought about Olivia, the way her sister sometimes snorted when she laughed, how her sister had actually thought about things like getting married and having kids, and sometimes seriously worried if she could be both a mom and a professional athlete. How her big ambition was to play in the World Cup and then become the coach of the Women's National Team and if not a life of professional coaching, she would be a teacher. Two kids; hopefully, twins. A husband who was fun. That had seemed like such a low bar to Ayanna at the time.

The most unexpected thing about grief was when there was finally progression—new friends, new interests, new crushes—it hurt more because the loved one wasn't there to weigh in. Olivia would tell

Ayanna to get a cute new outfit and ask someone out. While Olivia wasn't sure if she was going to have sex before marriage, she had already told Ayanna she wanted to hear everything when she decided to do it. Tell me everything, Olivia had said once. I can't promise I won't judge but I still want to know you.

For a moment, she heard Olivia's voice in her head. A little higher pitched, a faster talker critiquing the shots Ayanna had missed during her last match. Bad timing, hitting with your toe rather than through the laces. She used to roll her eyes or freeze her sister out when she did that.

It was getting cold out. Ayanna pulled out the pill, weighed it in her hands. Olivia, I miss you, she thought. Olivia, I've had a weird day; I don't need you to tell me the world will be better, I just need you to listen to me tell you about it and then to hear you tell me about your day. Olivia, I want you to tell me that somehow you survived. Olivia, I want you to tell me you forgive me. Olivia, I want you to be annoying to me again.

The more she thought about her sister, the more spirits descended, so many it reminded Ayanna of watching a movie where a smirking actor cut his hand a little and let blood drip into the ocean. An enormous number of sharks appeared, fins and fangs, and the main lady swooned with fear. A familiar voice thanked her for reaching out to Marlie: I will help you when she's there, thank you. The more the spirit spoke, the more electronic it sounded.

Ayanna was relieved to see them. When Matthias had said she was cured, Ayanna assumed in some way it was from this. It was frightening and annoying to be able to see the world as it was for everyone else, and see the spirits; but with the doors gone, this was, she knew now, the only chance of getting to see Olivia again. Their soft-pink bodies stretched, elongated, blobbed. They made the world seem like a vast lava lamp. The glow relaxed her.

"Liana, you seem so lonely," the voice said. A cloud coalesced into a figure taller than Ayanna. She could see his face clearly, large eyes with long eyelashes. He put a hand on her shoulder, and she could feel it. Light and a strange texture, like a hand made from Play-Doh.

Ayanna took a step back. Twice in one day, she thought, men not respecting my personal space. She knew it was a hand on her arm, but still wanted her boundaries respected.

"I could feel it."

"I miss you so much."

"I'm not Liana."

He told her about the summer of his affair with Liana. Looks at parties, kisses stolen in the dark, in empty rooms, a weekend at a hotel spent only in desire. They would exchange books and he would tuck notes in, sometimes note cards or cardboard cut to be a bookmark. Gin and tonics, a night when they walked to look at each other's windows but met in the middle and fell into bliss that almost got them caught. Her skin smelled like cedar and violets.

"If Liana loved you so much," Ayanna said, "then why didn't she leave her husband?"

The spirit paused there.

"I forgot about this side of you, Liana."

"Ayanna."

She continued: "Maybe," and Ayanna had never heard her voice be so cold and measured, "you were just fun for her for a summer. She was bored, and she loved the attention you gave her, but not you. Maybe she just liked sleeping with you but thought you were annoying as a person. She knew you wanted someone to love you and it made you easy to manipulate."

"I don't like this," he said.

"I don't like you calling me Liana, sending me those weird notes, telling me to kill myself."

"It's romantic. We can be together. I've been waiting so long for you, Liana. I can't believe you chose to be reborn again without me."

No one had ever spoken to Ayanna with so much need.

"I never had a family," he said. "I had you and only such a small time. I wanted years together. I wanted children. I wanted holidays."

The wind rustled the entire woods. He shook with it, moving from solidish man to cloud, and back. Above, the moon was a fingernail clipping left for someone to find in the navy quilt sky. I wish I was home, Ayanna thought. I wish there was somewhere that felt like home. I wish I was someone who was worrying about midterms or rush or my weird roommate instead of all this. I wish I was the one who died. I'm so tired of feeling.

And then she thought of all the years before, when she had loved being complicated, had happily thought of adventures and discoveries, had read biographies of explorers, and had dreamed of other worlds filled with not just golden paths and indigo meadows, but all the creativity and glory the universe might hold. She had wanted to discover without colonizing or cruelty. Ayanna immediately apologized to the person she had been. At heart, she still wanted to be brave, to be relentless, to be in a pursuit of knowledge, to feel the thrill again of seeing a new vista, to want to approach living with an open heart. And if not that, despite her intrinsic dislike for Matthias, Ayanna thought of his face when he felt certain he had saved someone's life.

"Liana, you're ignoring me," he said.

She hadn't realized he had been talking.

Ayanna reached out to him. Touched his wrist and felt it soften beneath her grasp. She avoided his eyes. "I need you to stop."

He stepped closer. Moved his head to her own, leaned down as if to smell her hair.

"No," he said, and disappeared.

19

For another week, Ayanna's dorm room persisted in smelling like rot. Her mother had texted her more frequently—you ruined my life, I wish I had taught you to love God, I am tired of you thinking you can do whatever you want, Olivia says I should forgive you but you are the reason why everything is like this—and once sent a meme of a cat wearing round black sunglasses that had the text no stress, just vibin. Sleeping felt impossible. The one time she had fallen asleep deeply was at Felix's apartment while everyone else was watching *Boyz n the Hood*. She'd wiped the drool off her mouth and listened to them arguing over who was more fire in the movie: Nia Long or Angela Bassett. Regina King, they felt, was someone who was next-door cute (a sparkler on the fire scale) when she was young but so hot it hurt now (somehow stepped in lava on the fire scale). Ayanna felt a million miles away, more concerned with how dry her mouth felt. The ghost kept coming in and knocking her things off the desk. All food tasted like salt.

On the Sunday night before Halloween, Ayanna could not stop thinking: Would anyone really care if she wasn't around anymore?

She could not think of a single person who would notice if she was gone. Was there anything she truly wanted? She wanted to make the world a better place, but that felt impossible and foolish. Arrogant too. Ayanna felt certain in her ugliness, her selfishness, her smallness. If she was dead, well, maybe, at least, she might be with Olivia. There was no proof everyone got to be a spirit, but there was a chance. Ayanna paced her dorm room, digging her fingernails into her palms.

What would Olivia think if she was waiting for her?

Maybe she would understand. And if she didn't understand at first, she would convince her over time. Hopefully.

She went on the forums for supernatural encounters and read obsessively. It was the same old shit of voices speaking backward, cold air, malicious presences, Civil War ghosts, slave ghosts, dead-husband ghosts, and beautiful-murdered-lady ghosts. It was exhausting to be so alone. Usually, Ayanna tried to avoid reading these because it made her feel like she was the crazy one. They always began an insidious refrain in Ayanna's head about the spirits, the way she moved through the world: I am making these up because I am unwell. I am making these up because my brain was irrevocably damaged by going through the door. I am making these up because I am forever traumatized by losing my sister. I am a terrible, sick person and I shouldn't be alive any longer.

It did not matter to her that she had seen Felix feed them at the park. Or that other people had studied them. Nothing rational mattered. Anything she could use as an argument against herself, Ayanna's brain latched on to.

Ayanna put her sister's things in her backpack, went back and forth with herself about taking her phone with her, ignored the mess on her floor and the note cards that again had been slid beneath the heavy door—STOP MAKING ME WAIT; KILL YOURSELF, YOU SPITEFUL BITCH; I'M SORRY, I LOVE YOU, LET'S BE TOGETHER—and put on her favorite coat as the one courtesy to herself. If this was the last hour of her life, she would be in one of the few things she unabashedly loved.

The city was still alive with people. Girls dressed sexy and wearing fake eyelashes, a couple making out in front of the library, the shorter boy on the higher step so he could get a sense of what it was like to be the taller lover, a group of visibly drunk friends trying to harmonize "Kiss from a Rose," and some people in costumes even though Halloween was finally a Saturday this year. But zombies and cowboys and people dressed as bananas were out among the usual black the North Face jackets and brown Ugg boots.

In the park that held the woods, a cluster of spirits was at the gate. The brightest pink Ayanna had ever seen. They were speaking to one another about the last things they could remember eating. Almost everything was a terrible meal in a hospital room, but one braggart who had, it sounded like, died by being hit by an errant driver had had an incredible four-course meal: duck with miso soy and greens, a mung-bean-and-kimchi fritter with a razor clam on top of yuzu custard, and an amuse-bouche he was struggling to remember. The spirits around him were torn between wanting to hang on to every word he said and wishing they could find a way to make him die a second time.

"Why are you all here?" Ayanna asked.

The moon is full. Je m'ennuyais. A boy will sometimes give us cake here. I saw a crowd. Ich bin einsam. I was once a tree in this very park and now I'm this. A sound like static heard from down a hallway. A voice like an owl hooting but the words sounded like no language. I love hearing him talk about his last meal. Why not?

None found it remarkable or especially interesting that Ayanna could see them.

She continued on. Swiped her card to enter the woods, and if her brain had been feeling even a little better, Ayanna would've felt a small wonder at how beautiful it was that evening. The moonlight was so clear among the gloom, its light felt like a river among the trees, something that could've been grabbed by quick hands, forced into a bottle, and distilled into a miraculous tonic. She might have seen the little white cat hunting in the night, the way its eyes were bright and reflecting green in the moonlight, and how its bottom half couldn't resist wriggling a little with the excitement and pleasure of the hunt. She could have absorbed herself in how tall the trees were, indulged herself in thinking about all the weather and winds they had felt, and wondered at how they conceived of life. What was it like to be alive in such a passive way? But she was crying, and Ayanna's brain was empty with the pull to be nothing. It hurt too much to keep living this way. The wind swirled dead leaves along the ground, plucked those who could not hold on any longer away from their branches.

Ayanna lingered near the path, making sure no one was there. There was a shadow that for some long, scared moments, she was sure was Felix. He would not be able to change her mind, crush or no crush, and she did not want him to have to think about this night for the rest of his life. It felt cruel to make him wonder if he had said something, noticed something, would everything be different?

On the small golden path, she pulled out her sister's pajamas, her nail polish. Olivia, Olivia, Olivia, she thought. You don't have to forgive me. I should have been the one who died. Will this be enough to make you forgive me a little? I don't want to do this anymore. I've ruined everything. She did not expect, or even hope, her sister to appear after last time. It was the only way she could think of to say a penance before what she was about to do.

The spirit who had been harassing her briefly appeared, kissed her forehead. "There's a tall parking structure less than a mile from here. I'll be waiting for you when you've done it. Thank you, thank you."

She nodded. There was no point in fighting with him. He kissed her face again and she could smell his nidorous breath, feel the wet of his impatient lips, and knew he was becoming more and more solid with his desire to reunite.

After ten minutes of thinking of her sister, a small part of her disappointed that even now Olivia refused to come to her, to tell her to live, realizing that must mean Olivia, too, hated her, and then feeling even more swallowed by self-loathing for being remotely angry at her sister, Ayanna stuffed her sister's things back in the backpack and walked to the parking structure.

The parking structure was high. She could see all the way to her dorm, past that even to all the small, expensive houses the professors lived in. The city lights: yellow, pink, white. And the moon, so big and close and orange. A mist in the chill air. Ayanna thought when she jumped, maybe instead of the ground, she'd fall into the mist instead. She stood at the very edge, felt all the night and its pressure on her shoulders, but still could not do it. Ayanna hated herself more, tried to will herself to be clumsy, to slip. She had been clumsy in so many other situations, but her body refused to plunge into the night while her brain thought: I hate you so much, I hate you. This could finally be over.

The moon, a large judging eye, refusing to tell her what to do. Silver cars around her and feet that refused to die.

She went back to the elevator, noticed how dirty the buttons were on the way down. Why couldn't she even do this? It was what she wanted. And for a moment, Ayanna was so angry with herself she considered going back up. But she knew this wasn't right and shuffled out of the elevator.

What she was supposed to do: Call her grandmother and tell her she was in trouble, call one of her old high school friends that had known both her and Olivia? Ayanna knew she could call Jane or Felix or Stephen. She could try calling her father. She was supposed to eat something, drink a glass of water, and do things that helped her remember she was responsible to herself. She was worthwhile and life was a gift. What a bunch of bullshit.

Ayanna walked to different open convenience stores and bought enough migraine medication that maybe, if she was diligent and took them all, and did not vomit, they would finally make this end. At first, she bought a lotto ticket or a lighter to make it seem less weird, but then it became clear the cashiers on their Bluetooths, their eyes on the security camera footage coming from the liquor aisles, did not care or even notice her.

On the street walking back to her dorm, a girl from her postmodernism class, Lisa, bumped into Ayanna. Lisa was swaying, she was dressed as a beer bottle, her makeup was running down her face. She turned to Ayanna and mumbled something, then turned and vomited on the street. Some hit the sidewalk, some hit people's shoes, and a guy yelled, "What the fuck is wrong with you."

Lisa said the world felt like it was choppy, and she had drank only two mixed drinks. No, drunk, she said. No drank, she corrected herself. Then Lisa sagged down on the street next to her vomit, and Ayanna had to squat quickly to pull Lisa back up and helped her lean against the brick building.

She asked Lisa where her friends were, who had given her the drinks, where she lived. The girl kept sagging, her face making an expression that Ayanna could describe only as melting. Her words were slurred. And Ayanna couldn't believe no one else seemed to notice her or the situation. A few people from that same class even walked by, including one of the boys who had argued with Lisa just four days ago in class when she had said she thought *The Crying of Lot 49* had to have a woman protagonist to highlight how distorted reality truly felt. They had spent what felt like an eternity arguing about gender essentialism while the teacher watched with half-closed eyes. Jane had doodled what looked like a cat riding a motorcycle with a speech bubble coming out of its mouth: *but you had to go to college.*

"I think you've been roofied," Ayanna said.

She weighed whether to call 911, wished they were back at the dorms, wanted to at least get away from the terrible smell of Lisa's vomit, wished she had retained any of the information from the campus flyers about date rape drugs, and for the first time in days, did not think about how much she fucking hated herself. Ayanna guessed maybe Lisa was lying, maybe she had just drunk too much, but this didn't feel like that.

Ayanna had Lisa wrap her arm over Ayanna's shoulder and she wrapped her own dominant arm around Lisa's waist. They walked first into the store, because the one thing she remembered was you should have the person drink water if they are able to do that safely. She bought two liters of water, Lisa knocked over the gum display on the counter, tried to clean it up, and was waved off by the cashier. It was hard to maneuver Lisa in her beer-bottle outfit. It would have been a little funny, this usually petite girl in such an onerous bottle costume crashing into everything and creating chaos, if it hadn't been so discomfiting for Ayanna. Closer to Lisa. She smelled like she had maybe pissed herself as well.

"Your friend is really fucked up," the cashier said, and laughed. "God, I miss college."

Ayanna ignored him and helped Lisa outside. They walked slowly to the closest bench, then when it became clear it was a bad idea to try to get Lisa to drink anything, Ayanna called 911.

AT THE HOSPITAL, while Lisa spoke to a nurse, Ayanna sat in the waiting room. She thought again about all the pills in her backpack, how despite everything, here she was again thinking about ending it all, but mostly she thought about Lisa. How much she wanted her to be okay. The TV showed the latest late-night TV talk show, where a handsome man was interviewing another handsome man about what it was like to be handsome. Everything was bright and washed-out. The nurse at the desk was wearing bright turquoise scrubs and a Halloween hat meant to look like a pumpkin top. People around Ayanna were bleeding or holding their stomachs or were in some way in distress. A woman she had to avoid looking at because her wrist was so clearly broken. Most of them were alone. She half watched the interview but spent most of her time wondering if Lisa was okay, and how she had ended up alone on the street like that, and she let out a breath she had been holding. A few spirits wisped above seats. Had they died waiting for care?

Hours of waiting. The television moved to reruns of a sketch show, all the Halloween episodes. Each one seemed to have a joke about wearing a sexy costume to a completely inappropriate situation. Yet some of the people around Ayanna kept laughing at it. She stood up a few times to stretch; the chairs were hard and unyielding. A moment or two where Ayanna dozed off, only to jolt herself awake. *SVU* reruns and those seemed wildly wrong to be shown in the ER waiting room, but people were watching them with the glaze of relaxation spread across their faces. When Lisa came out, she didn't say anything, just waited for Ayanna to gather her things. She was pale and some of her thick black hair was stuck to her chin.

"Are you okay?" Ayanna asked.

"No," Lisa said. "Yes."

They walked back to the dorm together in silence. The birds that remained in town were starting to wake up and sing. Soon, they would all head south, except for the crows that appeared in great flocks in November and December. Why did they like to be here, even when everything was miserable? Ayanna's thoughts swam with lack of sleep. She tried to calculate what she had to snack on in her dorm room and thought maybe there was half a granola bar in her top desk drawer.

"Are you hungry?" Ayanna asked.

"I never want to eat again," Lisa said. Her shadow was so large. "I smell so bad."

They walked again in silence, Ayanna watching how the other girl still moved a little clumsily and wondering if she should offer her an arm. Ayanna couldn't believe the hospital had let them leave. They were both so tired that neither had considered calling for a ride.

"You saved my life," Lisa said.

"No," Ayanna said. "Not really."

"You didn't have to help me."

"I did," Ayanna said, and was surprised by it. She repeated herself before Lisa could say anything again. "I did."

She stopped walking, took off her backpack, and pulled out the pills she had bought. Held them in her hands while walking down the street and threw them into the nearest trash can. Lisa didn't seem to notice.

"I'm just glad you're okay," Ayanna said.

Back at the dorms, they realized Lisa had somehow lost her swipe card that would let her in and back into her room. They knocked for a while at Lisa's door, but her roommate didn't answer. The RA on duty was nowhere to be found. Ayanna took Lisa to her dorm room. Handed her a towel, some pajamas that were far too big for her, and walked her down to the showers. When Lisa had taken off the costume, Ayanna held it gingerly between her hands, and walked it out to the dumpster behind the dorm and stuffed it in. Her body was so tired, she felt like she could feel her skull vibrating. Then she went back upstairs, cracked the window open a little, pulled out her yoga mat and extra pillow, and made herself a bed on the floor. There wasn't any food, just some mints rattling in their steel container, and she ate them slowly, one at a time, trying to savor them.

When Lisa came back, they argued briefly about who got the bed. Ayanna won and settled down onto the yoga mat. She listened briefly while Lisa cried herself to sleep, felt certain that if she tried to comfort her it would be the absolutely wrong thing to do—sometimes people needed to cry after terrible experiences and let it out—and put her head down on the pillow.

Ayanna assumed she would fall asleep immediately, but instead stayed listening to Lisa. It was only when she heard her start snoring that her body began to relax. There wasn't any satisfaction or certainty in her, just relief Lisa would probably be okay. If I keep living, Ayanna thought, the only way it's possible is if I do something for other people. She did not think she had what it took to be a doctor or a therapist or even a bus driver, but it was worth thinking more about what that could look like. The world was filled with people in trouble, and it seemed like maybe the only true skill she had was being someone who didn't want to look away when someone was in distress. It didn't, she thought, make her an especially good person. Or someone who could give herself self-regard, but it was something. Ayanna sighed. Tried to relax her body even more. Her stomach grumbled. If she was a good person, Ayanna thought, she wouldn't resent how often she noticed other people's troubles, their negative emotions, and wonder why people couldn't give her the same attention. The noticing only made her feel even more alone.

Day was stretching its way into the world. Ayanna realized that for the first time in weeks the room smelled fine; the most prevalent smell was the mints she had eaten as a desperate breakfast. Lisa rolled onto her back, back onto her side, the bed loudly announcing her movements. Ayanna shut her eyes. You should help people, she told herself, because you don't want to tell Olivia that you wasted your life.

Once, the spirit sang and then there were stars. Then the stars sang and there were planets. The planets clapped and stamped until there were trees and seas and birds.

And when the first bird began to trill, the spirit was glad and rested. The spirit knew death would never know it because song and truth would forever echo. The whales joined, then the elephants, then the people.

The spirit sang back to them in a voice of lightning and mist of all the universe's mysteries. Each tried to sing it back but the tune distorted. Words dropped, chords changed.

The spirit sang a command: Your time here should be spent finding a way to return to my melody.

20

Someone was knocking on Ayanna's door. It was evening. On the other side of the door, Jane was waiting for her. After a mix of *are you okay*s, incredulousness that it wasn't Ayanna who had been struck by the bike despite all the gossip, and why hadn't Ayanna answered her phone for days, why had she ignored emails and texts, everyone was asking about her and worrying, you're not alone, Ayanna, and that was pretty fucked up, why didn't you come to class, they almost had a fight, Jane's voice getting slower and louder with each sentence, then they laughed.

"I was being a pretty uptight mom there," Jane said.

"Make that into a shirt," Ayanna said, "Uptight Mom."

They walked together in the chilly October air to get late-night food. Jane was wearing a pink leather jacket and a T-shirt that read *What Would Prince Do* in purple Sharpie. Ayanna felt the pleasure of walking with Jane, a female friend who, finally, was taller than her. They talked briefly about how much money Jane spent on her T-shirts and Sharpies—she could find a six-pack of men's shirts for eighteen dollars, sometimes eight dollars on clearance—and Ayanna watched her breath in the chill night air, the waft of it, and it reminded her of the dead. Maybe souls and breath are connected, she thought, then refocused on her friend.

"Are you okay?" Ayanna asked Jane. "You've seemed so down lately."

"I've just been processing. And besides, I should ask you the same thing."

"I'm fine," Ayanna said, and it was almost true.

At the diner, they both drank decaf coffee and split a mountain of Tater Tots.

"I've been mourning not having a faith anymore," Jane said. "I've known I was queer for so long. And even if I wasn't queer, you've met me. I'm outspoken and bossy and weird. I'm not the right kind of lady."

"I like you." Ayanna forked three Tater Tots, felt pleased by how they looked like a line on her fork.

"Yeah, and I wish we had met ten years ago when I was ten and could've used a best friend."

Ayanna waited for Jane to change the subject or to get embarrassed by how earnestly they were talking to each other, but instead they met each other's eyes and smiled.

"Faith gave me someone who would love and always like me," Jane said. "I used to talk to Jesus every night, tell him about my day, tell him about my big crush on Gina Simmons and what her hair looked like that day. She had a mom who was always mixing it up—braids, beads, curls."

"I always feel like my heart fills up all the way to my throat when I see a little Black girl with beads in her hair. I want to say, your parents think you are the cutest thing on Earth if they took time to do that."

"But it's what I miss so much, I miss feeling like no matter what, there was someone out there who would love me, who would like me. Only God offered me that. And now, I don't have God, I don't have parents who will love me unless I'm closeted and unhappy. I feel so alone." Jane took a deep breath. "And my mom is sick. My dad says it will be too stressful for everyone if I come home because I keep causing issues."

Ayanna shook her head.

"Please don't say anything," Jane said. "I already know I can't change. I know this is a problem only because they choose to make it a problem. I know I've been being crazy lately. So." She took a sip of water, looked up at the ceiling. "What's going on with you?"

"I had a twin sister," Ayanna said. "Olivia. She died. I don't want to talk about how, but my family, we just fell apart in the aftermath. And my mom, she's always been rough on me, but because of this, there's nothing there."

Jane paused for a long moment, then reached across the table and took Ayanna's hand. "I'm not trying to replace your sister, but let's be family."

Ayanna's throat shut with emotion, eyes watering at how simply Jane offered this. She wanted to get up from the table and walk out into the cold night. I don't deserve to have a family, she thought. Her rational self knew this was why her therapist said she had PTSD. These thoughts were because of the guilt she felt around Olivia; she hadn't been able to say it yet in therapy, but she had written it after, the way her head ached even when she thought about her parents. All her feelings were sharp and jagged inside her, it felt impossible to crawl through them, for things to ever change. Then, she thought about lying on her bedroom floor, listening to Lisa's breathing. The way she had looked at the pupils of the boy who had been hit by the bike, made him talk, tried to understand if he was okay. How much she was willing to care for someone else even though she barely knew them. I want to live, she thought, and I want other people to live well. It was her new mantra. It would not ever make depression and anxiety go completely away, but it was the best thing she could think of to make living feel bearable again. Tomorrow, she would see her therapist, and discuss her medication dosage.

"I know you're scared," Jane said. Her eyes big and wet, and the music behind them a song about partying every Saturday night. "But we should try. We'll both fuck up, but we can forgive each other."

Ayanna forced her shoulders down. She nodded and picked at the remaining Tater Tots with her free hand, Jane seemed to be fascinated by the swirl of creamer in her cup. A tear was on her nose and dripped down onto the table. She wanted to ask Jane how she could believe in families at all. Instead, Ayanna squeezed her friend's hand twice and then sat quietly holding it across the jam-stained table.

They felt too young and tender while surrounded by drunk people sobering up in the early morning. Sitting in silence and hearing the loud conversations swirling around them, the world felt large and filled with people who had never brushed fingers with tragedy. Each Tater Tot was perfect to Ayanna, a little crunchy on the outside, soft on the inside. Somehow, not at all greasy. They agreed to order more.

Jane told Ayanna she'd kissed Marti earlier today. Ayanna knew she was on their soccer team but couldn't remember if Marti was the tall half-Chinese right back or if Marti was the short Black girl who had joined the team to "have a new experience" but who looked terrified anytime someone asked her if she wanted to be subbed on. She wondered if Jane was a campus celebrity like the white guy everyone pointed out to her who liked to wear a cowboy hat every time he got intimate and had convinced two girls to let him get on their backs and ride them like horses before things could really get started. But the dick was great, everyone said, ten out of ten. Wild that someone so cringe could give it out so well, both girls had said.

"Do you think it makes me a bad person to keep hooking up with people?"

"Well, this one was only a kiss."

Jane nodded. "But it's not always that. And while I think it's fun, and I always have, you know, consent, it's still people's feelings." She paused. "I'm glad you're not one of those people who say 'Well, men do it all the time,' as if that means it's okay."

"Oh, I hate that as a justification. There are plenty of people who pull bullshit moves and get away with it. People deserve better."

Then, they decided the time for earnest conversations was over and instead discussed Jane's upcoming Halloween party. It would be the night of the holiday for once. A friend was making a punch that he called "Dracula's Draft," which felt very Midwestern mom.

Drinking a cup at the party, Ayanna thought nothing had tasted less to her like something a mom would make. It reminded her of whiskey and apples, and she was pretty sure she would feel undead in the morning. There were so many girls there dressed like sexy zombies, sexy rabbits with little tail puffs on bodysuits, or wearing onesie unicorn pajamas bought from the same big-box store. Jane was dressed as Sailor Neptune, wearing a green wig, a short green kilt, long white gloves, and ballerina flats that had ties up to her knees. A guy Ayanna had never seen before was very drunk and telling Jane if she ever wanted to try men, just for a weekend, please, please call him. Jane was telling him he was being annoying.

Ayanna had promised herself she wasn't going to drink too much or stay out for too long. The next day, she was having lunch with Marlie and the creative writing professor, who insisted that Ayanna call her Mere. Ayanna was scanning the crowd for Felix, who had refused to tell her what his costume would be.

"Are you Dionne Warwick?" a guy dressed as a cow asked.

"No, she's Aretha!"

"I'm Ronnie Spector, you guys," Ayanna said.

She adjusted her wig and boots and then got another cup. The party was already sloppy. There was someone on the porch throwing bottles into the street. Someone was smoking a cigarette and swigging straight from a vodka bottle in the corner. Ayanna realized she did not want to be that girl wandering a party looking for her potential crush and went back to the dance floor. The playlist was on a Rihanna song and people were treating it as an opportunity to do different poses rather than really dance. Stephen shuffled toward her, alternated between posing like his hands were a picture frame, posing like a bat, and laughing, then went back over to the girl he was flirting with that night.

Ayanna danced a little more before feeling a hand on her neck.

"Liana." She could feel warm breath, lips touch her ear.

"I'm here for you," he continued. "It's me, Vincent."

She turned, but no one was there. Ayanna leaned against the wall, googled, for what felt like the millionth time, *how do you get rid of a ghost?* The suggestions were, as always, wear silver at all times, have an exorcism, take acre and listen to a Prince album backward, where you'll hear that what sounds like music when played normally is just him praising God when played in reverse, chug holy water, find God, move into a new house, burn sage, pay reparations, accept it, go back to an old save in your *Sims* game and stop the neighbor from dying in your house. Ayanna went upstairs, got in the bathroom line behind a guy wearing a fedora and a suit and holding a fake cigar.

"I know you," Ayanna said. "You're the guy who got hit by the bike."

"You saved my life," he said. "Well, I mean, you made me feel better. But I can't stop thinking about the guy who touched my face."

"This is a weird question, but how did it feel?"

"Too hot. Like accidentally touching a skillet. I keep looking at my face, expecting burn marks."

Bike Guy was obviously a little wasted, but she was happy to see him alive and well. He showed her how there were still some scrapes on his arms. He talked about how he hadn't even seen the bike coming, how one minute he was listening to his headphones and then he was on the sidewalk. It felt like he thought dying might happen like, you're upright, then you're on the ground and you don't know what's going on.

"Did you call your friend?"

"I did," he said, "and then chickened out and instead we talked about this movie we had both seen."

"What's your name?"

"Turner. I have a fancy mom."

"You can't even nickname that."

"People try and it's always a mess. What's your name?"

"Ayanna."

"I'm glad we got to see each other again. Seeing you, knowing your name, it makes what happened feel more real."

There was a beat where they both looked ahead to see how long the line was taking.

"Anyway," Ayanna said, deciding to let alcohol guide her decision-making, "you're clearly in love with that girl. You should tell her."

Turner drained the beer he was holding. "What we have right now is also important to me. And it's not like I think it will ruin everything to say something. I'm not that kind of person where if she doesn't feel the same way, I'll have a grudge. But I also like where I am now. I like having a crush, I like how I am right now. I don't want to change. That's what I learned from getting hit by a bike. I walked home and realized, whoa, I'm happy right now. Not about getting hit by a bike, but in general."

Ayanna felt this was unexpectedly wise, but also a little annoying. They exchanged numbers, Turner promising to let her know if anything as weird happened to him ever again. One of his friends stopped to chat and Turner pointed her out as "the girl who saved my life." It was embarrassing when he said it and it felt worse when his friend smiled and said, "You're famous."

"Turner, if you were being haunted, like by a weird ghost, not a chill ghost, what would you do to get rid of it?" Ayanna tried to say it like she was asking a fun, offbeat question.

"Ask what it needs and try to do it. And if that doesn't work, I guess shoot it with a silver bullet."

"That's werewolves," Ayanna said.

"Wear a cross all the time," said Turner's friend, "and hold it up at it every time it appeared and yell 'Get out of here.'"

Finally, the line moved. Everyone booed or catcalled the couple who had been hooking up in the bathroom as they walked out smug and disheveled, and after her turn, Ayanna had lost Turner to the party. It was one of those off-campus houses only rich kids could afford. Three bedrooms on this floor, one in which a bunch of people were clearly smoking weed, another with the door slightly open and where four girls were gossiping while all dressed like sexy bats. The party wasn't making her feel connected to anyone, but there was a pleasure in walking around, sipping a glass of punch, and watching so many people trying to have a capital-*E* Experience. She was not in the mood to try dancing again and was not drunk enough to enjoy most of the conversations happening around her. Ayanna knew having breakfast with Jane and Stephen and Felix the next day would be more fun for her; they had already planned on it. As she watched two girls from the soccer team making out while dressed as witches, one smearing green face paint on the other, Ayanna was pleased to have some gossip. For a while, she tried to find Stephen, who was texting her after their brief encounter on the dance floor, but every time she glimpsed him, he either was in a group or was flirting with a girl who was clearly there as All-I-Want-for-Christmas-Is-You Mariah Carey. Every time she moved through the thickest parts of the crowd, Ayanna felt a mouth near her ear, a hand touch her arm or graze the small of her back. It was impossible to tell if it was just being accidentally touched in a packed space or if he was there, messing with her. Finally, while she was in the backyard, splitting a joint with some people she recognized from the postmodernism seminar, including Lisa's friend who kept giving her significant looks and their biggest smiles, and trying to feel less anxious—I hate David Salle, one of them said in her most sophisticated voice, I will lose my shit if we have to talk about what he's making us feel again—Felix found her.

"This party is too cool," he complained. "Do you want to take a walk?"

"What are you?" she said, looking his costume up and down.

"Sasuke Uchiha."

He was wearing khaki shorts with leggings under them, a half-zipped dark fleece that he had cut at the elbows, a headband, and some elaborate bindings and wraps around his arms and wrists.

"I'll send you my personal *Naruto* and *Shippuden* mixes," he said. "Perfect winter viewing when the weather sucks."

"I feel like I haven't seen you in forever," he continued.

She didn't know what to say to that. It was true. "I kept trying to find you, but it's packed."

"You didn't answer my emails or texts," he said. "Sorry. That sounded needy."

Ayanna finished her drink in a glug, held on to the cup. "Can I ask you a personal question?"

Felix nodded, guided her beyond the party's remnants out into the cold, blue night. The streetlamps were orange on this side of town, and a few people had decorated for the holiday with string lights wrapped around porches, and one house with a seven-foot-tall ghost wailing and watching all comings and goings with glittering red eyes.

"Why are you working with Professor Collins?"

He cleared his throat. Ayanna offered him her arm, and he looped his own through it. The breeze played with Felix's costume, making him seem bigger as he started talking.

"Seven years ago—on May seventeenth—I died."

21

Felix Wilson was fifteen, well-liked and well-hated because he was the type of kid who was good at everything. Easygoing, on the track team where he ran the two-hundred- and four-hundred-meter hurdles, vice president of the Film Club where he earned his one and only week of detention for screening Spike Lee's *Do the Right Thing* and then John Singleton's *Boyz n the Hood* after already being warned that all film choices had to be approved by the club's academic adviser. He wanted to be a filmmaker. Weekends spent watching movies and writing in a black notebook, sometimes making embarrassing movies with his friends, and wanting to cultivate an appreciation of light. To be great, you couldn't just care about movement, about finding the right script, about the right actors, you had to know about color and what it made people feel.

Other things he wanted Ayanna to know: at that time, he had braces, he went to the fancy art school on scholarship, it was pretty white, but it was the place where he got to take the AP classes his parents cared so much about, and he got to write his scripts, have his nerdy little discussions about how Michael Mann uses sound, and think deeply about the ways the length of scenes isn't just about disseminating information, but about establishing time, emotion, and tone.

"I was insufferable," he said.

"I think you have to be when you're younger, if you want anything *big*," Ayanna said. She winced thinking of herself reading books about cartography, the way she sometimes drew imagined worlds instead of taking notes in high school. "There's something about cultivating obsessions, maybe?"

"Maybe," Felix said. He took a breath and puffed out into the night as if exhaling from a cigarette.

The week before he died, there had been a weird energy around school. Fights were breaking out. Everyone was still disagreeing on the number. Felix felt certain there had been nine broken up and noted in the register, but as many as fifteen that the teachers didn't know about. All the adults shrugged it off as boys, even art-school boys, just getting wild sometimes. It didn't feel like that to Felix. There was a mean humidity in the hallways and in the parking lot and on the gym floor.

Felix said, "I had a good friend, Amir, who believed in all sorts of woo shit. Amir was the only teenage boy I knew reading tarot cards, he wore an evil eye all the time looped around his wrist. He went to cemeteries and recorded audio, listening for the sound of ghosts. Amir said all this, the unrest, the unhappiness, it was because of a ghost or a curse. If it was a curse, his grandma could come and do a ritual sometime. A ghost, one seeping out anger, well, that was worse. It reminds me of what you told me about your dorm room."

Ayanna moved a little closer to him, both for the heat and to let herself feel a little thrilled by the way they were touching, the way he was confiding in her. There were still packs of people walking around, moving from party to party. They stopped to gawk at a group of people dressed as sexy Mushroom Kingdom. The girl dressed as Waluigi was truly beautiful, over six feet tall, clomping in her large black boots, playing with the large fake mustache she had pasted to her face. They both agreed it made them uncomfortable, and for a little while, because Ayanna was a little buzzed, their conversation digressed into a consideration of what made a good Halloween costume. When they agreed to disagree about a formula of pleasing yourself, potential sexiness or discomfort, and whether punning was fun or obnoxious, they returned to Felix's story.

He told Ayanna on the night of May 11, he and Amir talked on the phone for a long time. Most of the conversation was about *The 400 Blows*. They felt like the movie's title was cooler than the actual movie, but there was still a lot to talk about. It seemed dated in some ways, and so, so white, but there was also something in it that they both keenly thought spoke to how they felt being in mostly white schools, of having classmates and teachers who sometimes didn't see them, saw only their expectations of how intelligent they should be. Together, they had a three-hundred-movie-deep list to watch and discuss. Amir wanted to be a screenwriter and director; Felix sensed they were always dancing around the fact that they wanted to make movies together for the rest of their lives, but saying it aloud, affirming the feeling, wasn't masculine. Both of their parents had big ideas about how men should be, and they felt that hovering around all their interactions was a hand always pulled back to swat them into place.

Ayanna could feel the weight of what he was saying. His tone was similar to her own whenever she talked about Olivia.

"I think about this all the time," Felix said, "how he kept saying 'I feel like we shouldn't go to school tomorrow.' He couched it in a *Star Wars* reference, 'I have a bad feeling about this.' And then we laughed, because we always had bad feelings about going to school."

They walked in silence. Leaves crunched and rustled beneath their feet. She weighed telling him he didn't have to keep talking if he didn't want to, but it was clear he wanted to talk about his friend.

"One of the strange things about memory is, I feel like I can remember almost everything he said, but thinking about it, I'm almost completely obliterated out. I know I wasn't sitting there silent, but every part of it is him."

His voice was quieter.

"On May seventeenth, I woke up and also felt like I shouldn't go to school. I'd had a dream I couldn't remember, but I woke up knowing it was about something very bad happening. My mom, of course, was like lol, is this a joke. You are going. And then we fought a little bit. I got to school early, met up with Amir in the library. His mom had also been the same way, lol, no, go to school. We continued storyboarding this movie, about a kid who meets an alien in the woods. It was deliberately supposed to feel like a knockoff of *E.T.*, then midway through the cute alien eats one of the kids and takes off toward prom. We were bickering about the sequence, about my ability to draw the alien in these moments. And out of the corner of my eye, I saw a kid wearing a black ski mask and a black T-shirt. I didn't even see the gun. Just the outfit was enough."

Ayanna stopped walking. Felix stopped too. He gripped Ayanna's hands but didn't look at her. His head was turned toward the house they were in front of. It was decorated for Halloween: purple lights, a wreath with glowing spiders, and carved pumpkins with flickering lights inside them. On the porch, a garland of plastic candles dangling in the air.

"I pushed Amir down, I felt like the wind had been knocked out of me, I think I heard the sound of the shot after some of the bullets had already hit me."

Felix's voice was shaky. Ayanna's heart was in her throat.

"I remember thinking this is such bullshit. And it was dumb, because it was like the thoughts I had in class when a teacher was being a power-tripping asshole, it made me almost want to laugh that I could think the same thing after being shot. And I thought maybe I had saved Amir, but he was bleeding too. And then I knew I might die at school, and the rest of their lives my parents would have to deal with the fact they were part of the my-kid-died-at-school club, and my brain moved so quickly when I was lying there bleeding. I know I heard some kids crying and calling to one another, gunshots, people yelling. Someone kept saying "Mom" until she was silent. But it felt like I was trying to think every thought I was ever supposed to have. Amir was talking but I could barely hear him. I know he said thank you, I know he said we should hide but neither of us was capable of moving."

Felix said then everything was dark, and he dreamed about climbing up a mountain made entirely of silver stones. He could not see what was below, except it was very, very blue. There was music in every stone, and maybe he was trying not to fall into the ocean. Felix was gripped by a feeling of needing constant momentum and if he stopped, he would sink back into all the blue, and would be devoured. Later, he would read about the doors and notice how many people who had gone through had written about similar experiences. "Was I dead? Was I elsewhere? I call it a dream, but I know it wasn't."

Ayanna wrapped his fingers between hers. He squeezed back. Down the street, someone yelled, "Is that a skunk?"

"When I woke up in the hospital room, it was almost August," Felix said. "My mom kept thanking Jesus, my dad wrote thank-you cards for every single person who came into my room, from the surgeons to the hospital cleaning staff. At one point, I had died for three minutes. I had been in medically induced comas, there were times where I had been awake, but I didn't remember them."

"Your friend?"

"I didn't save him."

She could hear Felix was crying, and Ayanna felt guilty for even asking the obvious question.

"Anyway, for a long time, I felt like a part of me didn't come back from the experience. My therapist said it's not unusual to feel like that when you go through a big traumatic experience. You feel a divide, you mourn who you used to be; if you lost someone in the event, you feel guilty for mourning yourself when you should only be thinking about the person you lost. You want to move on, you don't want to move on."

"I know. When my sister—" Ayanna's throat shut. Then they were hugging and crying on the sidewalk. Down the street a mechanical witch cackled. Wind gusted. Felix's eyes were so big, dark, and sad. And when they were done crying, they were looking at each other, and there was a question between them. Ayanna nodded and tilted her head up, and they kissed each other softly, and Ayanna hoped it was fine her mouth tasted like salt and weed and whiskey. Felix's mouth was a little salty, but she didn't mind.

"Anyway, when I heard about Professor Collins's work, I wondered if it would help me get to speak to Amir again. And I wondered if somehow, I would maybe be able to find that piece of myself again. And I still get really scared sometimes in classrooms. I'm doing some of this as an independent study."

They were holding hands and walking down the street. A giddy part of Ayanna was thinking, *This is the first time I've ever walked down the street holding his hand.* Another part of her was melancholy, wondering if on some level, the attraction between them was because they sensed each other's grief, the connection she felt to him might only be based on their shared sorrow, and now that they had been real with each other, nothing between them would ever be truly fun or sexy or all the things she also wanted from her first adult relationship. His hand was warm, his fingernails were short, and his fingers were so much bigger than her own. She felt how nice it was to have a hand gripping hers with care. How even something as small as this could give her an insight into him. Before they walked into the party, Felix stopped Ayanna and kissed her again.

This time, a real one, the kind of kiss she could tell Jane about and not feel as if she were betraying something private and fragile between her and Felix. Ayanna knew Jane would say something like "The affairs of straight people do not concern me," but would then ask for more details. It wasn't only the feeling of kissing someone Ayanna had been longing for on and off for the past six weeks, it was the feeling of being so intimate with someone who felt truly important to her. There was a sense that no matter what happened, whether things became serious between them or they forged a new friendship that reckoned with this night, here was an experience with someone whom she would always consider tenderly. It was a choice Ayanna wanted to always make in her romantic life, to only feel for those willing to be vulnerable.

The music cut and the lights went out. People screamed in a this-is-fun way and then realized as the darkness persisted, it was not done for the purpose of sexy shenanigans. Ayanna and Felix walked into the house, Felix said he knew where the breaker was. A man's voice was yelling, "Liana, Liana, once a cheater, always a cheater. Liana." It smelled terrible. Rotting meat again, spilled beer, and the smell of too many people sweating and cheap Halloween makeup chemicals.

If she were dealing with a still-living man acting like this, Ayanna knew she would not acknowledge him, tell all her friends what he was doing and what he looked like, and ask them to keep him from her. She would go to the campus center around sexual violence and ask them for help in figuring out how to make herself completely locked down and invisible on the internet. It seemed impossible to do these things to a ghost.

Ayanna crossed her arms. She made her way back through the crowd in the now semidark, people were turning on their phone flashlights, a small group of people were looking for candles to light, and there was music coming from one of the upstairs rooms. She had the urge to go home, hoping the spirit would follow her, rather than continue to trouble all these people. But wasn't that what he wanted? For her to be alone, to hope to force her isolation into a shape that would make her think he was the only person she could depend on.

In the darkness, with only the light coming from the spirit, a light she assumed only she could see, Ayanna whispered once, twice, a third time: "Go home and be at rest."

She went upstairs and brought the music, the Bluetooth speaker, and the people still willing to dance downstairs. The playlist on the kid's phone was actually good. Songs at the right tempo that most people could follow, solid remixes, a few kitschy Halloween songs, and Ayanna thought the only thing that felt truly right in this moment was to join them. It was hard at first, despite the room's lighting; Ayanna was self-conscious, felt like she was always moving on the ones and threes, and despite the lightness she felt when running or chasing a ball and reading the movements of others around her, the dance floor felt like it was an obstacle course. Whispered it again and again as she danced, "go home and be at rest." Then, she drank some more beer, went back, and they were playing a song she always associated with her dad.

A rap song that for years he would put on every time he'd had a hard day and still needed to cook. Something about the first beats always eased his shoulders, and by thirty-five seconds in, he wouldn't just be seasoning meat or chopping vegetables, but dancing, moving his head, letting the beat move to his torso, spin and twirl him around, making him wonderful, making him embarrassing, making him all body and shedding everything but the pleasure he felt in being able to dance in his own home. And some of the happiest moments of her life had been in that kitchen with him, Ayanna trying to dance while passing him the garlic, laughing at the moves he was trying to pull, inventing the moves they called "chop-chop," "soup shuffle," and "low simmer."

And then, Jane was on the dance floor, and she seemed to only know how to dance by mostly staying still and doing handwork, sometimes moving all the way to doing hot-girl-in-a-music-video where she moved her torso and butt slowly and waved her hands over her head. Ayanna was bobbing, drinking from her friend's cup, and more and more people were gathering on the floor again, some graciously setting up their phones so that the flashlights made it a dance floor and not a potential comic swamp of people bumping into one another. Felix was there, and unfortunately for Ayanna's tender heart, he was a good dancer, someone who could look happy and confident, and he spun Ayanna and a laugh burbled out of her mouth, so relaxed and happy, when had she ever sounded like that before, and the party grew wings again and became one where you could feel people's desire to only care about pleasure and to get it from moving, from laughing, from playing together.

First, the orange string lights flickered on around the dance floor, and only a few people noticed, then the kitchen, and then for a moment they all turned on so bright everyone winced before settling back into their ordinary lumens. Some noticed the return and applauded, but most continued on dancing.

On the walk home—Felix's arm a warm weight across her shoulders, Jane click-clacking on the uneven sidewalk while laughing and swaying with two girls from the soccer team—Ayanna shut her eyes and let herself be guided for a few moments by Felix's warmth and certainty. She knew these streets; she didn't know the last time she had felt loose like this or cared for like this. Ayanna's eyes watered. Blinking away tears, she opened her eyes, and moving down the street was a great current of spirits. Bright pink and weaving together, pouring from the older buildings, leaking from the tree branches and bark, slithering out of grates. The streetlamps dim in comparison, the night's black sharper. Even the moon's remaining slivers of this cycle were shadowed pink. The moon, too, was filled with its own dead. The way the spirits shifted from light and cloud- and human-shaped to so many other things that they once had been or, maybe, would someday be. Later, Ayanna would wonder if this was the first time she saw a spirit and didn't feel her heart aching for it to be Olivia.

"Can you see them?" she whispered to Felix.

"I can never see them without the board," he said. "But there's a feeling in the air. Often when they're around, I think the air feels a little warmer, a little thicker."

"There's so many. And the way they're moving—" She paused and moved in even closer. "It's like a dance."

"Do you ever wish you couldn't see them?"

She shook her head. They were close enough that she could hear some were singing. Bird voices, person voices, horse voices, and something so gravelly, maybe it was the spirit of a mountain or earth that had died years before people had even been a part of the universe's considerations.

"I'm tired of not wanting to be me," Ayanna said. "But, hearing them, seeing them, I feel like I'm half here. Alive. And half dead. I mean you know how it is." A relief to know that was true. "When someone you love dies, a part of you does die with them. And then you wait to be resurrected."

"Time helps," Felix said. His voice so soft she almost missed the words.

The wind blew. She knew soon they would be in his warm apartment. He would keep her feeling safe and seen enough for her to say yes over and over through the rest of the night's dregs. Ayanna walked slower. She raised her left arm and let it slide through the spirits as she walked. They felt like nothing, but they spiraled and slid back together again and again. The spirits opened their mouths and sang. Then, the trees, the dying grass poking up between slats in the sidewalk, the birds, even the clouds joined in. Ayanna understood almost every word. The hair on her arms stood at full attention. The song was in her heart and lungs. She walked, letting it be her guide, her body moving to its rhythm.

22

Marlie Evans was wearing an oversized navy blazer that made her look even smaller with her fingers just poking out. Pure-white short-cropped hair, a gap in her teeth, and an attitude, in general, like she was always looking for something to enjoy. On her porch were a sweet potato pie and cups of coffee. She insisted on being called Marlie, not Miss Marlie, as Ayanna had initially addressed her. The *miss* made her feel old.

"You are too lonely, Meredith," she was chiding the creative writing professor. "I read your books and think: this woman needs to have fun."

"I have fun." She put a dab of whipped cream on top of a piece of pie.

"No," Marlie said simply. "You don't."

"I write literature," Meredith said. "I spend my life looking at life's complications."

Marlie laughed. "I read romance novels about interracial relationships that deal with politics and pleasure. They feel more like real life to me than the last story you sent me."

Ayanna watched them go back and forth while sipping her coffee. It was strong, and while it was doing nothing to make her feel less hungover, here was another pleasure, to watch these two disagree, to sit on a small porch and be happy the leaves were still clinging to the trees, and to look down the block and see what jack-o'-lanterns had survived the night before. The women were arguing, but it felt like being around a mother and daughter who had a malleable relationship moving between familial to platonic to bantering. Ayanna had a low tolerance for bickering, but there was something about watching an eighty-two-year-old obliterate a thirty-five-year-old that made her heart sing.

"I read your books and everyone is having bad sex. Everyone is getting hate-crimed in big and small ways. That's what my niece calls it, 'hate-crimed literature.' Feels a little too cute to me, but I can't stop saying it now. Your next book better be more fun. You keep thinking about these negative things all the time; it's going to hurt your soul."

Meredith rolled her eyes. "Thanks, Goodreads."

"What?"

"Nothing." Meredith took a big bite of pie. It was clear to Ayanna that it infuriated her that it was so good. If she was less nervous, Ayanna would have trolled both women by asking "Can any literature be good if it was written for profit?" She didn't even believe in the question, but Ayanna knew it would set them both on a wild argument.

"The pie is delicious," Ayanna said instead. "I like the marshmallow topping."

"I like you," Marlie said. She told Ayanna about the history of her book club, how all her friends seemed like they were looking for something to talk about that wasn't kids or men. And the easiest thing seemed to be books. She told Ayanna the secret to getting older and enjoying it was to always give herself time to talk to friends about everything, not just hard things, not just small talk. "We still talked about our children, our loves, we all did. But we talk about the world, how we feel, we disagree, we eat well, and books gave us the space."

Ayanna felt certain she was absolutely joining this book club, while feeling her anxieties about asking Marlie about Valerie ratcheting up.

"You look like you have something serious going on in there," Marlie said.

"This is going to make me sound crazy," Ayanna said. "Sorry, I mean make me sound wild. But I have a message for you from a woman named Valerie."

Marlie was nonplussed. "I've known a lot of Valeries over the years."

"She's one who died when you were twenty-one."

"What do you mean?"

"Can we go inside for a little bit?"

IN MARLIE'S SHOES-OFF HOME, the carpet was marshmallow-thick. On the living room floor, Ayanna spread out the board and placard from the project. Meredith, as Ayanna now had to think about the professor, was lighting candles. Ayanna wrote Valerie's name on a piece of paper over and over, with one variation: I am in the same room as Marlie. Felix had recommended it as part of the process. At breakfast, he said the only time he had gotten Amir to talk to him was by doing this.

She nodded, grateful for the advice. There was a moment when she stopped herself from asking if talking to Amir had given Felix closure. Ayanna had decided instead to trust he would tell her when he was ready. She also wasn't sure if closure was something she actually wanted and didn't want to have that conversation. Ayanna wanted to reach a point where she could think about Olivia every day without feeling guilt or recriminations; she wanted to keep her sister close. Closure still felt to her like being able to forget Olivia ever happened.

Marlie walked over and sat close to Ayanna, looked at what she was writing, and held out her hands to her. They were cold and soft in Ayanna's own, her fingernails were painted a pink that seemed barely worth the effort because they looked so close in shade to the matrixes of Ayanna's own nails. Why paint your nails fingernail-pink?

"I've been waiting sixty years for this," Marlie said as they looked down at the board and placard together. In the corner of the room, a pink mist was forming; soon, Ayanna knew, it would be a woman, eager to say her truth.

"You never got over it?" Ayanna asked. "Even after sixty years."

For the first time, Marlie looked sad. Old. "No one ever told you that you're not supposed to get over grief?"

The mist continued to take shape, a hand forming on the left, a head forming with long hairs sprouting.

"You don't get over it," Marlie said. "You let it shape you. You don't let it metastasize in you." She struggled on the word *metastasize*, had to repeat it before Ayanna realized what she was saying. "You appreciate that you could love someone or something so hard. You promise to keep living your life loving hard."

Before Ayanna could respond, or know how to respond, Valerie was there. Fully formed, beautiful and young, tinted pink, but looking mostly like a person.

She sat on the floor between them, took each of their hands. Valerie's and Marlie's eyes were locked on each other. Both were smiling.

"We loved each other when we were girls but couldn't be together," they said in unison.

"When we were twenty-two," Valerie said, her voice with a hint of static woven between each word, "we went swimming at night together."

And Ayanna could see them. Younger, laughing and splashing water at each other. Old them on one side of the room; behind, young them just as real and whole. Looking around to make sure no one noticed them and gently kissing. Neither had a swimsuit, they were both wearing what looked like T-shirts and underwear. They were clearly in love. Especially Marlie. Young her was looking at Valerie with a soft look in her eyes. They kissed goodbye; Marlie had to be home because her mother was strict and perceptive. Valerie wanted to swim more. She didn't care about her hair or if she got in trouble. She didn't care that Marlie said it was unsafe to swim alone. What she wanted was to feel the water on her body. Ayanna's teeth were chattering, her tongue felt dry in her mouth, but still she continued to see. Valerie hit her head on a rock while swimming. She screeched, held it. The skin hadn't been broken. She tried to shake it off, keep swimming. It was clear she was disoriented. And then, she went under.

"Oh," Ayanna said, and looked away. All of that was gone. She was back in Marlie's living room, the two—spirit and woman—holding hands.

The creative writing professor excused herself and went out to the yard. Ayanna couldn't tell what she was thinking, what she could or could not see.

"I thought your parents found out and made you leave. I thought you were scared and decided to take off. I thought so many things," Marlie said.

"I'm sorry," Valerie said. "I wanted to live a full life with you. It felt impossible then, but I wanted it. I wanted to be your wife."

"I've loved you my entire life," Marlie said.

Ayanna looked between them. It felt so painfully unfair. Around the room were pictures from Marlie's life. There were grandchildren and two pictures from a wedding day. She had married a man, but later in life, a woman who had eyes that looked like there was always a joke in them. Minutes ago, she had told Ayanna, "You keep loving things hard," and here was the evidence in each frame.

"You don't have to wait for me," Marlie said to Valerie.

"I needed you to know the truth. I wanted you to know I would never leave without saying goodbye."

Marlie reached out and took Valerie's face in her hands. "It's rude of you to come here looking like this, while I look like this now." Valerie let go of Ayanna and reached for Marlie's face, holding her cheeks.

"It's rude of you to say that. I wish I could have wrinkles. I wish I could've spent years of my life sitting on that porch with you."

Then, Valerie started to fizz and crackle. Both reached out and kept a hand on Ayanna's wrists.

"We won't take all your time," Marlie said.

"No, take as much as you need," Ayanna said. "And if you want, I can put in earbuds, so you can talk privately."

They spent most of the time just looking at each other. Marlie sometimes told Valerie things about her life. Valerie spoke a little about what might be next, how despite everything, it was beautiful. But mostly, they smiled and gazed into each other's eyes, sometimes Marlie teared up, sometimes they laughed.

Ayanna tried to look away but couldn't. She was seeing something important here, something worth learning.

Once, the spirit sang of two mountains that were kin. One silver, one gold. When they were born, they arose from the same womb of magma, heat, dirt. Time pulled them farther and farther apart. Their mother was all the soil and rock, a daughter of the spirit. She loved Silver and nurtured her as best she could. Gold was always out of her sight; of her body, but not of her heart.

The mother went to visit the spirit because her favorite daughter was falling apart slowly and surely from wind and rain. The spirit was building rivers and piecing together oceans. It worked slow while the mother spoke.

"And what of your other daughter?" the spirit asked when she was done.

When the soil and rock could not speak of Gold, the spirit sang that your love must not be like a net, letting some of your catch fall through. Your love must be as firm as a clasped fist. If you cannot love like this, you do not know love.

PART THREE

23

It was a perfect summer Saturday. Felix was finally home after a trip to visit his parents. In the car, he kept doing an imitation of his dad complaining about *Star Wars*. We watched six *Star Wars* movies in six days, Ayanna, and he hated every single one. The bakery across the city had no line for once. They were obsessed with the silky quiche with firm peas in it, the biscuits with za'atar, and sludgy coffee. The waitress kept talking about how hot it was going to be, but in the Midwestern way where yes, it was small talk, but also an acknowledgment about how inside each of them was still a little February frost that needed melting.

"I can't believe we've been doing this for thirteen years," Felix said while they sat at the little round table.

Ayanna had been talking to him about a book she was reading about the Ming treasure voyages. Every time she read about any expedition, she couldn't stop thinking about traveling for months just to get to one place and knowing it was a place where you would probably die. Wasn't it a miracle anyone was alive? How could people write books about these voyages and write dull email-style sentences? Treasure hunting was, to put it lightly, problematic, but she was there for the thrill of it.

"I've been talking about this book for ten minutes max," Ayanna said. She was never comfortable reflecting on their years together.

He ignored her attempt to push away sentimentality. "Us." He pointed at himself, then her. "This, bobo."

They had taken to calling each other "bobo" because Ayanna could not stop watching a clip of one of her favorite soccer players saying "Que miras, bobo." A friend had told them it was the equivalent of calling someone "dummy." It always made her laugh because it felt like the most perfect word for dummy and it was funny to hear Felix—someone who people always described as kind or gentle—call her a dummy in Spanish.

"Ayanna, you're my best friend."

The tone in his voice made her pay more attention. She set her fork down.

"Let's get married," he said.

On her plate was still a chunk of quiche crust and a few errant peas. The espresso machine sounded like it was going to explode. *I can't promise anything*, she thought. She wished the bakery were playing music, something she could use to pretend she couldn't hear what was being said.

"We've been together for over a decade." He reached across the table for her hand. "And I want to make it clear, you don't have to answer. And I could do it more formally. And I know that you have complicated—"

"Can we talk about this somewhere else?"

He nodded. Felix stood up, went to the counter to pay, and came back with a bag. Ayanna knew inside it would be the strawberry-lemon-basil scone she had been coveting and a piece of carrot cake with tahini buttercream frosting. Outside, without talking about it, they walked toward the park they liked to go to after eating at the bakery. A dad was walking around with his son draped over his shoulders and holding on to his head. The boy kept raising his hands up to pull and push on leaves. Gourmet Harvest's parking lot was packed. A white man with dreadlocks was playing the guitar beautifully and singing in an off-key voice that made everything seem like a terrible premonition. A spirit bobbed near his open guitar case. It was maybe the only one enjoying the music.

At the park, Felix turned toward Ayanna, and immediately apologized. "Sorry, I shouldn't have done that."

"No, don't apologize." She crossed her arms. Uncrossed them because she felt like crossing them made her seem like she wanted to fight. "I want to say that I trust and love you. More than I thought was possible for me."

Felix set the bag down. Stepped toward her.

"I know you're uncomfortable with the idea. But you're already my wife. That's how I think of you," he said. "We've been together so long and it always feels so intense and new. Each conversation. Each kiss. Each touch. And I want you to be officially my family."

"I love you," Ayanna said. She took a step back. Her voice had been so small.

Felix shook his head. "It's the doors, right?"

The pain of being known so well, the gift of being known so well. Her back was already sweating from the day's heat. It was only past ten.

"You want to be able to go if they ever come back."

Ayanna nodded. "I want to tell you you're wrong."

IN HER MIDTWENTIES, the phone ringing at three in the morning often meant Jane had been out partying or Jane was in Europe and was hoping Ayanna was still awake so they could hear each other's voices; someone was missing her, someone wanted sex, someone was drunk. All those nights, the electric annoyance of seeing 3:30 a.m. on her phone, then shaking it off to feel the pleasure of here, in this time, where someone should be resting, here she was, Ayanna, still on their minds. In her thirties, it had slowed into the cliché: someone had died. That night after meditating as always on Olivia, Ayanna was dreaming, as she had been for the past week, of walking in a city that did not exist because it was a jumble of her childhood hometown, the city where she had gone to college, and a small European city filled with beautiful white buildings with facades that had carvings of men's faces peering down with judgmental, wide eyes at those walking. As always, one of the carved men was singing but stopped when she looked at its face. The ground shook, Ayanna stooped and curled up like a pill bug. In the dream, she thought: I'm going to die. Everything shook and shook, windows shattered, then the singing started again. People sat up, brushed themselves off, and went about their business. Ayanna stayed on the ground. Her phone rang again, making the nightstand rattle. She reached for it, still mostly asleep.

This time, it was Stephen calling her. Her heart worried that somehow it would be a call about Jane, even though they had texted hours before. There was still a possibility, though, that Stephen was drunk or high and wanted to tell her about a record he had listened to or complain about another listing romance.

"My dad died," he said when she answered the phone.

Before she could say anything else, he continued. "I want you to come to the funeral. But it's going to be weird old-rich-white-guy stuff."

She had never heard him sound like this. Stephen was speaking slowly, his voice creaking from emotional weight. They had known each other for almost a third of their lives now but the things she knew about Stephen's father could be summarized as: he was very rich, he had been married four times but twice to the same woman, who was not Stephen's mom, he was a white dad who was willing to see Black women as desirable but not willing to consider the complications of raising a Black son, he did not like that Stephen referred to himself as Black and thought it was a way to erase "his contributions as a parent," and thought most minorities "should just get over it and stop complaining," and he had season tickets to Pistons games. Oh, and he was a phenomenal gift giver. The man had met Ayanna three times, but because she was important to Stephen he had added her to his Christmas list. Last year, he'd sent Ayanna a luxury perfume from Ireland that was hard to find in the United States. She'd resented being sent a scent—too personal—but now wore it out to dinner or to events she deemed "nice." The year when Stephen had graduated, he had given their entire friend group a trip to a cabin he owned on the Oregon coast. A place with a hot tub, fifteen bottles of good red wine waiting for them, and an exorbitant Tillamook gift basket. It was a trip Ayanna thought about every time depression told her she had no friends: walking on a beach just talking wild bullshit with Stephen, kissing Felix below an ancient tree, and sitting in the hot tub with Jane late at night and pointing at clouds and stars.

Stephen told her when and where, said his dad had left funds for people to use to attend the funeral if they needed it, and kept saying, "It was unexpected."

"I'll be there."

She listened to his breathing.

"When my sister." Ayanna paused, still uncomfortable saying the word, especially to other people who had just lost someone. "I was desperate to hear people talk about her, and then whenever they talked about her, it reminded me that she was gone, and I resented them for it."

"Yeah, I really don't want to talk about it."

Ayanna wondered if he wanted to ask her about the work she was doing. If he was going to ask her whether she could help him speak to his father one last time.

"Can I tell you something fucked up?"

"Yes, of course." Ayanna switched her phone to her other ear. She shifted in the bed, winced at the creak of it. This was the call-and-response of their friendship. Phone calls, glasses of wine, a walk in a beautiful park, filled with "fucked-up things" brimming up to Stephen's lips and Ayanna's eagerness for that level of vulnerability.

"Whenever I'm sad like this," Stephen said, sounding more like his normal self, just a little distant, "where I know I'm feeling the emotion, where I know why I'm feeling the emotion, but still I'm not consumed by it, I think of this messed-up thing a kid used to do in high school. I was in all the nerd classes, and this white kid in my AP English class would call me a 'tragic mulatto' whenever he saw me like looking out a window for a minute or listening to my headphones by myself."

"That's a very literary way to bully."

"It started with this really bad lecture by our teacher about Faulkner and how 'the tragic mulatto was an important literary trope.' But she was also talking in a way where you could easily think, 'Oh, this white lady really doesn't believe in race-mixing.' It was one of those things that like years later you have the distance to say 'That was fucked,' but when you're a teenager and you're used to being in a classroom with an adult who hasn't done much planning for good and bad reasons, and they just need to fill the day, and you're also just kind of checked out because one thirty p.m. at high school is like being under light anesthesia."

Ayanna nodded. She remembered he couldn't see her and said, "Yeah."

"But for all my senior year, this kid would call me that in passing whenever I seemed a little melancholy, and today, I thought about it again, how I was kind of just looking into the void after hearing about my dad and thought that and started laughing."

Ayanna wasn't sure what to say.

"I wanted to tell you because if I told Jane, she wouldn't care about the circumstances. She would be like, 'Stephen'"—and he did an imitation of Jane doing a tirade, which while sounding nothing like her actual voice did have her exact cadence and tone—"'finding things like that funny at all feels like you are siding with oppression.' And Felix is Felix. I tell him something like this and he's so nice and finds a gentle way to remind me that if I'm carrying things like this with me, maybe I should talk to someone and analyze why this is something I'm still hanging on. But you."

It was embarrassing for Ayanna how eagerly she wanted to know how her friend perceived her. She balled her own toes into fists, held them, even though they cracked, as a slight punishment.

"I like you because when I do something really bad, you call me back in, but most of the time, I feel like you want me to be myself."

"I like knowing you," Ayanna said. "When I'm friends with someone, I want to know all of them. Not just the cute parts."

"Yeah, and that's why I'm glad you're still in my life. You have the gift of making me feel liked."

They talked for ten more minutes, about a show Stephen had seen where an artist had made cakes out of metal and assault rifles out of cake and while it seemed very stupid at the time, well, here he was telling her about it, how when his mother had FaceTimed him to say his father was gone, she was wearing one of those Korean face masks, and he could tell she had forgotten that she was wearing it, how she was so upset he couldn't say anything about it, but how disturbing it was to see only her eyes, and how big and frightening they looked against the white papery substance, how she was crying, but the tears were disappearing into the skin-care slime of the mask. "It seemed like a weird prank at first," Stephen said.

Sometimes, when they spoke like this, Ayanna would remember the first time she had met him, he had been wearing a velvet blazer with no shirt on beneath it and would be tempted to laugh that somehow this person had become family.

Ayanna told him about how when her grandmother died, one of the last things she had said to Ayanna was, "You have to make a cake on my birthday every year and have a slice for me, but if it's one of those dumb vegetable cakes, chocolate zucchini, carrot, I will come back with a belt." She had never joked like that ever before with Ayanna, and because her grandmother had always been gentle and kind, they had laughed so hard that both felt it in their stomachs and throats, and then her grandmother had rolled over, said she was very tired, that she loved Ayanna, then died in her sleep five hours later.

"I know I'm going to be thinking about my mom in that sheet mask, telling me about my dad, for the rest of my life."

"I mean, me too, now."

They said good night and Stephen promised to text details after he had slept.

Ayanna got out of bed, walked down the hall without turning on the lights, and poked her head into the office. The lights were still on, Felix had fallen asleep on the couch, a book on his chest and papers and pen on the ground.

She crouched close to him. He smelled like her expensive moisturizer, the one he claimed never to use. "Felix."

His eyes fluttered. "Are you okay?"

"Your back is going to feel terrible in the morning."

"I write. My back always feels bad in the morning." She had heard him say it so many times now that she wondered if he had progressed to being able to say it in his sleep.

"Stephen's dad died."

Felix opened his eyes. This was one of her favorite things in the world, to get to see those big, dark eyes still soft with sleep and watch as they grew even softer when they focused in on her face. Whenever Ayanna noticed him looking at her this way, she knew it was working between them. How many people get looked at with such pleasure? There had been an excruciating year where they had broken up—her mental health had been bad, he'd been away at graduate school—where she had dated other people. Sometimes it was fun, sometimes it was sexy, sometimes it was consuming, but there seemed to be no one else on the entire planet who wanted her to feel as loved or desired as Felix wanted to make her feel. Then, it was clear he had registered what she said. Shook his head, his eyes suddenly wet. Felix sat up and looked at his phone, she sat on the small couch next to him and leaned her head on his shoulder.

"Are you going to help him talk to his dad?" Felix asked.

Ayanna sighed. Kept her eyes shut.

"I would, of course. But, I also don't want to. I kind of think it would change everything."

Felix leaned into her, rubbed his head against her shoulder. "You can say no. You don't have to do things that make you uncomfortable."

Ayanna shrugged away from him, stood up, and stretched her arms and shoulders. She could hear in his tone he wasn't just speaking about Stephen. The office was a mishmash of them. It worked because she was a civilized person who liked desks. He was a chaotic back destroyer who could only write with his butt on something soft and his back propped by huge pillows. In the bookshelves were all the black notebooks Ayanna had filled with her own automatic writing, with the things she remembered about the golden path, her write-ups of the memorable encounters she'd had with the dead, and the thank-you notes from people who claimed to feel some sort of peace from the encounter. A box filled with FOIA requests about government research on the doors, mostly blacked out, but every once in a while, a long glimpse into a different, more neutral view of her childhood.

A printout she had done of an internet thread about a mysterious woman who appeared to people that sometimes Ayanna allowed herself to fantasize was Olivia. She turned around and faced him.

"It's fine," she said, and immediately wished her voice had sounded more neutral. "I leave tomorrow anyway for work, and then, I guess, I'll fly straight from there."

For a brief second, Felix made a face Ayanna could only describe as "I'm making the same mistake again." Then, he nodded, smiled, and said they should go to bed.

24

On the plane, another dream about an earthquake, this time a city where every door was blue. If she opened the right one, Olivia would be on the other side. Ayanna had woken up with a start. She tried to watch a critically acclaimed television show about mean white people in the past keeping secrets from one another and being wittily cruel to one another. But she couldn't focus on it, even though almost every person on the show was beautiful. The door, the door. Her therapist had said maybe she was overvaluing her dreams. Sometimes, truly, they're just your brain processing the day. The more the dream recurred, the more Ayanna thought it was a vision. She did not want to tell her therapist that, though, because it sounded like the first step to being diagnosed with delusions of grandeur.

When watching TV did not take Ayanna away from her thoughts, she leaned her head against the plane's side, close to the small window. All her friends seemed to have felt an uplift when they hit their thirties. Stephen was killing it at work, Felix had sold a book based on his dissertation about fringe Black faith groups, and Jane was having a baby. They had all been lost and uncertain in their twenties, still made gestures toward having those feelings whenever Ayanna broached the subject, but Ayanna perceived them all as being mostly content.

They seemed to know how to create new things to want, how to enjoy the up-and-down progress of being alive. Ayanna felt like they were all coasting on their bikes, arms spread wide, and she was still trying to get her shoelaces unstuck from the gears. She knew, had articulated it in therapy—how she loved the formality and rigor of calling it "articulated"—that sometimes she was resentful of how Felix could move on from his grief. Yes, he had lost a friend, not a sister. But he had been through something deeply traumatic and loved living.

Felix kept a list of all the foods he wanted to try in his cell phone notes. He knew the names of the bakers and the owners of the bakery, was part of an experimental seeds exchange where he was trying to grow mythical-sounding blue beans, he chatted with Rose, the cashier at their closest Trader Joe's, about her terrible son-in-law, whom he had never met but whose off-the-grid misdeeds he knew all of and judged severely while buying his blue chips and chocolate-covered snacks, and was spending the summer learning how to skateboard because he had always wanted to be able to grind down a staircase's handrail and why not now. Felix genuinely wanted to see Ayanna grow old; he wasn't just being nice! Everything about life, even when it was explaining to an ER doctor that he was a grown man learning how to skateboard and that was why he had to get X-rays, made a part of his brain say "more, more, more." Ayanna saw that in his eyes instead of the embarrassment she would have felt. Meanwhile, Ayanna couldn't even look at pictures of rescue dogs because she knew her poor, dumb heart could not bear to love something that was certain to die before her. She knew for a fact there were children out in the world who were more sophisticated about death, grief, and love than she was. Beyond that, Ayanna often had to remind herself that anytime a person indulged in the process of emotional mathematics, jumping into ratios and equations to calculate someone else's sadness or lack thereof, it was only going to result in finding their own unhappiness.

It was lucky Ayanna hadn't paid for Wi-Fi on the plane. This high, this melancholy, she could see herself being tempted to drop in the group chat: Teach me how to be sustainably happy. Tell me how to live!! A bomb to drop among all the back-and-forths about the trip they were going to take before Jane had her first baby. When the flight was done, she bought an Auntie Anne's pretzel, told a spirit to reconsider spending eternity in an airport, and finally got a rideshare to pick her up. Everything will be fine, she told herself for, at least, the one thousandth time.

Most of the time, Ayanna's job thrilled her. She thought maybe it was the truest way to honor the spirit of her childhood ambitions to be an adventurer. Other people were now the universe's biggest frontiers to her. They were filled with mysteries and surprises, and the ability to come in, to help them connect with their lost or to examine why they thought they were haunted in some way, filled her with the old rush of wanting to see a sudden river or the desire to head all the way into the silver mountains or through the golden path's thickets. In people, there were always possibilities, if she was optimistic enough, if they were optimistic enough, for change. Anytime she felt worn down or cynical about dedicating herself to mediumship, Ayanna remembered the look on Marlie Evans's face when she'd said goodbye. How soft her eyes had been even though she was crying. "You've given me a peace I never imagined I could have," she'd said.

But this one was the kind of job Ayanna liked working the least, going to a beautiful historic home, doing some "rituals" to make a too-wealthy person feel better about the amount of money they had spent. White-saging a home felt too problematic to Ayanna, so she had created a ritual that involved what she called "sacred incense"—a scent she claimed was passed down from mother to daughter in her family but was actually an out-of-fashion designer brand's tomato-and-earth scent. She brought in white flowers and placed them around the house as offerings and asked the future homeowner to write a letter of peace and introduction to any spirits that might already be occupying the home.

For these events, Ayanna wore a uniform. Black pants, white shirt, a black blazer with birds, ladders, doors, eyes, and celestial elements embroidered on it. By far it was the most expensive item of clothing she owned but it felt necessary. Sometimes, she wore a wig over her natural hair, put on big fake eyelashes. Ayanna felt like the rich always wanted a capital-*E* Experience. They longed for faith that came with glamour and exclusivity. They had accumulated so much; they often didn't want to be in reality. Everything should feel composed and well lit, to make them feel that they were a distinguished director of living well. They should always feel a deep lie of complete and total control over their days.

In truth, few homes were haunted. The last home Ayanna had gone to where there was the serious presence of the dead was a thirtysomething-year-old movie star's home. He had been popular to a harrowing degree when Ayanna had been a teen, starring in films where he was always tortured by his big emotions and big love for a girl while dealing with his drunk mom or his criminally disturbed older brother or with the fact that he was a vampire or with the fact that he was secretly dying of tuberculosis. Even in his thirties, he was working, appearing as a troubled math genius or a musician who could only think by pushing his lustrous black wavy hair away from his forehead. His house had been filled with the spirits of lonely teens who had died loving him and who wanted to be with the actor for all of eternity. Somehow the actor had become slowly attuned to them, had told Ayanna that he could not sleep at night because he would feel hands stroking his hair, the brush of lips on his forehead, sometimes the feeling of a head pushed against his chest as if attempting to snuggle in. She had somewhat solved it by taking the movie star's manicured and well-moisturized hands between her own and calling all the spirits forward and organizing them into a fan club. The fan club president and the movie star struck a deal that one evening a month he would watch one of his own movies and comment on his feelings, speak his memories, and let them chastely lean their heads on his shoulders or their bodies against his long legs. Ayanna had been surprised by how chill he had been about the whole thing.

At this house, the owner was waiting for her. She looked vaguely familiar to Ayanna. The woman was very thin, wearing leggings and a large, oversized men's silk shirt. Blond with light blue eyes, and Ayanna felt certain she had maybe scrolled past this woman on social media talking about the power of celery juice or about how her skin was so clear because she drank a "tea" of hot water, apple cider vinegar, and lemon juice every afternoon.

"Before we start the ritual," Ayanna said, "tell me about the house. What made you certain it was haunted?"

Especially because this was the South, Ayanna expected the usual borderline racist nonsense that the owners heard slaves clanking and shuffling along the hallway. It was the trend lately. Now that there was a willingness to even consider slavery as something that might have had an impact on the present, a new flavor of white people who appeared to be obsessed with absolving themselves of inherited sins seemed to have emerged. They appeared to have only two contexts for Black people in the US, their imagined ideas of what slaves were and those of the popular filmmakers and writers whose focus was the enslaved people of the United States. She was tired of walking through a house that was large and unattainable and being asked by these people to banish any potential trace of a Black person who might have a claim on it. What made white people so certain that the people who had been enslaved hadn't had their fill of dealing with white people? Maybe, Ayanna would think as she threw white flowers around those spaces, just maybe, those ancestors were relishing in the rest and peace they deserved.

"I think my brother is here," the woman said.

Oh, Ayanna thought, and felt a little guilty for assuming.

The woman said she had recently sold a screenplay that was loosely based on her brother's life. He was older than her, had been very comfortable in life, an explorer. She said those facts as if they were normal things to say about a sibling. Her eyes seemed a little glazed, she kept looking behind Ayanna and around the house. As far as Ayanna could see, no one was here.

"Can I have a glass of water?" Ayanna asked, not because she needed a drink but to calm the woman down. She was annoyed at herself for forgetting her name. Preoccupied with Felix, with herself, she was trying as hard as she could to remember every single aspect. Ayanna could only fumble for the client's name: Maggie? Missy? Margaret?

The woman was grateful for the break. She led Ayanna to the kitchen, shuffling in her platform slippers. Most of the house had already been redone, the floors painted ivory, the walls other cream tones. The colors that appeared were a camel-colored couch, black trim around a door, and gray. It was supposed to be, Ayanna knew, peaceful and luxurious, but all homes like these did was make her wonder how much everything cost and look for the discreet cash register. Unremarkable art on the walls. A container of those rich-person roses that were guaranteed to last for an entire year in their suede containers.

In her refrigerator, the woman had either water with some rosemary and lemon or quartz-charged water.

"Quartz," Ayanna said. Maybe it tastes like minerals, she thought. They sat together at the long table, shiny enough that it reflected a distorted view of their faces.

"Let me try again," the woman said. "Actually, is it okay if I show you a video?"

Ayanna nodded, sipped more of her water. If she weren't working, she would have a million questions about how the water had been charged by the quartz, or whether the quartz had been charged by something and then dumped into the water, and what it was supposed to do. The woman pulled out her cell phone, scrolled and fussed, until she found the video she wanted to show Ayanna.

"I look so young," she said. "I've lost all of my lips."

Ayanna could not see what she was talking about; neither woman really had lips to lose. The difference in the faces was fullness, aesthetics, and movement. There were more lines on the younger face. Her skin was not shades of milk but had the color of a white person who sometimes used tanning beds.

In the video, the woman began. "I am Margot Cherry, I am twenty-six years old, and I am the only survivor of what I am now calling the Septaria Expedition. The US government claims this never happened. They have perpetuated a lie that my older brother died in a yachting accident in the Caymans. My brother was Jason Cherry."

Ayanna made her face blank. She could feel Margot's eyes on her.

"We went on a sanctioned expedition through the Michigan door, paying the US government and Pathsong each a million dollars for permission to go through and use our own guides."

Ayanna had to take a deep breath. Margot was one of the rich people she had talked shit and complained about that whole summer. Her father had told her they had ignored everyone's warnings after she and Olivia went through the door. He had told her, shaking with emotion, about the snow, how the path had changed, how they had watched as almost every member of the expedition horrifically died. How the woman had run through the snow, screaming, and everyone on the other side had been too scared to go through and make her return.

She had never heard how much the church had gotten and the amount made Ayanna's eyebrows want to creep up all the way to her hairline.

"This movie was meant to clear up the lies and conspiracies around

Jason's death, but everything I tried to write came out wrong," she said. "No one would buy the original draft."

On her screen, the video cut from her face to footage from years ago. The four of them in the fields Ayanna had known so well. They were wearing socks on their hands for some reason. Jason was smiling and giving the camera a thumbs-up. Ayanna could see her father in the background. He looked so young. He was clearly distraught in the video. She had never seen him like that. Someone was trying to comfort him. The expedition took a photo. All of them were clearly trying to look important. Margot paused the video.

Ayanna wasn't sure what to say. She was fascinated now by the woman in front of her. There had been a cut, Ayanna remembered, one that had oozed gold, maybe? She could not believe this woman was alive and well.

"I make other videos too. You might have seen my series. It does good numbers. About the power of kombucha, kimchi, and probiotics to cure depression."

"I don't go on social media much," Ayanna said. "It stresses me out."

"Try sea moss powder. Two teaspoons in filtered water after a long day. Sip it while listening to some relaxing music." Then Margot laughed. "Sorry, sometimes I'm just on. But finding this kind of medicine, it saved my life. I was so depressed after my brother died, after the incident. I had this weird illness that did not go away for a long time. I saw people made from static, I heard a voice telling me to repent, I felt hands when there was no one there. I had a wound that would not stop bleeding gold for years." She made an unpleasant face like she expected Ayanna would ask to see the wound or its scar.

Ayanna wished Felix were here. Not just because she felt certain he would somehow know what to say to make this situation easier for both her and Margot, but because she felt the weight of her time away so profoundly in this instant. She wanted it to already be two days from now, away and having a drink with him over dinner, and hearing his thoughts about this. He would encourage her to be her best self if he were here. He would also go to the hotel after this was done, look at this woman's Instagram, and do the exact, precise math on how much all these things cost and how even with bad insurance, you probably would pay less overall in a year's time for a low dose of Lexapro than for all these powders with well-designed labels. Enough money to probably pay off all the school-lunch debt at the closest elementary school went into powders. Ayanna, it hurts, she could imagine him saying.

"I felt certain that what I had walked into on that expedition was hell," Margot said. "You can probably sense them too, but sometimes at the edge of the room I still see them. Sometimes, I think they can manipulate the people around me."

"Tell me more about that." Ayanna could not figure out what to do here. She hoped if they walked through the house, there would be something. This was the other hard part. Most of the time, Ayanna accepted she was coming into these places and making a lot of money not to do what she had grown to love, communing with spirits, but to mostly act as a low-key, unaccredited therapist. Here was someone's potential suppressed shame at having too much money and having to see the tangible proof of it. Here was someone's anxiety at having worked so hard to get to this point in their life but not sure what was left to live for after working toward something for so long. Here was someone's desire—despite all their self-absorption and all the cruel things they might have had to do along the way to get to this point—to have someone say, "You are a good person and you matter."

Margot crossed her arms, one guarding her body, the other on her opposing shoulder. "This is silly, but when I was jogging, I swear to you that a bunch of kids called me a bitch."

"How old?"

"Young, like six. They were walking with a teacher, and she didn't even notice. All these little African American kids calling me a bitch."

"That's messed up, I'm sorry." Kids yell stuff all the time. Yeah, maybe, Ayanna considered, a bunch of six-year-olds called Margot a bitch, but it was probably not as easy as they were possessed by malevolent spirits who wanted to cuss out all joggers. But it was also probably, Ayanna felt certain, just as likely that it was a white woman uncomfortable living in a community that was not all white, and letting her anxieties get away from her. She wanted to give her the benefit of the doubt. Ayanna wanted to be a person who could give almost anyone grace, but she was also so tired of being expected to only give the powerful and rich her empathy. Maybe she had kicked some mud by accident at the kids. Maybe the kids were being bad and quoting a song they had heard on the radio. Every popular song on the planet seemed to have lyrics about being a bad bitch who werks it; kids love radio and pushing boundaries.

Margot relaxed her posture at hearing Ayanna's sympathy.

"And this is going to sound like a loaded question, but it's something I ask all my clients before I begin." Ayanna said the lie casually and was quietly impressed by herself. "What do you do to help other people? Especially in your community?"

"My videos. You should see the comments. I'm bringing so many people peace and, you know, knowledge that has been kept from them for a long time."

Ayanna nodded. She felt the self-righteous teen she had been bubbling inside. Maybe that version of herself would have found a way to get this woman to be explicit about how she found her cures for people's ailments. What companies did she have agreements with? And why was her only community online? Why couldn't she automatically think of those kids as being a part of her community? Ayanna also knew she could excuse herself to the bathroom, look up how much money this woman was worth, and probably get even more indignant. It wasn't even the most egregious circumstances Ayanna had walked into on this job, and she understood deeply that the world ran on a vast cycle of fear and punishment. There was nothing novel and new about this. Humanity would always harm itself, would never really be at peace, until people learned to look past their own self-absorptions. She understood all this intellectually. But still, Ayanna had to unclench her jaw, force a smile on her face, look away from this woman, and stare at her inoffensive blob wall art with feigned interest.

It was not remarkable, because everywhere on Earth people suffered—even the worst people on Earth probably loved someone or something enough to make them weep and mourn—but in this particular city, the quality-of-life disparity was plainly written in a font size that could probably be seen from space. They were sitting in a multimillion-dollar home in a state that had an almost 20 percent poverty rate. Elementary schools in this very city were in the national news because of their outdated textbooks, their crumbling buildings, mold; there were cities dealing with lead pipes, water-treatment facilities struggling to cope with the rising salination of the life-giving river, and each new climate disaster was devastating more and more of that bottom 20 percent who could not afford to evacuate and who could not afford to rebuild or even bury their dead. But this was also the city where people went to regress. Just on the way to this appointment, Ayanna had watched as different packs of fiftysomethings carrying expensive handbags yelled at one another while holding mixed drinks and ignoring the people around them who were holding up signs asking for a dollar so they would be able to eat tonight. Everywhere was a party.

And these videos. That was it?

Ayanna did not want to take away this woman's ability to cope. She had clearly been through it. And Ayanna felt that as long as it wasn't hurting anyone else—although she felt certain if she researched and watched this woman's social media channels, there would be proof that this was not harmless coping—it was mostly fine to quietly believe in the things you needed to, to keep living and heal yourself.

"Let's tour the home together," Ayanna said.

They walked again in the cream-and-ivory downstairs rooms, Margot pointing out corners where she had seen something evil or wrong, kicking up a beautiful rug to show a stain on the floor that to Ayanna looked like maybe the wood's grain showing through the paint, but Margot said it was an evil symbol.

Ayanna ran a hand over it, muttered to herself, then nodded at Margot.

Upstairs, there was more character to the house. Large white sculptural lamps made from paper, which Ayanna liked a lot but thought she would also find frightening alone at night in this big house, and patterned rugs that still fit the beige aesthetic but with glimpses of rust and black. There was a bathroom like a dungeon, a semihealthy monstera Ayanna felt was lonely and discomfited by the lack of bright colors, and one room that seemed to be almost a parody of the city's heritage: velvet curtains with beguiling gold trim, a hurricane lamp, a fainting couch, the arched Spanish windows, bits of maybe the ornate metalwork that had originally been out of the house now framed. There was a large vase Ayanna was drawn to, and when she looked inside, a spirit was lodged in the bottom.

"Don't worry about me," it whispered. "I got this vase on a deal, and I never really got to savor it."

"Do you interact with her at all?" Ayanna asked.

"No," the spirit said, "she's annoying."

"You found something?" Margot asked.

"The vase is one of those positive forces. Sometimes, when you find an object someone made or they really cherished, it kind of just vibrates with good energy."

"Oh," Margot said. "I thought all of this was about, you know, banishing demons. Getting rid of dark forces."

Ayanna adjusted her blazer. Wanted to touch the wig she was wearing, but always worried that doing so would emphasize how fake it was.

"If you're uncomfortable with it, I'll buy it from you. Or I can have it treated."

Margot shook her head. "No, it's fine."

Ayanna was suspicious the instant she left the house, the vase would be smashed or tossed out into the night. It was unfortunate that the vase was too big to steal. "Let's light some incense in here."

They went into the room where Margot made her videos. It had a small kitchenette, superb lighting, a vanity, shelves of cameras and makeup and products. A spirit was wisping around, mostly cloud but with long arms and hands with what looked like press-on nails still there. Ayanna didn't react this time, even when the spirit said, "Kombucha is not better than Lexapro."

She rubbed her left eyebrow, then smoothed it.

The spirit lingered over the products, tried to knock them down, her hands unable to solidify enough to make a mess.

"What do your friends think of the house?" Ayanna asked.

Out of the corner of her eye she could see the spirit's attempts at destruction, each hand going through an intended target, an almost promising attempt to dramatically flip one of the tables, which rocked for a moment, then lost energy. It shrunk down to a small blob shape and went over to a far corner of the room.

"I don't really take a lot of visitors to this town. I mostly work here. I had people over more when I was back home, but I took a trip here last year and felt destined to live here. At least for a little while."

So, all you have are nice things and internet comments, Ayanna thought.

"I always wonder if I would be happy here too," Ayanna said. "Despite everything, it's beautiful. I always feel inspired. There's always music in the air. People looking to have some kind of fun. It's rare to be somewhere where you feel like you're meant to feel pleasure."

"Exactly," Margot said.

In the bedroom, they sat on the love seat. Ayanna listened to Margot talk more through her unusual circumstances in the house. Creaks, a lot of construction delays, bad dreams, the feeling of being watched. Guilt that she felt like wasn't emanating from her, but from the curtains and the downstairs rug, and leaked out of the vents.

"We'll do the cleanse, but you're right, there are spirits in this house. My impulse here is to tell you that you're going to have to start donating into their community. They have lived and loved and lost in this city. They want you to help the children of their descendants." Ayanna paused. She could not read Margot's face. Her eyes were downcast, her mouth was set into a line. "Clean out the school lunch debt, see if you can make a fund that pays all their lunches, work to help the kids not just in this neighborhood, but throughout the city."

The longer the woman was silent, the more Ayanna knew that nothing she was saying was getting through.

"I also have a message for you," Ayanna said. She thought about what she had wanted from Olivia for all these years. She leaned her head back, let her eyes flutter, made her body quake dramatically, kicked out her legs, then sat up again and made her voice deeper. "He—I want you to live a full life. You are continuing my legacy and beginning your own in the ways you help people. Diversify. Pollinate. Use love. Use kindness."

If you need something to worship, Ayanna thought and knew it was a rare person who didn't need money, God, or attention as something to follow, *let it be gratitude*. She would have been embarrassed by the earnestness of the thought if she hadn't been so fed up.

"Jason," Margot breathed. "What do you think of the movie?"

"I'm proud of you. You could have gotten a handsomer guy to play me but I'm proud of you."

Margot was crying. Ayanna made herself quake harder. "I'm proud of you," she said again. Her eyelashes fluttered and she moved her mouth into different shapes, then sat up abruptly.

"Whatever I said in the trance was meant only for you," Ayanna said. "Please don't tell me."

Ayanna wiped at her eyes. Pretended to feel a little lost. "This always takes me out a little."

Margot nodded. She rolled up her sleeves and looked around the house. They went downstairs, gathered some of the flowers and incense. Together, they left flowers in each area where Margot had mentioned a negative encounter, put some in the vase, and lit sticks in each room. Margot still seemed on the verge of tears, but Ayanna felt like she had already done enough. When the ritual was over, Margot clasped her hands together.

"The house is different now. I'm different," she said. "I'm going to change the world. I feel so alive. I deserve life."

Margot paused. "I deserve a life."

"I'm glad I could help," Ayanna said, and walked out into the evening. Outside, the world smelled like humidity and spilled trash. Her hair stunk of the incense she had used. Inside, as Ayanna had been gathering her things and putting on shoes, Margot had already started scripting and practicing a new video. "Hello, followers, I'm here to remind you that life is worth living." She kept saying this, practicing her smile differently each time.

25

It had been months since Ayanna had seen Jane in person. There was her friend, tall with barely a bump despite being in the eighth month of pregnancy. She hugged Jane, said hello to her, also said, "Hello, baby," and then they went to breakfast talking about how it was ridiculous that a death was the thing to bring them back together.

"Is CeCe coming to the funeral?" Ayanna asked.

"No, she wanted to save days for when the baby comes." Jane was looking around the restaurant with almost malevolent intent. "I can't tell if this place's coffee is good enough for me."

Ayanna couldn't stop looking at Jane. She had never understood the ways people described pregnant women, talking about glowing or some sort of radiating. Quietly she had sometimes thought those descriptions said more about how culturally uncomfortable people were with curvy women. Maybe she was a little jealous of her friend? Not because Ayanna felt a deep longing to be a mother, but because her friend could see the world—so often harsh and mean, especially to children, especially to Black children—and still feel confident in her ability to try to give a child a good life. She wanted to be that radically optimistic. Or maybe it was because Jane looked great. Buzzed hair, moisturized, toned arms, always interested in the world around her in a way that Ayanna felt certain meant she would forever be a little young.

"How are you feeling?" Ayanna asked.

"Honestly?"

Ayanna nodded.

"Insane." Jane placed one hand on her stomach as if her long fingers could cushion the fetus from hearing. "This fool in here is constantly kicking and tossing and turning every night. People are judging the size of my bump and feel comfortable accusing me of exercising too much or worrying about my size. I have put on thirty lbs." She sounded out the abbreviation *lbs* and Ayanna laughed. "I'm sleep-deprived and last night I was up late arguing with randos on social media about empathy." She made a point of looking at the menu, even though they both knew she was going to order a mushroom omelet, hash browns, crispy bacon, and a glass of orange juice. Jane rubbed her head, seemed to get pleasure out of the fact that she had shaved her head so only a light cover of down was on top, and smiled at its texture.

"What about empathy?"

"Oh, that it's so often treated as this purely positive force in the universe. But even empathy is about social power, and it feels like no one is questioning that."

"Like whenever there's an election and newspapers are interviewing old white men about their economic insecurities?"

"Yes, but I even see it tied to, like, gun rights. Those assholes are always saying 'my freedoms this' and 'my freedoms that' and they want you to empathize with them to act like it's the same type of social freedom as being able to send your child to school. People act like if you just have the power of empathy even a book can change you and make you a better person, sure, cool, I wish. Most of the time, you have to have the ability to even notice who you're empathizing with and consider why."

Behind them an older couple was holding hands and speaking in a language Ayanna could not identify. There was a little girl in a sparkly dress trying to escape from her parents every time they tried to take a bite to eat. The restaurant was playing soft yet tedious jazz. Ayanna was trying to figure out if this was about Jane's parenting anxieties in some way that should be addressed or if it was mostly her thinking about the world. A spirit swirling in a shape between dog-tree-old-man was peering over an older man's shoulder as he did the crossword.

"Anyway, as you can guess, that was not a popular take to have on the internet. So, last night at four a.m., I started drawing this insane diagram of what I thought were important social freedoms that valued human life and what were ones that only valued death and/or money." Jane, reading the look on Ayanna's face, waved a hand. "I threw it in the trash in the morning. Although some were really good. I felt like if I kept it, it would be something I would have to take to my therapist. And I think I'm still burnt out from IVF. And how few people seemed to get how hard it was. And I'm still mad about how scared I get."

Ayanna reached across the table, squeezed Jane's hand. "I love you. You should've sent me your nuts diagram."

Jane smiling at her from across a restaurant table was one of her favorite homes.

"We should live in the same city. I should come over sometimes just to like watch TV and then do the dishes." Ayanna took a sip of water. "We should have bought a huge house for us all to live in together."

"You should move," Jane said. "I'm watching this dating show right now that is all about the worst queer people in the world trying to date one another and CeCe can't handle it. I can't believe I married a woman who hates mess. All she does is shake her head whenever I put it on."

"Felix wants to get married."

"Why wouldn't he? You're incredible. You're hot, smart, and interesting. And you've been together for a million years." Jane pushed the menu away from her. "But you don't have to marry him. You know he'll stay with you no matter what."

"I want to be able to compromise. There are so many good reasons to get married. Taxes, health care, hospital visits. It's so practical. And yet."

"You love him, though."

"This is going to feel very sad-girl, so I'm going to apologize in advance, okay? But he gives my life gravity. I don't mean like he's the center of everything. But he's this quiet force in my life that keeps me feeling like me."

She could tell Jane didn't quite understand but wasn't sure what to say.

"Just sit with it," Jane said. "I didn't think I ever wanted to be the pregnant one. And then, well. I listened to CeCe, I listened to what I didn't want to hear. One of life's great pleasures is figuring out when and how to change your mind. But you're not wrong. Marriage is an inequitable trap for most women. Do a civil partnership instead. Most of the same benefits. And you know, he's patient. It took you eight years to officially move in together."

Even that made Ayanna pause. She was fully committed; they lived together.

Ayanna wondered if this was the process already. Wasn't telling Jane a step toward wanting to compromise? She didn't want to tell Jane about Margot, not before she had told Felix. That, too, was a reminder of how much she had built her life around him. There were things she always wanted him to be the first person to hear. Maybe the problem on some level was that she felt guilty. Here she was, far older now than Olivia would ever be. Olivia had wanted a husband and kids and a house filled with plants and dogs. Why should she—the person who'd never wanted to get married—have an approximation of that?

"No matter what you do," Jane said, "you already have something beautiful together. You don't have to do what everyone else does."

IT WASN'T THAT AYANNA had expected a normal, quiet funeral for Stephen's dad. It would've been deeply out of character for him to have a church service or to pick only one hundred of his closest friends and associates to pack into a funeral followed by a buffet. Stephen's dad had been rich in a way Ayanna could not truly understand: not homes but estates; owning seemingly unrelated businesses or at least shares in them that were interesting to him only based on their ability to generate disparate sources of income; dollars springing up from making the right eye contact with someone at a party who knew a good idea. As Ayanna stepped out of the rideshare, a woman dressed in all black was waiting to serve them vodka martinis or some sort of blackberry tonic mocktail. While they watched her shake the martini, Jane pointed to what appeared to be an elaborate art display celebrating Stephen's dad. There was a painting of him with his head shown in a regal style juxtaposed against an abstracted background. An even bigger black-and-white photo of him and a maybe four-year-old Stephen wearing tuxedoes and holding hands. A statue of a child holding a terrier. And below each one, an elaborate display of deep-red, almost black, roses.

"Have you ever worked a funeral like this before?" Jane asked the bartender.

The bartender poured the martini, tipped in olives with a custom *B*—for Brandon Butler—toothpick. "I'm not allowed to comment or remark on the service," she said while shaking her head no.

"Can I tip you?" Ayanna asked. There was no jar on the table, and if they were already not allowed to comment on the funeral, it felt worth asking.

"That's kind, but I'm getting paid very well." She slid the drinks gently toward them. "Cheers."

Closer to the art display, Ayanna and Jane read the informational placards that had been put up. All the work had been done by famous artists and were part of Stephen's dad's private collection. The roses were a prize-winning hybrid he had helped fund to be even darker than the black baccara. There was more art spread around the grounds, both inspired by the Butler family, and also to show off some of the more remarkable pieces of the collection.

"Do you think," Jane whispered, "this is meant to be just a part of the memorial service, or do you think this is supposed to get people hyped for an auction?"

"Both." Ayanna took a sip of her martini. "This is the first vodka martini I've ever liked."

"Rich-person vodka is no joke. Baby, I love you so much that I'm turning down rich-person vodka," Jane said. Then she looked at Ayanna. "I'm sorry. I'll stop talking to the baby now. I know it's weird."

They followed the path set up. There were different stations offering water, the signature drinks, and snacks, and showing off more and more art. One area had actors performing award-winning poems from a press that Mr. Butler had funded for fifteen years before it became too much of a money sink for him to endure. A statue that was supposed to be of Stephen's mom but looked mostly like hunks of marble with a fantastic juicy butt. There was a portrait of Stephen that captured how hazel his eyes could look under the right light, his skin darker than usual, probably from a summer spent hiking, and in the background his father holding a black umbrella and drinking a martini. The light made his white-blond hair look almost like it was aflame, the black sunglasses he was wearing made his skin look almost as pale as the hair.

"Stephen should take that photo to his therapist," Ayanna said. "I think it would explain a lot."

Jane kept studying it. "I feel like if Stephen had showed this to us, we would've understood exactly how weird his life has been." They had not yet seen Felix or Stephen. Felix had come early to take a long walk with Stephen and keep him from drinking too much before the funeral.

As they walked, Ayanna was aware that despite the circumstances, she felt lighter. Feeling this way was complicated. Here there was people watching, there were beautiful gardens, the pleasure of noticing a raptor soaring up in the air and of pointing to it and hearing her best friend say, "Well, who does he think he is? Being that majestic at someone else's funeral." Simultaneously, there was Ayanna's irrational fear that her brain was addicted to getting depressed. She was willing to feel disconnected and slow because of how much pleasure she felt on days like this, when everything felt sudden and clear. Days when she was able to think and feel, oh, I'm happy in this moment, which was so monumental and like a gift in contrast to the hours of alienation and exhaustion that preceded them. Ayanna knew intellectually that depression did not work in that particular way but it was hard, even on good days, not to implicitly distrust and blame herself.

Another display was of Mr. Butler's love of Manchester United. Signed kits he had collected over the years, a replica of the seats he had somehow gotten season tickets for over the years, a picture of him shaking hands with what looked like a mildly bored Wayne Rooney. A note on personalized stationery from Sir Alex Ferguson that seemed impossible to read. Manchester United scarves from the nineties in exquisite condition behind glass.

Ayanna shrugged at it. "Cool."

Jane pursed her lips. "The man is dead. You don't have to keep fighting with him about soccer."

"It's wild to me that someone could have such pristine taste in art and have such embarrassing taste in football clubs." Ayanna raised her eyebrows. "People are complex and irrational beings."

"You are American. Call it 'soccer.'"

They walked away from the display, Jane stopping to stretch a little and then to lean over and murmur to the baby.

"How often do you talk to it?" Ayanna said. "Also, I didn't mean that in a judgy way."

"Oh, on and off through the day. It helps me feel less self-conscious. I know it doesn't really know anything or see anything, but it's also my kid in there. I already want to tell it what's going on."

"That's sweet," Ayanna said.

"Are you sure you're not going to find out the sex?" Ayanna asked after a brief pause.

"It is perfect for right now." Jane rolled her eyes. "Everyone looks great in blue. Buy some onesies and don't worry about it."

Finally, they made it to the building where the service was happening. In an atrium, long rows of black seats, more photographs of Stephen's dad up on a stage, and in the front row were Stephen and Felix talking to each other. Ayanna could hear some people muttering about how much the coffin had cost. It appeared to them to be a $90,000 model, gold with silk lining and international signs of rest and rejuvenation and safe passage engraved on it.

"I heard his body isn't even here, that he asked to be buried like an ancient Egyptian, full process, full tomb. All the shit outside is going to be placed in it after this."

"There's no way his lawyers would have let him do that. Those are assets."

"Let's go say hi," Jane said.

They walked up the aisle and Ayanna tried to ignore all the heads turning toward them. It was a crowd that was trying to figure them out—girlfriend to either Stephen or Mr. Butler; illegitimate kids; probably not rich because of their shoes; maybe Jane was an artist with her short hair and confidence. A few, Ayanna knew, probably recognized her. She had worked for some of them, either purifying homes or sometimes helping them to reach out to their dead. The attention made her feel itchy. It was strange, too, for there to be no spirits at a place like this. Ayanna had seen them now for so long that she always noticed when they weren't present. For a while, she had tried to understand it, hoped it would give her a greater sense of how they or death itself worked. But in her thirties, Ayanna had decided to accept the fact the dead, like the living, were idiosyncratic and resisted easy explanations for their behavior.

She hugged Stephen first. He had bags under his eyes and the expression of someone who just wanted everything to be over. Then hugged Felix and couldn't help but linger, touching his back, letting her face bump up against the top of his shoulders.

"I missed you," she mouthed at him. He smiled and mouthed it back.

"I was just telling Felix about what my dad decided to do." Stephen was scanning the room. He paused and looked at Jane. "Please sit down. And do you need more comfortable shoes? Your ankles."

"I'm fine."

"Are you?"

"I might ask you later, but right now, I promise I'm not just being polite."

They sat down and Stephen told them everyone had purposefully not told him—until it was too late to do anything about it—that his father had been frozen. His body was in a facility somewhere in Minnesota, where people would take care of it around the clock, and sometime in the future, when technology had advanced, doctors would be ready to do the procedures to bring Stephen's dad back to life. It also looked like, according to his papers, he had paid for Stephen to have the same procedure if he wanted to opt in. All that ancient Egypt stuff was a cover.

"Did you know he was that weird about death?" Ayanna asked.

"No. I thought he was normal weird about death."

"I would be so pissed off if this was my dad," Jane said. "He is dead. He's wasting all that money, wasting energy, and time."

"He's just being a job creator," Stephen said, then laughed a little too hard.

Ayanna had mulled over on the plane ride what the right thing to do was. But she loved Stephen and couldn't help but say, "If there's anything you need to say, I could help."

He put his hands on Ayanna's shoulders. "Ay, I love you and I respect your work, but no thanks. Death is final. That's the world I want. Healthy boundaries."

Stephen paused and let go of Ayanna. He looked around. "I don't want to ruin the surprise either. Maybe he's actually right and the process works. He's not dead. Just chilling, waiting for some genius surgery robot to be invented."

Felix was about to say something, but then the lights dimmed once, twice, and Stephen said, "The service is starting."

Stephen's mom gave a eulogy about the history of the Butler family. How they had come to the United States on a boat, how they had survived uncertain times over and over and how they were an example of true American resilience, and then the history of their money, all the capital Mr. Butler had inherited and somehow quadrupled over the years. From nothing to something. And Jane snorted a little at the idea that a $400,000 inheritance was nothing. The room smelled like expensive candles and many people who had been drinking for hours. Ayanna wished she could stand up and stretch without being rude. The next eulogy was vague platitudes about a better place and the great Butler legacy to the arts. Ayanna adjusted herself so her pinkie was always brushing Felix's. It felt rude to tenderly hold hands at the funeral of someone you did not love. No one was crying. It didn't really feel to Ayanna like anyone had really died. Maybe that was the point, because Mr. Butler had chosen to freeze himself, and maybe almost everyone else believed he was right and would return a hundred, two hundred years later, in a fit and healthy body, and continue another life of making money, betting on racehorses, and drinking expensive tasteless alcohols.

But it felt so profoundly wrong to Ayanna. She thought the point of a service like this was to be surrounded by mutual love for the lost person or to hope the beloved was in some way present and could feel how much they'd mattered in their short time on Earth. All these years, and still she was furious with her mother for not inviting her to Olivia's memorial. The last time she had spoken to her father, he said Opal had created a shrine to Olivia and told him it helped her hear Olivia's voice clearer. "It helps her grieve," he said, "but I don't think what she's hearing is your sister." Ayanna had not heard from her mother in years.

As the service continued, Ayanna thought what she always did in quiet moments: *Olivia, I'm here and ready to listen. I'm sorry.* There was the sound of several people shushing someone.

The officiant said, "We walk in life to seek meaning and to give meaning. That is God's will."

After the funeral, Stephen turned to them all and said, "My dad loved Japanese city pop, he believed in good, tailored suits with high armholes, he once bought a signed Steven Gerrard jersey just to burn it, and I think the only thing he liked that wasn't about status or money was roses. Almost anywhere we went that had a rose, he would stop to look and admire the color, the shape. He was disappointed whenever they were in bad condition. Every rose was a gift to him. I don't know if we ever even really knew each other and that's weird. But I miss him."

"I'm going to say one more fucked-up thing," Stephen said, and looked directly at Ayanna as always. She nodded.

"He had so much money, so much stuff, and he only ever had little bits of people. What a dumbass."

Then he stood up before anyone could say anything, and went over to his mother and told her she had done a great job, and he was very proud of her. He greeted some of his stepmoms and hugged some of his siblings. Most of them didn't look like one another, but they all had similar facial expressions. The room was loud with conversations and high heels on hard tile floors. There was more liquor being poured, people were probably already trying to figure out which artworks would be on sale soon, and there was the wheeling of the carts covered in silver trays for the dinner that was to follow.

"Sometimes," Felix said, "I feel like funerals are meant to kill the person one last time."

Jane gave him an interested look. "Say more."

"They're meant to make you feel like time is moving on. You rarely go to one where you hear about the person as they were. It's all gendered stuff, money, history, potential if they're young. Sometimes all you hear is some half-assed talk about God and callings. The dead aren't even talked about. It's so depressing." He turned to Ayanna earnestly. "When I die, I want you to remind people I could also be very annoying. Tell them about how often I leave wet towels on my side of the bed."

She laughed, and he said, "I'm not joking. Make me be alive one last time."

"I'll tell them you stole expensive lotions and lied about it. You leave towels in the bed. You're not as good of a driver as you think you are. The way your snore can sometimes sound like a bird."

"Keep going," he said.

"I'll say nice things too."

"Like what?"

Jane took a few steps away from them, maybe uncomfortable with their flirting, and started listening intently to someone else's conversation, not even bothering to pretend she wasn't eavesdropping. Her face was growing more and more concerned as Ayanna reminded Felix he was a good listener, had excellent taste in music, was somehow capable of making turkey taste good even though that felt like an eldritch secret to her. Turkey is meant to taste bad, Felix. It's tradition. She leaned forward and whispered in his ear what else he was excellent at, and felt flush with the way he smiled at her. Ayanna stayed close. He truly was content to let her think about what she wanted. There was only pleasure on his face as she stood close.

Then Felix paused and asked if everything was okay with Jane. Together, they studied her. Ayanna couldn't help but assume Jane was listening to something scandalous, like confirmation that most of Stephen's dad's money had come from money laundering or grifts, or that one of the young men she was listening to was Stephen's secret half brother. Jane touched her side. And for a moment, Ayanna worried she was misreading the situation and, somehow, maybe Jane wasn't hearing something bad but was concerned about her health or the baby's. Jane fished her phone out of her purse.

"Something up?" Ayanna asked. Felix came over and offered Jane an arm. They hovered around their friend.

"Do you need some water? To sit down?" Felix and Ayanna were asking at the same time.

Jane handed her the phone. It was open to a breaking news article. At first, Ayanna didn't understand what she was reading. Around her more and more people were looking and talking on their phones. Felix was speaking to her, his hand was on her shoulder, and Jane was talking too, looking into her eyes. Jane's eyes were so dark, the whites so sharp, and she had dusted gold above and around, and it was easier for Ayanna to pay attention to those details because her brain was still reacting to the headline's slap. Then, Ayanna looked down at the screen. Once, her father had thought aloud to her, told her it probably wasn't right but maybe the ways we perceived the world, the universe, were all wrong. People were always thinking in terms of distances, but maybe everything in the universe, excluding people and animals, was speaking together. Gravity, light, heat were maybe also tools of communication between planets, between stars, between gases. Sometimes, meanly, Ayanna had wanted to hear him say these things again but to an astrophysicist, to hear him try to explain his half-baked but poetic understandings of these things and how the doors maybe tied into what he called "celestial forces for communication and understanding." It was easier, Ayanna knew, to think of him reading the same headline and to wonder about him instead of the doors and what their return meant. Her father had two more kids, was living abroad, and was raising them to believe in nothing. They were lucky, Ayanna had thought, because they were being raised to be realistic. Ayanna scrolled. There it was: her door. There were no longer fields around it but brown soil tinted with gold, long light-green grass in the background, the barn where she had prayed standing behind it.

26

After dinner, Ayanna quickly went back to her hotel. Inside her suitcase, a spirit had stuffed itself in among her untouched clothes and she ordered it out. It lingered, pretending it had somehow not heard her, and she said "now" in a voice that made her sound like her mother. The spirit sulked its way into the minibar, misting and leaving a basement scent behind it. Ayanna rolled her eyes. She packed quickly, until there was a soft knock on the door. Dreading a confrontation with Jane, Ayanna ignored it, but the person kept insistently and evenly knocking. Knowing it could only be Felix, Ayanna opened the door. He hugged her, said nothing, and in silence helped her pack. He looked under the bed and gathered her toiletries from the bathroom.

"You don't have to do this," she said at least three times.

Finally, Felix said, "I know but I want to."

She stopped then, and hugged him, tipped her face up toward his and kissed him. Ayanna felt certain it wasn't a goodbye.

"You should talk to Jane," he said. "She is freaking out."

"I can't."

"She's your best friend. You love her."

It annoyed her, as always, that things were so simple for him to express. Yes, of course you have to have an awkward confrontation with your best friend. No, you can't just ghost and drive off into the night and then apologize later. Once when they were fighting, he had told her it was exhausting that she could be so good to people who would never truly know her and be so willing to disappear on the people who loved her. The unspoken sentence after he'd said that to her was: it was like she had learned nothing from her sister's death. And then he had immediately apologized and said that wasn't fair for him to say. He hadn't even said the hard part aloud. The apology, somehow, had been the thing to truly enrage her. She had uttered an embarrassing little screech and walked out of the apartment, then out into the night. And now, in this hotel room, a part of her was waiting again for Felix to point to something too true about her.

When she said nothing, he said, "You'll feel better if you do this right."

A part of her relaxed.

"I hate the art in here," Ayanna said. "Why do they think ducks are restful?"

"Better than geese," Felix said. "Nature's true evil."

Then he crossed his arms and looked her in the eyes. The hotel room was dim enough that there was no way for her to see the difference between his pupils and irises. She met his gaze but could not tell what he was thinking. Before he could speak there was a knock, much louder, and Ayanna knew it was Jane. Felix turned and opened the door, let in Jane and Stephen. She was barefoot and carrying her shoes. Stephen seemed a little buzzed.

"You can't do this," Jane said. And she turned to Felix. "How could you let her do this?"

"Feminism in action," Stephen said. "You're being very get-this-ho-in-line."

Jane turned toward him and gestured with the hand holding the heels, nearly grazing him with the shoes' toe boxes. "Excuse me?"

"Sorry," Stephen said. "We did 'Dad's dead' shots."

He flopped onto the couch. Stephen spread out and dangled his feet over the edge. His shoes were beautiful. Black leather, embossed florals shining under the unflattering hotel room overhead lights.

"What is the point of going there?" Jane said. "Are you going to go through the door? You won't find her."

Ayanna said nothing.

"I thought everything was fine with you."

Ayanna fiddled with her bag, refused to meet Jane's gaze. It was easier to watch her lips form words—it looked as if she had put on a fresh coat of lipstick on the way over—and to watch the way her bump moved in the dress as she gestured. It felt lucky that Jane was so pregnant. The baby was sacred to her, expensive too. IVF, time, anxieties. Sometimes, Jane referred to the baby as Lambo, because of how much of a luxury it felt to her. There was no way she would follow. There would be, if Ayanna even decided to try to walk the path again, potentially no coming back.

She had told Jane everything when they were in Oregon, years ago. They'd stayed up the entire night talking. The questions Jane had asked about Olivia. Small like favorite color, precise like how had she eaten pizza, crust-eater or not, and big like what did you love most about her. Jane hadn't had much to say about the doors. She'd been rapt while Ayanna talked about walking through, the way everything had changed. Jane was engaged and thoughtful about her seeing spirits. But it was clear that for Jane, what she wanted was to be another person who could love Olivia. Ayanna understood Jane was afraid of elsewhere. She was the kind of person who couldn't even go camping. Life for her was never meant to be unruly or dangerous. Ayanna half listened as Jane continued to promise her nothing good would come from any of this.

When it became clear to Jane that Ayanna was going to let her yell until she was exhausted, she turned to Felix with a mix of: You could stop this, are you going to let her go, is this what a good boyfriend does, come the fuck on. I thought you wanted to marry her. Why are you letting me do all the hard work.

"Don't," Ayanna said, and it surprised all of them. Stephen sat up a little straighter. It seemed like he was in danger of falling off the couch with its slick material.

"Then talk to me."

"This is my decision."

"You should have to explain stupid decisions."

Ayanna sighed. It wasn't stupid to her. And it was barely a decision. She'd known immediately, when she had seen the door's return, that there was proof, she had to go back. It was impossible for her to know what she would do. All she knew was there was nowhere on Earth where she could be except back in the field, sitting in the warm dirt. There, maybe, Ayanna would know completely what to do next.

"If you walk through that door, you will die," Jane said. "Popping or not, you will never come home."

"I mean, yes, that's a possibility," Ayanna said. "But maybe not. When has walking through a door ever had only one outcome?"

FELIX AND STEPHEN CARRIED Ayanna's luggage downstairs for her.

"This feels like a bad idea," Stephen said, "but I respect it."

"Text me if you need anything. Any day, any time. Even if it's just to talk," Felix said.

"I told Jane the only way she could get you to stay is if she faked some contractions," Stephen said. He pulled a vape pen out of his pocket. Smoked from it, handed it to Felix. Ayanna paused, watching the two of them. Stephen was clearly considering doing a fake contraction of his own, Felix watching and preparing both to laugh and to tell him one was enough. Here they were, standing around, being a little stupid on purpose, making her laugh, and that was one of the small, good homes she'd had for years.

She hugged them both and said she loved them. "You more than him," Ayanna said to Felix. He grabbed her again and pressed her into his chest, let her breathe in the pine scent of his deodorant. Ayanna took her time, hoping Jane would come around and not punish her. She didn't want to leave on those terms. And then Jane was there, hugging Ayanna's back and saying nothing. The taxi pulled up. Ayanna hugged all three again. She hoped the feel and pressure of her arms was enough to say everything she wanted. Sitting in the backseat and pulling away, Ayanna turned toward the back window, but they were already gone.

27

Ayanna tried to do the math on how much of her life she had spent thinking about the doors. Spacing out on public transportation or in cars, lying awake at 3 a.m. with the feeling of being hyperaware of her heart and breaths, posting anonymously on a forum with other people who grew up in faiths based on the door, and sometimes in therapy while looking at her hands or the paint on the walls, the thought of its return or refusal to return would burst out of her. But she'd never had the imagination or willingness to consider how a return would make her feel. There were so many things out of her control, Ayanna's feelings about the situation had become mostly irrelevant to her.

The rental car was parked. She smelled better than expected for driving so long and sleeping in the car. Everything felt unchanged. Red-tinged dirt. The large tree that had to be at least one hundred years old. Smaller pine trees planted by a neighbor that should have been bigger by now. Lawn mowers roaring and complaining through the air. Summer warm-cut-grass scent. In the distance, Ayanna could see the red barn's black roof. She considered driving to a gas station and changing out of the workout leggings and oversized T-shirt she was wearing. Her dad had always made her dress nice despite the dirt and mud. Under her breath, Ayanna was humming the song members of the church had sung while digging out the rows while she meditated in the dirt. The eyes of love.

Almost everyone in the forum had said they were going to stay away from the doors. That time in their lives was over. Ayanna, not that she was keeping score, felt like she had been in the most benevolent leaning of all the faiths. Most had been more like cults: people thrown through the door for angering leaders; teenagers tasked with harvesting the seeds people used to create acre; weird sex stuff; and rituals of saying the door measured your soul on each visit. If you were holding disbelief and cruelty in your heart, of course you would pop. Ayanna's only contributions to those conversations were platitudes. It seemed rude to say, Well, I mostly had a pretty positive experience until my sister died!

There were no dead here. That was what also made it feel like the past. The closest she had seen one was ten miles away, wafting between horse shape and teenage-girl shape on a bridge next to a very low river. She had considered calling her father and had decided not to because he had done nothing to reach out to her. Ayanna hoped he had stayed in Spain, not flown here or to Germany. The closest she could get to a prayer in this situation was to hope he would stay home and raise his young kids. That he would always put being a responsible father first. She did not want to think about the money he had probably embezzled from the church. It was still strange to be here without him and her grandmother.

Ayanna got out of the car. Stretched until she felt a welcome pop in her shoulder. Retied her shoes, once, twice. Then, carrying a tote she had bought near the Michigan border filled with snacks and a water bottle, made her way down the road. She tried to think only of the gravel her shoes crunched over, the way the tree branches reached toward her, birdsong, and attempted to remember the Japanese word she liked so much that meant "sun coming through tree leaves." There was a feeling, though, that Ayanna tried to say was anxiety, of being pulled forward.

The closer she came, the more she heard other people talking, not even the lawn mowers and leaf blowers could drown them out. More had come than she'd expected. Ayanna had thought there would somehow be little interest. This had felt so particularly hers. By the time she had been born, the church had maybe two hundred parishioners who were treated by the locals as annoying weirdos. Car after car on the roadside, parked precariously near deep ditches and streams and blocking people's long driveways. A few houses had signs, offering parking for twenty dollars cash or best offer; thirty dollars for adult bathroom privileges, five dollars for children. There were a few familiar faces, an older woman who hugged her and couldn't stop talking about how she had watched Ayanna grow up. It was clear the woman wanted to ask about Ayanna's father, and Ayanna let the crowd pull them away from each other. There were people selling waters, paper fans, and fruit. When people balked at the prices, Ayanna heard the salespeople saying, "Well, we take Venmo."

There were some cops trying to maintain order. A man saying instructions through a bullhorn, but his voice was hard to understand. People were knocking into one another. Shoulder after shoulder clanked and crashed against one another. The procession forward was hot and unsafe. Ayanna moved to the side, until she was mostly out of the crowd, and forced herself to slowly drink water until she calmed down. All the signs this was not going to be just her or this would be an uncomfortable experience had been there, Ayanna realized. She remembered how expensive gas was, how high hotel room rates were, the feeling that so many cars were on the road, but she had been so inside herself as to not infer what these things could have meant on her drive. People loved spectacles.

She was unsure of what to do next. The safer, saner thing would be to go back to the car. Maybe use her savings, stay in a hotel for a week, then drive back here. But what if the door left? Yet Ayanna felt the heat, the number of people, anxious police officers, the way there was no discernible order, made everything feel too volatile. Then she saw her mother walk past and move into the crowd.

They had not seen each other for fifteen years. Hadn't spoken or texted in five. Her mother, Ayanna thought, looked young. Her posture was still good, always making her seem taller than she was. Opal's hair was processed and straightened, so it gleamed black under the August sun. She was wearing a long dress with a floral pattern that felt so her. Dinky little roses. Ayanna couldn't stop following her. She had nothing to say to this woman. The years had made that certain. She did not want to forgive her. She did not want or need a mother any longer. To invite her into her life would feel like a desire for conformity rather than for love or self-worth. But still, Ayanna followed her. Mesmerized by seeing the way she walked, the pure white Nikes on her feet, Ayanna felt her heart beat quick because that was Olivia's stride, her way of walking, heel-toe, head high. A long scar on the back of her mother's left forearm. Had her legs always been so thin? In one moment, they were so close to each other that if her mother had turned around, they would have been face-to-face.

Opal smelled different now. No more sweetie-pie perfumes and Irish Spring soaps. Her mother smelled like the sun was boiling the bourbon out of her. The large brown purse slung around her was probably filled with a pint. Ayanna didn't think she was imagining it. Almost everyone else around them smelled like sweat and deodorant. Here was the sharp scent of liquor. There was a sway to Opal's movements whenever the crowd had to pause. She bumped into people and made no attempt to apologize. Ayanna felt worse knowing her mother was still drinking. For years, Ayanna had worked to remind herself the whole thing with Olivia had been a series of bad decisions, that the end had been an accident, that there was nothing that could be solved by dealing out faults and blame. But smelling this proof, assuming the drinking was still because of Olivia's death, it felt cosmically unfair her mother was here in the crowd after a night of heavy drinking and her dad—who, if there was blame to lather people in, deserved at least a healthy scrub of it—was comfortably at home with his nice new wife and cute sons, probably having a siesta right now.

"You can't control anything but yourself," Ayanna muttered. When she looked up, her mother had disappeared again.

Ayanna wished it was possible to lie to herself, to say she had not seen this woman. But looking at her now was the closest she had felt to being able to do something for Olivia. It felt like it would be a betrayal to her sister not to try to discreetly watch over their mother in these moments. A man bumped into Ayanna and said, "It's too hot." The closer they got to the long gate, the church, the fields, the louder the crowd was. It sounded like someone was breaking something. The man on the bullhorn was saying things but they kept coming out as squawks.

"It's like he swallowed the microphone," someone said, "and is trying to talk through his stomach."

A woman yelled, "I will give you ten thousand dollars to let me go through."

She found her mother again. Now she was yelling, "Let me in, let me in." People ignored her. "They killed my daughter here," she yelled. And now people were looking at her. Opal pushed through the crowd, long steps, shoving, and Ayanna followed as much as she could in her wake. It was as if most of her aging had happened to her voice. An octave lower, louder. People were talking, but still her yells cut through. Opal was at the very front now, speaking angrily to a man in military uniform. Stamping her feet, gesturing. Behind her, the door was open, but it was open to somewhere Ayanna had never seen before.

It was a desert with golden sand. There were things that looked like a mix of mushrooms and trees. A tree's gray with dark blue fungus with light tan spots. They moved in a way where Ayanna could not tell if it was because of wind or if they were alive in a different way than plants were on Earth. A violet sky. There were hills in the distance, but they were so bright Ayanna had to make a visor out of her hands to feel comfortable looking. Was there music? A voice singing softly from far away. Maybe a lake? And her feet longed, like she was a teenager again, to walk right through. She wanted to hold the golden sand up at eye level, let it run between her fingers and weigh it on her palm, to feel her body work to climb those dunes. If there was water, it would probably be a shade of purple like the sky.

"Is this it?" a man said to another next to him. "Is there where the wife was?"

The other man didn't understand, and Ayanna listened to the familiar story again. A lost wife, a virtuous man, a pilgrimage, a walk together from death to life.

"My daughter told me this is where she was," Opal was saying. "I have to go to her. I can bring her back."

"It's not safe," Ayanna thought she could hear the man say. It was hard to tell. The crowd was getting louder. More people were saying they heard music, some said they could smell things like cake baking in an oven. One of the few people ahead of Ayanna had sweat through the back of his shirt. It clung to him and so did the dirt kicked up by so many people walking on the road. Most of the people up here were taking pictures of the door, making videos of themselves, talking quietly and earnestly into their cell phones. They were on the very edge of where cell phones stopped working. A teenage girl in front of her stepped closer and the screen fritzed black.

Ayanna shook her head. Her mother pushed a man and leaped to scale the gate. He tried to pull her down. She swung and clawed at him while scrambling. Opal pushed him into the gate, hard enough to rattle it, and there was a thud when his head hit the metal. He seemed dazed and he staggered. Ayanna longed to melt into the crowd. *I don't know this woman and I don't know why I'm here*, she willed herself to think. Instead, Ayanna walked closer. Tried to pull her mother down and took a surprise kick to the chest. It winded her and she leaned back for a second and gasped. The second time, Ayanna pulled roughly, no longer caring about being nice.

"You can't act this way."

Her mother turned. "Olivia?" She reached for Ayanna, her eyes bright, her smile bigger than Ayanna had ever seen it.

Then she squinted and the smile melted. "Ayanna?"

Ayanna closed her eyes for a second underneath her mother's gaze. Tried to think of what to say. And in that hesitation, her mother leaped up again, began pulling at and squirming over the gate, not caring about scratches or pain. Finally, she was over the fence and running toward the door. Opal fell and was still for a moment. Near the door, there was one plant, an allium maybe, purple and green, that stood proud and thick. Despite everything happening, Ayanna realized it was probably one she had planted. It had persisted here, all these years.

"Do you know her?" the security guard asked. He stood up. Still seemed a little disoriented. His eyes were red and distant.

"That's my mom," Ayanna said. "She's drunk."

"She's in deep shit," he said.

"I know."

"We have to stop her from going in." He rubbed his head. In the scuffle with her mom, he had lost his blue baseball cap. Ayanna could see scratches from her mom's nails and the slight impressions of the cap on his mostly bald scalp.

"I know," Ayanna said. She knew on some level that this was a responsibility she had now. They were no longer family, but they had love in common. Ayanna was old enough now to know there were no strong arguments to be made around fairness. Life was fundamentally unfair. People were doomed to continually replicate in ideas and systems and attitudes an intrinsic unfairness learned from being a part of nature. Yet she couldn't help but think, *This is monumentally stupid and unfair.*

The security guard waved a key card and opened the door. They stepped in together. Opal was lying in the dirt, seemingly out of energy. Ayanna and the man approached her. The music was louder here. She could feel the vibrations of it coming up from the soil.

"I can hear Ruby's voice," he said. "She's calling to me." He took a scared step back.

Ayanna ignored him, offered her mom a hand. She turned over. Her leg was swollen. Ayanna handed her some water, pulled a bag of beef jerky out of her bag. It took all her willpower not to tell Opal how to behave, to tell her how much trouble she was in, to lay into her about her drinking, to say something harsh still about Olivia's memorial service. It was all there and waiting to be said. Instead, Ayanna sat next to her on the ground and said, "This isn't where Olivia went. It was a meadow. Long blue grass, blue sky, silver mountains. We were both thrilled by how beautiful it was."

Opal opened the bag of jerky. She pulled a piece out and chewed it contemplatively.

"I can't stop you from going through. I definitely can't stop you from getting arrested. This is probably trespassing. You assaulted a security guard."

Her mother continued eating the jerky.

"There's the barn where I spent so much time when I was growing up. I used to sit here with Dad in the summer and fall. We would pray somehow that these doors would make the world a better place, that they would end suffering. Oh man, I wanted to believe that so bad."

"Badly," Opal said. She reached for her purse, dug around, took out a small shooter of vodka, and downed it. Ayanna handed her the water bottle again. She waited for the security guard to do something, but he had gone back to the gate. Opal dug in her purse again, pulled out a cell phone, and looked at it. Ayanna knew they were close enough that phones no longer worked.

"What do you want from this?"

"I'm going to wait here until the door opens back to the meadow you described. I am going to go through and get Olivia back."

"You could die."

"I don't care."

"She's dead. You'll be doing it for nothing." Ayanna could hear how uncertain she sounded. They were here for the same reason.

"You don't know that."

"This isn't like normal death," Ayanna said. She clapped her hands together. "You could literally pop. Think about how painful that must be."

"Why are you here?" Her mother finally turned and looked at her. Opal, Olivia, Ayanna all had the same big, sad-looking eyes. "You got lucky the first time. This is tempting fate."

Ayanna opened her mouth. Shut it. She was unsure of how much longer she could do this. For years, her mother had texted her on and off, blaming Ayanna for Olivia's death. And now this?

Felix once had said to Ayanna, "Forgiving isn't the same as love. You don't have to do either with your parents unless it will make you feel better." They had been driving home after a long weekend with his parents. On the last morning, his parents had woken up early and made green-garlic omelets because they knew it was one of Ayanna's favorite breakfasts. They hugged her like they meant it. Ayanna wanted them to feel like family but, every time, their kindness and grace made her think about all the things she wanted to yell at both her parents.

"I want to want to forgive them," she'd said, then leaned her head against the passenger window. Felix had taken her hand and said after a minute of silence, "Let's go buy some fries." *I'm loved*, she thought. *I learned how to do it again.*

There was a rumble. Ayanna could no longer feel or hear music. Opal looked up at the sky. The door slammed shut. Closed, it was more beautiful than Ayanna remembered. So bright. It was like coming down from a hill and seeing Lake Michigan in June. It always was a shock, the richness of it against the pale sand, the neon-and-white-striped beach towels people liked to use. Strange, too, to see the door again and despite everything feel no fear. It was like returning to an old friend. She wanted to tell it everything that had happened to her in the past years, to let it know her. If her mother had not been there, Ayanna knew she wouldn't have been able to resist kneeling in the dirt, muttering all these things to it.

After twenty minutes, it opened again. A grotto. Silver stone in front and still orange water. Only the light from outside the door made everything visible. What was maybe a statue could be seen. A base of large stones, a skirt that looked like it had been assembled from driftwood, a torso of mud and stone. Five arms. No face. *It's dim*, Ayanna told herself, *my mind could be playing tricks on me.* She had forgotten the dissonance of being in a mundane Michigan field and being able to see improbable elsewheres. And had the door always felt like an optical illusion? As an adult, Ayanna noticed the space of the doorframe shouldn't have allowed her to be able to see so far, so wide. The day grew hotter.

Humidity made the air feel closer and closer to solid. Ayanna tried to keep her water intake slow and steady. It would storm, Ayanna knew, around five. Enough lightning to make most of the crowd disperse until it was done. After what Ayanna estimated was around two hours, the door shut again. More police arrived, increasingly concerned with the growing crowd and the danger of a crush than with

Ayanna and Opal. Around a half hour passed. The door opened out into a long meadow, this one bronze and filled with spirits. They were all speaking in languages Ayanna couldn't understand. Some sounded like instruments, she couldn't help keeping her eyes on one that kept changing from cat and slender person to what looked like a waterfall and who was speaking only in marimba noises. The sky behind them was flickering between colors.

Maybe her sister had seen all this. Maybe she was still alive. Walking between worlds, finding a way to adapt each time. Ayanna wanted to believe it was a possibility. Her sister eating the sweetest, most impossible berries. Drinking violet water and being astonished that it tasted like syrup. Lying in one of the orange swamps, hot-tub-warm against her tired bones. Olivia seeing each world and carving her name into a stone.

At one point, her mother admitted she needed help to make it to a bathroom. Her ankle was swollen. They walked slowly together to the barn. After helping her mother to the bathroom door, Ayanna paced the barn. Sat in her old makeshift pew. The concrete floor was cracked and less even now. There were no longer books on the shelves or photos of the parishioners or the pinboards where people had put note cards of their intentions and the small things they wanted to do to help bring about world peace. It didn't smell like coffee or chili or potluck. It was far cooler in here, thanks to a small air conditioner desperately trying to fight against the heat.

There was nothing Ayanna thought she could say to change her mother's mind. Ayanna made her drink more water in the cool barn, sit for a while.

"This is your fault," her mother said.

"Sure." Ayanna was surprised by how neutral she felt. She wasn't eighteen any longer. A part of her could imagine Felix, Jane, and Stephen reacting to her telling them about seeing her mom. The different ways they would find to turn the situation into something easier to discuss, from making jokes about it to getting indignant on her behalf. Once on a demented tangent, Jane had described a fantasy she had of following Ayanna's mom with a bucket of snowballs, just chucking them at the back of her head, luxuriating in the thought of the ice that would fall down the back of her coat, making her clothes beneath cold and wet. She deserves it, Jane had said. Looking at Opal, Ayanna could hear Jane saying, "True justice is a snowball to the throat," and almost laughed. Ayanna refilled the water bottle and handed it to her mother. She didn't need this person to treat her well. Her cruelty no longer made Ayanna feel lonely.

Outside, the door had changed again. A golden jungle where snow was falling and parrots that looked cut from night were swarming near the door's edge and looking out. Opal said she could hear Olivia's voice here and tried to go in, Ayanna held her back by the arm and refused to let go. I can't hear her, Ayanna kept saying. I would be able to hear her if she was here. They argued until the door slammed shut. And the sky above cracked open, rain falling so fast and thick that it was a relief to Ayanna.

The rain stopped after only a few minutes. Still, the birds watched from their side of the door. The door kept following its new whims. Closing in one-to-two-hour intervals. Opening up to new vistas. The more Ayanna saw, the more she alternated between being dazzled and feeling unspeakable dread. For each place that stirred up her desire to walk through, to draw a map, to bring back proof of the place's existence, another would open that made Ayanna feel certain here was where she would be. There was one door, all white light, and a sound that was barely able to be heard that made Ayanna nauseated. A susurrus quality, like an unwanted mouth next to her ear. Even those remaining in the crowd behind the gate backed away. A woman fainted.

"You should get help," Ayanna said to her mom after the door had shut again. "I don't mean that flippantly. But you don't have to live like this."

Later, Ayanna said to Opal: "You still have time to start over. I can't promise you'll be happy, but you should try to live a life." Ayanna handed her some beef jerky.

Up close, Ayanna could see lines on her mother's forehead, the kind that made her feel like she could see all the nights of being upset and furious and lonely spread across a decade of her life. She no longer cared about tidiness or keeping her nails polished and even. There were times when her mother was more interesting to her than the door. The way she cleared her throat now or crossed her legs. The way she sometimes spoke quietly to herself, "Opal, this is your chance."

So many therapists had asked Ayanna if she had anger at her mother she needed to express. At both her parents. Mostly in these moments, Ayanna felt annoyed with herself for thinking about her father, not her mother. Maybe it was because it would've been easier in some ways to deal with him. Ayanna felt certain she could convince him to go home. She still occasionally spoke to him and did have things to say to her brothers. They were funny and sweet. She didn't mind being twenty-five and twenty-eight years older than them. But her mother had become only a string of obnoxious words on her phone over the years. She hadn't realized how little she thought of her mother as a person until being confronted by her again. They continued to share bags of salty snacks and say very little to each other. It was a relief, too, to be in her presence and no longer feel like she wanted or needed anything from her.

"What if I took you to church?" Ayanna offered. "When's the last time you've been to Mass?"

Opal ignored her.

Olivia, I am trying, Ayanna thought.

"You told me once that God made everything worth doing."

"Why would I listen to you?" Opal leaned back, dug her hands into the dirt. "You don't believe in anything."

It was almost impossible not to shrug like she was sixteen again.

Finally, when Ayanna was so exhausted that she could feel every bone in her body, like their weight was making her muscles tired, the door opened again to the blue meadow. The grass seemed longer than before, the blue sky a little lighter, less like a gloaming and closer to daybreak. In her apartment, the map she and Olivia had discussed was tucked into a folder. Still, Ayanna thought she knew the way. It was burned in her brain.

Give me a sign, Ayanna thought. *Please come home.*

Ayanna let her mother stand up. She refused to walk her to it. Her mother limped over to the door. Stood on the cusp. Reached an arm. Pulled it back before it went all the way through. Ayanna couldn't get any closer. She knew one step more would become all the steps. Ayanna held on to her knees as if her legs would walk over. *I am meant to be here,* she told herself. *Staying here is the right choice. Going through won't change things in a way I want.* Thought it over and over again and didn't realize that she was rocking with the effort of keeping herself on Earth. Opal continued trying to get herself through the door but could not do it. Ayanna couldn't watch. She did not know if she was making the right decision. A part of her hated herself for not walking through, striding through the long grass, looking in the distance for signs of Olivia and how she might have survived, going down the hill to the berry bushes, to the spot where all the lights had converged into a new door. Waiting there for as long as it took for Olivia to appear. Ayanna wanted to walk through all the universe's wilds, calling her sister's name. She forced herself to watch. Her mom tentatively reaching an arm or leg forward, swaying back. Ayanna told herself to look past her, to see if a figure was approaching. She would go through the door only if she saw her sister, to bring her home.

She watched and waited. Muscles tense. The grass swayed but there was no sign of what moved the blades. The door slammed shut again.

"I didn't hear her," Opal said.

"Me either," Ayanna said.

They sat next to each other, waiting to see what the door would bring next.

28

The next morning, the door opened again to the blue meadows. It was so beautiful that Ayanna teared up. Azure morning light where everything felt wrapped in its soft embrace. A blue that made you want to whisper because it felt so impossible. Real life would break it. The grass was swaying. Everything was quiet. Opal patted Ayanna's knee. "This is what I want," her mother said.

Ayanna nodded. Throughout the night she had tried church, getting help, calling her father, offering to take her out to eat, anything. Opal had laughed away the suggestions. None of those things mattered. Here, she had pointed at the door, was something she could see. Something she could do. They had slept next to each other in the dirt, refusing to touch one another. Ayanna spent a few minutes awake, remembering how there was a time when listening to her mother breathe at night, moving in and snuggling close, was enough to make everything bad feel miles away. Her mother's breathing was even. She still slept on her side, facing right. Ayanna handed Opal her tote bag and water bottle, taking only her wallet, keys, and phone from it. There were snacks, aspirin, tampons. Ayanna shut her eyes. Opal stood up. Ayanna refused to watch her die. Her fingers dug into her knees. The sun was a kiss on her upturned face.

"Be safe," Ayanna said.

"Olivia," Opal called. "Olivia." She called the name over and over until it sounded like a melody. Ayanna opened her eyes. Opal was through the door, standing still. The long indigo grass came up to her waist. Ayanna watched as her mother grew smaller and smaller. In her head, she traced Opal's path. There would be the berry bushes. The hill to climb that would let her gaze upon the silver mountains. She hoped her mother would do what she couldn't and find Olivia. And if not that, maybe she would walk all the way to the mountains. Discover the secrets hidden up high, or at least get to relish in how beautiful all that blue must look from a higher elevation.

Maybe they would find each other as spirits.

The door shut. Ayanna did not think she would ever see her mother again. When she tried not to hate Opal, Ayanna liked to think about the time when her mother had taken her alone to watch a women's soccer match. Olivia had been sick. They'd eaten popcorn together, hugged when the National Team scored their first goal, and when they were five up because they played together like a ludicrous eleven-headed being, running and moving together in awesome sync, they'd agreed this was beautiful. They'd judged the people around them who kept saying the women should be better sports and go easy. The memory did not help Ayanna to cry. When the door opened again, hours later, it was the golden path, where again it was snowing. Cold air blasted out the door, but it felt good to Ayanna against all that heat, like lingering in a grocery-store freezer door pretending she was indecisive about ice cream. She walked over to it and turned her back on it. Let it soothe her. For the first time, from the golden path she heard nothing, smelled nothing. Ayanna knew she could no longer stay.

"Please be good to yourself," Ayanna said, hoping somehow it would reach Opal. "Tell Olivia I miss her." Then, Ayanna got the guards to let her out. She looked at the bald one and suddenly realized he was her dad's old friend, Malik. He saw the look of recognition on her face and smiled at her. She realized why he had let them be. No one asked what had happened to Opal.

"What will happen here?" Ayanna asked.

He sighed. "We'll lock it down further. When things get calmer, some scientists will be allowed to come." Malik looked around. "Some rich guy has already offered a lot of money to go through. Everything that happened before, it will probably happen again."

Ayanna slowly walked to her car. Let each step be its own farewell. The crowd was heavy again, but now with people calling the door "Satan's evil, a disgusting temptation." She listened to the sounds of people, lawn mowers, her feet on the gravel. She wanted to never come here again, even though it was still beautiful to her. *There would always be a part of her*, Ayanna felt, *that was these roads and trees*. Always pointing up toward the wide open sky and big white clouds. Her rental car was covered in bird shit and dented from hail. She fished out her pajamas, changed into them, not caring if anyone saw, then got in. Ayanna bought a plane ticket out of Detroit for this evening and began the long trip downstate, stopping once to nap in a Walmart parking lot, and a second time to slam an energy drink in a gas station where a few of the dead were misting around the beef jerky and corn chip aisle. She bought another bag, took it outside, tore it open, and dumped it onto the hot parking lot asphalt. They devoured it and one even said gracias.

When Ayanna's phone had charged, it buzzed with texts and alerts, even a missed call from her dad. It was the day before Jane's forget-baby-showers-I-want-a-vacation. There would be time to talk for days. Ayanna slept briefly in an airport hotel room, took a shower, then slept deeply on the airplane as she had never done before in her entire life.

When the plane landed, Ayanna bought more toiletries and a sundress from an airport shop. It was so clean and quiet that she felt like buying everything and giving each cashier a compliment on how soothing the stores were. After about thirty minutes of puttering around and wheeling her suitcase, Ayanna tired of picking things up and then deciding not to buy them. In the last store, a Muzak version of her and Olivia's favorite Bone Thugs-N-Harmony song played, and she lingered near the speaker.

The door had opened the night before to a land that had seemed all sky, no ground. The air was a northern lights swirl of greens and teal, and two spirits, both shaped like people and never changing or misting, were calling to each other "It is safer to be dead than to be alive." They walked through the lights, saying it over and over as if the phrase were their version of Marco Polo. Ayanna blinked away the memory, stared at a wall of different kinds of trail mixes, gourmet to midnight snacking, until she felt fully back in the world. Ready to get out from the bright lights and white tiles, Ayanna got in the rideshare. It smelled like someone had tried to Febreze out cigarette smoke and like someone who had worn musty rich-lady perfume had cooked herself in the backseat. The driver looked as if she could have been Ayanna's cool younger sister: box braids, red-boned, wearing dark green lipstick and sunglasses that matched the shade.

"Your whole vibe. I love it," Ayanna said.

"Thanks, baby. I do this for me but I'm glad you appreciate it."

There was a song on the radio about flying to the moon over a sick beat. Ayanna wondered if it was actually about the moon or if that was the new thing everyone was saying instead of rolling or tripping. It made her feel old and out of touch. Most of her thoughts again were about elsewhere.

Tell the moon I love her, a voice with a lot of reverb crooned on the radio.

"Someone wants to speak to you," the driver said.

"What?"

"Since I was a girl, spirits have moved through me," she said. "It's rare. But there's one here."

Ayanna looked around but saw no one. Then, she met the driver's eyes in the mirror. She had taken off her sunglasses and they were as pink as a spirit, no pupils or irises.

Even people who had no idea of doors or spirits or believed in ancestor worship or ghosts knew this city was the place on Earth closest to the beyond—whatever that was—that if you died here, you couldn't help but come back sometimes. It was also Jane's favorite city in the world, where she insisted they all go to eat too much, to say too much, to listen to too much good music, and to give her all the blessings to bring her baby into the world. Was the driver possessed or had she died driving a similar car? There were tours of haunted houses on every street that were guaranteed to make anyone's blood run cold. The hotel Ayanna was going to stay in advertised the ghost of a famous writer who had come to the city to write four hours every morning and party eight hours every night. Critics had loved to call his books "gin-soaked." Altars on different street corners, where everyone was encouraged to leave flowers and dollars for their beloved dead. The last time Ayanna had been here, she had left a fifty and a designer lipstick she had seen in a duty-free shop that felt like something Olivia would have coveted. Each altar was always crowded with every color of roses, which you could conveniently buy down the corner for three dollars a stem.

"Who is it?"

There was always the fear that Vincent's spirit had returned, sensing her unhappiness, to begin another span of tormenting her. In her bag was a ring Felix had given her, sterling silver and with an evil eye on it. He had told her when he gave it to her that he had followed Amir's advice for protective objects. He had slept with the ring for a week, he had held it every day and thought about how much he loved her. Ayanna wished she hadn't put her bag in the trunk.

"She loves you." Her voice was different. It was like a harmony; Ayanna could hear a familiar voice mixed in with hers. Younger and soft. She recognized it but refused to put a name to the voice. Hope was too much. "I love you."

Ayanna nodded. She hoped it was a trick to try to get her to tip more. Sometimes, the dead imitated their living selves. Maybe this driver had been a grifter, knowing that pretending to be mystical and engaged was a great way to get extra tips from visitors here. When she had thought about the possibility of this, it was on different terms. Ayanna would walk through the door, her sister would be waiting, and somehow, she would bring her back into the world of the living. She would be somewhere private where she would, could, say everything, and all her emotions, her feelings, would be healthy, and she would have great posture.

"You need to take care of yourself. It's impossible to make it through this world with the way you're living and treating yourself. You're making yourself so unhappy. I've seen you do it over and over again."

"Okay."

"Don't just say okay." She turned off the radio. "I have a wild thought."

Ayanna's eyes teared up.

"I've been watching you your entire life and you have everything anyone could want. You have a person who loves you, you work to help people and make money from it, you have close friends. And still, you won't give me up."

"I killed you," Ayanna said. "And the world is ugly, people are cruel, and no one values life and it all feels fucking hopeless. How can I do this for forty more years? Fifty? And it should have been me. You should be here."

Then, she cried a little because it felt so childish to say aloud. Ayanna reached a hand forward to the front seat. Olivia took it and clasped Ayanna's palm, and in it, she felt the squishy soft of the dead in her touch, immediately let go, then reached for it again. She knew her sister was saying it was an accident, there was no way they could have known, and trying to get Ayanna to say it back, to confirm she understood. Say it, Olivia said. Stop hurting yourself, she said. Ayanna mouthed the words. Tried to make them feel true.

"Why wouldn't you talk to me before this? I miss you so much. You're the only person—" Ayanna said. She had to stop to swallow, her throat so thick with tears. "I love you. Every day still hurts without you. You're my sister."

"My turn isn't finished. You're being selfish. You're wallowing. You complain so much about how other people treat life, and still, you're afraid to really live. And it's such bullshit, Ayanna. You know what's next isn't half as pleasurable as it is here. You could be living for both of us. And you're getting old."

"Thirty-three isn't old." Ayanna rolled her eyes. She held on to her sister's hand.

"Okay, fine. It's not that old, whatever. I'm not here to bicker about age. If it feels hopeless, you do things for other people," Olivia said, and Ayanna heard the echo of their grandmother in her cadence. She heard herself too.

"I love you," Ayanna said again.

"Prove it."

Rose shampoo, mint gum, moldy bouquet water, and a smell that she could not articulate but that her nose knew was Olivia. She had known it since they were in the womb, growing from legume-sized to seven pounds, and snuggling together in their amniotic sac, and relearning again when they rolled together on floors and blinked at one another from their parents' exhausted arms. Home smell.

"Here's my wild thought. Even though things are better, they are so much better, a small part of me still wants you to say that I'm not meant to be alive, that we're meant to be together. I want you to forgive me. I feel like the only way you can forgive me is if I die too."

The car was gliding through traffic, missing pedestrians who were stumbling out into the street holding cans of beer in paper bags, pausing at red lights, and her eyes were on Ayanna. They were shining, and Ayanna wondered for the first time if the dead could still cry. And then felt ashamed that of all these years now of seeing the dead, speaking to them, wondering why she was mostly alone in this, she had never considered something like their ability to cry. The air was cold in the car, and Ayanna wished she could hear breaths other than her own. *Stay. Please. And if not that*, she thought, *if I could live the rest of my life in this car, telling you the truth. Stay.*

"Promise me you'll live a long life. Promise me. Ayanna, the only person you can save is yourself."

"Why didn't you say anything before?"

"Because you were looking for an excuse to die for so long. I was so mad at you. You have to live. You deserve to live. And I had to take care of Mom. I know she wasn't good to you, but I didn't want her to be alone."

"You were really there?"

"Mom is a bad listener."

Ayanna shut her eyes. All this time, she had been so close and so far.

"Don't be mad," Olivia said.

"Are you waiting for me?"

"Not really."

"Then why are you still here?"

"I was born. You were born. I died. You live but don't live. You live and you will live. I will live again."

There were other things the sisters spoke about on the drive, things Ayanna would never tell anyone else. Sometimes, Olivia said things that made no sense, she spoke in circles, offered to tell Ayanna what it meant to be alive in a universe like this. "I've seen so many wonderful things," Olivia said, "and so many awful people." Ayanna kept holding her sister's hand, didn't care how it felt, all Ayanna wanted was to be able to hold on to these moments for the rest of her life. She tried to tell Olivia about their mother, but Olivia said she already knew. Why talk about it? There were so many things Ayanna wanted to say, but the power of listening to Olivia's voice, being with the person who could make her feel alive. *That,* Ayanna thought, *is maybe the only way to know if you truly love someone. You feel more alive in their presence, more capable of wanting to feel pleasure when you are in their orbit.* She told her sister about Felix, Jane, and Stephen. That they had half brothers. Olivia laughed at one point. It was a mix of cackle and giggle and it hurt to realize she had forgotten exactly how it sounded. Will I see you again? Ayanna kept asking, and each time was met with a shift in the conversation. "Could I have brought you back?" Ayanna asked. "It's possible," Olivia said, "everything is possible." The answer was so annoying that Ayanna pushed back, but Olivia changed the subject. Golden deserts, a brief haunting of their favorite women's-soccer-team player, the bush in Dad's old front yard, the wonder of being able to understand anybody and everyone, and the song of stars and gravity sung by whales and children.

Finally, the driver let go of her hand. She placed it back on the wheel. Her eyes went back to the road. She put on her sunglasses. The air smelled again of loud perfume and cigarettes.

"It's on the left," the driver said.

Ayanna got out of the car. Her heart had never felt bigger in her chest, or more painful. Every bone in her body felt like it was on fire as the car drove away. Without thinking, despite the pain, Ayanna sprinted after it, clunking her carry-on bag on the sidewalk, almost losing it on an uneven patch. "Olivia," she yelled. Again. When her breath was jagged, she stopped and bent over. Tried to catch a deep breath.

"Buy something or move on," a man said to her sharply.

Ayanna looked up. She was in front of one of the rose stands. Pink, duck-egg blue, lavender, yellow, rainbow, royal blue, so many shades of red, white. She gathered as many as she could, didn't care about the cost. Tried to cobble them into something organized while the man watched with a bemused expression. He gave her a dusty vase on the house and seemed a little ashamed for being so terse initially.

The statue down the street looked like an off-brand Mary. Her eyes a little too close together, an actual smile instead of the wan smile of sculptural holiness, brass. A spot on her cheek rubbed shinier. Seven swords piercing her chest. Ayanna set the roses down. Taped on the wall next to the sculpture was a little index card with the words *Our Lady of Sorrows*. Ayanna was all feelings and soreness. All the roses, the ones she had bought, the ones left from others before her, felt almost like too much to look at. Someone had left a T-shirt of Garfield on a skateboard, a photograph of two girls hugging in front of a bar, letters, postcards, an expensive gold lighter. *I should have told her life is so hard because you have to keep relearning over and over how to keep living and being alive. To the world. To other people. I should have found a way to say, to me, you will always be alive. I should have said thank you. I should have said let's do this forever.* Ayanna touched the rose petals, the top of the lighter. There were people waiting for her, but she lingered here where other people had also stood missing their dead.

Soon, she would go to a dinner and hug her friends and laugh too hard and eat something that felt like art. A pot of mussels in saffron and lemon broth for everyone to share. She promised herself that every time she and Stephen got together to drink and watch movies and talk, she would remind herself it was a blessing to be alive at the same time as him. She would commit over and over to enduring the strain, the breakdown, and the growth of loving again and again. Ayanna told herself that every time she would come home to the sound of Felix listening to music and chopping vegetables, she would thank herself for being alive for so long. This is a gift, Ayanna. Don't act like it's not. Love life. When she met Jane's child, she would hold on to the delight of seeing her best friend's big, beautiful, mean eyes on that infant's wrinkled face. They would talk for hours over the baby's head, over the child's head, and with the baby when it was old enough. Her family was getting another member. She was loved. Each conversation would be its own kind of offering. Ayanna would endure, even when it was painful. It was the only path she wanted to know, and Ayanna vowed to walk it the rest of her life. Ayanna finally knew: love, with all its intertwined loss, was her penance.

ACKNOWLEDGMENTS

First, if any of the mental health issues Ayanna experiences in the book resonate with you (from anxiety to depression to PTSD), I want to make you aware of some resources. In the United States, you can call the National Suicide Lifeline by dialing 988. You can also reach the Crisis Text Line by texting the word, "start," to 741-741. Even if you're not in crisis, but something resonated with you, your mental health is important. Therapy can be hard and awkward—lol, trust me, I know—but it might be the step you need. There are even places that will give you free therapy services, such as Walk In (in the Twin Cities), either in-person or virtually.

Second, some notes about the book. The painting *the courage to venture to the edge of reason* is a real painting by Caroline Kent. I do not own it, but I love it. If the Lucille Clifton reference caught your eye, yes, I was hoping you might consider reading her novels *Two-Headed Woman* or *Generations*. I also read *Familiar Spirits* by Alison Lurie, listened to *Ghost Church* hosted by Jamie Loftus, and watched video of/looked at archived artists books and several paintings by Agatha Wojciechowsky (and the spirits). There were several other texts read and considered, including folk tales from the US and scholarly research on ghost figures in Black literature. Tarot cards, Ouija boards, and one Uber driver in New Orleans who claimed to be psychic were consulted.

Honestly, this is one of my favorite parts of writing a book, getting to pause and thank everyone who helped make it possible. I hate the myth around writing I've heard since growing up about the writer as a lone genius. Yes, I did the writing, but many, many, many people helped get it to the point of being the final product you're reading now. Besides, life is short, and there are less and less socially acceptable moments—or ones that have not been co-opted by a capitalist culture to sell mindfulness (whatever that actually means)—to be grateful.

I began writing *Meet Me at the Crossroads* in 2018. I thought what I was writing for a long while was a part of *The Women Could Fly*, but it clearly was not. This novel wouldn't have been finished so quickly if it wasn't for the support of Hedgebrook, the Picador Professorship in Leipzig, and the University of Minnesota's English department. I want to especially thank Kate Nuernberger, Sugi Ganeshananthan, Julie Schumacher, Krys Malcolm Belc, Doug Kearney, and Aamina Ahmad for making it very easy for me to be away for a semester. Thank you, too, to Noelle Ziersch for all her kindness and patience helping me navigate Germany; I might have left early if it hadn't been for you. Noelle, you are brilliant.

I also need to thank the two early readers of this book, Dan Conaway and Jami Attenberg.

Dan, of course, yes, you had to. That's your job as my agent; and, see, here I am again anticipating your arguments about why I should not thank you. But your creative and emotional insights and your ability to remind people in every situation, whenever necessary, that I am a person and not a product makes it so much easier to keep writing. Jami, you made the second section of this book so much better with your feedback. You are one of the best mentors I've ever had because, yes, you are my friend who wants the best for me, but you also always let me ask, "Yo, is this crazy (positive)" and "Yo, is this weird (derogatory)" and are immediately honest with me. Everyone, especially in the arts, needs a Jami.

Thank you to everyone at Amistad who worked on this book from Ryan Amato to Abby West to Judith Curr to Alison Cerri to Hanna Richards, but especially Paul Olsewski and Rakesh Satyal. Rakesh, your intelligence, creativity, and kindness make me a better writer. I'm lucky I've gotten to work with you on two books now. Paul, you are incredible at your job, and I'll always be grateful for our correspondence during Covid. Thank you, thank you, thank you. There are also many people from Amistad/HarperCollins from production staff to sales staff to interns who made this book possible, even if we didn't get to speak during the process.

Thank you to Sanjana Seelam and your staff at WME for your tireless work. And thanks, too, to Chaim Lipskar, Peggy Boulous Smith, and Sydnee Harlan of Writers House.

Thank you to every librarian and bookseller that has hand sold, written a recommendation, or suggested one of my books to a patron, but especially Kathleen Kondek, Daniel Goldin, Alyson and Janet Jones, Annie Metcalf, Sarah Hollenbeck, Oscar Gittemeier, and Miranda Sanchez. And thank you to every person who has invited me somewhere to talk about books and writing. It is always a pleasure.

Thank you, too, to the excellent students at the University of Minnesota whom I've been lucky enough to work with. One day, you'll all get to read their books and then you'll be lucky, too. And thank you also to the workshop attendees that I've had at Tin House; again, you will get to read their future books and be richer for it. Listening to all of the writers who are clearly still in love with fiction and put so much care and effort into reading and writing inspires me.

Thank you to Aaron and Hanna for feeding me goose blood soup; Scott, Paul, and Hilary Leichter for helping me to get to Germany and for every conversation I've had with you about writing; Claire Comstock-Gay for making Minneapolis feel like home; Jeff, Romayne, Ruth, N, H, C, K, U, A, P, and I, Alyssa, and Laura. And if I forgot anyone, I'm sorry! I will thank you again and buy you a coffee in person.

Some of this book snapped into a place after a long, strange encounter with an Uber driver in New Orleans in 2021. Yes, you were right about many things. Thank you for your kindness.

Finally: Jon, you encouraged me to dedicate this book "to the haters, thou shall inherit the Earth" or the 2024–2025 Liverpool starting 11 because of how much happiness they've given me, but this book wouldn't have been possible without you. You give me the time and space to write and the love and encouragement to make the writing better.

ABOUT THE AUTHOR

MEGAN GIDDINGS is an assistant professor at the University of Minnesota. Her novel, *Lakewood*, was one of *New York* magazine's ten best books of 2020, one of NPR's best books of 2020, a Michigan Notable book for 2021, a nominee for two NAACP Image Awards, and a finalist for a 2020 Los Angeles Times Book Prize in the Ray Bradbury Prize for Science Fiction, Fantasy, and Speculative Fiction category. Her second novel, *The Women Could Fly*, was named one of *The Washington Post*'s best science fiction and fantasy novels of 2022, one of *Vulture*'s best fantasy books of 2022, and was a *New York Times* Editors' Choice. Her work has received support from the Barbara Deming Foundation and Hedgebrook. She lives in Minneapolis.